THE
DARK
HOUSE

Praise for John Sedgwick and

The Dark House

"A compelling story, wonderfully told. John Sedgwick is the real thing."   —Robert B. Parker, author of *Gunman's Rhapsody*

"A scary tale of ancient feuds, midnight stalkers, and buried clues. Sedgwick weaves a finely tuned plot leading to a wild chase sequence and a chilling ending."—*St. Louis Post-Dispatch*

"A tense and intriguing debut. . . . A multilayered mystery which does not immediately surrender its secrets [and] . . . keeps the reader in suspense until the very end."   —*BookPage*

"Unique and absorbing. . . . A spellbinding story of obsession, greed, and redemption."

— Barnes & Noble, Discover Great New Writers

"*The Dark House* is an engaging first novel, both a mystery and a love story, with a most curious and memorable main character and a plot that twists and turns to a wholly unpredictable end."

—Jonathan Harr, author of *A Civil Action*

"Deftly touches on themes of seeing and being seen and touchingly portrays the struggles of a man crippled by his emotional solitude."   —*Time Out* (New York)

Richard Howard

About the Author

JOHN SEDGWICK hails from the same family that has produced the early speaker of the house Theodore Sedgwick, nineteenth-century novelist Catharine Maria Sedgwick, and Andy Warhol protégée Edie Sedgwick. He has written for *Newsweek*, *GQ*, *Atlantic Monthly*, *Worth*, and other magazines. He lives in Newton, Massachusetts.

THE
DARK
HOUSE

A NOVEL

JOHN SEDGWICK

 Perennial
An Imprint of HarperCollinsPublishers

For Josie

THE
DARK
HOUSE

One

"Eleven thirty-eight P.M.," Rollins said quietly into the tiny Panasonic in his palm. "North on 93, just past Exit 32. The Audi's two cars up, holding steady at"—he glanced down at the speedometer—"about fifty-seven, fifty-eight miles an hour." The Audi was navy blue, or possibly black, with green-on-white Massachusetts plates. Rollins put the tape recorder down by the newspaper on the passenger seat of his Nissan. As far as he could tell, the Audi was occupied only by the driver, who was thin and fiftyish and had a look of concentration that was unusual for this time of night. Because the man was wearing a suit coat and unfashionable glasses, Rollins at first had guessed banking. Then he spotted an umbrella on the rear dash, and he reconsidered. Insurance? After all, the forecast had said nothing of rain, just the endless steam heat so typical for Boston in late July.

The trees were set well back from the raised highway, opening up a wide night sky. A blurry moon rose through the glass by his left shoulder. Before him, the asphalt gleamed like open water. As Rollins followed along, he knew enough to keep out of the Audi's rearview mirrors, both center and side. He was sensitive that way, almost as if his skin were allergic to another's sight. He stayed well back, and one lane over, to make it clear that he just *happened* to be traveling this road tonight. His slim hands curled lightly on the wheel, Rollins was ready to move when the Audi moved. It was a kind of dance, Rollins supposed. A dance with a shadow.

On a pursuit, Rollins never flipped on talk radio or whistled, as he might do at other times—when he was staring at the stock prices floating across the bottom of his computer screen at the office, say, or sitting in the big chair by the phone in his apartment. He didn't want to break the mood of the evening by cutting the white noise that enveloped him. He was comforted by the steady drone of his engine, the wavelike rush of passing cars, the buzz of the tires on the asphalt, the whoosh of humid air from the vents. Inside the Nissan, he felt snug as an astronaut, tidily enclosed in his bubble of glass and steel. But keyed up, too, on the cusp of a new adventure.

Rollins couldn't know where the driver of the Audi had been before their paths first crossed in front of the Mid-Nite Convenient newsstand, with its red awning, in Somerville's Union Square some miles back. The man's past was a blank, and the car bore no SOCCER MOM bumper sticker, no Northeastern University parking pass to help fill out a history. Only his future could be known. So different from the way life generally worked, Rollins mused with a shake of the head. The only thing noteworthy about the Audi's exterior was a slight dent on the housing of the left rear wheel. "The kind of ding you get in a parking lot," he told the recorder. "Nothing major."

In Rollins' experience, people rarely went anywhere just once. Rather, their lives were an endless loop of going, coming back, and going again. Most likely, where the man in the Audi was going was where he had come from. He was returning to his source. By now, Rollins was something of an expert on Boston's greater metropolitan area, its thoroughfares, one-way streets and cul-de-sacs. He knew precisely where one town ended and another began; and he grasped the subtle differences between exclusive Wellesley, say, and reclusive Weston, which lay right beside it. And of course, it meant even more to see the exact neighborhood within the town, and still more to see which street.

And what sort of house? A gated estate in Beverly Farms, on Massachusetts's gilded North Shore, where the driveways are a half mile long? Rollins had had a comfortable childhood in a big house on a private road in upper-class Brookline, and he was always on the lookout for one of his own, just to see how that person had managed it. Or would it be a more traditional suburban home—with a tight yard, neighbors pressing in on either side? Were there kids in the picture? Would a voice call down to him from an upstairs window when Rollins's man came home? If so, would it be accented? With luck, Rollins might spot other revealing details—some Spanish artwork in the bedroom, or a projection TV in the paneled den, or antique doll furniture arrayed on the living room mantelpiece. Small points, but telling ones to him.

He clicked on the tape recorder again. "Eleven forty-seven. Passing Exit 33, no change in speed." So his subject was not the Exit 33 type after all. That is, not one to take the Fellsway up to Stoneham, with its tract houses, its drab Redstone Shopping Center, its tiny zoo, seventeen baseball fields (Rollins had once passed a slow evening counting them), mediocre schools, three cemeteries, and Empire Bowl-a-drome, so favored by overweight smokers. Likewise exits 34, 35, 36, 37A and B, 38, and 39.

Past Exit 39, however, twenty miles north of Boston, where signs of roadside activity finally started to thin, the Audi signaled for a right turn, its blinker impatient, Germanic. (Rollins could write an interesting monograph on taillights: their flame-colored stripes, circles, dots, and wraparound curves were so much more variable and expressive than those tedious twin orbs of white up front.) After an interval that affirmed his man's deliberate nature, the Audi moved gently to the right lane and slowed to fifty. Rollins, in the far left, eased off the gas and shifted two lanes over. He could feel a film of sweat where his fingers touched the steering wheel. He was closing in. The Audi turned at

Exit 40, eastbound on Route 62. "Twelve oh-three," Rollins said, glancing at the dashboard clock. "East on 62. The Audi seems to be slowing a little, so I think I'll stay back."

Route 62 led past a sand and gravel supply yard, its great mounds of earth dark except for a few security lights, then wound around through several ill-landscaped subdevelopments. The Audi's turn signal flashed again, and the car made a quick left, then—this time without signaling—a right, and another right, finally turning onto a tree-lined street.

"Something's a little off here," Rollins whispered into the Panasonic. He didn't like that last flurry of turns. Plus, he'd cast his man as a homecoming father. But he could tell when an individual was driving into a neighborhood as a visitor or as a resident: Visitors grope their way along, while residents steam through as if they know every turn in the road. The driver of the Audi was definitely groping. More perplexing still, the car halted in front of a split-level ranch that had some ersatz grillwork over the windows and faux medieval paneling on the front door. It couldn't go for more than $175,000, well below the price range suggested by the Audi. It seemed to be the residence of an aspiring middle-manager, or a department supervisor with a single income. Rollins stopped several houses back on the other side of the street, cut the engine, and killed the headlights.

The dome light inside the Audi flashed on for a moment as the driver opened the car door. He was more gaunt than Rollins expected, with thinning hair and a wispy mustache he had not noticed before. His suit wasn't badly cut. Rollins upped his salary estimate into the eighty- to ninety-thousand-dollar range. The gaunt man took a quick, nervous look around as he stepped out of the car—another unexpected move for a homecoming father. He paused momentarily as he surveyed Rollins' car. Rollins stopped breathing. But the man turned back to the Audi, closed the door, and made his way up the limestone walkway to the front steps. At the door, he fished in his pocket and pulled out a single key. He slid it into the lock, pushed the door open, and stepped inside.

There is a rhythm to such entries. Rollins had seen hundreds. At this hour, he typically would wait no more than three seconds for the lights to come on. But three seconds passed, then ten, then thirty. A full minute went by, and still no light burned in the house. That got Rollins' pulse going. It was conceivable that his man had somehow gone straight to bed in the dark. It was also possible that he had walked to the back of the house, or down into the basement, where he might have flipped on a light that did not shine onto the street.

A more alarming thought formed in Rollins' mind: that the man was fully aware of his presence, and had been for some time. And that the driver was, at this very moment, staring out at Rollins from the darkness, performing his own evaluation, for his own ends. Light was everything at night. One saw from the darkness into the light. The lighter environment was the one observed. If the house remained dark, *Rollins* could be the subject. His intestines turned watery, and his skin felt flushed and prickly. He was being watched. He could feel it.

Five minutes flickered past on the dashboard clock; it felt like an hour, or a day. His arm heavy, Rollins flipped the switch on the interior light so that it wouldn't shine when he opened the door and slowly released the door handle to step out of his car. He went around to the sidewalk and strode away from the house to give his man, if he was indeed watching, the impression that he, Rollins, wasn't interested in that house at all. No, sir, not *at all!* Once he was out of sight, he crossed the street and walked around the house's block to view the back of the dark house through the rustling trees. It was completely black against the gauzy night sky. Circling the block to return to the dark house from the other direction, he put his hands in his khaki pockets to convey casualness while he peered as far around to the back as he could out of the corner of his eye without actually turning his head. The neighboring houses screened off some of his view, but, again, every window in the house that he could see was pitch black.

Rollins returned to his Nissan. "No lights on in the house," he told the tape recorder somewhat breathlessly. "I just looked around from the back. Not one light. Jesus." He watched the house through the driver's-side window. A few cars went by, and a jogger in a reflecting vest chugged along the sidewalk, but otherwise nothing changed. "All right," he said, starting the car. "Twelve fifty-three. I need a toilet." It was the night's last entry.

Two

"Well, you're getting a lot of work done, I see."

Rollins swiveled around in his chair. It was Marj, the new girl in an adjacent cubicle. She had two earrings in each ear, auburn hair that Rollins was pretty sure was not her natural color, and, apparently, a hunger for attention. She was twenty-seven, he knew from her job application, and, to judge by the unadorned ring finger, single. And, for reasons he wasn't quite clear about, she seemed to have been trying, from the moment she arrived two months ago, to befriend him. At present, she was wearing a black skirt slit a couple of inches up the side, a tight green blouse and matching eyeliner, which, for a man like Rollins, was probably not the right way to go about it.

"You've been staring out the window for, like, the last half hour." Marj leaned up against the edge of his desk and plucked a pencil out of the pencil holder to drum against his desktop. "What's the matter, out late last night?"

"Not terribly." Every tap on the desktop pounded directly on Rollins' brain.

Marj chewed her lip. A fold of her skirt slanted across her pelvis. One of her high heels tipped sideways.

"Mind if I ask you a question?" Rollins asked finally.

Marj brightened. "Shoot."

"When you come home at night, do you turn on the lights?"

Marj crossed her arms in front of her chest, a gesture seemingly designed to protect her from a man she may have wildly misjudged. "Usually."

"I'm serious—do you?"

"Yeah, I turn on the lights." Marj looked at him warily, her blondish eyebrows furled in horizontal S's.

"Even if you're going straight to bed?"

"Sure."

"Always?"

"Yeah, always," she replied, her voice rising. "Or I might bump into something. I'm not a freaking bat." She gave out a little crackle of a laugh, as if to discharge some accumulated voltage. "Why all the crazy questions?"

"Oh, just research. You've been most helpful." He smiled. "Thanks."

Marj remained where she was. "Research? What kind?"

"General."

Normally, Rollins would have taken Marj's puzzled look as a perverse kind of compliment and let it go at that. He liked being secretive, even a little squirrelly, at times. But the possibility of having been watched last night had sobered him. He took a breath while he contemplated the matter. "Okay, I saw someone go into a house last night without turning on the lights. I was thinking about it just now. I thought it was odd."

"That the sort of thing you think about?"

"Sometimes."

There was a pause in the conversation as Marj pondered that. "Which house?"

Rollins told Marj the full story that afternoon over lunch at a soup-and-salad place named Georgio's. He hadn't meant to tell her—or anyone. He'd planned to file away the night's tape with all the others on the long row over his bed. A subject for future review, perhaps, but not active concern. Yet the sight of the dark house—as he'd come to think of it—had stayed with him. More than that, it seemed to grow in his memory, like a plant that had accidentally been released in a new, more favorable environment. What was, in fact, a stubby suburban ranch house had now taken on some of the characteristics of a towering Gothic. The whole business seemed somehow momentous, and he wasn't sure where to go with it. He spoke to his brother in Indianapolis on occasion, but never about anything like this. There were other, more distant, relatives around, like Aunt Eleanor and Uncle George out in the western suburbs, but they were hardly confidants. He'd had his crowd at Williams (fellow classics majors and black-and-white film buffs mostly), plus a few holdovers from prep school. But the gang had drifted to New York since college, and the truth was, he found himself a little short on genuine friends at present.

That decided it. She was right there, and, despite her quasi-punk appearance, she seemed genuinely curious. Plus, the fact that he barely knew the first thing about her (and, presumably, vice versa) made him think she might be a harmless recipient of his news. Some history was operating here: He'd once confided in a young woman on a train to New York City, revealing to her a few details of his driving life that he attributed to a nameless friend. The woman seemed mildly intrigued, especially once Rollins made it clear that his friend was not some scuzzy peeping tom, but rather a kind of cultural anthropologist. She said that Rollins' friend reminded her of a distant cousin in Washington state who used a radio scanner to monitor police reports. "Kind of an interesting guy, actually," the woman said. Rollins had been so encouraged, he thought that he might try to get together with the woman for a drink in the city, but it turned out she was continuing on to Philadelphia. He never did get her name. Still, he left the train whistling; it had been so wonderful to unburden himself.

He didn't tell Marj everything. He glossed over the fact that he'd made a hobby of following people back to their homes for the last several years. He focused on the part that was too large for him to take in alone, namely the monstrous peculiarity of the gaunt man entering a dark house and never turning on the lights.

Marj listened to his tale intently, without interrupting.

"So what do you make of it?" Rollins asked finally.

"I'm amazed you did that."

Rollins colored. He was in deeper than he'd thought. "Haven't you ever wondered about people? What they . . . do?"

Marj looked at him. "You've done this before, haven't you?"

Rollins reached for his water glass and took a long, cool drink.

"Well, you *are* a devil!" Marj's eyes flashed. "And here I thought you were some boring Republican like all the other creeps in the office. God, what a relief."

Rollins set the glass down. He was startled by that glimmer in her eyes. Did it convey interest, or—he didn't quite know how to think about this—a kind of ferocity? It was like a car with its brights up, coming straight at him in his lane. As far as he could remember, no one had ever lingered on his face quite so shamelessly. He'd had a girlfriend or two, years back, but nothing that went anywhere. But these eyes of Marj's, they were like twin suns. He tried to match her gaze, but after a few moments he had to return his attention to his water glass.

Still, he did hope that, despite his shyness, she might find him reasonably attractive. At thirty-seven, he was still fairly young. He dressed well, all his clothes—like the blazer, rep tie, and summer-weight flannels ensemble he was wearing right now—were selected with care at the Exeter Shop, where he was on a first-name basis with the owner, a charming Trinidadian. He hadn't gone gray, or bald, or fat, like some of his Williams classmates. If anything, the years had given his face a sleek angularity that he thought might possibly be considered handsome in the manner of certain thirties' film stars he admired. As he followed Marj in his peripheral vision, her gaze felt tender, like her hands (or so he assumed) now slowly bringing a bottle of Sprite to her lips. A good sign, surely.

Their lunches arrived, and Rollins took refuge in his salad, while Marj turned to her gazpacho. He ate in silence, concentrating on each bite: the satisfying crunch of the lettuce, the little explosions of the tomatoes on his tongue, the tang of the dressing.

"You should go back, you know," Marj said finally.

Rollins dabbed at the corner of his mouth with his napkin. "You think?"

"Or perhaps I should go," Marj added.

It was remarkable how a new bit of information about a person could transform all that had come before. Suddenly, he didn't mind her extra earrings and dyed hair. "By yourself?"

"He's never seen *me*."

"Absolutely not. It wouldn't be safe. Who knows, the fellow might have a gun."

"Then maybe we should go together. You can protect me from this 'fellow.'" The corner of her mouth quivered as if she were trying to suppress a smile.

This was trouble. Rollins didn't have many guiding principles for his nightly pursuits, but one of them was the Garbo rule. He had to be alone. That had always been inviolable. Solitude allowed him to focus his energies on the object of his pursuit. The sole attachment had to be to the stranger in the car.

Marj finished off the Sprite and set the bottle down. "I'm not doing anything tonight, you know."

Marj lived in an apartment building on Washington Street just down the hill from the sprawling Saint Elizabeth's Hospital in the Brighton section of Boston. As arranged, Rollins double-parked out front at exactly seven-thirty and honked three times. Marj threw open a window three flights up. "Be right there!" she shouted, waving. Her hair was wet and she was wearing only a bath towel. Rollins had seen such things before, countless times. He had seen more. But it's different when you know the person. There's an extra connection, a line of unspoken communication, that makes the sight all the more revealing. He put the car in neutral, pulled the hand brake, and switched on the emergency blinkers.

Fifteen minutes later, he heard a rap on the passenger-side glass. He leaned over to pop the lock. From that vantage, peering up at her through the side window, he could see an inch or two of the downy flesh under her loose cotton T-shirt.

Marj jumped in with a rush of perfume. "Hey." She had a Walkman draped around her neck like a necklace, and artfully torn jeans. A rhythmic scratchiness leaked out from the headset. Everything about her seemed strange, but it was the immediacy of her being there, right there in his car, that got to him most of all. The Nissan hadn't seen many passengers. He tried to assure himself that it wasn't so unusual for a single man in the city to be so private about his car, but deep down he had his doubts. A few months back, he'd driven his brother Richard out for Thai food in Central Square when he'd come through on a business trip from Indiana. And he'd had a woman in the Nissan last fall. That was adventurous. A Cindy someone, whom he'd met at the Laundromat around the corner from his apartment. They'd gone to a Red Sox game for a few innings before Cindy started to complain about the noise and spilt beer. Actually, Rollins had started to enjoy himself, the marvelous expanse of green that was spread out before him, the leisurely pace of the game. He'd held open the possibility of dinner, but Cindy insisted on being driven straight home.

"You okay?" Marj tipped her head to look at him at an angle, as if trying for a new perspective. "We don't have to do this, you know. If it's too weird."

"It'll be fine." Rollins switched on the ignition. "Really." He moved the car out into traffic and headed across town.

"Sorry to be so slow. I got a phone call."

"No problem. It's still a little light out." He pointedly didn't ask who called. Out of habit, he scanned the license plates on the nearby cars, checking for vanities.

"Say—look at you."

As usual for his night work, Rollins had dressed down considerably. He wore his driving clothes—loose chinos, an old pair of sneakers, and a sweatshirt his mother had once sent him in a failed attempt to get him to exercise.

"I wanted to be comfortable," Rollins explained.

Marj looked at him again. "You're not married, are you?"

"Me? No." He nearly laughed at the thought.

"I didn't think so," Marj said. "But my mom thought I should ask." She paused a second, looking out at the other cars on the road. "Since you're older."

"You asked your mother about me?"

"I'm from the Midwest. Well, originally. Morton, Illinois, the heart of the heartland." She practically sang it out, as if it were a jingle from an advertisement. "Just east of Peoria. Got it? White frame house, picket fence, the whole bit. I split about ten years ago, but my mom still likes to check in. Don't worry, I just told her we were going out for a drive. That's something people do in Morton."

"I'm from Brookline," Rollins said. "I've spent about my whole life around here." Marj seemed to incline toward him a little, but Rollins stopped short. It didn't seem like enough of a life to merit a conversation: dancing school; woodworking classes at the Brookline Community Center (his one experience with what his mother termed "mixing"); the "pre-prep" Grant School, with its faint smell of sawdust; puberty at Middlesex; then going west to Williams, his one big adventure. Why go into it? And as for the other life—the one he really lived—God, where to begin?

They were up on the turnpike now, passing the big screen over the famous left-field wall at Fenway Park. He passed through the dim tunnel, done in grimy bathroom tiles, under the plastic-looking Prudential tower to the expressway—reasonably clear at this hour—and across the nameless bridge at the mouth of the ruffled Charles to 93.

For a while, Marj rode quietly, too, and Rollins let the silence enfold the two of them. In his car, he was used to silence, but it had an unaccustomed edge to it now, with Marj there. Usually, as he embarked on a pursuit, the silence tokened concentration, focus; now there was a pervasive sense of expectation that Rollins found unsettling, but that he didn't know how to dispel.

Once they were up on 93 heading north, Marj shifted in her seat. "So—any family?"

This was one of Rollins' least favorite topics. For simplicity's sake, he decided to leave out any reference to the illustrious, so-called greater family: that vast herd of overenthusiastic near-strangers who gathered for the annual fall family clambake at his grandmother's big place by the sea in Gloucester. Ditto the first cousins, whom he knew fairly well, but who were an impenetrable thicket all their own. Several moments passed—until Rollins realized that, despite all the thoughts that had coursed through his head, he hadn't actually said anything, and, further, that Marj was waiting for him speak. Finally, he explained about his younger brother, Richard, in Indianapolis. "He's married with two children, the V.P. of the Coca-Cola bottling plant there. I guess he's the big success in the family." He tried to keep a sound of complaint out of his voice.

"That's it? Just the brother?" Marj asked.

If his sister Stephanie had lived, she'd be older than Marj. "That's all."

"How about your parents? They still alive?"

Rollins kept his eyes on the road ahead. "My mother lives in a retirement center outside Hartford. My father is out west."

"Divorced?"

"When I was eleven." He'd clung to his father's pant leg the last time he came to the house, a ridiculous scene. His father was so tall then, over six feet, but Rollins himself was fully that height now. Harder to believe, he was almost exactly that age. Rollins reflexively stroked his chin. He seemed to be inheriting his father's jawline, too, along with his deeply inset eyes. Hawklike, he'd always thought as a child. "My father remarried—twice, actually. He has a young wife now. About your age."

"You're older than your *mother*?"

"Stepmother," Rollins corrected her. "I haven't met her, actually."

"You're not close to your dad, I take it."

Father down on the oriental rug with him. The living room of the big house. Father in his greatcoat, his silk scarf drooping, as he held one of Rollins' treasured toy cars, an Aston Martin, in his gloved hands. "Vroom, vroom," Father was saying, as he flicked the wheels with the tip of a leather-clad finger. The gloves were black. The tone icy.

Mother beside him, her hair up, her pale neck glittering with jewels. "We should go, darling. The car's waiting."

Then he was off with Mother again, to another party.

"Well?" Marj persisted.

"Not particularly." Rollins had heard of the most recent marriage only by postcard. A Hawaiian beach scene, if he remembered right, from their honeymoon. He should check; he still had the card somewhere. He tried to keep such things.

"My dad's dead. My real one, I mean." Marj finally switched off the Walkman. "He died before I was born, so it's okay. Well, okay for me. Well, relatively okay." Her hands fluttered in her lap, several silver rings flashing. "He was stationed in Germany during the Vietnam War, and something exploded. I never got the full story. My mom married my stepdad when I was six."

"I'm sorry."

"Yeah, well, what can you do?"

As they went along, Marj told Rollins she had the man in the dark house all figured. He was either passing nuclear secrets to foreign governments or molesting children. Rollins smiled, sure she got such wild ideas from television. His eyes roved to a crimson Mercedes with darkened windows.

"I'm boring you," Marj said.

"Not at all."

"I tend to talk too much. Especially when I'm nervous."

A flutter pulsed outward from his heart. Rollins slowed the car a little and turned to her. "We don't have to do this, you know."

"No—that's not what I meant."

She did sound jumpy. This was going to be like that Cindy. A big mistake, he just knew it.

"I want to," she continued. "It's just, oh, *I* don't know." She lapsed back into silence. Her glance turned to the other cars on the road. "You could follow any of these?"

"I suppose."

A sly look came over her. "Ever see anything good? Sex or something?"

"Heavens, no," Rollins said. "You'd be surprised how boring people are."

"So why do you follow them? You some kind of pervert?"

He smiled, hoping that was her idea of a joke. When her eyes stayed on him, his smile dimmed. "I don't do it very much. Very often, I should say." Her eyes stayed right where they were. "I mean, I don't."

"But when you do, I mean."

Rollins took a breath, hoping the fresh air would clear his mind. He had never put this in words before; he wasn't sure there were words. "Just to see where they're from, what they do. I mean, look around." He gestured to the other cars on the road—several Hondas, a couple of minivans, a Jeep. "Don't you ever wonder about all these people?"

Marj glanced about her. "Not too often."

"Well, I do," Rollins said.

"Jeez," Marj muttered. "You might have followed *me*."

"Don't be silly."

But, of course, he had followed her, a month ago. He had been waiting at a corner not far from the downtown Boston high-rise where they worked. Because he had splurged on a very nice '42 Côtes du Rhone the night before, he decided to tail the forty-second car. It was Marj's, a beat-up Toyota Corolla. He recognized her immediately. Rollins had a policy against tailing people he knew, but, having settled on car forty-two, he had to see the matter through. Marj proved to be an erratic driver. She never signaled before turning and routinely scooted through intersections well after the light turned red. This made for a challenge, but Rollins had stayed with her, his visor down. There was something about knowing her that roused him, gave the evening an even sharper edge than usual. She seemed remarkably care-free, and Rollins had to admire that. His own cautious introspection could be a burden. He followed her back to her Brighton apartment and waited there for two hours while she passed from one of her apartment windows to another in various states of undress. Finally, she emerged again in a lovely little red dress and heels. This time she hailed a cab, which ran a red light, and he lost her in traffic. He had not followed her again, although he had been tempted.

It was after eight when Rollins and Marj turned onto Elmhurst Drive in North Reading, and pulled up at the dark house.

"It's that one." Rollins pointed to number 29. All the other houses along the street were lit up, with sounds of life streaming from the open windows. But number 29 was dark and silent. The driveway was empty. Next to it, the metal-sided exterior glowed dully in the lamp-light. The few shrubs and one scruffy hemlock were nearly black on the unlit side.

"Creepy." Marj scrunched down deeper in her seat.

"I thought you were interested."

"Well, I was." Marj hesitated. "But it's . . . it's not what I expected. It's like seeing a corpse or something."

"It's just a house."

"With maybe a guy inside!" Marj exclaimed. "And he might have a gun, you said so yourself."

"I doubt he's home. Besides, I really don't think he has a gun. He didn't seem the type."

Marj seemed unconvinced. "Can't we go get a coffee or some-thing?"

"Let's wait a little, since we're here."

They sat there for a while in silence. Time didn't mean much to Rollins. It was an abstraction, something to pass through. But Marj started plucking at the crease on her jeans, then smoothing it out again.

"All right, Rolo," she asked finally, "are we going to stay here all night?"

"Just till something happens."

"Like?"

"Somebody comes in, somebody goes out. Something like that."

Marj crossed her arms in a sulky gesture that Rollins suddenly found irritating. He said nothing, however, and merely continued to sit there. That's what a pursuit was, after all. Watching and waiting.

"Why don't you go look around? Do *something*, at least."

Rollins was tempted to explain his principles of pursuit to her. He'd have declaimed them with an edge in his voice, laying down the law to her with a sentence that started "Look here . . ." But he didn't dare be too combative with this nymph, for fear he might only provoke more questions about the frequency of his nightly travels or, worse, scare her off. So it was with only the slightest pique that he reached for the door handle. "And you?"

"I'll wait here, thanks."

Rollins opened the door and climbed out. Black shadows sliced this way and that from the streetlamps. He regretted leaving the protective cocoon of his car and striking out toward the dark house. But so much of life is a matter of simply getting started. You start out in a certain direction, you keep going. Rollins kept on, across the road, along the sidewalk, up the steps, all the way to the door of the house. He stood there on the landing, his heart pounding as if he had sprinted the whole distance. He glanced back to the car, to see if Marj had noticed how daring he had been, but Marj had ducked down out of sight. Rollins was afraid she'd pulled on her Walkman again, tuning him out in favor of acid rock. He paused, weakened, and retreated down the steps. He went around to the side of the house and, pushing between some rough shrubbery, squeezed through to a window whose interior shade had not been pulled tight to the sill. He bent down, cupped his hands on the glass, and peered inside.

The whole house was empty except for the wall-to-wall carpeting. Not a stick of furniture anywhere. His nose was still up against the cool glass when he heard the crackle of tires on loose asphalt close by. He felt a bright light on him. He turned. A huge car had turned into the driveway and lit him up with its headlights. All he could think to do was to raise his hands. A door opened and a man got out. The headlights remained on. Squinting, Rollins braced himself for a bullet.

"So, you're in the market?" the man asked.

Rollins moved his hands a bit to screen off the lights. He could make out a shadowy figure against the car—a big green Land Cruiser, he could see now.

"Great little piece of property, isn't it?" The man laughed a comfortable, genial laugh. "Hi, Jerry Sloane, Sloane Realty." He extended a hand in what was obviously a practiced gesture. "And you are?"

"Harris." Amazing how easy it was to lie.

"Harris, you say?"

Rollins nodded.

"Great to see you. That the Mrs.?" Sloane turned back toward Marj, who, Rollins could see, had gotten out of the car and crossed to their side of the street. She was standing on the sidewalk, her hands up by her face protectively.

Rollins said nothing. He wanted to keep Marj safe from all this.

"Oh, girlfriend, huh?"

Rollins looked over at Marj, who looked back at him.

"Doin' pretty well," Sloane whispered to Rollins conspiratorially. Then he clapped him on the back and spoke up. "Well, come on, come on. What are you waiting for? Let me show you the house. Believe me, it's a steal at a hundred seventy-nine."

"It's really for sale?" Marj called from the sidewalk.

"Jeez, sweetheart, I hope it is," Sloane replied. "We wouldn't want to be caught trespassing, would we?" He gave out a big laugh and flicked out a forearm at Rollins in an unsuccessful effort to get him to join in. "I got the listing a few days ago. You're the very first one to check it out." He handed Rollins a business card.

"Anyone living here?"

"God no. You'll see—it's all cleaned out."

Rollins went up the path to the house, aware that he was following in the steps of the gaunt man from the night before. "It just looked like someone might be living here, that's all." Somehow, Rollins thought he needed to explain.

Sloane dug into his pocket, pulled out a key, and fitted it into the door.

"You know who owns it?" Rollins asked.

Sloane pushed the door open. "Off the record?"

Rollins nodded.

"Can't tell you." Sloane laughed again. A real joker, that Sloane.

While Sloane went inside, Rollins returned to Marj and laid out the situation.

"So the guy's a realtor?" Marj asked quietly, obviously confused. "I thought you said you thought he was in insurance."

"This isn't the man I followed," Rollins whispered. "This Sloane fellow *is* a real estate agent, at least he says he is. He gave me his card." He handed it to Marj, who looked at it very carefully. "He thinks I'm looking to buy the house. I told him my name was Harris."

"Is it?"

Rollins ignored that. "I thought I'd take a look around inside, since we're here."

"This is majorly weird." Marj took a step toward the house. "You're going to get in trouble, I just know it."

Going up the walkway together, Rollins thought they might be a couple of newlyweds, then dropped the idea.

"Jerry Sloane." The realtor thrust out a hand to Marj at the top of the stairs.

"Hi." Marj did not give him a name.

Sloane looked from Rollins to Marj and then back again. "So, you two house hunting?" he asked. "Or"—he turned to Marj—"you just giving him real estate advice?"

"I'm afraid that's personal," Rollins interrupted.

"Oh, absolutely! The wife says I shouldn't be so nosy. Bad habit, but it goes with the territory." Sloane flipped on the lights and ushered them inside. The place was completely empty, just as Sloane had said, and it smelled of mildew and industrial cleaners. "It'd help to have a little air in here." Sloane raised some shades and threw open a few windows.

Rollins glanced about. All that remained of the previous occupants were some ghostly rectangles on the wall where a few pictures had hung. While Sloane lectured Marj on the details of the house's closet space, taxes, and proximity to local schools, Rollins slipped away to go through the kitchen cabinets, the drawers under the built-in bookcase in the living room, the hall closets. Nothing, hardly even any dust. Leaving Sloane to show Marj the back porch, Rollins crept downstairs to the basement. It was damp, with a small furnace. Rollins stepped warily, sure the gaunt man would jump out at him at any moment and put a knife to his throat. Still, he kept searching for a memento, a photograph, a vault, a passageway, a secret compartment—something, anything, that would explain the mystery of the night before. But he found nothing. As he trudged back up the basement stairs, he couldn't imagine why the gaunt man had come to such a place, why he'd had a key, what he'd done inside, what had become of him.

He could hear Sloane's voice, a low monotone, from the master bedroom as he moved back through the living room. It was a small house—the living area all flowed together, the kitchen, dining room, and sitting area all merging into one. No privacy, Rollins thought. At the big house in Brookline where he'd grown up, space was all there was. Everything and everyone seemed so far apart—shut away in that vast house behind thick, oak doors down long hallways that were hung with oils and silenced by thick Persian rugs. But here, the slightest sounds rang through the walls like gunfire.

"Harris?" It was Marj calling from the master bedroom. It took Rollins a moment to realize that she meant him. He turned and found her coming toward him. "I didn't know where you were." She sounded frightened.

"I was showing her the Jacuzzi," Sloane explained. Was there a note of guilt in his voice? "Worth the price of the house right there. Want to see?"

He guided Rollins back to the master bath. Water was pouring into the tub through a golden spigot, pooling with a froth of bubbles.

Rollins didn't like the look of it. "We should be going." He headed back out of the bedroom and down the hall to the front door.

"You want to leave an address or phone number or something?" Sloane shouted after him.

"I don't think we're interested after all," Rollins replied. "Thanks anyway."

"Well, you have my card if you change your mind." Sloane stood just inside the screen door, watching them. "People do, you know, all the time."

Outside in his car, Rollins could feel Sloane's eyes on him from the threshold as he released the hand brake and switched on the ignition. It was like being X-rayed. He shouldn't have been able to feel anything, but he did. The whole left side of his head seemed to buzz where it was exposed to Sloane's gaze. He eased the car away from the curb.

"Find anything?" Marj asked.

Distracted, Rollins didn't quite take in what Marj was asking.

"I said, did you find out anything while I was in with el creepo?"

"No. Nothing." He took a right, to double back onto 62. He still felt Sloane's gaze.

"You sure he wasn't the guy you followed?"

"*Yes.*" Rollins nodded emphatically.

"Then why do you suppose he was so interested in you?"

Sometimes, Rollins felt things before his brain registered them: His palms suddenly felt oily, and there was a murky pulsing deep in his chest. "What makes you think he was?"

"Are you blind? You didn't notice the way he looked at you?"

"Of course not." All his senses had been on high alert. But he had been distracted, first by Marj and then by Sloane's suddenly pulling up out of nowhere, his headlights blazing. If only he'd had a little warning, time to prepare.

"It was like he was trying to figure out if he knew you from somewhere," Marj went on. "You *sure* you never seen him before?"

"Positive."

"Then, when he had me alone with him by the Jacuzzi, he kept asking me stuff about you—like where you worked, where you lived. He kept it casual, but I could tell he really wanted to know. That's why I yelled. Freaked me fucking out."

Sloane's face loomed up in Rollins' mind, big as a billboard. "You didn't tell him, did you?"

"I had to tell him *something*!"

"Why?"

"He'd think I was holding out on him. Rolo, it would have been strange. I kept it real general, don't worry. I said you were in mutual funds, and you lived, like, in town."

"Oh, Jesus."

"Look, maybe he was just trying to tell if you could afford the house."

"Anybody could afford that house."

"I couldn't."

An offhand remark, Rollins was pretty sure. Marj hadn't meant anything by it. All the same, it shamed him. Clearly, his parents had been right about one thing: It was never wise to discuss money. He vowed to avoid the topic with Marj in the future.

The rest of the ride back to Boston passed uneasily for Rollins. He dropped Marj off at her apartment building. Despite her demurrals, he saw her to her front door and opened it for her.

"Thanks." Her voice seemed to be almost all breath. "You don't suppose anything bad will happen, do you? I mean, we were just playing around, basically, right?"

Rollins assured her that nothing would come of it.

Marj smiled. "Well, good night then." She extended a hand. Still smarting from the pushy way that Sloane had thrust out his hand, Rollins was determined to be more suave with Marj. But somehow he miscalculated and, rather than lock onto the meat of her hand, he ended up grasping mostly her fingers.

Instead of driving home, he went through the first intersection, then curved back to watch her windows for a few minutes from a taxi stand. Things were starting to swim a little, and he just wanted to make sure that she was okay. That's all. He saw her speak on a cordless phone as she paced back and forth in front of what he guessed were the living room windows. He watched her gesture with those very same fingers, the ones that had touched him. He watched her run them through her hair.

Three

It was past eleven when he returned to his own apartment building, a former row house on Hanover Street in Boston's North End. The neighborhood was home mostly to Italian-Americans, but also to an increasing number of well-heeled young professionals like himself, who were drawn to the cappuccino bars and not put off by the lingering mob associations of the place. At that hour, Rollins was surprised to find his landlady, Mrs. D'Alimonte, still up. "Oh, Mr. Rollins!" she cried, bustling out of her ground floor apartment with a plateful of cannoli. She was wearing a faded housedress, and her hair looked limp from the heat. "I baked them for you special."

Rollins was in no mood for dessert, but he didn't want to be impolite. He selected one of the pastries and delicately bit into the end, careful not to make a mess of the ricotta filling. "Delicious," he said. "Thank you."

"You're out late tonight," said Mrs. D'Alimonte, widening her round eyes. "A pretty girl, I hope."

Rollins flushed, then realized she was just fishing for information. He headed upstairs, eager for the solitude of his apartment, his wide bed and soft pillow.

He had made it only a few steps up the stairs before Mrs. D'Alimonte called out to him again. "I'm glad you like the cannoli, Mr. Rollins." She raised her voice a little. "Because I—well—I meant to tell you—this came for you the other day." Rollins craned his head around. She was holding an envelope by one corner as if it were some sort of legal evidence. "And I—oh dear—somehow it ended up in my apartment under the newspapers and—"

Rollins returned a few steps down the stairs and took the envelope from her hand. As he did so, Mrs. D'Alimonte's jaw started to quiver. Rollins hadn't thought he could have such an effect on anyone, least of all his oversize landlady. He inspected the envelope. *Rollins* was handwritten in ballpoint on the front, nothing more; there was no stamp, postmark, or return address.

"Someone must have dropped it off for you," Mrs. D'Alimonte said. "I—I found it on the floor just inside the front door."

"When?"

"A week ago? Maybe ten days? I'm afraid I don't exactly remember."

"Mrs. D'Alimonte, I have to ask: Do you usually examine my mail?"

"No, never, Mr. Rollins!"

But Rollins had made his point. He pocketed the envelope and continued back upstairs.

"Mr. Rollins, are you in some kind of trouble?"

Rollins stopped again. "Whatever makes you think that?"

"You seem—oh, nothing. Never mind. Good night, Mr. Rollins. I'm sorry about the letter. I should have given it to you sooner. I'm just a mixed-up old lady."

Rollins waited until Mrs. D'Alimonte had retreated back into her apartment before he opened his door. He had installed several dead bolts, and it always took him a while to unlock everything. Inside, he punched in the code disconnecting his burglar alarm, then flipped on the lights and checked to see that all the shades were pulled.

Rollins lived in a one-bedroom apartment with dark wallpaper he'd selected to bring out the dusky hues of the oil landscapes on the walls. Restfully English in their gilt frames, they'd been acquired by a great-aunt for a song at Knoedler's nearly a century earlier. Another family heirloom stood by the window, next to the radiator. It was an early Victorian mahogany sideboard that had come down from his maternal grandfather. It was a little large for the space, but Rollins had always been fond of it. As a child, he had liked to hide in the lower cabinets, especially during his parents' dinner parties. That was how he'd learned his father considered him "withdrawn" and "enigmatic," two words he'd had to look up. Now, the sideboard was decorated with a scissored angel from the younger of Richard's two children, an eight-year-old named Natalie; it had come two Christmases ago, but Rollins hadn't thrown it out. The angel stood, somewhat faded and curled up, beside some ceremonial silver and an extremely handsome, inlaid Parisian humidor. Since Rollins didn't smoke, the humidor had remained empty for years until, through a previous job, he got to know a private investigator by the name of Al Schecter. Actually, Schecter always called himself a "professional investigator" to downplay the lurid Hollywood associations of his career. Rollins hadn't talked to him in years, but he thought of him fondly every time he looked at the humidor. Schecter had given him a dozen cigars—illegal Cubans from his collection—to fill it. In tribute to Schecter, Rollins had never removed them.

Envelope in hand, Rollins settled into the large leather chair that stood by the bookcase stuffed with a few of his Latin texts from college, some business books, an Arnold genealogy volume (covering his mother's side of the family), and a complete leatherbound edition of James Fenimore Cooper that his grandmother had given him as a graduation present. He switched on the antique lamp that curved over the chair, pulled on his reading glasses, and looked at the envelope. The *Rollins* was written with a definite scrawl, whether it was a mark of haste or slovenliness he couldn't guess. A cheap pen, anyway. A blob of ink had congealed at the top of the *R* and on the second *l*.

He took a breath, poked an index finger under the flap, and ripped the envelope open. There was a note inside, written on plain paper. It bore no name or letterhead, merely a number scrawled with the same blobby ballpoint: *9427503*. At first, Rollins assumed it was some sort of account number or possibly an entry code. But then he noted the seven digits and decided that it had to be a telephone number, even if it lacked the usual hyphen separating out the exchange. He glanced over at the telephone, the heavy, black, rotary type now considered old-fashioned, at his elbow. He considered dialing, but it was nearly midnight, no time to phone.

The note on the side table glowed slightly yellow in the tawny morning light that filtered through the window shades. Rollins was tempted to crumple it up and toss it into the wastebasket like other unsolicited correspondence. It was rude, after all, to be so inexplicable. The note seemed to demand something from him that he wasn't sure he wanted to give.

It brought back to mind all the strange events involving the dark house, events that were likewise inexplicable. Could those events and this obscure note be linked? On the face of it, two oddities in close succession seemed likely to be related. That's the conclusion that he'd come to last night, anyway, as he was struggling to go to sleep. But now, in the daylight, he wasn't so sure. If Mrs. D'Alimonte was to be believed, the note had arrived well before Rollins had gone to the dark house, before he'd ever thought of going to the dark house, before there ever *was* a dark house so far as he was concerned. And it was as pointless to contemplate a link between these two unrelated occurrences as . . . well, as it would be to project matrimony between him and Marj based on the previous evening's car ride. After all, that night's pursuit had been purely arbitrary, as always. Rollins had simply looked up from the *Herald*'s gossip column in front of that newsstand in Somerville, spotted the Audi going by, and followed it.

He took the sheet of paper into the kitchen and propped it up against the salt and pepper shakers on the table and sat down before it, bringing his head low to study it. It was just a number. A number from nowhere. That was all. No watermarks, stray doodles— or any indentations left from other correspondence, which a cop show recollected from his childhood inspired him to check for.

For comparison, he retrieved the envelope from the telephone table and tipped it up against a candlestick. He looked from one document to the other. On both, the handwriting was light, almost spidery. Looking closer, he thought he detected a trace of femininity in the delicate loop of the first *9*. In Rollins' experience, men's handwriting tended toward jagged angularity, women's to a more supple roundness. The idea came to him in a spasm: Might Marj have written it? In a kind of brain-burst, he pictured her laboring over the paper, tongue protruding through tightened lips, ballpoint in hand.

He hurried to the telephone book to see if Brighton might be covered by the 942 exchange. But no: 942 was for Watertown, across the Charles River from Brighton. While he was at it, he checked Marj's home telephone. There was an M. Simmons at her address on Washington Street, but the phone was 367–9836. Another wild possibility struck him. Both the name Rollins and the number 9427503 were seven units long. Was 9427503 the numerical equivalent of his name on the telephone dial? Was someone playing an elaborate joke on him? He checked the telephone. No to that, too. Rollins and 9427503 did not overlap in the slightest; the telephone equivalent of Rollins was 7655467.

He was tempted to dial that number, just for curiosity's sake. But he returned to the kitchen and, leaving the two pieces of paper on their easels, he prepared his breakfast (toast with peach jam, orange juice, black coffee). He continued to stare at them from various angles around the little kitchen throughout his meal. When he had cleared away his dishes, he could postpone the inevitable no longer. He carried the note over to his telephone table, picked up the receiver, and dialed. He got two rings, then a click. Then the shrill whine of a fax/modem line shrieked into his ear, and he hurriedly replaced the receiver.

* * *

It would have been about a ten-minute walk from his North End apartment to Johnson Investments in Boston's financial district, but Rollins always drove. That took fifteen minutes, what with the lights, the tangle of one-way streets, and the parking. With the windows rolled up and the visor down, he felt safely insulated from the world as he glided along. Irritable this morning, with so much on his mind, he applied the horn liberally to scatter the pedestrians in his path.

He settled the car into its space four levels down from the street, then boarded the elevator to the lobby floor, its gleaming Tuscan marble and polished brass a testament to the firm's prosperity, if not to that of its employees. For himself, he liked being part of such a big, gleaming success; it took off some of the family pressure to accomplish something personally. He enjoyed the smart click of his heels against the marble, the expansive echo, the surge of other well-dressed employees hurrying along to keep up with the demands of the global markets. He crossed the hall and, passing up two elevators that looked a bit too full for comfort, rode in silence to the fourteenth floor in the company of Kent McMillan, the twenty-nine-year-old stock picker whose Emerging Sector Fund had of late defied gravity. For three flights, Rollins watched him in the shiny reflection of the elevator doors. Then he spoke. "Mind if I ask you a question?"

McMillan's eyes turned to his.

"Do people ever send you things out of the blue? People you don't know, I mean."

"Fan mail?" McMillan flicked some lint off a lapel. "Sure. Goes with the territory."

"I meant something more along the line of . . . anonymous notes."

Clearly, McMillan didn't grasp what Rollins meant. "I get pictures sometimes. Women send 'em to me. You'd be surprised. Some of 'em—whew." He rolled his eyes.

"They send them to you at home?"

"God, no. I'm not listed. The office. Why—someone been bugging you?"

"No, no." Rollins coughed up a little laugh that he hoped would sound dismissive. "Nothing serious. I just received something a little unusual—handwritten, no name—and I thought you might—"

McMillan interrupted: "If it gets weird, you can always call security. They're tigers."

The elevator reached Rollins' floor, and he stepped out. "Well, thanks."

"Sorry it happened," McMillan called out behind him.

McMillan had ten more flights to go, but Rollins got off on fourteen to join the other drones in operations, or ops, which amounted to the custodial department of the growing Johnson empire. If Rollins were ever blinded, he could find his way here by smell, or the absence thereof, for it was the one part of the entire building that bore no scent whatsoever. The other departments, to Rollins' refined nostrils, nearly reeked of greed and fear, the dueling emotions of high finance. But ops was safe from all that. All the drones did was run the numbers on the numbers—determining the profits and losses of the big egos upstairs. By most standards, it was dull work. It involved no travel, few telephone conversations even, just the steady click of computer keys and an occasional amble down the hall for a cup of decaf or a Diet Coke.

But ops was Rollins' domain, his lair, and it comforted him to see the place this morning, just as always: the blue-gray carpeting that covered not just the floor but three feet of the walls as well; the chalky, acoustic-tiled ceiling; the shiny faces, unmarked by strain. The sounds evoked an electronic rain forest: the driplike patter of the computer keyboards; the murmur of subdued, unenthusiastic voices; the warbling sort of ring that the phones gave off. Rollins had been here five years, a tenure twice the duration of the next-longest inmate, the irrepressible Sally James in overseas. But unlike the others, Rollins had no plans to leave.

One of the attractive points of the job for Rollins had always been the narrowness of its emotional range. He didn't go to many parties, but when he did he usually accompanied the inevitable description of his job with a brief, wry lecture on the value of monotony. To him, the work represented security, reliability, steadiness—qualities that were important for reasons he had never fully explored and did not intend to. He let the big egos grapple with the vagaries of the investment trade, whether interest rates would rise or fall, where the unemployment rate would be six months out, whether the bond market would be spooked by an inauspicious military buildup in some piddling third-world country. Rollins merely put the day's figures in a row and added them up. Well, there was more to it than that, but who really wanted to go into it? Leave it at this: Some days the sum was positive, some days negative, and he didn't particularly care either way.

Rollins always arrived well before nine o'clock, to give himself time to get settled before the numbers started to fly when the domestic equity markets opened at nine-thirty. This morning, he passed through the glass double doors at 8:47. Happy not to be waylaid by Harmony, the gabby receptionist, he embarked on the twenty-three steps that led him to his small office with its one window, a prized emblem of his seniority. Marj's workstation was about ten feet past his own, off to the right, and concealed behind a gray baffle. Rollins would catch sight of her only if she was standing, which she evidently wasn't doing now. He was burning to ask her about the note, but he was not prepared to go and actually peer in her doorway to see if she was there. That would be a public declaration of interest in Marj that he wasn't prepared to make. She was little more than a temp, after all, one with double earrings in each ear, like some Hottentot.

He veered off toward his desk, sat down, and scanned the windows of the office building across the way. But his eyes did not linger there. He felt edgy, restless. He flipped on his computer and tapped his foot on the carpeting until the machine booted up. He checked for e-mail messages, but found none. He felt a moment of relief that at least one avenue to his awareness remained uninvaded. Then disappointment set in. Marj might have sent him something. He could imagine it: clumsy but affectionate, signed—who knows?—"me." He drummed his fingers on the desk. Maybe she hadn't arrived yet. Unlike himself, her daily schedule was more variable. Some days, she rushed in well after the market had opened, a bit of tardiness that was nearly unforgivable at Johnson. Other days, she arrived even before he did. Was she here?

Rollins stood up and quickly scanned across the baffle tops. No sign of her.

He grabbed a mug off the slender shelf above his desk and headed down the corridor toward the kitchen nook. He slowed as he passed Marj's desk. He glimpsed a bright summer outfit. Marj was leaning back in her chair as she talked to Jenette Manglen, the matronly senior executive from sectors. Rollins' and Marj's eyes met for only a moment. Marj's fingers flicked a slight greeting. Before Manglen could spot him loitering there, Rollins accelerated again.

He lingered in the kitchen area, sampling the doughnuts. He bit into three of them, found them all unappetizing, and dropped them in the trash. He checked his watch, then slowly made his way back to his office, coffee in hand. This time, Marj was alone. She looked up toward him expectantly, but, right then, Rollins could not bring himself to speak to her. What would he say? It was enough to know, simply, that she was there. He continued on back to his desk, where he sipped his coffee, his door open beside him.

"You could at least wave." It was Marj, close by. He sensed the brightness of her dress.

Rollins pretended to be absorbed in his computer screen.

From the way the air moved, he could feel her lean down to him. "Hello?"

He turned around to face her. He noticed the thin, wobbly line of yellow eyeliner on her eyelid, the youthful softness of her cheeks and chin.

She leaned back against his desktop, her pelvis nearly at his eye level. "What, not talking to me?"

In his youth, Rollins had been prone to migraines that whipped up out of nothing, forcing him to lie under cold compresses in bed with the shades drawn for days, and he lived in fear that they would someday return. They tended to come out of a feeling of being overwhelmed, as if he were caught in a net from which he could never clear himself, no matter how much he flailed and flailed. Certain colors could do it, some smells, even a noise if it was the right pitch. But some emotions would do it most of all. Now, despite his eagerness to be here with

Marj, Rollins felt his temples pounding in a way that was not auspicious. He needed silence, solitude. Rollins got up from his chair and stepped past her, inadvertently catching his fingertip on her skirt as he brushed by. "Excuse me. I'm sorry." He headed briskly down the corridor. Rollins could sense heads turning toward him as he rushed by, but he was past caring. As he passed the kitchen nook, he hurriedly set his coffee mug down in the sink. Behind him, he could see Marj pursuing him.

This was not good. He hurried on down to the end of the corridor, past the boss's glassed-in office, took a right, and dashed to the men's room, sure that he would be safe there among the porcelain urinals. He pushed open the heavy door and rushed headlong to the sink, desperate to plunge his head under ice-cold water. But just as he was reaching for the spigot, the door opened again behind him, and he heard a pair of heels click on the tiled floor.

"Rolo, you all right?" It was Marj, coming closer.

At first, Rollins didn't answer. He ducked down silently to check the toilet stalls, which, mercifully, were empty. "You shouldn't be in here," he said quietly. He soaked a paper towel with cold water and dabbed his forehead.

Marj stepped closer and took the towel from him. "Bend down." She spoke softly.

Rollins grasped the edges of the sink with his hands, bowed his head, and closed his eyes. He felt her hands push into his hair as she pressed the cool towel down on his temples, first one, then the other. Some water trickled down toward his eyes, like backward tears.

Warm water slurping in his ear, and suds threatening his eyes, and her hands on him, Neely's hands, digging into his scalp, pushing and pushing, from behind him, as she bent over his back. "Keep your eyes shut," she'd say. "Squeeze 'em." And his snuffling as he said okay.

He closed his eyes tight, his head filled with the soothing sensation that came from Marj's fingertips. He was eager for it, but uncertain, too. He was too aware of Marj's body, pressing against his side; with Neely, he'd sensed only her hands.

"Headache?"

"A migraine. I could feel it coming. I'm sorry. I should have said."

Marj continued to massage his temples. Rollins was terribly afraid someone might come in. "You sleep all right last night?" she asked.

"Not particularly."

"Me neither. I kept thinking about that weird house, and that real estate guy."

Rollins let his head sag, trying to let the soothing coolness from her fingertips work into his brain. A long time passed in silence as her fingers went around and around on his temples. For a while, her gentle strokes achieved wonders. It seemed that her caresses were actually reaching into his consciousness. But finally, the sheer proximity of this near-stranger, delightful as she was, unnerved him. He thought about how awkward it would look if someone came in and found them there, his head bent low before her, his left ear so close to her breast. He stepped away from the sink. "Thanks." He pulled out some paper towels to dry his hands and the sides of his face. When he looked up, he was surprised she was still there, considering that he had delivered her cue to leave. But there was no denying it—she was definitely attractive just now, her hair rumpled, her lips parted as she looked at him.

"I found this when I arrived home last night," he said after a moment. He reached into his jacket pocket and handed her the envelope.

Marj wiped her hands on her skirt and took it from him.

Rollins watched her open up the envelope and slide out the paper. "You didn't leave it for me by any chance, did you?"

"This?" Marj read off the digits, then checked on the back. "God, no. What's 9427503—the winning lotto?"

"I figured it was a phone number."

"You try it?"

Rollins nodded gently, not wanting to bring on a headache. "It's a fax line."

Marj brought her hand to her mouth. "Oh, God—you got that, that screech? No wonder you have a headache."

"You sure you didn't leave it?"

"Rolo, I don't even know where you live."

That nickname seemed to have established an intimacy that Rollins wasn't quite ready for.

"Yesterday, you told Sloane I lived in town," he said evenly.

"Will you get off this, please? In town—that's just an expression, okay?" She looked at the note again. "It's not even my handwriting. I don't do script—not like that anyway. Look—"

She reached into Rollins' jacket for a pen and wrote his name out in her own handwriting below the other *Rollins*. When she was finished, it was strange to see his name there twice, as if two different people—both of them strangers, really—were calling out to him.

"See?" Marj asked. "What would I send you a bunch of numbers for, anyway? If I wanted to write you something, I'd use words."

"I guess I wasn't thinking."

"So who did send it?"

"That's what I don't know."

"We'll have to try the fax line, then." Marj snapped up the paper and headed for the door.

"Wait a second—you can't just—"

But Marj didn't stop. Conscious of his incipient migraine, Rollins tried not to jostle his head too much as he hurried to catch up to her outside in the corridor. "You can't just send her anything."

Marj turned around toward him, puzzlement on her face. "Her?"

Somewhat sheepishly, Rollins told her his theory of female penmanship, afraid Marj might find it sexist. Women could be touchy about such things.

Marj looked at the letter again. "Maybe. We'll have to find out, won't we?" She led him back to the fax machine and pulled out a blank sheet of paper. "Here. Write something."

"But if I send a note, it will have this fax number on it. Whoever-it-is will know where I work."

"They already know where you live."

Rollins rubbed his temples, feeling the hot skin slide around on either side of his head.

"Besides, you were willing to call from your home phone. That's traceable. Ever heard of caller ID?"

"Yes, but—" It hadn't occurred to him that such a modern innovation might apply to his own calls from such an antique phone. It distressed him to think how visible he was—he who had always prided himself on his ability to stay hidden. It seemed that he was scattering calling cards wherever he went. "Oh, never mind."

"Go on. Write something. It probably won't go through anyway. It's probably just a computer modem."

Rollins leaned over the table on which the fax machine sat. After a bit of thought, he wrote: *Who are you and what do you want?* He showed the line to Marj.

"Perfect." She gave him an admiring look, then took the sheet and fed it into the fax machine, punched in the number on the telepad, and pressed the green START button. There was a dial tone, then the chirp of the numbers going through, and then the scream of the machine at the other end of the line. Finally a click, and the paper started to slide slowly through.

"Looks like it's working," Marj said.

Both of them watched the paper disappear into the machine and reemerge into the collecting tray beneath. Marj scooped it up from there and handed it to Rollins, who dropped it into the wastebasket. "I guess it was a fax number," he said.

All Rollins could think was that he had sent a message off into the void. But he didn't have a chance to ponder this for long. The fax machine soon gave out another click, then it started to rumble, and slowly a piece of paper rose from the machine's hind end. Rollins swept the fax off the receiving tray. It was his own message sent back to him. But this time, each *you* was underlined, so that the sentence now read: *Who are you and what do you want?*

"Well, looks like it was a wrong number after all," Rollins said, relieved.

Marj looked astonished. "Are you kidding me? Somebody's on to you, Rolo. Who are you, what do you want—it's what *I'd* want to know."

"Come on. It's just some clod who's irritated to get a fax from a stranger."

"Well, let's find out." Marj snatched the message from Rollins and grabbed the pen that was still in his hand. She added her own note to the bottom of the fax: *What's that supposed to mean?*

Rollins watched as she slid it into the fax machine, pressed REDIAL, then START. The fax worked its way through the machine's digestive tract.

For several minutes, they both hovered expectantly over the fax machine. But no message came back.

"See?" Rollins said. "It's nothing." He returned to his desk, glad finally to be right about something.

It was hot and steamy when Rollins left the Johnson building in his Nissan—eighty-six degrees according to the electronic sign on the U.S. Trust building on Congress Street. To get his mind off this non-sense with the fax number, he latched on to the first car he saw whose license plate ended in 86. He was desperate to lose himself in a pursuit again. On the road, he was nothing and nobody, just a pair of eyes and a pair of lips to record what he saw. He longed to empty himself out again.

The vehicle with the 86 proved to be a maroon Ford Windstar. He'd caught sight of the minivan turning right off Commonwealth Avenue onto Arlington Street, by the Public Garden with its roses and fruit trees, and he dutifully made note of this fact into the tape recorder. "Seems to be a fan of the governor's," Rollins added, refer-ring to the sticker on the rear bumper. He followed the minivan into the Callahan Tunnel and up Route 1A by Logan Airport to a parking lot beside a litter-strewn baseball field, where three uniformed young ballplayers piled out. "Little Leaguers, looks like," Rollins whispered into the tape recorder as he glided by. "Three of them and a dad." His own father's sporting interests had always been confined to an occasional round of golf at the country club. Rollins parked farther down the lot, then stepped out of his car. The kids played for JOE'S DONUTS INDIANS, as it said in block type across the front of their uniforms, the O's enlarged to look like doughnuts. Rollins watched the driver lead his charges to the diamond. He waited a bit, then followed behind.

It was a pleasant evening, if a little moist, and Rollins took a seat high up in the stands to watch the Indians go through their warm-ups. A clear violation of the code: Customarily, Rollins remained hidden in his car throughout a pursuit. But as he had seen with Cindy, he was drawn to this great American idyll, one he'd scarcely experienced as a boy. He'd played only a little ball, never very well, of course. Richard was the athletic one in the family. Besides, it was good to get some air.

The Indians were taking on the Werner Ford Mustangs. The game itself was slow to get going, and then proved to be a sloppy affair with muffed grounders and errant pitching. Rollins' attention wandered to the distant trees, the various advertisements on the outfield wall, and finally to a youngish redhead in cut-offs and a tank top who was leaning against the side of the backstop. For a fleeting moment, Rollins thought it was Marj. Her fingers grasping the fence's wire mesh, the young woman's arms were up, giving Rollins a provocative glimpse of her underarms. She had a touch of Marj's brightness, her ability to liven things up.

After a couple of innings, she gave the Mustangs a last shout of encouragement and headed for the parking lot.

Rollins followed her.

Rollins' palms tingled, and his breath came faster than normal as he strolled along. He was conscious of being exposed on all sides, not just from a narrow angle or two as he would be in his car. He was aware of his skin, the visible parts and, also, the invisible parts that, with each step, were being rubbed and pressed by the insides of his clothes. But mostly he concentrated on the woman he was following. Each purrlike scuff of her sandals put every part of her in intriguing motion—her hair swinging across the back of her neck, her muscled calves flexing with each step, her thighs quivering inside her clingy cut-offs. He wasn't at all sure where this would lead, but he couldn't stop himself.

He'd crossed a line—into a place without lines.

She climbed into a Chrysler convertible with the top up and exited the parking lot quickly. Rollins had to hurry to his car (without being too obvious about it) and then zip after her to catch up. She went right onto 1A, and then U-ed back at the first rotary. Rollins stayed with her, several cars behind. Ten minutes passed as Rollins pursued the Chrysler, the driver's hair flowing behind like a windsock. His thoughts locked on to her, Rollins wondered if, like Marj, she also listened to hard rock and spent her evenings yakking on her cordless. This time, he left the recorder off.

He followed the Chrysler back to working-class Chelsea, where she wove through the grimy downtown. He felt a ripple of anxiety as, stopped at a light, he thought he caught her stealing an extra look in her rearview. He flipped down his visor to obscure himself. Then he had a jolt of fright a few blocks later when he saw her reach for a cell phone. Still he pursued. He charged in after her when, without signaling (so like Marj!), she made a sharp right turn into a narrow alley by a pizza parlor. He'd gone in about twenty yards when, with sudden terror, he saw the Chrysler jerk to a halt. The woman whipped around in her seat and pointed right at him, rage on her face. "He's right there!" she shouted.

Off to his right, Rollins saw a large bearded man come racing up a side alley at him. He was wielding a baseball bat. "Get the *fuck* away from my wife!" the man screamed. Rollins slammed the car into reverse and shot out of there, every nerve on fire.

What—what had gotten into him? What had he been thinking of? He thought he'd been so careful, so cunning. And for what? For nothing. It was wrong, wrong, wrong. He shouldn't have followed that poor woman. This exact situation was what his rules were for! He must have frightened her horribly—to see him following her like some stalker. And the risk to himself! That bearded man—the husband. He could have— Well, who knew exactly, but it might have been dreadful. He might have been hurt. Or the police might have been involved, or reporters. Just the thought of the shame, the embarrassment. The humiliation. And for what? What *had* he been seeking? What if the bearded man had *not* charged at him—how far would he have pursued? What had he hoped to see? What might he have done?

His thoughts raced this way and that. But they always returned to the same place. To one idea, one feeling. He wanted to get closer. That was all.

Four

Rollins kept the tapes of his pursuits, filed by date and time, in their original clear-plastic cases on a long shelf over the wide, maple-framed bed in his bedroom. It seemed safest to have them there, where they would be close to him while he slept. Even though they did not concern him directly (*he* was not the subject of his pursuit, after all), they were still extremely personal, and revealing in their way.

The very first pursuit had occurred a few weeks before he'd arrived at Johnson—almost five years earlier, on November 18, 1995, at 6:17 P.M., as it said in black felt-tip pen on the spine of the left-most cassette box. He'd come off a career in journalism, or something of a career (it lasted only a few years and ended badly); he'd been accustomed to taking elaborate notes and often used a tape recorder. That first one wasn't much, just a kind of private journalism, a way of keeping his hand in. He'd spotted an interesting-looking car, a '63 Renault, as it happened, two cars up on the expressway, and he'd gotten curious about its owner. That proved to be an elderly retiree who lived alone in a small beachfront cottage in Harwichport, out on the Cape. After that, he tailed a magenta Ford Fairlane, drawn to the unusual color. It was driven by a frizzy-haired student who parked it in a tow zone in the Back Bay, removed a pair of stereo speakers from the trunk, and disappeared into a brownstone that belonged to Emerson College.

In those early days, when he was still caught up in the drama of each chase, Rollins had recorded practically everything, not just the objective details of a pursuit. He imagined elaborate romantic histories for his subjects (often replete with scandalous divorces and abandoned children), described the weather in adjective-laden detail, critiqued the architecture, reviewed the cars (particularly savagely where low-end Japanese imports were concerned). . . . Now, he was embarrassed that he could ever have gone on so.

But he was younger then, and a bit of a romantic. Listening to these early tapes again, he sometimes sensed in them a tone of—what? explanation?—as though he'd imagined, even in the act of speaking, that he might share them someday with someone else. Here and there, he also picked up a note of unhappiness and longing that he hadn't meant to express, hadn't even been aware of at the time, and it startled him to hear himself sound so low. He'd always thought he'd come across as reasonably happy. He attributed those occasional bleats of dissatisfaction to an uneasy adjustment to the solitary life back in his early thirties, when it became clear that dating was not his game.

It struck him now how young he'd seemed and how much he'd matured in those five years. He'd straightened his life out a great deal since. He had a job, a good job, as well as what was surely one of the most exciting hobbies imaginable. Objectively, things may not have changed a great deal, but he had adjusted to them so much better. When he listened to the recent tapes, he figured he sounded all right. (Then again, it had taken a few years for the sadness of those early tapes to become apparent, as if his deepest feelings were recorded on a film that took a long time to develop. He tried not to dwell too much on that distressing possibility.) In any case, he figured he'd probably never find anyone to listen to the tapes, so he'd gradually cut back on the verbiage, which was the safer course anyway. Now the verbal record was purely an aide-mémoire, a few basic details to kindle his recollection. In most cases, he confined himself to the make and model of car, time of sighting, route, destination, the subject, and any activities witnessed.

Those early tapes, even when stacked three boxes high (ten tapes to a box), covered almost four feet of shelf. He'd switched to the much handier microcassettes after six months—on July 7, 1996, at 9:17 P.M.—and they continued, six to a slim case, another two feet, leaving only about a foot more for future recordings.

It was a hot night, and Rollins (who didn't believe in air-conditioning) was stretched out on his bed in his white boxer shorts, his head back on pillows, trying to get his mind off the sight of the redhead's husband coming at him. Because of the heat, he thought he might enjoy a winter recording, and, choosing pretty much at random, he'd selected the box from December 19, 1995, one of the early ones. Rollins removed the thick Sony tape player from the bedside cabinet and placed it beside him on the pillow. He slipped the tape into the slot and lay back with his eyes closed.

"Tuesday, December nineteenth, nineteen ninety-five. Eight-fourteen P.M.," the tape began. "I'm on Boylston Street in the Back Bay between—what have we got here?—all right, yes, I see where I am now, between Berkeley and Clarendon." The sound of his own voice was hypnotic. "The man I'm following is in a tan Mercedes S600. Married, I bet. But it wouldn't surprise me if he had somebody on the side. Seems like the type. A little too handsome, if you ask me. Too sure of himself. Too smooth. He left the Prudential garage seven minutes ago." On the tape, the Merc's driver double-parked and hurried inside a Bath 'n' Bed shop. "Probably a last-minute Christmas-gift pickup for the wife he's forgotten all about."

The tape went on: "A couple of boys just went past. Five and seven is my guess, nicely dressed, matching parkas, holding tight to their mother. I'll bet a dollar they're headed to F.A.O. Schwarz." Listening to his earlier self, Rollins tensed, just as his earlier self probably had. At roughly the age of the older boy, he'd gone with his brother Richard to see the Santa Claus at F.A.O Schwarz one December. The boys were taken by the handyman, Gabe, who sometimes doubled as chauffeur in his Buick Skylark, its wide interior fragrant with pipe tobacco. After Stephanie died, their parents usually offloaded such tasks, giving young Rollins the impression they couldn't bear the sight of him anymore. So Gabe drove them to the toy store that day. Of course, when Christmas came, none of the gifts that Rollins had discussed so carefully with Santa—a rare German edition of a prewar BMW was particularly longed for—appeared under the tree.

"Only six days until Christmas," said Rollins' voice on the tape. "Look at everyone, all weighed down with packages, trudging through the goddamn slush. Nobody looks too joyful, if you ask me."

As the words brought the scenes to mind—the parked cars buried in snowbanks, the Christmas lights twinkling in ice-glazed trees (it had been a particularly harsh winter, he remembered), Rollins had the unusual sensation that he was getting inside his own head, and the even stranger feeling that his own head was all there was. In the background, he could hear cars splattering by. He could picture the ashen faces of the package-laden shoppers, the leaden skies overhead. He had the over-whelming impression of soot-smudged snow, of concrete-colored skies, of dull tasks being repeated endlessly. It was distressing, suddenly, to think that there might have been an actual world out there that was in fact quite different—cheerier, mostly—from the one that he detailed to his Sony. To Rollins' disturbed surprise, the voice cried out: "Is gray the only color of this Christmas season? Shouldn't I be seeing a little more red or green or white out here? Is it really this gray?" Rollins clicked off the machine, nearly quaking with amazement that his younger self had come to the same realization—and he hadn't remembered it. He sat up and looked again at the cases over his bed, wondering what other disturbed perceptions were locked away in them.

The telephone rang. Rollins glanced at the bedside clock: It was well after eight, too late for telemarketers. With a jolt, he remembered the possible fax number. Was its owner now calling him? Rollins didn't always answer his phone; if he was tired, he sometimes counted it a victory to hear the caller give up after six or seven rings. But he switched off the recorder, hurried to the sitting room, and plucked the receiver from its cradle. "Yes?"

"Rolo, that you?"

It was Marj. Her telephone voice was more full-throated than he had imagined. It seemed to thrust her toward him, mouth first.

"How did you get my number?" he asked cautiously. It wasn't listed.

"From Harmony." The Johnson receptionist. "She's got all the home numbers. Look, I'm out by the house. I think you should come."

"What house?"

"The house house. You know. The—dark house."

"You went *back*?"

"Just—oh, come on, would you please?" Marj sounded like she might burst into tears. "It's on fire, Rollins! There are all these fire engines and shit everywhere."

Rollins went silent, imagining the blaze, the streams of water arcing from fat hoses.

"Hurry, okay?"

"I'll be there as soon as I can." Rollins restored the receiver to its cradle. He returned to his bed and, with some reluctance, unplugged the recorder and returned the tape to its place on the shelf overhead. It offered some serenity, this scene he had recorded so many years ago and tucked away in a plastic case like all the others, all of them completely over and done with. But then he thought of the house engulfed in flames and Marj there watching, the fire flickering in her eyes, the heat on her skin.

Mrs. D'Alimonte must have been hovering by her door, because she charged into the hall as soon as Rollins put his foot on the staircase. "Oh, Mr. Rollins," she cried out breathlessly, "is that you?"

Rollins continued down the stairs, his head down.

"Mr. Rollins?" she repeated.

"Mrs. D'Alimonte," he said frostily. Nothing more.

"The most wonderful news. I'm finally renting the other apartment on your floor." It had been vacant for months. "To a single mother with a lovely little girl. I don't usually take children, as you know, but she was just so adorable. And now I'm so excited!" She brought her hands together like a preteen. "A little girl, Mr. Rollins, isn't that wonderful? And the mother, I think you'll find her very attractive. I do hope you'll look out for them, Mr. Rollins."

"Yes, absolutely." Rollins gave her a big smile that he hoped would not seem too artificial.

"Going out again tonight?" Mrs. D'Alimonte asked. The way she stood there, her back against her apartment door, Rollins thought suddenly that the old woman was not just trying to marry him off to some new renter, but had designs on him herself.

"I have to see someone."

"Oh, really?" Mrs. D's eyes seemed to bore in on him.

"Good night, Mrs. D'Alimonte." Rollins closed the door behind him.

As he proceeded to his garage, he sensed something and turned: There was a man on the far side of the street moving away from him. Rollins felt sure that he had not been in motion before, that he had been standing, facing Rollins' apartment building until he came out. The man was reasonably well-dressed for this part of town. Once he'd turned, Rollins could make out only a skeletal quality to his features. A gaunt man. Rollins crossed the street and hurried after him, but the man hooked a left at the next block. When Rollins hurried to the corner, he had disappeared. Rollins glanced in a window or two of the cafes and restaurants down the street, but, seeing nothing of him, thought better of it. He didn't want the gaunt man—if it was *the* gaunt man—to think that he was looking for him. It was better to feign detachment, unconcern. Rollins returned the way he had come, glancing back only once to see if he was being followed. At his garage, he avoided the elevator and climbed the stairs to the third floor. Then, his eyes darting about the shadows, he rushed to his Nissan in slot 37. He sped out of the parking garage, tires squealing.

As he passed along the narrow North End streets, across the Charles, and then headed north—*again*—on Interstate 93, he paid far less attention to the cars up ahead than to the ones behind. He thought about the back of his head, how it would look from behind. He didn't see a dark Audi. Might the gaunt man—if, again, it had been the gaunt man he'd seen—have changed cars? Rollins tried to examine the drivers as he cruised along. But, searching by mirror in the fading light, he could barely see into the interior of adjoining cars. Possibly, the gaunt man had enlisted an associate to follow him.

The thought shot through him: The gaunt man might be in league with Sloane! Panicky, Rollins checked around for the realtor's hulking Land Cruiser and was relieved to see no sign of it.

The Nissan hummed smoothly along in the middle lane, but Rollins had the sensation he disliked most in life—of being intruded upon, of being physically disturbed. What's more, he was filled with foreboding that his private pursuit was now about to go public. By now, the TV news vans would have swarmed the tree-lined Elmhurst street by number 29. Blow-dried reporters would be addressing TV cameras before the house's smoldering embers for their eleven o'clock report.

Yet as he drove east on 62, he heard no sirens, and, as he scanned the moonlit horizon, he could see no smoke rising over the trees and the smattering of colonial houses that dotted the narrow highway. As he wound through sleepy North Reading and turned in on Elmhurst, he saw no sign of a fire at all. Number 29 still stood, the faux medieval door intact, the metal siding gleaming dully just as before. The only difference was that a FOR SALE sign from Sloane Realty now adorned the front yard.

He was still gazing in astonishment at 29 from across the street when he heard a rap on the passenger-side window. He snapped his head around. It was Marj. She gestured for him to roll down the window, which he did. But, annoyed, he didn't pop the door lock, just straightened up on his side of the car, his arms folded across his chest. From there, he could see her thin hand, with its silver bracelets, several rings, and bright yellow fingernails, slither over the glass to pluck the lock button. She climbed in beside him, then quietly pulled the door shut behind her.

"Hi," she said.

"Not much of a fire." Rollins looked back at the house.

"Maybe I exaggerated a little."

Rollins turned toward her again, so that their eyes met.

"It gets lonely watching a house all by yourself," Marj continued. "I don't know how you do it."

"How long have you been here?"

"Couple hours."

Rollins felt his eyebrows flicker involuntarily, the way they did when a driver he'd been following took a sudden, illegal U-turn on the highway, losing him. The girl was a mystery. By now, he thought he was a decent student of human nature, but clearly some things were beyond him.

"The whole thing was starting to bug me, all right?" She rubbed her hands together between her knees, as if she were cold. She had on a denim jacket and a tight skirt that revealed a lot of leg. Not what he'd have recommended for a pursuit. Her reddish hair flopped down over her forehead. "I hope you don't mind," she said.

"Why would I?"

"I don't know. It's your house—at least I think of it that way. I don't want to, like, barge in."

"What about Sloane?" he asked. "Weren't you afraid he'd see you here?"

"I brought something for that putz." She pulled a small silver canister out of the pocket of her jacket. "Mace." She pushed it to Rollins' face, close enough to make him pull his head back. "If he comes near me. *Pshhhh.*"

"Careful with that."

"Oh, relax. The safety cap's still on. See?" She waved that in front of his face, too.

Rollins shifted in his seat.

"You're mad at me, aren't you?" Marj asked.

"You did lie."

"Oh, poor baby." Marj slid over near him and pressed an open palm against Rollins' cheek. Her hand felt damp and cool—a misery after the sight of her long, lean thighs on his passenger seat.

"Please don't." His brother used to press his hands on him, just to be annoying.

"Okay, okay." Marj withdrew her hand. "Sorry."

Seeing her pull back, he was sorry, too; he shouldn't have said anything.

He looked at her, then out the window at 29 Elmhurst, then at Marj again. She had lured him back here. Not for the second time either, but a third. This violated a precept almost as inviolable as his Garbo rule: no repeats. He followed a car for one night, and that was it. Any more than that and he risked getting involved. He might leave a bit of himself in that car, that house, that life. Instead of him owning it, it might own him. He might become a part of the scene he'd meant only to witness.

"So, how'd you get here?" he asked.

"I brought my car." She gestured across the street, maybe five car lengths down from number 29. "Over there."

"You parked with your back to the house?"

"I used the rearview. I figured it'd be less conspicuous."

The girl could think.

"You see anything?" Rollins asked.

"Zip." Marj scratched her forehead with her yellow fingernails.

Rollins wondered if Marj was wearing perfume. He couldn't smell any, but perhaps that was because he'd gotten used to it. He tried to remember what the perfume had smelled like when he'd first ridden with her. Was it fruity or flowery? He closed his eyes for a second, thinking. With his eyes shut, he couldn't sense her presence, and that was strange, too. Normally, he could feel when people were close by. Perhaps she was becoming too familiar to him.

When he opened his eyes again, he saw her looking at him. "Headache?" she asked.

"I'm okay."

She sighed. "Pretty weird out here the other night."

"Maybe a little."

"All the pretending, I mean."

"I wasn't about to tell that man my real name," Rollins said defensively.

"I wasn't talking about you."

Rollins looked at her from a different angle.

"I meant me." Marj smoothed out her skirt, then fumbled with the hem. "I didn't tell you the full story about my dad. Remember how I told you he died in an accident?"

Rollins did remember. That and how envious he'd felt when she'd told him her father had died. Not that he wished his own father dead. Heavens. No, he simply wanted the relationship resolved. Two marriages later, was his father still his father? Or more exactly, was that *all* he was—not friend, mentor, fan? It was all the more confusing now that he lived somewhere on the opposite coast, and was virtually incommunicado. For all Rollins knew, his father could have had more children by now. For that matter, he could be dead.

That crumpled postcard announcing Father's remarriage. Just a few words on the back, scrawled in a lazy diagonal. Signed: Your father. *No* Love, *no* Fondly. *Just* Your father.

Marj looked over at him. "You still there?"

"Yes."

"You get so quiet sometimes." She waited a moment. "My dad didn't have an accident. I guess I like to think he did. I didn't want you to have the wrong idea about me." She turned away.

"So what did happen?"

"He just never came back. I guess he couldn't quite face up to the idea that he was a dad. My dad. So he just stayed over there, even after his time in the army was up. He's still there, far as I know."

"You never saw him?"

"Nope."

Rollins stared over at her. "Why are you telling me this?"

"I just didn't want you to think that you were the only person who was looking. I look all the time."

Rollins shifted uneasily in his seat. He did not take easily to change. He never rearranged the furniture in his apartment. He revised his list of favorite restaurants only when one closed. For almost a decade, he had taken the same vacations—a week in a small hotel called the Harborside in Florida's Pigeon Key in mid-February, and another at a tiny rented cottage on Sober Island, off Nova Scotia, in early August, now barely a fortnight away—and always alone. He belonged to no clubs, subscribed only to *National Geographic*; and, as for movies, he attended only the revivals of his adored classic black and whites at the Brattle in Harvard Square. Now, with Marj in the seat beside him, her hands tucked under her armpits, he feared that all of this was in danger.

Rollins stroked his chin with the tip of his right index finger, then turned away from her toward number 29. It was an unprepossessing house, but it was, at least temporarily, a fixed point in his universe. He started to trace the lines of the down spout up to the gutter. Then he caught himself and put the car in gear. "We shouldn't stay here."

"But my car—"

"We'll come back for it, don't worry."

"What's the matter?"

"I think I saw that gaunt man again."

"What gaunt man?"

"The guy in the Audi who led me here in the first place."

"Oh, *shit*. That guy? Where?" She looked around.

Rollins gave her the details of the possible sighting that evening. "I can't be sure," he wound up, "but we better get moving."

Marj fell silent for a moment, her brow tight, her head slightly cocked. "Wait—so you think he might be following you?"

"It's possible, yes." Rollins moved the car ahead slowly, in low gear, while he checked the rearview.

"Oh, *shit*," Marj said. "Shit, shit, shit, shit, shit." She struck him lightly on the shoulder. "I *knew* this would get scary. I just knew it."

"I'm not absolutely sure it was him. I didn't get a clear look at him."

"Did he run off at the sight of you?"

Rollins hesitated for a moment, then nodded.

"It was him," Marj said coldly, her eyes ahead. "I can feel it."

Rollins glanced over at her. "How?"

"I just can. After everything else, Rolo, it just makes sense." Marj rapped her open palm on her bare thigh. "I bet he's paid to watch you. I bet it's his job."

"Oh, come on. I followed *him*, remember?" Rollins had had about enough of Marj's melodramatic theorizing.

Marj lifted her arms in mock surrender. "Okay, okay. It's crazy. All right?"

Rollins softened, his eyes on the road ahead as he moved along. "Who'd pay him?"

She turned to him. "That's what I keep wondering about, Rolo. That's the part I don't get. Okay, you tell me you just happened to follow this guy home. I think: 'All right, that's kinda weird.'" She threw out a hand as if to dismiss it. "But we all have our little things. Maybe it's cool. I don't know. I try not to be prejudiced, okay? But then this other guy, this Sloane, I see him look at you like he knows you. And you go, 'Wow, I didn't even notice!' And then you tell me somebody dropped off a secret number, like, a couple of weeks ago. And you say, 'Gee, I can't imagine what this is. Did *you* send it?' And I go, 'Noooooo.' And now you say that this skinny guy is, like, staking out your apartment. It's a bit much, wouldn't you say? So what is it, Rolo? You dealing, or what?"

Rollins eyed her for a second, startled by her directness. "For goodness' sake."

"Well, what then? There's more here, Rolo. That's what I've been thinking about for the last two hours. There's got to be something more. Because what we have here, with the house and Sloane and the crazy number and everything—it doesn't make any sense."

By now, Rollins had passed the right turn that led back to 62, and had instead gone left and pulled over. But it wasn't until he pulled the hand brake that Marj suddenly sounded panicky. "What are you doing?"

"I want to see if we are being followed."

"Oh, shit," she said again, but the word had a new quality to it, a hint of thrill. She swung around to look behind her. "What if we are?"

"We leave."

Marj swung back to him, fear on her face. "But suppose we can't? Suppose he and Sloane come at us, like, from both ends of the street?"

"Don't be so dramatic."

"Well, how do you know what they'd do?"

"Look, all I know is, if we are being followed—and I'm not sure we are—we are being followed very discreetly. Do you know what that means?" Rollins felt a need right then to lord it over her, to demonstrate that he was fully a decade older, and he didn't wait for an answer. "It means that they won't come at us like some German panzer division."

Marj squirmed again in her seat. She fell silent for a while, but Rollins could sense the wheels spinning in her head.

"You still didn't answer my question," she said finally.

"Which one?"

"About what you're hiding from me."

"Nothing." Rollins realized an amendment was in order. "Well, nothing pertinent."

"So you don't deal?"

He laughed. "No."

"You in debt?"

"Hardly." Rollins balanced all his accounts on the first of the month. If it weren't for his rule against discussing money, he would have pointed this out to her, gleefully. He'd have added that, thanks to various trusts that had come down to him on his mother's side of the family, he was personally worth, according to the most recent quarterly summary, over $1.75 million. Money was a private topic, but not an unhappy one.

"You're not screwing a mafioso's wife."

"Oh, stop."

Marj's eyes swerved around toward his. "Or somebody's husband."

That did not even merit a response. Rollins merely eyed her coolly in return, his jaw tight with irritation.

Both Marj's hands flew into the air. "Look, I don't know what you're about, okay? You could do it with dogs as far as I know." That was hurtful, as Marj must have instantly recognized. "Okay, I'm sorry.

The thing is: I'm just trying to figure why all these people seem to be so hooked on you right now."

"I don't know." And Rollins truly did not. With his night work, he was a vacancy, a being without substance or history, drifting through other people's lives. He was nothing to the people he watched. He didn't have to worry about what they might think of him, because they would never think anything of him.

"Maybe they blame you for losing money at Johnson."

"But I don't have anything to do with the investment side. You know that. I just keep track of the numbers."

"Maybe they *think* you do something more."

"They can't be that stupid."

That quieted her, and the two sat silently in the dark together, while the crickets throbbed outside the car. Occasionally, a light would come on or go off in one of the houses around them, all of them, modest, low-slung affairs like the one around the corner at 29 Elmhurst. There was an occasional voice, or a burst of laughter from a TV, through an open window. But otherwise, the neighborhood was quiet and still. Rollins became conscious of Marj's breathing. He imagined the whole car filling up with her breath and his breath, mixed. If he had been a different sort of man, he might have slid a hand over onto her knee.

But Marj had thoughts of her own. "What about before Johnson? Somebody told me you used to be a journalist."

"Who?"

She shrugged. "Oh, it was just some gossip in the ladies' room."

"About me?" Rollins didn't like the sound of this. He glanced in the rearview again, checking one more time for a sign of the Audi or the Land Cruiser. Then he let out a sigh. "All right, yes, I worked for a tabloid in Boston called the *Beacon*. It went out of business a few years ago. I had a great beat. I covered commercial real estate transactions downtown—high-rise office buildings, hotels, that kind of thing."

"But you quit?"

"I was fired."

"Well, whaddya know. I thought *I* was the only one at Johnson who'd ever been fired."

"It's a long story." Rollins could still see the balding Grant Bowser gesturing angrily toward him in the glassed-in managing editor's office, while outside in the newsroom all the staffers continued to work away at their desks, pretending not to notice. "The short of it is, I wasn't much of a reporter."

"And the long version?"

"I wasn't much of a writer, either."

Marj smiled. "Well, I guess you did have a problem."

Rollins was glad that she could see the humor of the situation. "It was more than reporting and writing, actually. It had to do with *what* I reported, and *what* I wrote. I'd have been fine if I'd stuck to my real estate column. But I tried to branch out, and I got into some trouble."

She stared at him a moment. "Am I supposed to beg you to tell me about it? Is that what I do now?"

Rollins took a breath and began. "It was about a woman who disappeared six, seven years ago," he began. "She'd been living in Londonderry, New Hampshire, and then, well, and then she wasn't anywhere. She hasn't been seen since." He explained that he hadn't gotten on to the story until she'd been gone for almost two years. He spent months on it. He could have written a book. He turned in something like 125 pages, which at a paper like the *Beacon* was ridiculous. He might have dropped an encyclopedia on his editor's desk. That was Grant Bowser, a slender, bespectacled gentleman with possibly too great a fondness for bright bow ties. Bowser didn't know what to do with the story. He hacked most of it away, rewrote much of the rest himself, and buried the piece deep inside the next issue. Rollins wanted to go back to it for an update three months later, but Grant said he never wanted to hear of the story again. Telling Marj now, he was seized again with the massive feeling of frustration that had consumed him at the time. He had killed himself to do that story, worked himself absolutely to the bone. It had come to mean everything to him.

"But how did you get fired?"

"I guess I made a scene."

"What did you do?"

Rollins supposed that he had to tell her, even though it had not been his best moment. "I yelled a little and knocked some things off his desk."

"Oh yeah?" She looked over at him, flashing that same feral look he'd seen at Georgio's. "You?"

Rollins nodded.

"I wish I'd been there."

"I was younger. Anyway, he told me I'd gotten too close to the story. I said, 'Damn right I have,' and threatened to quit."

"Uh-oh."

"Yeah. Big mistake. He said, 'Fine, go clean out your desk then,' and that was it."

"No more journalism for you?"

"Nope." Rollins looked out the window, toward the houses lining the street. "I suppose it was good practice, though."

"For—?"

"For finding out things. Used to be, back when I was working on that disappearance case, I'd go up to any of these houses." Rollins gestured out the window. "I'd bang on the door, start asking questions."

"Sounds ballsy."

"I guess." A trace of weariness came into his voice. "But it could get to you after a while."

Rollins checked the dashboard clock: 9:21. "It's been a half hour. I don't think anyone's following us." Rollins started up the car again and drove clear around the block. He cruised by number 29, which was still dark. But 31 next door was well lit. There was a rusty Oldsmobile in the driveway, and a light was on over the front door. Rollins opened the car door.

"Where are you going?" Marj asked.

Rollins nodded toward number 31. "I thought I'd try this one." Rollins leaned over to the glove compartment and took out a small notebook and pen. "Might get some answers."

"You're not leaving me here." Marj scrambled out of her seat.

Outside the car, Rollins checked up and down the street. You get a different feeling for a place when you're out in the open. Rollins could feel the breeze on him, the same wind that rustled the leaves as it moved through the trees, could hear the cars rushing along 62.

Marj was standing beside him. "You all right?"

"Fine." His body felt tight as he started across the street and neared number 31. But then he heard the car door thump shut behind him and, although he didn't turn to look, what must have been Marj's shoes scudding after him. It was a comfort to have her there. Despite all his brave talk, he wouldn't have been able to do this alone. Watching, yes. But not entering. Entering was different. In his limited experience, entering meant submitting to another person's consciousness, attitudes, and, potentially, control. Still, it wouldn't do to acknowledge such fears to Marj, and he did his best to step lightly as he climbed the brick front steps to number 31.

BEULEY, it said in gold stick-on letters under the mailbox, although the final *Y* had peeled loose. Up close, Rollins could hear a TV going inside the house. "Follow my lead," he told Marj as he pressed the buzzer. Inside, a dog yapped and scampered toward the door, then scratched at it with its claws. But no one appeared. Rollins buzzed again. Finally, a dead bolt was released with a click, and an elderly woman in a bloodred wrapper peeped out at them.

"Mrs. Beuley?" Rollins asked.

The woman nodded.

"I'm Christopher Black—from the *Chronicle*." Rollins referred to the local paper, the *Reading Chronicle and Daily Gazette*. It was liberating to lie. "And this is my assistant, Meg Jones."

The woman started to shut the door. "I get it already."

"Oh, we're not selling the paper, Mrs. Beuley." Rollins gently blocked the door with his foot. "We're reporters."

The dog growled at Rollins, and Marj added brightly: "We're doing a story about the effect of the various leash laws on the different neighborhoods, and we'd like to ask you a few questions."

Rollins wanted to cup his hand over her mouth.

"Would that be all right with you, ma'am?" Marj continued sweetly.

Mrs. Beuley looked them over. "Well, you two don't look like murderers."

"Well, I'm not," Marj said. "But I don't know about him."

Mrs. Beuley gave Rollins another look. "Yeah, I see what you mean." She closed the door for a moment to release the chain, then opened the door wide. Rollins took one last look back at the street—still nothing—before he stepped inside.

Mrs. Beuley continued to act a little put off by Rollins, but she'd obviously warmed to Marj, who was now busily petting the dog. She offered to take Marj's denim jacket.

"No thanks," Marj replied, laughing. "I don't have much on underneath."

Mrs. Beuley smiled at that. "Oh, gracious." She herself was reed thin. But to judge by the way the skin hung off her, Rollins guessed she probably had been heavier once. She was a little older than his mother—seventy-five, maybe eighty. Rollins had always been conscious of shut-ins, since they tended to be watchers. He was inclined to stay away from houses that were too quiet.

Mrs. Beuley moved silently across the spongy carpeting in her well-worn pink slippers, carefully stepping around a pile of old newspapers and *TV Guides* in the front hall. "Pardon the mess." The house smelled of Lysol.

Mrs. Beuley led them down a short hall lined with yellowing family photos and into a small kitchen, where she sat her guests down at the oak table while she put the kettle on the stove for tea. "What is it you want to know now?"

Although Rollins shot Marj a glance to get her to quit with this nonsense about the dog ordinances, Marj stuck with it and soon had Mrs. Beuley prattling on about her many experiences with neighborhood canines while Rollins doodled, pretending to take notes. Mrs. Beuley directed most of her remarks to her poodle, Prince, who was gazing eagerly at her from his mat by the refrigerator. Eventually, after pouring out some Lipton's for the three of them, Mrs. Beuley let slip a few details about her late husband's career with General Electric, and her oldest son's alcohol problem.

"How about your next-door neighbors over there?" Rollins prodded with a nod toward the dark house. "They had any dogs?"

Mrs. Beuley gave a fairly detailed history of number 29. The house had been built two years after her own, in 1948. First came the McGrews, who'd had a spaniel at one time. Then a childless couple, the Reids, moved in. With that, Mrs. Beuley got up to heat some more tea.

"The Reids still there?" Rollins pressed.

"Oh, no. His work took him to Minnesota. So they sold the house to a family named Holtz. I didn't know them very well. I don't remember any dogs, though."

"They still have it?" Marj persisted.

"Heavens, no. Sold it three, four years ago."

"So who owns it now?" Rollins asked. It had been a long time since he had asked such pressing questions, and he couldn't tell if Mrs. Beuley was holding back or truly didn't know.

"The place is for sale. Didn't you see the sign? Besides, I don't know what this has to do with leash laws."

"Sorry. Just curious." Then, on inspiration: "I thought I saw someone walking a dog around there. A slender fellow, fifty, fifty-five, maybe, with a bit of a mustache." Rollins drew his index finger across his upper lip to emphasize the idea. "Drives an Audi?"

"No one there ever had a car like that," Mrs. Beuley replied. She sounded quite adamant, then added, "That place is quite a story, but not for any article. You won't be writing any of this down." She wagged a bony finger at Rollins.

Marj's eyes and Rollins' eyes moved to Mrs. Beuley. A few moments passed, but she did not elaborate.

"How's that?" Rollins finally asked.

"Oh, just the things that went on there."

"Such as?" he pressed.

"I don't think they'd want me gossiping about them. Ask that Sloane fellow. He knows all about it."

* * *

"*Leash laws?*" Rollins asked when he and Marj were back in his car. "Whatever were you thinking?" He shook his head to convey his displeasure, but not too vigorously. That gambit of hers, it wasn't what he would have done, that was for sure. But, in fairness, it had worked out well enough.

"It was the first thing that popped into my head. It got her talking, anyway."

"You're lucky she didn't call the police."

"She was *not* going to call the police. She was happy to have somebody to talk to. You're the one who blew it. If you hadn't been so pushy, we could have gotten a lot more out of her."

Rollins sat unhappily in the driver's seat. There was some truth to this. "At least we found out that the gaunt man never lived there."

"So why would he go in?"

"That's what I don't know." It was quite maddening.

"And what's it mean that the house would make 'quite a story'?"

"I don't know that either." The questions were starting to multiply, just as they had when he'd written that story about the disappearance five years before. He glanced through his notebook. He'd taken only a few genuine notes. Mostly, he'd doodled a forest of question marks.

Five

The more they talked, the more certain Rollins became that Marj wanted to ride back to Boston with him. Not that she said anything about it; it was the way she stayed there in the passenger seat, wondering about Mrs. Beuley and not making any move toward her car as the crickets thrummed and the night descended all around them. But Rollins didn't think it would be smart to leave her car overnight anywhere near the dark house, and there was no question about leaving his.

"You should probably get back to your car, don't you think?" Rollins finally asked.

"Oh, right," Marj said, as if she'd forgotten. "I guess it's getting kinda late."

To make sure she got home safely, Rollins followed her back down

93 to Boston. He whistled a bit of "Moon River" as he drove along behind Marj's little Toyota, with its ruddy rectangles for taillights. He drove with the window down, his elbow resting on the door frame, the wind howling in his ear, tossing his hair. It was a nice night, fairly clear, with the balmy air that reminded him of Florida in February, and palm trees and pink sunsets. There were few other cars on the highway, and he kept Marj no more than thirty feet in front of him the whole way down, past three malls, all nearly deserted at this hour, and countless road signs showing routes that Rollins, for once, felt no interest in exploring. It was wonderful to have her car right there in front of him, and to know she was happy to have him following right behind. For the first time, he felt joined to her, as though their futures were linked.

The Charles River was choppy, with little swells that lapped against the docks on the Charlestown side, when they drove back over into Boston. Figuring she could make it the rest of the way on her own, Rollins gave Marj a quick farewell toot of his horn as he veered off the expressway for the North End while she continued on around to the turnpike toward Brighton.

When he got back, the lights were out in the front hall, and Rollins felt all his anxieties return as he moved through the shadows to the staircase. His skin felt dead as he pulled out his keys and climbed up the carpeted stairs. He hurried inside and quickly bolted the door behind him. His eyes jumped about after he hit the lights, checking for anything amiss. Could someone be in the apartment with him at this very moment? He stood for a moment on the oriental carpet in his sitting room, listening for the sound of another's breathing. He might have been trying to find a ghost. He rounded the leather chair. "Hello?" he called out. "Hello?"

He had a start when he saw the lone silver candleholder out on the kitchen table. Then he remembered he himself had put it there just that morning. He glanced around the nook kitchen, then recrossed the living room, and snapped on the light by his bed. He cringed at the sudden explosive brightness. His room was just as he had left it.

The bathroom door was shut tight. Before touching the knob, he flipped on the switch just to the right and listened for a moment. When he heard nothing, he opened the door and poked his head in. The closed shower curtain swayed lightly. He counted silently to three, then charged forward and flung it open. There was nothing in the shower except the soap and the shampoo bottle on their little shelf by the shower nozzle. He retraced his steps, searched the bedroom closet, and then the one in the front hall. When he was finally assured that he was alone in his little apartment, he got out some Pouilly-Fuissé from the refrigerator, poured himself a glass, and quickly downed it, and then two more.

Light slicing across his bedroom from a crack in the door. Late. All so quiet, except for the ticking of his Baby Ben clock—and the creak of his rocking chair. She was in it, slowly rocking, as if in a dream. Neely. In her pale blue nightie, her hair down past her shoulders.

He'd turned to her. Not scared, just sleepy. "You all right?"

"Fine. I couldn't sleep, that's all."

His head back down on the pillow; the gray ceiling up above. Breathing. She continued to rock.

"You ever get lonely?" she asked him. Her voice so gentle.

"I don't know."

"I mean, even when you're with people?" Neely added.

Too confusing.

"Never mind. It's a dumb question." She returned to her rocking. "You sleep. I'll be okay. Sleep."

When he looked again, the rocking chair was empty.

As he passed back through the living room, a little dreamy now, he thought of Marj. Did she ever get lonely? He should call her to see if she'd gotten home safely—but really just to chat. No. He didn't want her to think him fretful.

When he finally stepped into his pajamas and slid into bed, someone was playing a Verdi opera in one of the apartments high up off the echoey courtyard in the back. He kept thinking he heard footsteps in the hall, or, once, a hand rattling his doorknob. When a breeze ruffled his bedroom draperies, he was sure someone was trying to sneak in the window—even though it was a good fifteen feet up from the ground. Still, like an idiot, he got up to check, then closed the window and locked the sash. The window had offered his only breath of air, and he passed the rest of the night sweltering on top of his sheets.

In the morning, he left for work with just a few gulps of water in his stomach. His worries seemed stupid in the bright light. Still, he did check around once or twice as he made his way down noisy Hanover Street to his car, but he saw only the usual pedestrians hurrying by, and a steady stream of traffic passing his front door. At his garage, he impulsively glanced in the trunk of the Nissan and even checked under the hood—not that he knew what he was looking for—before he climbed in the car and started the ignition. Even then, he braced for an explosion when he turned the switch. When the car came to life just as usual, he told himself that he *had* to relax. He actually mouthed the words.

It was a relief to get to Johnson, to settle into his little office with just the one doorway to worry about. Marj came in a little after nine. She was wearing a long skirt and black boots that seemed to pound into the carpeting as she surged by his doorway with barely a glance toward him. At first, he figured she'd gone into stranger mode, as befitted office workers who were "seeing" each other. He felt a little rush of pleasure at the prospect—but then wondered if he wasn't being premature. And had he detected a trace of irritation in her tightly set mouth as she charged by?

He tried to attend to the numbers that were starting to stream across his computer screen. The overnight returns on the Asian markets augured a good day on the Street. Then the little mailbox in the lower right corner of his screen flashed on. He had e-mail.

It was from Msimm@jinv:

u cd have calld, u know
m

He felt that in his chest. He should have called her when he'd thought to. Something might have happened to her, just as something might have happened to himself.

Rollins typed:

Sorry.

Then he thought that might not be quite enough. He wished he had a good excuse, such as his phone was out of order, or he'd fallen sick. But he couldn't think of anything, and he didn't want to lie, not to her. After a few moments' thought, he decided to leave it at that, and he clicked on SEND. Moments later, his e-mail box was lit again. It was Marj:

its ok. Im fine. just thought ud call
m

It wasn't until lunchtime that he actually saw her. She dropped into his office quite jauntily, as though nothing could possibly be the matter between them. She slapped a thin file folder down on his desk. "Get a load of this. I just got it from Sally up on twenty-one. She's incredible at research." She picked up a pencil off Rollins' desk and drummed it against the desktop. Rollins flipped the file open. It contained a brief computer printout from the third page of the "Metro" section of the *Boston Globe*. TEACHER NABBED IN DRUG BUST was the headline. It reported that Jerome Sloane, a substitute English teacher at Madison Park High School, of 43 Sandler Avenue in the Jamaica Plain section of Boston, had been arrested on charges of possessing three ounces of cocaine with intent to sell. The piece was dated February 17, 1989.

"I had her try Gerald, Jeremiah, Jeremy, and Jerome," Marj said, still drumming. "This was the only thing that came up. You think it's our Jerry?"

"It's possible."

"Think they put him away?"

"This the only story Sally found?"

Marj nodded.

"Then probably not. Somebody would have followed up. He probably got off with a fine or probation."

Marj stepped over to Rollins' window and leaned against the sill, hands outstretched, filling up the view. "That might have been what that Mrs. Beuley was talking about." She stood up again. "Hey—maybe the guy you saw was running drugs. Like, that was why he seemed so edgy. Maybe they were using the Elmhurst house for drug deals."

"I looked all over the house, and I didn't see any sign of it."

Marj tapped Rollins' shoulder with the pencil. "Like they're going to leave powder and stuff just lying around."

"I'd think there would be some indication. But the whole place was spotless."

"So they cleaned up." Marj put the pencil back on the desk.

"Sloane didn't seem exactly reluctant to show us around."

"Like I said, Rolo, they cleaned up. All right?"

"Maybe." Rollins had stopped listening. He'd glanced down at the printout again and noticed that there was another sheet behind it. He slid the printout over to the side and found a fax that came with a cover sheet from the *Boston Globe*. Behind it, a black-and-white photograph that nearly stopped his heart: an attractive, thirtyish woman with long, light hair flowing down her shoulders. Neely.

CORNELIA BLANCHARD, the caption said in block letters, AUTHOR OF *MEMORIES OF EDEN*. A publicity photo, it looked like. The image had turned blotchy coming through the fax machine. Still, seeing it, Rollins could feel the blood drain from his head, and he felt a strange inward pressure at his temples, as if his skull were being hollowed out. He pushed his hands out to the desktop to steady himself.

"What's the matter? God, Rolo, you're *sweating*! Are you all right?"

Rollins didn't answer for a moment, he was so lost in the photograph. Neely's eyes—not their black-and-white facsimiles, but the actual hazel orbs themselves—seemed to be staring right at him.

"What's this doing here?"

"What do you mean?"

"I thought your friend Sally did a search on Sloane."

"She did. Why—who is it?"

For a moment, Rollins was reluctant to say. "The woman who was in that big story I was telling you about."

"The one that got you fired?"

"Yeah."

"She was a writer?"

"A poet. *Memories of Eden* was her first book. Published in eighty-eight, I think. I have it someplace. She had a bit of a following. She was always reading at some coffeehouse in Cambridge."

"Cornelia Blanchard," Marj said again, staring at the picture.

"We called her Neely."

"We?"

"The family. She was my old baby-sitter, a cousin on my mother's side. She lived with us for a while."

"Wait, she was your *cousin*? It was your *cousin* who disappeared?"

Rollins nodded.

"Why didn't you say so?"

Rollins took in some air and shook his head. Why hadn't he? To give himself some space from his past, he supposed, not that that was much of a reason. And, possibly, to spare Marj, too.

"I don't know. Maybe I should have. I'm sorry."

Marj plucked some tissues from the box on his desk and handed them to him wordlessly. He blotted his forehead and temples, where he could feel the perspiration starting to drip.

"Well, no wonder you spent all that time on that story of yours," she told him. "She was your cousin, Rolo. And your baby-sitter. And all the time I was thinking, 'Here's another nutso thing.' Going crazy writing this huge story about someone you didn't even know." Marj looked down at the photo again. "Kind of nice-looking."

Rollins nodded. He continued to stare at the photograph.

"The last time I ever saw her was at Williams, my junior year. It must have been nineteen seventy-five. There was a bang on the door, and there she was. In my room."

A drafty single. His narrow bed, a nonworking fireplace, and hardly anything on the walls. Silence there, too, except the muffled voices through the walls.

"She told me she was just driving by. She seemed quite disturbed, but wouldn't say why. I couldn't imagine how she'd found me, or what she wanted. I asked her if she needed a place to stay, and she shook her head. Then she said she'd made a terrible mistake, that she shouldn't have come. I told her I was glad to see her."

Neely in glasses; her golden hair dulled. His hands reaching through the air toward her. And her hands up sharply to deflect them—"No, please don't"—as she backed to the door.

"But she pushed me away. She was out the door before I could stop her. And that was it."

"What do you suppose was going on?"

Rollins shook his head. "I have no idea."

Rollins looked down at the publicity photograph again. For the piece on Neely's disappearance, he'd accumulated quite an archive of photographs, but he'd never seen this one before. He'd taped the images up all around his desk. Snapshots, newspaper photographs, even sketches that friends had provided. There must have been fifteen or twenty of them. Neely had filled practically the whole wall of his partition at the *Beacon*.

"Where do you think this was taken?" Marj asked.

"Looks like the side porch at her house in Londonderry." Rollins had gone there many times when he was working on the story. (Not in, though. The house was locked up tight as a drum.) He still went back there, from time to time, if he was in the area. He thought he might pick up a feeling for her, a sense of what had happened, where she had gone. But nothing had ever come to him.

"How'd you find it?" Rollins asked.

"The Sloane file was cross-referenced to a file on Twenty-nine Elmhurst."

"But what did Neely have to do with the dark house?"

Marj shrugged. "Beats me."

Once again, the dark house was swelling with portent and significance. It was sprouting black towers and creeping vines; it was looming up against a night sky. He wanted to discharge that ominous specter, to break any connection to it. He wanted to turn it back into a house like any other. He didn't at all enjoy the idea that Neely—and through her, he himself—might be linked to a house that he had visited only at random. For that would force him to reconsider his understanding of chance, which was, after all, the basis on which he had constructed his many years of pursuits. If his arrival at the dark house was not arbitrary, then it was planned. And if it was planned, it was certainly not planned by him. So, who planned it, and why and how? These were large, immensely troubling questions, and Rollins recoiled from them.

He slapped the photograph down on his desk. "Why would this have ended up in a file on Twenty-nine Elmhurst? Why would there even *be* a file on Twenty-nine Elmhurst?"

"The librarian said there were some handwritten notes in with it. They referred to some rumors about the place that a reporter was trying to track down for a 'Metro' story."

"What sort of rumors?"

"The librarian wouldn't say anything about them, except that they were 'a little bizarre.'"

"What's *that* mean?"

"I don't know, Rolo," Marj said irritably. "I'm just passing on what Sally told me. Apparently, the librarian tossed them. She said they shouldn't have been there in the first place. Supposedly, those files are only for published material."

"Well, it's probably nothing," Rollins said.

Marj's eyes flared. "Oh, stop."

"I mean it."

"You're going to tell me this is nothing? Look at me."

He didn't mind. She was so lovely, particularly around the eyes. They didn't speak, but he felt something pass between them.

Marj reached for his hand where it lay outstretched on his desktop and ran her fingers lightly over his knuckles. "Trust me a little, okay?"

"Okay." Rollins smiled. "Sorry."

"Good." Marj picked up the pencil and started her drumming again. "So where are we going tonight?"

Six

The house was a two-story Cape, somewhat run-down, with cracked shingles and peeling peach-colored trim that seemed all the more drab in the fading light. The houses around it were all neatly landscaped with well-tended shrubs, lush grass, and weedless flower beds. The Cape had only a parched lawn and a pair of scraggly rhododendrons by the front steps. But it did have a small satellite dish and, by the walkway, a sign out front bearing the words THE SLOANE RESIDENCE in cast iron.

"Will you look at that," Marj said from the driver's seat. "That little fucker."

Rollins was in the backseat, his head low. The whole trip from Boston, he'd been scanning the rearview for any signs of the gaunt man. More than twenty-four hours had passed since the episode outside his apartment, and Rollins was beginning to feel a little silly about his continued vigilance. As he kept telling himself, he had only sensed the gaunt man, after all, not actually seen him clearly. Still, as a precaution this evening, he was also wearing a Boston Red Sox baseball cap—a memento from that abortive baseball game of almost a year ago—with the brim down low over his eyes. Al Schecter had once mentioned how a hat helped conceal your identity.

Rollins and Marj were in her Toyota this time. Marj had said she'd been afraid Sloane might recognize Rollins' Nissan from the Elmhurst house, but Rollins had the odd idea that she was trying to assert control.

"You sure you want to?" he'd asked, as they left work.

Marj hadn't hesitated. "Sure I'm sure." Then she'd thrown it back at him. "Why, you're not?"

"No, no, it's fine with me."

It had taken Rollins a little while to get used to her driving. She went a little faster than Rollins might have liked, and faster still when approaching yellow lights. But she was an attentive and confident driver, and before too long Rollins had stopped sneaking anxious looks at the road up ahead, and concentrated entirely on the road behind, watching to make sure they weren't being followed.

Rollins had found the address—14 West Marshfield Road, in this modestly upmarket section of Medford—on Sloane's business card. Driving out tonight, Rollins had half-expected the address to turn out to be a vacant lot or some other dead end. But here it was, with that SLOANE RESIDENCE sign as a giant advertisement for itself. Sloane's green Land Cruiser was in the driveway, by a rusting basketball hoop.

"Slowly now." Rollins tapped Marj's shoulder (hitting bare skin on either side of the strap of her halter top) for emphasis as he craned around to get a good look at the house from the side window. The downstairs drapes were pulled, and the lights were all off on the streetside rooms above, making it hard to see anything inside. But, from the dilapidated exterior, Rollins picked up a strong impression of negative cash-flow.

Marj drove down to the end of the street, then U-ed back for a second look.

On the return, Rollins checked for possible sight lines from behind the house, but it backed up onto the wide waters of the Mystic River. "See any good angles from the back?"

"Not without swimming." Marj stopped again two houses down from Sloane's, where they could see the murky water flowing past. "What about from over there?" She pointed to what looked like a kiddie park on the river's far shore, maybe a hundred yards off.

Rollins could barely make out a swing set and some tiny plastic horses in the twilight. "You kidding?" Sloane's window would be barely the size of his fingernail from there, not to mention blurry. "My eyesight isn't that sharp, you know." The girl still had a lot to learn.

"That's what you think." Marj reached down to the floor in front of the passenger seat and handed Rollins a small shopping bag. "I got you something."

Rollins pulled it back over the headrest, then held it for a moment in his lap, unsure how to proceed.

"Open it, dummy."

Rollins reached into the bag and extracted a small, bright-blue cardboard box. He popped the masking tape with his index finger, and, from the tissue paper inside, he fished out a pair of binoculars. NIKON MONARCH, it said on the label that dangled from one eyepiece. They were small and demure, a sleeker version of old-fashioned opera glasses. He felt a thrill, a kind of brightening within him, to realize that Marj had given him a gift. And such a personal one, too. But then he worried that the two of them might be achieving too great an intimacy. His pursuits were meant to be solo.

"Pretty light," Rollins said, placing them in the palm of his hand. "Nice workmanship."

"Go ahead, try them."

As Rollins put the glasses to his eyes to look around, the world swelled with possibility. The distant houses suddenly seemed enormous. They almost pressed in on him. "Amazing."

"Aren't they great? They were on sale at the drugstore. I had to go in for Tampax, and I thought of you. When I saw the binoculars, I mean." She colored a little, which surprised him.

He almost kissed her. But he waited too long, and the moment passed. "Thanks," he said instead.

"So you don't already have a pair?"

"No. Never even thought of it."

"Well, I wasn't sure."

It was past nine when they swung open the low gate to the kiddie park on a slight rise up from the river and across from the Sloanes'. Marj climbed onto a spring-mounted, polka-dotted horse and started careening wildly about, her hair flouncing with each bounce. But Rollins took up position beside a thick maple. A bright moon was out, and he figured the tree would offer good cover. He had some trouble focusing the lenses, since his right eye was weaker than his left. He called out: "I can't get these to work."

Marj dismounted, took the glasses from him, adjusted the outer ring of the right eyepiece, then handed them back. "Better?"

"Much." Rollins quickly lost himself in the view. The binoculars were marvelous. They seemed to put him right inside the house, even though it was indeed nearly a hundred yards away. There were no shades on this side, where no neighbors encroached. Rollins roamed around the dated, yellow countertops and hulking maroon refrigerator of the Sloanes' kitchen. A slightly overweight brunette was laboring at the sink. He almost flinched when his eyes settled on Sloane. He was leaning back comfortably in an oak chair. At that magnification, Sloane nearly filled the lenses, and Rollins was suddenly afraid Sloane might reach out and grab him by the throat.

"Got anything?" Marj asked.

"Not too much. Sloane's sitting in the kitchen while his wife does the dishes."

"Typical."

"Want to look?"

Marj took the glasses and adjusted them slightly. "Jeez, the guy doesn't even lift a finger." She watched silently for a few minutes. "Look out, we've got movement."

"Oh?" Rollins looked over to the house, but couldn't make out anything from that distance.

"Jerry's headed to the TV. Oh, that's nice. He pours himself some hooch first. Wifey's stuck with the dishes, while hubby gets sloshed in front of the tube. I bet it's the porn channel." She fell silent, watching. "Wait a sec, he's leaving, the jerk. No, wait, there must have been someone at the door. He's coming back, with another guy. Some schmo. Take a look. Maybe you know him." She passed the binoculars back to Rollins. By the time Rollins managed to get the focus right, Sloane was sitting, drink in hand, on the couch in front of the TV. From this angle, Rollins couldn't tell if the set was on. Diagonally across from him was a slightly older man. The sight of him knocked the air out of Rollins for a moment. He had to clamp down on the binoculars to keep them from wobbling in his hands. The gaunt man. Here. He was nodding, as if in powerful agreement to something that Sloane was saying.

"It's him," Rollins said.

"Who?"

"The one I followed that first night, back to the Elmhurst house." He was thin, graying, mid-fifties, wearing a sport coat.

"With the Audi?"

"Yes."

Marj took the glasses from him again. "So, that's the guy."

"And they know each other," Rollins said. "What do you suppose they're talking about?"

"You, I bet. Just kidding."

But Rollins did have the feeling that a net was spreading out before him—and threatening to enclose him. He'd tailed the gaunt man to the dark house, only to find Sloane there when he and Marj returned. Then Marj had gone off to find out more about Sloane—and she'd come across a photograph of Rollins' vanished cousin Neely. And now, here Sloane and the gaunt man were together. Why? What did this have to do with him? He couldn't think—yet it was scary to see the two of them obviously allied. It was as if Rollins were exerting some unaccountable gravitational attraction, drawing these two strangers into orbit around him. He'd read stories of blind people who'd finally gained sight, and how overwhelming they'd found it to be confronted by a sudden profusion of dazzling colors. Now, Rollins feared that he, too, was gaining a shattering new sense of the world. For the first time since he'd started his pursuits, he suspected he may not have been invisible after all, and that thought made the world look like a new and far more dangerous place.

He took the binoculars back from Marj and watched more intently. After a few minutes, the light went off in the kitchen and the pudgy brunette emerged in the living room, where she dropped down at the far end of the couch from Sloane and stared at the TV, which must have been on, although neither Sloane nor the gaunt man had been paying any attention to it. Finally, as Rollins stared, the brunette got up from the couch and left the room. Rollins scanned the various windows and picked her up again at the top of the stairs. From there, she crossed into a child's bedroom—festooned with sports posters—where a boy's head was outlined against a glowing computer screen.

Marj was sitting cross-legged on the grass beside Rollins as he watched, her shoulder grazing his leg ever so slightly. She didn't interrupt him.

The brunette placed a hand on the child's shoulder. When the boy wobbled his shoulder in a "not yet" gesture, she grabbed him under the armpit and hoisted him out of his chair. The boy wriggled out of her grip for a moment, but she snagged his hand and swung him around and swatted him on the rear end. Rollins shifted his lenses to the living room window in time to see Sloane tilt his head up toward the ceiling, bellowing, furious. Perhaps the commotion upstairs had interrupted his conversation with the gaunt man. Sloane stormed out of the room; Rollins switched back upstairs as Sloane appeared in the boy's doorway. Sloane looked daggers at his wife, who gestured angrily back at the boy, now slumped on the bed. Rollins would have liked to hear the words. What was the language of their rage? His own parents had never yelled, not at each other, not within his earshot, anyway. He'd hidden in that sideboard, and other places, to eavesdrop. Several times, he'd sneaked out of bed when he was supposed to be asleep to listen at their bedroom door, hoping to discover a spoken truth that would explain everything. But he never did. For the most part, he'd heard only the silence that he always heard in that house, as if their voices were muted by all the plush rugs, the sumptuous furnishings. Or maybe the silence *was* the truth; his was a house full of nothing.

Sloane stepped toward his wife, a hand raised, as the boy cowered on the bed. The wife raised an arm to defend herself, but too late. With a great, sweeping motion, he smacked her hard across the face. The blow slammed the woman toward the wall, past the window. The boy cringed, but did not move. Rollins lingered there, waiting to see if she would get up. It was too terrible, this violence of husband against wife. If he'd had his tape recorder, Rollins would have made a note. He willed the boy to pay attention, offer sympathy to his mother, something. But the boy only looked on warily, his elbows tight. After a while, he got off the bed and drifted out of the room. When the mother did not rise into view again, Rollins searched for the boy and found him in the bathroom, using the toilet. Rollins checked for the mother downstairs, but he saw only Sloane in the kitchen again, where he poured himself a highball, drained it, then settled back down by the gaunt man once more.

Rollins lowered the binoculars from his eyes and looked around for Marj. She was standing barefoot at the river's edge, the water up to her ankles.

"It's polluted, you know," he called over to her.

"What isn't?" She waded slowly about, back and forth. "That guy still there?"

"Yeah."

"They doing anything?"

"No. Just sitting there."

"What do we do now?"

Rollins paused a moment, to clear his mind of all he'd seen. "I thought maybe we should drive back around, see if we can get a license plate number. Maybe we can figure out who he is, where he lives or something."

"Sounds good." Marj stepped out of the water. She sat down on a tree stump and started to dry her feet with her socks.

Rollins came over to help, not that there was much that he could do.

After what he'd just seen, he just wanted to be near her, for comfort.

"There was a bit of a fight, actually."

Marj looked up, amazement on her face. "Sloane and that guy?"

"Sloane and his wife. Just now. It was over their son, I think."

"Any blood?"

Rollins was relieved she took the news as a joke. "No. Tears, though." He'd seen the woman's body quake.

That got Marj's attention. "Oh?"

"He slapped her."

"No shit." She shook her head. "Right then, while you were watching?"

"Yeah, quite a blow, actually. He really smacked her."

"She okay?"

"I don't know. I couldn't see."

Marj continued drying her feet, but very slowly. "Can I ask you a question? Do you *like* seeing that sort of thing?"

"Not particularly."

Marj reached down and grabbed a shoe that she'd left on the shore and flung it at him, hitting him in the ankle. He backed off and looked at her warily. At first, Rollins thought she was being playful. He got a different idea when she pitched the other one at his chest. He was lucky to block it with his forearm.

"What *is* it with you?" She hunched back down again, her eyes on the mossy ground. "All my girlfriends say, 'What are you doing with this guy? He's *psycho*.' I tell them, no, no, no. Actually, he's kinda nice, you'd like him, blah, blah, blah. But now you do this weird shit right in front of me, and I wonder what the *fuck* is going on inside your head."

"I wasn't sure you'd want to know."

"Well, I don't think I do. I don't think I want to know any of this." This time, she picked up some loose dirt and flung that at him, too. It didn't carry very far in the wind, but it made Rollins keep his distance. He watched her carefully, not knowing what she'd do next. "This weird gaunt guy, the faxes, that lady who disappeared, and now this. I don't think I want to know any of it, okay?"

Rollins was afraid she was going to cry. He wasn't sure he could take that. He wasn't used to naked displays of emotion; he found them frightening. But he also couldn't bear to think that Marj, of all people, might be so overwhelmed—and himself the cause. He could live with his demons. He deserved them. But Marj certainly didn't. He came closer to her, with the idea that he might rescue her from them somehow. He felt like running away with her—to Scandinavia or the South Pacific, some place free of associations, where he could start fresh as a new and much better person. He and Marj would get in the car, right now, and start driving. Just go. Go and keep going until they reached the ocean, and then board a plane bound for a far corner of the earth.

He reached out for her, hoping to begin that journey. But Marj flung out an arm. "Don't touch me, okay? Just don't touch me." Almost frantic now, she busied herself putting her socks back on, but they kept getting bunched up. Finally she balled the socks up in her hands and stuffed them in her pockets. "Okay, I'll admit it. I'm a little scared right now. I was scared last night, too. That's why I wanted you to call. Now I'm scared worse." She swept a hand back to indicate the house across the water. "I'm not used to staring into people's bedrooms. All right? Yeah, okay, I bought you the binoculars. But I was just being nice. I thought you'd like having them."

Rollins clutched the binoculars in his hand. "I do. I am grateful, Marj." Sometimes, a certain arch formality crept into his way of speaking when he most wanted to be sincere. "Really," he added.

Marj didn't seem to take that in. "This might sound strange to you, but this whole thing is not my idea of fun, okay? At first, I thought, all right, I can try anything once. But now, maybe I don't really want to know. Maybe it's all really, really fucked up." She picked up more dirt, but this time threw it out into the water, where it scattered the reflection of Sloane's house.

She turned back to him. Even in the moonlight, he could see that her eyes were red. "And now you tell me you saw some poor woman get whacked across the face. And you watched as though it didn't bother you at all. Just—*pass the popcorn!*"

"It does bother me," Rollins said. "Marj, I—" He stopped. He remembered his own house, seeing the way his mother looked at his father after the separation and before the divorce. She had the same look on her face as the woman did here in Sloane's house, before the blow landed. Dazed, unbelieving. His mother's bitterness had set in later, but Rollins' own pain had hit right away. He wanted to tell her this now. But he could not.

Marj rubbed her shirtsleeve across her eyes. "I felt—okay, this is really stupid—but I felt like maybe I could find my real dad out here in one of these windows. I know, I know. It doesn't make any sense." She tossed a hand into the air. "He's a million miles away from here, if he's anywhere." She sniffled. "But I just thought I might see him if I got these binoculars and just, like, kept looking. . . . Oh, God, why am I crying? I *hate* crying."

"I'm—Marj, I'm sorry."

"This whole thing is so pathetic. I don't know what I'm doing here." She stood up and without so much as a glance back at the house or at Rollins, she headed toward the park gate. Rollins watched her go. At the gate, she turned back to face him.

"Aren't you coming? You'll want the stupid license plate number, remember?"

Rollins looked back at the house. His heart wasn't much in it.

"Rollins, let's go."

Back in the car, Marj drove in silence around to the front of the house again. The Audi was there, parked on the street. Rollins jotted down the license plate number on the bag the binoculars had come in. Then they left.

On the trip back, Marj tuned the radio to a rock station and jacked the volume up to a level that Rollins found almost painful. He had a sense of the car as some kind of massive four-wheeled boom box, drawing annoyed looks from the fellow drivers to whom he'd always hoped that he was completely indistinct. He figured this was his penance, not that he quite knew for what. He passed the trip looking out the window, his baseball cap scrunched in his hand, the cars around him an undifferentiated blur.

As they pulled up by Rollins' car, parked around the corner from Marj's apartment building in Brighton, Marj said something to him, but, with the music pounding, he couldn't hear what it was. He reached over and snapped off the radio. His jaw ached. He must have been clenching it.

"I was telling you to keep the binoculars," she said. "You might need them."

"I have them right here." He'd put them back in the box, which he carried in his hand.

He started to get out.

Evidently, she could think of nothing to add, for she let him climb out of the car in silence. When he closed the door, she was still looking at him through the window. He leaned down toward her hopefully. "Did you say something?"

She gave him a cold look. "I'm just waiting for you to move your car."

"Oh, I'm sorry." He stepped away from the car, then turned back. "Now, you sure you'll be safe?"

"Look, don't worry about me." She put the car in gear. "If it gets too crazy, you might want to call the cops."

"I'll keep that in mind."

Rollins squeezed between a couple of parked cars to the sidewalk, and then climbed into his Nissan. He pulled out of his parking space, and, in his rearview, watched her nip into the vacant space behind him. As he waited at the first light, Rollins turned and watched Marj climb out of her car and head toward her building.

Time slowed, freighted. Rollins took a left at the next corner, then another, then pulled into a municipal parking lot. He had a straight shot at Marj's windows from there, and he was away from the streetlights. Through his driver's-side window, he stared up at her apartment—the three windows at the far end of the third floor. He wanted to make sure she was okay. That's what he told himself. He thought of using her binoculars, but feared they might attract attention. He watched intently, without moving, for over an hour. He saw Marj only once. She was wearing a thin, pale-green nightie as she crossed her windows with a glass in her hand.

Finally, her lights went out.

He slipped out of the Nissan, and made his way back to Marj's building. Every step seemed like a major commitment. Somehow, he expected that the air would resist him, but, of course, it let him slide right through. He didn't slow until he reached the front door, where he dug his keys out of his pocket in an attempt at passing for a resident returning home. This was another of Al Schecter's old tricks. Rollins had to make a couple of passes by the door, but on his third crossing, he timed it just right. A young man burst out the door to the apartment building just as Rollins pulled up with his keys in his outstretched hand. The man actually held the door for him and nodded graciously at Rollins as he stepped inside the hall.

His heart started to pump: He was in Marj's building. He'd entered where she lived. He tried to detect her perfume, that subtle sweetness of her, there in the hallway. But no, the air only smelled old. Still, it was a pleasure to suck it into his lungs all the same; it was something of her inside him.

The mailboxes were to the right. M. Simmons was in apartment 3F. Rollins almost couldn't believe that her name was listed there, in plain sight. It seemed like a proclamation of some sort. *To him*, maybe. He could feel a steady blip on the right side of his neck where an artery throbbed against his shirt collar, and another on one wrist where his pulse pressed against his cuff. He was drawing near to her.

There was an elevator past the mailboxes, but someone else might come aboard, and he didn't want to risk sharing Marj's proximity with a stranger. He continued down the hall, and he pushed through a heavy door that led to the stairs. The stairwell was harsh and bleak. His shoes clicked against the bare metal steps as he climbed to the third floor. He opened the door to a dimly lit hall, its walls a shadowy green. A threadbare carpet deadened the sound of Rollins' footsteps as he went down the corridor past 3D and 3E. His heart thudded in anticipation. 3F was at the far end, the door decorated with an anti-handgun sticker and a feminist cartoon he couldn't quite follow.

He glanced behind him to make sure no one was about, then, ever so gently, tried the door handle. The door was locked tight. He raised his hand to the wood and, slowly, slowly, he ran his hands along it, feeling its glossy varnish. He brought his cheek to the cool smoothness of the door. He ran a finger along one panel. He brought an ear close to the door, hoping he might hear her breathing within. The door was too thick to hear through, but he liked the thought of her asleep inside.

He stayed there for as long as he dared. He shut his eyes, the better to imagine her. Finally, he stepped back again and reached into his back pocket and took out his wallet. He removed his Johnson business card and pulled a stubby pencil from his shirt pocket. On the back of the card, in block letters, he wrote, *SLEEP WELL, MY DARLING*, the only words he'd ever heard his parents say with any affection. He wished that, someday, he might be able to say them to Marj. He slipped the card under the door. He stood there for a moment, pondering the gravity of that act. Then he returned the way he had come.

Seven

Someone was banging on Rollins' front door. At first, the noise wove itself into the disturbing dream he was having about the fight at the Sloanes'. Then suddenly he was awake, searching nervously about the room. Yellow light from a courtyard high-intensity lamp seeped in around the edges of his window shades, barely illuminating the wooden chair in the corner—the binoculars and Red Sox cap hung over its back—and the few framed prints of vintage cars that adorned his walls. He checked his bedside clock—3:14. The knocking persisted, louder and more rapid, with an insistent, metallic sound.

"Open up," came a shout. "Would you please?"

The voice was female, and all he could think was that it was Marj: She had read his note and come to him. He jumped out of bed, threw on his bathrobe, and hurried to his front door. He moved as if in a dream, the sideboard, sconces, and other familiar furnishings of his sitting room somehow liquefied around him. He frantically unlocked the bolts and swung open the door, bringing a rush of cool air up inside his pajamas, ready to take Marj into his arms with a shout.

But it wasn't Marj. It was a slim, dark-eyed woman in a loose, gray shift that nicely revealed the soft contours of her body. She had thick brown hair, slightly wavy, that spilled down over her shoulders.

"Excuse me, Mr. Rollin—I'm terribly sorry—I know it's late—"

"Do I know you?" Rollins interrupted. In a weird vestige of his dream, he thought, briefly, that this was the woman Sloane had hit. But she was younger and slimmer, and she didn't seem nearly so helpless. He squared his shoulders, instinctively trying to screen off the view into his apartment. As he did, he realized his father would have done exactly the same. He would have risen up, tall and imperious, to protect the sanctity of his castle from the prying eyes of a stranger.

"Oh, sorry. Tina Mancuso." The woman extended a hand, which Rollins shook awkwardly. "Didn't Mrs. D'Alimonte tell you?" She smiled fetchingly, despite the hour. "I just moved in with my daughter." She glanced back toward an open door down the hall. "I'm your new neighbor."

Rollins rubbed his eyes. There were cardboard boxes inside 2A, he could see now. "Oh, yes, right," he said sleepily. He supposed she must want something from him, but he couldn't imagine what. He raked his hair with his fingers, dutifully trying to rouse himself to greater wakefulness.

"My five-year-old is sick, and I really don't know what to do." She tugged anxiously at her fingers.

"Have you called a doctor?"

"I don't have one yet. We just moved and . . . "

Rollins waited, but she didn't elaborate. "Well, isn't there some sort of HMO you could call? Some emergency room?" Rollins knew little about such things. He avoided doctors, himself. The nosy questions, the roughness of their hands on him, the chill of the stethoscope.

"I—we—don't have a health plan anymore. I'm, well, I'm kind of between jobs."

"I'm sorry." He felt groggy; this whole encounter was too confusing. "What did you say your name was again?"

"Tina. Tina Mancuso." She smiled determinedly.

"Right. Look, Tina. It's very late. I'm not sure what you want from me." He still had a hand on the doorknob. He was tempted to close the door and to push Tina and her troubles out of his life. But she had stepped across the threshold, blocking him.

A desperate tone came into her voice. "I have a sick daughter. Mrs. D'Alimonte said that if I had any problems, I should ask you. She said you were a nice person."

"Isn't she around?" Rollins asked.

"She had to go to Baltimore. A baptism, I think she said."

"But what am I supposed to *do*?"

"We need a ride to the emergency room."

"You don't have a car?"

She shook her head. "Mr. Rollin, you know how it is after a big move like this. I'll be honest with you. I'm flat broke."

Rollins wondered how she could swing the $1,200 monthly rent, but he said nothing. Her accent, her pattern of speech, her brassy style—all this suggested to him that she was definitely not one of his. He detected little education, no culture, no "class," in the sense that his parents might have meant it. Yet she did have a certain animal appeal, something that emanated from her wide, confident hips and full breasts. This was a woman who rarely lacked for boyfriends, he was sure.

"Can I give you money for a taxi?" he offered.

To his surprise, Tina's face fell. "I shouldn't have bothered you." She stepped away from the door.

The way she moved away, so defeated, tugged at Rollins. Clearly, her pushiness had just been a brave front; at heart, she was simply a young single mother in a panic. "No, please, I insist. I'd drive you myself, but . . . Wait just a moment while I get my billfold." He went to grab his wallet off his bedroom dresser. When he returned, she was standing inside his foyer.

"You've done the place up nice," she told him quietly. "You a collector?"

"No, no. This is all just family stuff." He quickly plucked out two twenties and a ten, and stuffed them into the woman's open hand, hoping that would end the matter. Money did have its uses.

She didn't look at the cash. "I shouldn't take this."

"Please," Rollins told her. "I want you to."

"Well, okay then." She smiled and brought her other hand lightly against his chest. It was only the briefest contact, but something about it caused a change, as he sensed they both knew. A sort of molten heat surged within him, and he nearly reached for her, despite himself, despite Marj. The whole encounter seemed so dreamlike, as if she didn't really exist, and therefore wouldn't mind if he touched her, even if he touched those full lips of hers, or between her prominent breasts, so smoothly outlined by the folds of her shift. Only an overwhelming desire existed. Shameful, unexpected, inappropriate, but undeniable. But before he could think this through, she had retreated back down the hall, her skirts swishing.

Rollins was sitting in his leather chair, trying to calm himself and regain a fix on things, when he heard her come down the hall a few minutes later. She spoke quietly—to her child presumably—as she started down the staircase, the carpeted steps creaking under her. "It's all right, Heather," he heard her say. "Don't you worry."

Rollins was suddenly afraid for them, stumbling out into the dark, where so many hazards lurked. At the last moment, he opened the door and rushed after them. He must have made a bit of a racket on the stairs.

"Oh, God, it's you, Mr. Rollin," Tina exclaimed. "You scared me." The little girl, Heather, was in her arms. She seemed to be about four or five, her round face was pale and sweaty, her dark blond hair sticking to her temples. Rollins reached down to her and swept a few damp hairs off her forehead.

Stephanie on the tile floor, stone cold. He could tell by the color—pale blue—around her mouth, and at the tips of her fingers. A pale blue, like a shadow.

"I'm terribly sorry," Rollins said. "I shouldn't have been so unhelpful before."

"It's all right, Mr. Rollin. The taxi is here. We'll be fine."

"Please, let me carry her," he said, reaching for the child.

"I've got her. It's okay." Tina continued on down the stairs, Heather's head rocking uneasily with each step. Rollins couldn't bear the idea that something might happen to the little girl. He trailed after them, not knowing what to do. "At least let me get the door," he said finally, and lurched toward the door handle.

"Sure," Tina said.

Rollins drew open the front door for them, and stepped out ahead of them onto the front stoop. A fine mist was swirling, dampening his bathrobe and pajamas. He looked out into the wet gloom: The taxi was waiting by the sidewalk, its headlights bright, its wipers beating. Before he let Tina and Heather pass by him, he checked around the sidewalk and the street beyond. No sign of Sloane or the gaunt man.

Stephanie's hair in ringlets where she lay dripping. Nothing moving but the water off her. And all his fault.

"Let me go with you," he told Tina.

She looked at him and laughed. "Like that?"

Rollins had forgotten he was still in his pajamas. "It'll just take a moment to change."

"We'll be fine. Thank you, Mr. Rollin, really." This time, she sounded truly grateful.

Rollins opened the taxi door for her, although the rain was beginning to seep through his nightclothes to his shoulders. She slid inside the car, the child on her lap.

He leaned down toward them. "The name is Rollins, actually. With an *s*. That's what people call me, just Rollins."

She smiled up at him as though she had accomplished something. "All right. Rollins."

Rollins turned to the front of the cab. "Go to the MGH," he told the driver. "And hurry—please."

"Yes, the MGH. Of course. Thanks," Tina told him.

"You're entirely welcome." Rollins shut the door.

As the cab roared off, little Heather shot Rollins a wave through the back window.

Rollins watched the taxi go down Hanover Street. When it was out of sight, he checked around again for the gaunt man, or Sloane, or any other fury that might be pursuing him. But, once again, the street and sidewalks were empty. Rollins climbed up the stairs and closed the door, then glanced behind him once more from inside, just to be sure. Then he hurried back up the dark stairs.

Rollins arrived at Johnson the next morning on the stroke of eight-forty-five, which should have qualified him for an award. When he entered his office, he lowered the venetian blinds and lay his head on his desk to rest for a moment. He had not been able to get back to sleep after the lunacy of the night before. He'd kept waiting for Tina's tread on the stairs. Just to make sure that the little girl was all right, he assured himself. And he did fear for Heather, she seemed so hot. But he'd heard nothing the whole night. Afraid he might have nodded off and missed them, he'd listened at Tina's door first thing this morning. Again, nothing. He'd held off knocking, though, for fear of waking them in case they were home after all. Besides, what would he say? Hello? Good morning? Everything all right? He was sure he'd made a complete fool of himself last night, first with his absurdly lustful thoughts (which he feared had been only too transparent), and then with all his belated, unwanted offers of help.

As he lay there at his desk, his nose buried in the sleeve of his jacket, the stiff material pressing against his cheeks, Rollins heard a light tread on the wall-to-wall carpet. He knew it was Marj. He might have been a heat sensor: She was a steady warmth that was moving toward him down the hall. Now that she was so close by, he was mortified that he could have let his thoughts stray from her, even for a moment. And after he'd seen Marj just a few hours before. It was appalling! Would he end up like his father, flitting like an insect from one woman to the next and the next? He should have turned to face Marj, but he couldn't right then. He sensed her slowing as she passed his door, then resuming her pace again as she moved on down the hallway.

He saw her later that morning when he passed her desk on his way to the bathroom. She was on the telephone, coiling the cord around her index finger. Their eyes met for a moment, and he thought he heard her voice catch as he went by.

In the men's room, he washed his face with cold water, trying to bring down a slight puffiness around his eyes. When he returned, she wasn't in her cubicle. An e-mail message from Msimm@jinv was waiting for him back at his desk.

Wat's the matter, u sick?
m

Rollins didn't know quite what she meant at first. Then he figured she'd seen him resting. He sent back:

Just tired.

Another e-mail from her came a few minutes later:

Me too. I culdn't sleep last night. No more litle notes under my apt dor, pls OK? They mkae me real nervus.
m

Rollins' fingers trembled as he typed his reply:

OK. Sorry.

It rained for the next three days, a steady drizzle punctuated by several terrific downpours that flooded the narrow North End streets and caused colossal traffic jams downtown. Now, the time seemed like the rain itself—interminable, pointless. He kept checking for signs of Tina and her daughter, but saw nothing of them. More agonizing, he wasn't sure if he actually *wanted* to see them or just wanted to know where they were, the way one wants to know where a loaded gun might be.

He asked an upstairs neighbor, a tall man he knew only as Pete, if he had seen them, but Pete knew nothing, and Rollins quickly dropped the subject, lest Pete begin to wonder why he was so interested. Still, the Mancusos had taken up residence in Rollins' head, and he felt the need for the sense of liberation that he normally found in his pursuits. But, after the scary experience with the Chrysler, he had vowed not to venture out onto the road for at least another eighty-six hours.

That first night, a Friday, Rollins tried to lose himself in talk radio, a relatively new vice. He had an old Stromberg-Colson radio that his mother had always listened to while she brushed her hair before bed. And while it didn't measure up to the current standards of high-fidelity, talk shows came through fine. The subject this evening was the difference between love and friendship. For some reason, the show was not attracting the usual quantity of earnest callers, which left the host with a lot of airtime to fill. Rollins was tempted to call himself, to offer his opinion that love was not a matter of degree, as the host had argued, but of kind. Rollins was ransacking his memory for some wisdom from the ancients that would back up his point that love was rare and exalted beyond anything offered by mere buddyhood. (He liked that phrase, "mere buddyhood," and was sure it would go well over the air.) He even thought he might consult his Latin texts, sure that he'd find something from Horace or Catullus that would drive his point home, and, for the first time in a while, he started pulling those tiny red volumes off the shelf, running his eyes along the much interlineated verses.

The telephone rang. Rollins looked at the phone for a moment before he approached it. It was past ten, late for a call by almost any standard. The telephone rang twice more, then Rollins picked up the receiver. "Hello?"

He received no answer. He listened for the sound of breathing, but heard only dead air. "Marj?" he asked finally. "That you?" He had a queer feeling that it was, but there was no response from the other end of the line. Rollins clutched the receiver with both hands, as if it were Marj's hand. "Marj?" he asked again, a little quieter this time. Still no answer. He almost replaced the receiver, but then couldn't bear to break his tenuous connection to this sylph. He brought the mouthpiece close to his lips, spoke softly. He wanted these words to enter her consciousness the way her breath had filled his car. "I never know what to say to you, Marj. I always say the wrong thing, do the wrong thing." Then it occurred to him that it might not be Marj at all. It might in fact be Sloane, or the gaunt man, calling to frighten or to plague him. He froze for a second, then he hung up the receiver and stepped back from the telephone, eyeing it.

A few minutes passed. His eyes were still fixed on the old-fashioned phone when it rang again. Extraordinary. It felt as though he had somehow willed the telephone to ring. He watched the phone ring once, twice, three times. Rollins finally picked it up. "Hello," he said warily.

"It's your mother." Her aristocratic voice, with its cool elegance, brought back the full image of the woman who had always styled herself a great lady. Even at this hour, Jane Rollins' voice had pearls in it, freshly polished silver, and thick linen napkins folded just so. But it did nothing to allay his anxieties. He was grateful, at least, that she hadn't addressed him by name.

"Everything all right?" Rollins and his mother didn't speak very often. Hearing her, he had to think that there must be some family crisis afoot.

"I just thought I'd give you a chance to wish me a happy birthday."

"Oh, that." Rollins lightened momentarily, but then he felt disturbed all over again that he could have forgotten such a thing. He quickly checked the little calendar that was propped up on a shelf in the bookcase. Today's date, the twenty-ninth, was surrounded by a jagged square of red he'd placed there at the first of the year. "I'm awfully sorry, Mother. Happy birthday."

Rollins was suddenly alarmed at the thought that his mother might have heard his cries for Marj. "You didn't just call, by any chance?"

"No, why?"

"The phone rang but there was no one there."

"Oh, I get those all the time. I just hang up."

On his birthday calls to Mother, Rollins sometimes sang a bit of the "Happy Birthday" song, slightly off-key. As the oldest child, he'd always led the singing in the family, after his father had left. It had cheered him to think that he had a few family traditions to fall back on. But now, he didn't quite have the heart for it. Without that routine, though, Rollins realized he was obliged to say something personal to his mother, something beyond "Hello," or "How are you?" He wished that he could merely stay on the line with her without speaking. For as long as he could remember, words had been a strain between them.

"You sitting down now?" Rollins asked.

"Why, has something happened?"

"Oh, no. I just wanted to be able to picture you better, that's all."

There was a playful quality to her reply: "Well, if you must know, I'm on the red sofa by the telephone in my living room." He envisioned her in her apartment there at her retirement center, Maple Hill. A small place, crammed with elegant furniture. While he saw her in Boston every few months, he had visited her there only once, two years before. It was shortly after Richard (always better at doing the right thing) had helped move her in following the death of their stepfather, Albert Crossan, a retired concrete supplier whom his mother had met at a bridge party when Rollins was in his late teens. It was Crossan who'd lured her down to Farmington, where he had a big modern house with a swimming pool. Rollins had found Maple Hill utterly depressing, what with all the ghostly geriatrics drifting down endless corridors or going through the motions in the dining room as they waited for the end to come. He suspected his mother did, too. Still, admirably, she had managed to retain a bit of grandeur there, even in her reduced circumstances.

"You remember, it used to be in the library in Brookline," his mother continued.

"I remember it well." Rollins could see her sitting there by herself before dinner in front of the fire in the postdivorce years. A highball would be in her hand, one of the fine crystal ones that were not to be used by the children. She was not to be bothered, that was clear, but she could be watched, slowly sipping her two fingers of bourbon, heavy on the ice.

"I'm on my leather chair," Rollins told her.

"Oh, that old thing you got at the dump."

"It was a rummage sale, Mother."

A light exchange, but it brought back other, heavier ones—accusations of hers that he had parried, more or less skillfully, through the years. Aftertremors of the one great shock of their lives—that's how he thought of them.

They discussed the weather for a few minutes, and his mother caught Rollins up on the news that Richard's wife, Susan, was thinking of going back to her job managing a chain of high-end housewares shops. "Now listen," his mother concluded. "I'm coming to Boston tomorrow to see Mr. Grove"—he was the family trust officer at Richardson Brothers—"about some investment decisions. I thought we might get together for lunch afterward."

It didn't surprise Rollins that his mother would take such an active role in her financial affairs at her advanced age, or that she would be able to arrange to meet with Mr. Grove on a Saturday morning. It surprised him only that she would save this piece of business for last. He wondered if their conversation had actually been some kind of test—and if this final overture had meant he'd passed or failed it. Had his mother detected some changes in him, ones that she thought she'd better monitor closer at hand?

"That would be fine," Rollins told her.

They worked out the time: Eleven-thirty in the grand Richardson offices at Post Office Square. "Please don't be late, darling," Mrs. Rollins closed. "You know how I hate waiting."

Afterward, Rollins couldn't get comfortable as he lay down on his bed atop the covers. He returned to the telephone and after consulting directory assistance for M. Simmons in Brighton, he dialed Marj's number. He'd extinguished all the lights except for the lamp by the telephone chair. He needed near darkness for this. He was wearing only his pajamas, a fresh white pair, with pale blue piping around the cuffs. When the call went through, he leaned back on the big leather chair. His right hand held the receiver; his left lay on his soft belly as Marj's phone rang—with a seductive, purring sound—four times. Then there was a click and an answering machine came on: "You know what to do." That was followed by a long beep. Rollins hung up without a word, then dialed her number twice more, just to hear her voice.

Eight

Rollins felt feverish that night. He was afraid that he'd caught something from young Heather. He slept little, and his few dreams seemed rushed. In the morning, the sheets were tangled and damp with sweat.

It was still raining. He could hear the steady, static-like hiss outside his windows, and there was a grayness to the light around his shades. Since it wasn't yet seven on a Saturday morning, he lay in bed until his old worries returned, starting with the Mancusos. Once again, he hadn't heard them come in during the night. But then, he had slept some this time.

He splashed some water on his face, pulled on his bathrobe, and crept down the hall to listen at their door. He heard nothing. "Tina? Heather?" he called out. "You there?" He kept seeing the little girl's pale, moist face as she descended the stairs.

When no one answered, he returned to his apartment and picked up the telephone. He dialed the patient information line at the MGH. When the operator came on, he told her he was trying to reach his daughter, Heather Mancuso. Lying was becoming automatic now. Rollins could hear the click of keys in the background, then a pause.

"How are you spelling Mancuso?"

Rollins told her with a *c* and an *s*. He couldn't think of any other way.

"I'm sorry, there's no listing. You sure she's an in-patient?"

"Yes, of course. Her mother brought her in." Rollins felt almost indignant.

"And when was that?"

"Two nights ago."

Rollins heard more keys click.

"I'm sorry. We have no record of a Heather Mancuso on that night either. Perhaps she went to another hospital?"

"Her mother said the MGH."

"Well, we have no record of her being here, sir."

Rollins hung up and tried four other hospitals in the area. He described himself as Heather's uncle, godfather, and twice as her elementary school principal. No other hospital had any record of Heather Mancuso, either.

On Saturdays, Rollins usually went out for breakfast at a local cafe. With the rain, he was tempted to stay in, but when he checked the refrigerator, he saw that he was all out of coffee beans, and the muffins he'd been counting on were moldy. Just for a moment, he wished that things might get done in his apartment without his being the one to do them. Perhaps he needed a maid. His parents had always employed a cook and a housekeeper, along with their factotum, Gabe. Such assistance hadn't, in fact, been in style when he was a child, but his father, whose own childhood had been spent only on the edges of the privileged life, had insisted on it, and his mother had quickly warmed to all the help. She had, in fact, become quite magisterial with the small staff. Unfortunately, given the size of his apartment, Rollins realized that it would be ridiculous to have even a part-timer come in. There was barely enough room for Rollins himself.

He wondered if Marj was any good at cooking. Somehow, he doubted it.

He took a shower and, while he was at it, knelt down to clean some grime out of the drain while the warm water pounded on his shoulders and neck. He shaved in the shower, then stepped out and toweled off.

As he was about to leave the bathroom, he noticed that the door was slightly ajar. He'd been pretty sure that he had shut it tight behind him when he'd come in. He secured the towel around him and pushed the door open. He felt a cool breeze on his chest and still-damp underarms as he peered out into his bedroom. "Hello?" he called out. Everything seemed the same: the unmade bed, his clothes draped over the chair by the window, the drapes pulled tight.

He pulled on a polo shirt from his bureau and stepped into a pair of undershorts, then advanced toward his closet. "Hello?" he asked again, feeling a little foolish this time, as he approached the closed closet door. Still, he thought that he should have something in his hand, some weapon, but nothing came to mind except an old tennis racquet in the front hall. He placed his hand on the doorknob and eased the door open. He braced himself, but no attack came. Nothing moved in his closet. He carefully parted the clothes on their hangers to examine the back. There was no sign of anyone, just his usual array of dusty old shoes, an abandoned TV, and a few cardboard boxes filled with winter clothes. He grabbed a pair of khakis off the hanger, and pulled them on. He felt better, but he still checked under the bed. Nothing.

He ventured into the other parts of the apartment. Nothing was amiss in the living room or in the kitchen. He pushed aside the coats in the front hall closet, just to be sure. The locks were still secured on the front door. Everything appeared to be in order.

He absolutely had to relax.

He returned to his bedroom, put on a pair of foul-weather shoes, then added a windbreaker from its hook in the front hall closet. He checked the locks on the windows before he went out, then was careful to set the burglar alarm and dead-bolt his door behind him.

The cafe was down past the laundromat; it was a small place called Della Rosa's. There were just a few people inside, most of them paging through newspapers. He found a seat by a window. He ordered a cappuccino and one of the flaky pastries he'd seen out on the counter.

The waitress brought him his food a few minutes later. She was youngish, in a tight tie-dyed T-shirt. She asked him if his name was Rollins by any chance.

Rollins felt a twinge at the back of his neck. "That's right."

"I thought it was you." She smiled. "A friend of yours came in." She made it sound like good news.

"Oh?"

"Yeah, some guy. Didn't give his name. Asked about you. Said he hadn't seen you in a while. He'd tried to call, but I guess you don't have an answering machine."

Rollins asked her what the man looked like, and, after pausing for a second to think, the waitress said, "Real skinny, that's all I remember."

Rollins felt those words in his stomach. "Mustache?" He dragged an index finger across his upper lip.

"Yeah, that's right!" The woman nearly shouted.

"What did he want?"

"Just if I'd seen you around."

Rollins waited. He sensed he wouldn't have to ask many questions to keep her talking.

"I told him, sure, I'd seen you in here a couple times. You live around here, right?"

Rollins glanced around the cafe. No one seemed to be paying much attention. He nodded.

"Yeah, thought so. Nice of him to check up on you, huh?"

"Isn't it." Rollins' mind drifted back to the sight of the gaunt man disappearing around the corner just a few blocks away.

The waitress moved back to the counter. Rollins had lost his appetite. He didn't finish his coffee or his pastry. He got up to go. When he reached the register, the waitress asked him if "that guy" had ever gotten in touch with him.

"Yes he did, actually." Rollins paid the bill and added a decent tip.

"Just the other day. He didn't say anything about coming around here, though. When did you see him?"

"Yesterday, I think it was. No, wait, the day before. I didn't work yesterday."

That must have been Thursday. Through Marj's binoculars, Rollins had seen the gaunt man talking to Sloane that very night. They might have been talking about him after all.

"How funny," the waitress said.

Rollins wasn't sure he followed.

" 'Cuz, like, he'd just seen you."

Rollins smiled, doing his best to keep his composure.

"Well, tell him hi for me next time you see him, okay?" she called after him.

"He knows your name?"

"Everybody does. It's Leeann. Pleased to meet you." She smiled.

Outside, the rain had let up. As he walked along, he was aware of his body, of the bodies of the other people he passed. None of them seemed especially lean, none had mustaches. He hurried down the sidewalk, took a right on Hanover. The rain must have backed up traffic downtown, because the street was choked with cars in both directions. He searched the faces of the drivers and was glad not to recognize anyone. When he reached the door to his apartment building, he clung to the knob for a second, grateful for its cool solidity, before he gave it a twist and stepped inside.

The staircase lights were still out, and it took his eyes a while to adjust to the dimness. At first, there seemed to be a bag of some sort on the front stairs. But then he saw that it was a little girl in a brown dress that reached barely to her knees. It was Heather. A teddy bear was perched on the step beside her. "Hi, mister," she called out to him. "Wanna play Old Maid? I've got the cards in here someplace." She rummaged around inside a purple knapsack beside her.

"Heather? That you?" He felt a lifting inside him.

"Yup."

"You okay? How's the fever?"

"I cooled down. I'm fine now."

"Where's your mother?"

"Out."

"And she just left you here?" That was puzzling. Whatever else she was, Tina had seemed like a devoted mother.

"I was upstairs, but I got kinda itchy." She sniffled and wiped her nose on the shoulder of her dress, then pulled a hand out of her bag. "Oh, here they are. See?" She showed Rollins the Old Maid pack. "C'mon, just one game?" She sniffled again. Rollins handed her a handkerchief from his back pocket. She thanked him and blew her nose into it. She started to hand it back.

"You can keep it," Rollins said.

"Really?"

Rollins nodded, and she zipped it into the pouch of her backpack. "Thanks, mister," she said.

Rollins didn't feel safe with her there, so close to the front door. He offered to play upstairs, but Heather said it was boring in her apartment with all the stupid boxes. So he suggested they go to his place. Heather, of course, had no idea how rare it was to receive such an invitation. Still, she brightened as if she had been given a free ticket to Disneyland. She stuffed her teddy bear and Old Maid cards into her knapsack as if she were packing for a long trip, then followed Rollins up the stairs. Her sneakers, with their untied laces, hardly made any sound.

Heather showed no particular interest in the lavish furnishings in Rollins' apartment. She merely dropped her knapsack on the floor just inside the door, wiped her hands on her dress, and asked if he had anything to eat.

Rollins led Heather back into the narrow kitchen. He thought for a moment of offering her the remains of some Thai take-out in his refrigerator, but decided instead on some Milano cookies, which he set out for her on a saucer as if she were a stray kitten. The candlesticks were still out on the table, and he'd propped the original notepaper with the strange seven-digit number back up on it, along with the return fax. He'd been looking at them at odd moments, waiting for inspiration. Now, he quickly snatched them up and set them aside in a pile before she, too, was drawn into the mystery. But it was too late.

"What are those?" Heather asked.

"Nothing important."

"They looked important."

"Well, they aren't really."

Heather took a bite of cookie. "Then why don't you throw them out?"

"I probably should."

Heather stopped chewing for a moment. "Then why don't you?" She was a persistent little thing.

"I will later, all right? Do you want any milk?"

"Yes."

"Okay then." He could feel himself loosening up. He was surprised how much he was enjoying this, the back-and-forth, the sound of another voice echoing off the pale yellow walls in the kitchen, the actual presence of another person—albeit a small, young one—to fuss over and be startled by.

Rollins checked the refrigerator. He had a carton, but, when he took a sniff, discovered that the milk had gone bad. "Sorry," he said. "Do you suppose water would be okay?"

"Sure." She sounded disappointed.

He set down a glass. The cookies were gone. "You *were* hungry," Rollins said.

"Yeah, I was!" Heather brushed off a few crumbs that had stuck to the corner of her mouth. He set out the rest of the bag, but Heather said she needed to use the bathroom.

Rollins ushered her through the sitting room toward his bedroom. He couldn't get over how small she was, how light on her feet. He kept thinking how forbidding his antiques must look to her, just as they had looked to him as a child. But she said nothing about them and merely tagged along behind him without a sound. He paused for a moment before pushing open the bedroom door. It was dark inside, with the shades drawn, and he had to click on the light. He was afraid she might ask about the long row of tapes over his bed, but, instead, as she stepped inside, she fixed on his pictures of antique cars. "These yours?" she asked, bringing her nose right up to them.

"The pictures are," he replied. "Not the cars."

"I like that one." She pressed a finger on the 1937 Pierce-Arrow, leaving a light smudge on the glass.

"Me, too." He left the smudge there, glad to have something to remember her by. The car had belonged to Rollins' grandfather. He used to take Rollins driving around his Dover estate when Rollins was very young. The property had seemed to him to be the size of a small town; they could drive around almost forever, a plaid blanket over their legs against the early morning chill. But, like so many things, that had all stopped with Stephanie's death; after that, Rollins seemed to spend all his spare time with child psychiatrists, when he would have much preferred to be tooling around with Gramps in the Pierce-Arrow.

Rollins went on to the bathroom to flip on the light over the sink. Heather followed closely behind him. But Rollins withdrew well before she made her way to the toilet. He told her he would be outside if she needed him. He was sitting at the foot of the bed when Heather came back out. She dug a finger under the waistband of her dress. She was such a pretty girl, with her golden yellow hair and sky blue eyes; Rollins felt happy just to look at her. Aside from the rare get-togethers with Richard's kids, he saw so few children. He patted the bed again. "Come here, would you?"

Suddenly, Heather tried to dart past Rollins, but he caught her tiny wrist just as she was turning the corner of the bed.

"Got you!" he shouted cheerfully. It was his father's mock-gruff voice, he realized, from the rare days when they used to roughhouse on the big rug in the living room.

"I was just going to get my teddy!" Heather pleaded, her voice quivering. Tears had formed in her eyes. "Can't I get my teddy?"

"My goodness, of course!" Rollins felt terrible to have riled her, and he tried to be as soothing as he could. "I'm sorry." He released her wrist and gently stroked her hair. He could feel the heat from her scalp. "Here, I'll get it." Rollins hurried out to the hall, grabbed the knap-sack, and returned to the bedroom. "There you are." He dropped the knapsack on the bed, and Heather dug the fuzzy, brown teddy bear out of it and hugged it to her chest. Rollins perched himself on the bed in front of her. "Can I show you something?" Heather didn't sit beside him as he had hoped, but she did lean against the edge of the bed, watching him. "Please?" he asked gently. Heather nodded. She was all eyes now.

He rolled to his left, pushed a hand into his back pocket and drew out his wallet. He flipped it open, dug a finger underneath all the slots that held his credit cards and teased out a small photograph, slightly brown from all its years pressed up against the calfskin of his wallet. As he did so, he could see Heather lean toward him trying to get a peek.

It was a baby picture of a tiny little girl in a white gown. She had wispy hair, a slightly dazed expression, and soft blue eyes. "This is Stephanie," Rollins said. "It was taken about six months after she was born. It's the only picture I have of her."

"Who is she?"

"She's my little sister."

"She's cute."

Rollins could sense the girl relaxing. "Yes, isn't she? You remind me of her a little."

"She doesn't look like you."

"You don't think so?" He held the picture up by his face so she could compare.

Heather wrinkled her nose. "She's a lot younger. Littler, too."

"This was taken a long time ago. Look how big her pupils are. They were the most beautiful blue."

Heather took another look.

"They were always looking for me, that's what my mother said. And her hands were so little. I had no idea they'd be so small. They always seemed to be reaching for me."

There was a shout from the front hall. "Heather? Heather? You up there, darling?"

Rollins turned to Heather. "Your mother's looking for you."

"I don't care."

"Oh, but you should." He stood up. "Take my hand?"

Heather hesitated only for a moment. "Okay."

Her hand was warm and light. He held on to it, and then picked up her knapsack and led her through the sitting room to his front hall. Tina was just inside Rollins' door. She was wearing a clingy shirt, and she had on makeup this time. "So you *are* here." Tina flicked her hair off her shoulders, then reached out and swept her daughter up into her arms. "I was looking everywhere for you!"

"I've been playing with mister," Heather said.

"You were? Well, isn't that nice." She turned to Rollins. "I didn't mean to be out so long." She smiled again, demurely. "You must think I'm the worst mother."

"Not at all," Rollins reassured her. "I know how things can come up."

"Mister showed me a picture," Heather said.

"Of my sister," Rollins quickly explained.

"Oh?" Tina said, with a look that compelled him to get out the photograph again. He handed it to her reluctantly. Tina studied it a moment. "Cute."

"I left the door open," Rollins assured her.

"Oh, listen—" Tina blurted out in a voice that Rollins took to be reassuring.

"I just didn't—"

"You've been real nice," Tina said, handing back the photograph. "Mrs. D'Alimonte was right about you." Rollins waited for a moment. He thought something might come—a gesture, an offer. Some overture that would put him in a terrible quandary. But Tina merely thanked him.

"You can borrow my teddy sometime if you want," Heather added. She held up the well-worn bear and gave it a little shake. "Everybody needs a friend, you know."

"I'll keep that in mind," Rollins told her.

Then, with Heather still in her arms, Tina made her way back down the hall to their apartment.

*   *   *

It was drizzling when Rollins set out to meet his mother an hour later. The traffic hadn't subsided, so he decided to walk to Richardson Brothers, which was across from the Johnson building, maybe ten minutes away. He felt anxious as he hurried along under his black umbrella, and he glanced about him periodically, but saw no sign of any pursuers. Halfway along, too late to do anything about it, he realized he was doing something quite unwise. The Richardson Brothers offices were practically the family vault, after all; the Brothers had held various family trusts for generations. The money itself was rarely seen of course, but it had certainly had its effects, funding that big house in Brookline, a country house in Vermont, the private schools, the European ski trips that Rollins never much enjoyed. If he was indeed being followed, it hardly seemed prudent to draw attention to the family's pile.

Richardson Brothers was located in one of the grand granite office buildings that fronted onto the small European-style park, heavy on marigolds, the blossoms clotted in the rain, in Post Office Square. He'd come here a few times before, the first being the most memorable. It had been shortly after his twenty-first birthday, and he had been summoned from Williams by a Mr. Grove for what he described as "an important conversation." When Rollins arrived in jacket and tie, Mr. Grove explained about his trust fund. Rollins had some trouble grasping the concept of a big bundle of money—it was $573,000 then—that had come, virtually gift-wrapped, down to him through the ages to do with *entirely as he pleased,* so Mr. Grove actually took him into a back room, through a thick steel door and into a vault to examine the stock certificates themselves. "Nothing quite like touching it," the older man had said with a laugh. The certificates had proved to be unusually large, ornate documents printed on the same paper as cash money, but adorned with the names of prominent American corporations like IBM, Ford, and General Electric. "I own all this?" Rollins had asked, flipping through all the paper as one might an encyclopedia. Mr. Grove merely nodded, a beguiling half-smile on his face. Since then, Rollins had often sensed that the money gave him a secret allure, an importance that went beyond anything that he actually did, which was another reason he thought it best to keep quiet about it. Still,

Rollins himself had gazed with fascination on his quarterly statements, watching the sums grow steadily, year by year, as if charged with a powerful vitality all of their own.

With one last look behind him, Rollins pushed through the revolving door to find a uniformed security guard behind the marble reception desk in the high-ceilinged front hall. Rollins explained who he was.

"Oh, yes," the guard replied. "You're expected upstairs."

The guard had Rollins sign in, then led him around to the elevators. The guard had to turn a key to activate one that would take him up to the seventeenth floor.

The elevator opened directly into the Richardson Brothers' quarters, where a grandfather clock faced him, along with an oil painting of a clipper ship. He turned left toward a window that gave a partial view of the Atlantic—foggy and gray this morning—between the other high-rises that had sprung up along the waterfront. Unlike Johnson, which was so bright it sometimes made him squint, the Richardson offices were dimly and soothingly lit. With their dark wood paneling, leather furniture, and plentiful antiques, the offices reminded him of the Somerset Club, where his father sometimes took him for lunch after the divorce.

The door to the reception area was open, and Rollins made his way across the thick carpet silently. That was habitual with him, especially around his family. He'd always recognized the benefits of silence as he crept about the house, the little things you could learn. Now, he spotted his mother sharing a leather couch with Mr. Grove underneath a portrait of the founding Richardsons, with their grim visages and bright watch fobs. If Rollins hadn't known better, he might have taken his mother and Mr. Grove for lovers, they sat together with such familiarity. Mr. Grove, a well-dressed, ruddy-cheeked gent who must be in his early sixties now, had been out to the house many times when Rollins was a child, often bearing a heavy leather bag filled with important-looking documents to sign. Now, he had something of a feminine aspect as he gazed over at Rollins' mother, who, in her businesslike blue skirt suit, seemed somewhat bemused by all the fawning attention.

Her hair was up in a tight bun, a new style for her, and it was grayer than before, and her face seemed somewhat drawn, but there was still the same glint in her eyes.

It was Mr. Grove who noticed Rollins first, and he caused Jane Rollins to turn. "Oh, there you are!" she declared, rearing back a little before she recovered herself. "What a pleasant surprise." She checked her watch. "So prompt."

Mr. Grove, seemingly oblivious to any hint of familial strife, immediately stood up and extended a hand. "Good to see you again, my boy." His voice was soft and welcoming, like well-worn upholstery.

"Buy and hold," Mrs. Rollins told her son. "That's the key. I learned that from my father, just as he did from his." She turned to Mr. Grove with a slight twinkle in her eye: "Wouldn't you say that our conversation this morning underscores the soundness of that principle?"

"Oh, definitely," Mr. Grove said obligingly. "I'm always glad to hear from you, and very glad you came in." He rubbed his hands together as if trying to warm them. "Now, are you sure I can't call you a cab or something?"

"I have a car waiting, and I've got my son here to help me along."

For the first time, Rollins noticed that a wooden cane leaned up against the couch beside his mother. As she grasped it in her right hand, Mr. Grove alertly stepped toward her to help her to her feet.

"Why, thank you, Nick," his mother said. She turned to her son. "I've been having a little trouble with my hip lately. But nothing to worry about. This damn rain doesn't help though."

Mr. Grove saw them out to the hallway. When the elevator arrived, he shook hands with them once more, helped his client into the elevator, and pressed the button for the mezzanine floor for them before stepping back out. He was smiling at them as the doors closed and the elevator descended.

Rollins' mother raised her cane just outside the front door, and a black Lincoln Town Car came around from its spot in front of a fire hydrant across the way. As Jane Rollins led the way toward it, Rollins did his best to shelter his mother with his umbrella. Once they'd reached the car, he glanced about, checking for onlookers. And again, he saw none.

"You coming?" his mother asked from inside the car.

"Of course." Rollins went around to the far side and climbed in.

"I thought the Harvard Club would be good," Mrs. Rollins said.

Rollins said fine, but he had the feeling that he often had with his mother: that her plans were settled and irrevocable regardless of his own wishes.

She looked at Rollins out of the corner of her eye. Her head had dipped with age, as had her eyelids, and, up close, they gave her appearance an unsettling reptilian aspect that was not fully countered by the gold pins in her hair and her faded lipstick. "I have to watch them in there. Oh, they're so very genteel. You saw our dear Mr. Grove. Such a kind man. But he'd ruin us in a second with some ghastly municipal bonds if I gave him half a chance or, God love us all, Internet stocks. No, I have to come show my face every few months, just to keep them in line."

They were passing the back of the templelike Boston City Hall, across from the bustling tourist trap, Faneuil Hall. "You live over that way, don't you?" she asked, tapping on the glass in the direction of the North End. "You'll have to invite me to see your apartment one of these years. After a while, a mother gets curious, you know."

"It's kind of small. I'm not sure you'd like it."

"I love small things."

"Not to live in."

"Well, perhaps not."

His mother returned to the view, and started reminiscing about Government Center's previous incarnation as Scollay Square, with its burlesque shows and prostitutes. Actually, she used the word "whores," much to Rollins' surprise. No doubt, she'd learned about such things from his father, who was always more attuned to what really went on in the world.

It wasn't until they were in the small dining room at the Harvard Club (a massive edifice built, Rollins always thought, far more to a towering New York scale than to a cozy Boston one) that Rollins dared to enter potentially dangerous conversational territory. His mother had pulled out a snapshot that Richard had sent her of his children, and Rollins had said, he thought, all the right things, especially about Natalie, whom he genuinely did like. The photo reminded him of Neely's picture from the *Globe*'s files and, despite his apprehensions, he decided to mention it. "I ran across a photograph of cousin Cornelia the other day."

His mother had been babbling on quite cheerfully about Richard's kids, but now a marked coolness came into her voice. "Oh?" His mother had never warmed to her niece, for reasons Rollins could never quite piece out. In attitude and temperament, they'd seemed perfectly suited. Like his mother, Neely had been very athletic and had gone on to captain the varsity lacrosse team at Smith. She'd always encouraged the children to play whiffle ball or croquet on the lawn in the two summers she stayed with them while her parents traveled abroad. She was a big sister to Rollins and his younger brother those summers, a bright bundle of good cheer. It went so well that Neely returned for a full year the following summer, even though her own parents stayed home. She was eighteen by then, and she'd finished boarding school, but her parents had decided she wasn't ready for college. Rollins' mother declared that she needed official duties, so she served as an au pair—baby-sitting mostly, but running the occasional errand as well—while she took art classes in town. His father was more enthusiastic about Neely than his mother was. Father could sometimes be roused to join in the merry lawn games that Neely organized, but Mother never could.

"A friend had it," Rollins said, referring to the picture of Neely he'd run across.

"Why'd he show it to you?" His mother rearranged the silverware at her place setting.

"She." He was happy to allude to Marj, especially if she remained unnamed.

"I guess everyone thinks you're the big expert on Neely now," his mother added dryly, answering her own question.

Rollins ignored the dig. "It was a publicity photograph taken for her first book."

"I never read it." His mother smeared some butter on her roll.

"Yes, you did," Rollins reminded her. He'd given her a copy for Christmas and saw her reading it at the breakfast table over her usual muffins the next morning. "You're thinking of the second one." That one, *Forced Blossoms*, had caused a stir, at least in the family, for its explicit sexuality. Words like "labia" had appeared several times in the text. "Remember, you said it was too gynecological?"

The old woman laughed gently. "Oh, yes, I suppose I did." She added: "Now, you're not going to tell me she's turned up somewhere, are you?"

Rollins was struck by her tone of indifference to Neely's fate. "No."

"I do wonder what will happen to her money." His mother said this idly, as if it were of no particular consequence. Rollins figured she had financial topics on her mind after the visit to Mr. Grove.

"There isn't that much." With the help of Al Schecter, who was looking into the case for an insurance company, Rollins had figured Neely was worth about $750,000 at the time of her disappearance, much of it in the form of her Londonderry property.

"Oh, but that was before her grandmother died—your uncle George's mother, Alicia Blanchard." His mother intensified a little, like a lamp turned up by rheostat. "She was extremely well-off, you know. Extremely." Rollins' understanding of that side of the family was somewhat dim, but he'd heard that Alicia's husband, Joseph, had started up a telecommunications business on the side while he was a professor at MIT. "After old Joe died, she bought a palazzo in Venice overlooking one of the smaller canals, I forget which. I visited once with your stepfather. She was an artist, you know. Did portraits. Sort of blotchy ones. I never much cared for them, but a couple of them ended up in the Worcester art museum. She probably paid to put them there, knowing her." Her face showed her disdain for such a maneuver. "She thought Neely's father was a pill." The dour and portly George Blanchard had gone into commercial real estate in Pittsburgh, although the family had continued to live up here. He'd done extremely well, far better than Jane Rollins' own husband. "But she did admire Neely. Thought it was distinguished to have a poet in the family."

The waiter interrupted to take their order. After some quick deliberations, Mrs. Rollins decided on the cod, while her son selected the chicken Caesar. They snapped their menus shut and handed them back.

"Neely's sexual orientation didn't bother her grandmother?" Rollins asked.

"Her what?" Jane Rollins interrupted.

"The fact that she was a lesbian?"

"Oh, that. Heavens, no. That might have been part of her appeal. Alicia was quite a freethinker. Left Neely just about everything, from what I heard. Ellie was *furious*, not that she needed the money, God knows." Eleanor was his mother's sister, Cornelia's mother. "She thought it was a terrible slap in the face."

"How much was it?" Rollins hadn't known any of this.

"After the estate taxes, it might have been as high as four or five million. And that was—what? Four years ago, something like that. You know how the stock market has been going. It could be twice that now."

This was astonishing. "Didn't she know that Neely was . . . gone?"

"Certainly she knew. She was fascinated by the whole story. Absolutely fascinated. We had quite a lively correspondence about it. But she never cared for Ellie. In-laws can be like that, you'll find. And George was so useless. She had no other children, and only the one grandchild. No, to her, Cornelia was the last great hope. I think she figured this might be some kind of inducement for her to come back."

"She couldn't come back if she was dead."

"I never could convince her that she was."

"You should have sent her my story, then."

His mother's face fell abruptly. The *Beacon* story had always been a sore point between them. Rollins knew, because she had never once mentioned it to him—although she had given her sister Ellie an earful, filled with terms like "appalling" and "public spectacle," which Ellie had passed on to Rollins one afternoon over tea.

His mother gazed at him openmouthed for a moment—a most unmotherly sight; she looked like a flounder—before she composed herself. "Oh, that," she said. "I don't think we need to discuss *that*." Then, perhaps realizing that she had raised her voice slightly, she smiled. Her public smile. The one she used to assure anyone who might be watching that she was, as always, enjoying herself immensely.

"I'm sorry you feel that way," Rollins said bravely, knowing that his words had some fight in them.

Jane Rollins did not respond, but merely glanced at her watch. "Where is that waiter? The service here is so slow." After a brief, uncomfortable silence, she straightened herself up in her chair, took a small sip of water, and returned to her story of Neely's grandmother as if, Rollins thought, the awkward intervening segment of the conversation had never occurred. "Alicia thought Neely had simply gone off somewhere. She saw her as a great romantic, with all her own—what do you call it? Wanderlust, that's the word. A very stubborn lady, Alicia."

"So what's become of the money?"

Her face hardened again. "You aren't planning to write any more about this, are you?"

"Mother, please." It had been a long time since he had felt so provoked by her.

"I'd like some advance warning, that's all."

"You know I haven't written anything in years."

"And aren't planning to?"

It was irritating the way she kept pushing at him, trying to control him, even now. Rollins was tempted to jump up from his seat, toss his napkin down on the table, and storm out of the dining room with a few choice words hurled in her direction. But such childishness—which he had never descended to, even as a child—would only have confirmed his mother's opinion of him. Far better to wait, to let the feeling pass, as he knew it eventually would. "No, mother," he replied finally. "That's all done. No more journalism for me."

She smiled again. "I can't say that I'm sorry. I never thought it suited you, darling."

Rollins said nothing. He missed his old job at the *Beacon*, burrowed in his tiny office, gathering his private store of information, then serving it up to the world in small, manageable doses. It seemed so much more meaningful than what he did now at Johnson.

"Do you?" she probed, clearly trying to press her advantage.

"Perhaps not," he conceded.

His mother gave him a sideways look. "You do surprise me sometimes, you know. Now, Richard, he is what he is. Totally transparent. But, with you, I'm never sure. Sometimes I feel I don't quite know you."

Rollins was stunned. This observation, so calmly delivered, felt like a knife slicing into him. Her lack of understanding was all his fault; that was the implication. He tried to think of a suitable reply. But nothing came to mind—or, at least, nothing that would improve the situation or bring him some relief. His one consolation was that his mother seemed not to notice his distress. Having delivered herself of her dire pronouncement, she merely adjusted her hair a little.

"I haven't any idea about the money," she added airily. "It's in her trust, I suppose."

Rollins knew that Cornelia had such an account overseen by an old-line firm called Hadley and Poor up in Concord, New Hampshire. Schecter had found it, and had had a strained conversation about it with her trust officers, who couldn't have been less helpful. Schecter told Rollins he sensed that they had been caught unawares by news of their client's disappearance, but were trying to conceal that fact. After Schecter contacted them, he heard reports from one of his associates that a man in a gray suit had come out to Cornelia's house to peer in the windows. After considerable back-and-forth, Hadley and Poor finally conceded that there had been no "activity" on Cornelia's account since August 27, 1993, about two weeks before the last day that she was known to be alive.

"So the money's just sitting there?"

"I suppose so. Odd, isn't it?"

"Very."

"I wouldn't have done it, I'll tell you that. To let all that wonderful money go to waste? It's absurd. But Alicia was extremely eccentric." Jane Rollins noticed the waiter passing by an adjoining table. "Excuse me," she called out to get his attention, and, when he came closer, she pointed out that she and her son had been waiting almost a half hour, a slight exaggeration. "I used to receive much better service here."

The waiter, a graying Pakistani, stiffened. "I can only do what I can do, madam." He turned on his heel, bound for another table.

"How unfortunate," Mrs. Rollins said under her breath.

Rollins felt the harshness of the exchange deep in his gut, but his mother merely finished off the last of her bread.

"Your father proposed to me here, you know."

"Here?" Rollins hadn't known.

"We were sitting right over there." She pointed to a corner table. "He was at the B-school then." The Harvard Business School, she meant. "He was so handsome." She glowed a little at the memory. "And very ambitious, which disturbed my father a little. Your father had great plans to start a company—I forget what, exactly—and make a vast fortune. He talked about it so, so fiercely. He was desperate for success."

"He never got it, though, did he?"

Mrs. Rollins smoothed out the napkin in her lap. "Not yet. Not so far as I know." She seemed lost in memory for a moment. "Happiest moment of my life, imagine that. Sitting right there. He got out a ring he'd picked out at Shreve's and had the waiter bring it on a silver tray, right after dessert. It was the most charming thing. Your father could be very gallant when he wanted to be." She turned to her son with new curiosity. "But now, this woman you mentioned, the one with the photograph, is she a . . . *close* friend?"

Rollins' matrimonial possibilities were never far from his mother's thoughts. Years back, she used to pester him regularly with questions about whether there were "any young ladies in the picture," as she once phrased it.

Fortunately, their lunches arrived, interrupting this line of inquiry. Mrs. Rollins gave the waiter a crisp "Thank you" and sliced into her cod while Rollins tried to distract himself with the chicken Caesar. After a few bites, he switched the topic to Richard's career, and the subject of Marj was buried—predictably and, in this case, happily—beneath her enthusiastic recounting of Richard's ascent up the ladder at the bottling company.

Lunch over, they returned to the Town Car, and his mother had her driver drop Rollins off in the North End. When they pulled up by his door, she took a great interest in the exterior of the Hanover Street apartment building, not that it was, in truth, all that distinctive. But Rollins told her, falsely, that his own apartment was three flights up.

"I'd probably have to carry you," he said.

"Very well then. Next time, when my hip is better."

He gave her a peck on the cheek, the first time he'd touched her with any intimacy during the whole visit, and then stepped out onto the street. Once he'd shut the door behind him, his mother pressed the button to roll the window back down a couple of inches. "Let me know if you learn anything about Cornelia." As the window rose again, Rollins could hear her add: "Poor child. It is a pity."

Rollins stayed in most of the rest of the day, leaving his rooms only once to receive some Chinese food that was delivered to the front door. He kept his shades drawn, as always, but he did occasionally peek down into the courtyard to check for the gaunt man. He almost telephoned Marj to tell her the latest developments, but decided he'd better wait until he felt calmer. It always rattled him to see his mother.

That night, around ten-thirty, Rollins was listening to an intense talk-show discussion of sexual harassment of state employees when he heard a knock on his door.

"Rollins?" came a voice. "It's Tina."

Rollins switched off the radio. "Just a moment." Afraid something had happened to Heather, he quickly unlocked the door and swung it open. "Yes?"

Tina was barefoot and wearing a skimpy black dress with a flower pattern. Her forehead was a little moist—from the heat, presumably—dampening some of the dark hair by her temples.

"Hi," she said shyly.

"Is everything all right?"

"Oh yes, it's fine. Heather's asleep, that's all. Finally."

Rollins waited, expecting something more. He glanced past Tina down the shadowy hall.

"I just wanted to."—she tugged at her fingers—"no. It's way too late. I've disturbed you. You were probably going to bed."

Part of him wanted to acknowledge the truth of that statement and close the door. The sensible part, which was usually in the ascendancy. Instead, he said: "Not at all. Perhaps you'd like to come in for a moment." And he said it quietly, conscious of how far sound could travel in such a small building.

"Would that be all right?"

"Why not?" Rollins opened the door to let her pass. As she did so, her bare arm brushed against his side. It was almost certainly unintended, and yet it made him aware of her presence all the more powerfully. She was in her early thirties, Rollins guessed. A few years older than Marj, at any rate. Slightly taller, too, definitely more filled out, and more knowing, it seemed. "Do you want me to leave the door open?" Rollins asked. "So you can hear Heather?"

"Oh, that's all right." She smiled at him. "I'm sure she's fine."

He swung the door shut behind him, and it clicked with a finality that gave him a pang of guilt, as if he had committed an irrevocable sin. When he turned back to follow her into the room, she was standing by his leather chair, trailing a finger idly along one chair arm. "Look, I just wanted to thank you," she told him. "It was nice of you the other night—and this morning, looking after Heather."

"Glad to help." Rollins watched her, fascinated. It had been ages since he'd had a woman alone in his apartment. Seeing the shapely Tina now, that fact seemed incredible to him. It left him not knowing what to do or say. It was as though he had been frozen and was just now beginning to thaw. He was overwhelmed by the very sight of her.

They eyed each other for a long moment, then Tina turned to study a framed illustration showing a pair of dragons, a sword, and a book. "Wow," Tina said. "All these things of yours, they're so interesting."

"That's just a family crest," Rollins said.

Tina moved closer to it, scrutinized the calligraphy at the bottom. "Blanchard?" she asked.

"That's right. On my mother's side of the family."

Tina dragged her finger meditatively across her lip as she moved to a group photo by the window. "Who are all these?" When Rollins didn't answer right away, Tina turned back to him. "I'm sorry, I shouldn't be asking all these questions. I don't get out all that much anymore, with Heather. I forget how to talk to grown-ups sometimes."

"It's no big secret. That's the film society I started at Williams."

"Oh, I love movies." Tina's eyes continued to rove around his place.

"We concentrated on older ones, black and whites mostly."

She asked what Rollins did now, and he told her about his work at Johnson in what he termed the "back room." As usual, he kept the details vague. He assumed that Tina wouldn't have much patience for the minutiae. But he also wasn't ready to get into genuine confidences with her. And he didn't want to be disloyal to Marj.

"You seem to do all right," Tina told him.

His eyes flared. From where she was standing, Tina could see through his open bedroom door to the tapes on their shelf over his bed, and she was starting to take a few steps in that direction.

Rollins rushed past her and drew the bedroom door shut. "Excuse me, but I'd rather you didn't go in there."

Tina acted startled. "Oh, I'm sorry. I just wanted to see which way you put your bed. The layout is the same as mine."

"Well, yes, but it's a mess. A terrible mess. Really."

"Oh listen, don't talk to me about mess. I must have unpacked twenty boxes today." She reached back with one hand to massage her own shoulder, inadvertently giving Rollins an exciting glimpse of her décolletage. "Kitchen stuff is the worst. All those tiny little things—tea strainers, my God!—and no good place to put them." She didn't move from the door, though. "Not even a quick peek?" She held her fingers an inch apart.

"I'm sorry. I'd really rather not." No one was to see his tapes until he chose to allow it.

"Look—I understand completely," she told him.

Rollins felt as if some threat had passed. "You must be thirsty," he told her. "I have some Pellegrino in the fridge." Rollins led her into the kitchen, where he brought down a couple of glasses from the cupboard, then poured out the fizzy water for both of them. "Please, sit."

She was standing by the table. Her eyes had turned to his little pile of papers related to the fax number, if that's what it was. Another mental alarm sounded, but more faintly. "Let me get that out of your way," Rollins said, reaching to clear away the papers.

She raised a glass. "To you," she said, clinking it against his. "Thanks for the hospitality."

"Any time."

She finished the glass, then set it back down. "Look, it's late. I should be getting back."

He followed her to his door.

Before she left, she gave him a light kiss on the cheek, the barest brush of her lips against his skin. "If you ever get lonely, come knock on my door. Okay?" Then she went back down the hall.

Nine

It kept raining, off and on, the next day, too. Rollins left his apartment only to pick up the *Sunday Globe*, some bagels, a carton of fresh milk, and a bag of French roast at a convenience store down Hanover Street. Despite the revelations from Leeann about the gaunt man, Rollins had started to wonder if he had imagined such a tormentor, just dreamed him and Sloane up out of nothing. He actually tried to determine how he might reassure himself that he truly had followed that Audi out to the dark house, for example. Thinking this way, he was too distraught to read much of the paper, but he downed a whole pot of coffee and was brewing a second when he heard some heavy thumping on his door.

Rollins went to the door and peeked out his fisheye lens. Heather, in bright red shorts, was out in the hall with a rubber ball in her hand.

She looked up at his door plaintively. "Can you come out and play, mister? I'm bored."

"Sorry, I'm making coffee."

"I'm really, really bored."

"What about your mother?"

"She's sleeping."

Rollins checked his watch again. "But it's the middle of the afternoon. She sick?"

"She was up late." There was another thump against the door. "Talking on the phone."

"Would you quit that, please?"

"You never played Old Maid."

Possibly, children were not always a total delight.

"Please? I've got the cards."

"Oh, all right." Rollins unlocked the door. "But quickly. We'll just sit down right here, okay?" Rollins ushered her inside and settled himself on the rug.

"Okeydokey." Heather dropped down beside him. She fished the cards out of her pocket, and slowly dealt them with her pudgy little hands, laying out the cards in two sloppy piles between them. The tip of her tongue protruded from between her lips. It wasn't long before she had a question for him.

"What's a whore?" she asked.

"Goodness, what a word."

"But what's it mean?"

Rollins thought for a moment. "It's a woman who needs money."

"Yeah, I guess that's my mom."

"Someone really called her a whore?" Terrible to think that such words were used around five-year-olds. Such an awful word, too.

"Yeah, Timmy."

Rollins asked who Timmy was, but Heather was busy scooping up her cards and sorting them in her hand. She set down a couple of matching pairs, then held up her hand toward Rollins, who looked at her, puzzled.

"You're supposed to pick a card," Heather explained. "Put down any pairs. Whoever gets stuck with the Old Maid loses." She looked at him. "Don't you know anything?"

"It's been a long time." Solitaire had been more his line. He picked a card from her hand. It was the Old Maid, but Rollins tried not to let on.

"Hah-hah," Heather said.

Rollins ignored her. "Who's Timmy?" he repeated.

"This kid I met. When I was sick, remember?" Heather took one of Rollins' cards. "A match!" She waved the pair triumphantly in the air, then set it down.

"Where?"

"I don't know." A singsong voice.

"Was it where you went in the taxi?" Rollins pressed.

"Yup." She held out her hand to him, but Rollins didn't quite register. "You didn't go to the hospital, did you?"

"Nope." She pushed her hand closer to Rollins' face. *"Your turn."*

Rollins picked. No match. "Timmy's house—was it a nice place?"

"Kind of. It was by some water."

"That sounds nice."

"But my mom's friend was mean. He kept saying it was 'very inconvenient' for us to come. I think she was talking to him last night, but I'm not sure. She talks to lots of people."

There was a noise out in the hall, and Heather looked over Rollins' shoulder, and Rollins' eyes followed. Tina stood in Rollins' doorway. Her hair was mussed, and she wore a bathrobe. "Well, good morning," she told Rollins with a smile.

Heather gathered up her cards and her ball. "I better go," she whispered to Rollins. "Bye."

"Don't stop," Tina said.

Rollins stood up. "I'm not much good at Old Maid anyway."

Heather returned to the hallway.

"She's quite a girl," Rollins said.

"Till you get to know her." Tina rolled her eyes. "Thanks for last night. I can really use adult company sometimes."

"Any time."

Rollins turned back toward his door, then stopped and faced her again. "So you didn't go to the hospital after all?"

A funny expression came over Tina's face. "Did Heather tell you that?"

Rollins nodded.

"That girl. No, I went to a friend's place instead. I can't afford a hospital. My friend's wife's a nurse. I figured they'd know what to do. But I'll pay you back for the taxi real soon. I promise."

Rollins dismissed the notion with a wave. "I'm just glad Heather's okay."

At Johnson the next morning, Rollins found a note from his boss, Dell Henderson, in his in-box. *Please see me*, it said.

With some foreboding, Rollins went straight down the hall to Henderson's corner office. He glanced in Marj's cubicle on the way, but she wasn't in yet.

Henderson's secretary, elderly Betty Marie, sent him right on in without any of the usual pleasantries. Henderson was at his desk, staring at his computer screen; the sky was a bright blue out the big window behind. Henderson was late twenties, balding, with the glossy, pink skin Rollins associated with the overpaid. He was in suspenders today—to add a little extra managerial gravitas, Rollins figured. It took Henderson a moment to realize that he had a visitor. "Ah, Rollins," Henderson said, rolling his chair away from the screen. "Take a seat, why don't you." Henderson pointed toward a slender, gray chair. "Spoke to Eberhardt Friday." He referred to Moe Eberhardt, the head of general accounting up on 22, the man to whom Rollins reported his daily figures. "I gather there was a problem in the paper numbers." That meant the Paper and Forest Products Select Fund.

"Nothing major," Rollins replied, trying not to sound defensive. "We worked it out." Rollins' tally of the offering price had been off by approximately three-hundredths of a cent. He'd neglected to check to see if the computer had included the day's results from a tiny firm called Evergreen National, which had temporarily been off the ticker because the share price had plummeted after a management shake-up.

Rollins' lapse could have cost Johnson a quarter-million or so, but Eberhardt had caught the mistake and messaged him. Rollins had fixed things up before the share price went out over the wire. He had made similar goofs a couple of times before, and he hadn't thought twice about this one. After all, no harm had been done.

"Just want you to know, they're getting sticky about such errors upstairs. Word to the wise."

"Right. I'll be more careful. Sorry." Rollins got up to go.

Henderson looked over at him. "Oh, and another thing."

Rollins sat back down in his chair a little heavily.

"I heard about an incident in the men's." Henderson paused significantly. "You and that new gal, Simmons?" He fixed Rollins with a penetrating stare that was all the more irksome coming from a lad ten years his junior. "Look but don't touch—know what I mean? Like a museum in here. No joke—we've had a ton of very tedious meetings on this."

"It's not the way it looks." Rollins was horrified to think that Marj had complained about him.

"You know how it works. Let's just say that I heard it might be more, all right?"

"She was just giving me an aspirin."

Henderson waved a hand in the air. "Whatever. Do me a favor and keep it zipped."

"Absolutely." Rollins stood up and crossed to the door.

Henderson stopped him again. "I was looking through your file." This was never a good sign. "I didn't know your old man was friends with Mr. Johnson."

"Mr. Johnson?" Rollins' mind went blank.

"*The* Mr. Johnson, the one for whom you work," Henderson said impatiently, referring to the owner and CEO of Johnson Investments, Inc.

Any connection between his father and Mr. Johnson was certainly news to Rollins. He hadn't thought his father was in that league. Henry Rollins had not gotten anywhere near developing the company that he had dreamed of at the Harvard Club. The closest he'd come was to start a small investment firm, Henry Rollins and Co., in the early eighties, bankrolled by a portion of his wife's inheritance. He'd done one deal with a former secretary of the treasury and a retired chairman of Kaufman & Smith, but the firm finally dissolved in 1992 amid whispers of an SEC investigation that never materialized.

"Through T. J. Lambert, apparently," Henderson went on. Lambert was one of the old warhorses of Boston finance and a founder of the fabled Boston brokerage house, Lambert, Delaney and Starr, which had ultimately been folded into the Tedesco financial empire. Henderson plucked Rollins' file from the holder on his desk and flipped it open. He sifted through Rollins' annual job reports. "Not a bad record here, you know," he said in passing. "Punctual, accurate, reliable. A little uncommunicative at times, maybe." He looked up at Rollins and delivered an artificial smile. "But so what?" He continued to dig through the papers in the file. "Yeah, here it is." He handed Rollins the letter on Lambert's thick, nicely embossed stationery. "Take a look."

It was a To Whom It May Concern endorsement, filled with high praise of the generic variety, but one sentence in particular caught Rollins' attention: *I've known his parents, Henry and Jane, for years, of course.*

Both his parents. Named in a letter written over two decades after their divorce, no less. Puzzling. Rollins had never told either of them that he was looking for a job. At that point, in 1995, Rollins hadn't seen his father for three years. He was in closer contact with his mother, but he hadn't breathed a word to her about his firing. He hadn't wanted to give her the pleasure of knowing that the story about Neely's disappearance had caused him grief, too.

Could his mother have dropped a line to T. J. Lambert about him? So she had been aware of his being fired from the *Beacon*? Might her networking have been—what?—her way of making up to him for her many acts of coldness through the years? It was certainly her style to work completely behind the scenes. And, even if Rollins' father's name had been invoked, he saw only his mother's hand. She'd always had the sounder business sense. Even when his father was trying to start up his investment company, his mother never trusted him with any of her investment decisions over her family money. On those many trips out to Brookline, Mr. Grove spoke only to her.

Whichever parent was responsible, the ploy worked. And it explained the great mystery of how Rollins had secured his Johnson job with such limited financial experience. He had been accepted in a matter of days, after only the most cursory interview. He'd only even thought to apply because his brother had happened to mention that Johnson was expanding.

In the lower left-hand corner, Rollins noticed a pencil notation. *Whatever Henry wants. F. P. J.*

Rollins drew Henderson's attention to the initials.

"Yep, that's Mr. Johnson," Henderson said. "That's what I'm talking about. Caught my eye, too." Henderson looked hard at Rollins, as if he were a sum that didn't quite tally. "Look, I'll be blunt. You got some powerful friends here. Do me a favor: Don't screw up."

"I'll do my best." Rollins stood up, glad for the opportunity to look down at Henderson, the man's bald head reflecting the fluorescent light.

Henderson looked up at him. "You're not on any sort of medication, are you?"

"No."

He waved his hand again, as if dispelling smoke. "Never mind. Forget I asked."

Marj's light blue raincoat was on her chair when Rollins went back up the corridor to his desk, but there was no other sign of her. When he returned to his little office, he found a manila envelope on his desk. His name was handwritten on it, along with the word *personal*, underlined twice, in red ink. Rollins stared at it for some time. Judging by the loopiness of the *l*'s and *o*'s, he thought—no, hoped—he recognized Marj's handwriting. The letters seemed to have air pockets in them. He experienced a keenness, a quickening. He shut the door behind him, then flipped up the metal clasps. In peeling open the envelope's lip, he sliced the tip of his right index finger, which nearly made him cry out. He sucked the tiny wound, savoring the saltiness of his blood, then carefully held that finger away from the others as he tipped out the package's contents.

The package contained blurry microfilm copies of a *Beacon* newspaper article headlined THE WOMAN WHO WASN'T THERE. It was the story he'd written about Neely. He set it down on the table and spread it out flat with both hands. It was like being able to touch a memory. He was amazed to have it right there at his fingertips. It brought so much back—not just the story itself, but the long days spent digging out the facts behind the mystery of Neely's disappearance, and then the longer nights spent trying to make sense of what he'd learned. Seeing the story again was like seeing a photo of the big brick house where he had grown up, or a birthday letter from his father, the few years he'd remembered to send one. It was still urgently familiar, no matter how far past it might have become. This tale would never leave him.

He scanned the lead paragraphs.

THE WOMAN WHO WASN'T THERE
By E. A. Rollins

The handsome late-Victorian house off a winding road in Londonderry, New Hampshire, is dark this chilly March afternoon. Dark as it is now every afternoon—and every morning and every night. There are no lights on in the upstairs study where Cornelia Blanchard wrote her two volumes of poetry. No music comes from the piano downstairs where she used to bang out her soulful jazz. And, down in the field, in the little pond where she used to swim, only an occasional waterbug splashes about.

Cornelia Sprague Blanchard is gone. For reasons that no one can explain, the 37-year-old openly gay poet and lecturer disappeared from this idyllic spot two years ago, vanishing without a trace one evening. Despite several painstaking investigations, no sign of her, either alive or dead, has ever been found. "I sometimes wonder if she ever really existed," says one mystified friend.

The cadences weren't too bad. The writing seemed authoritative, if somewhat halting and melodramatic. Of course, it had been heavily edited. He cringed at the phrase "openly gay," which Bowser had inserted to "juice things up" over Rollins' objections. Still, the piece had an atmosphere of intrigue. Rollins might have read until the end, several pages later, if he hadn't noticed the Post-it tab at the foot of the first page. *This you? M.*

Rollins stood up and glanced diagonally behind him. This time, Marj was standing up with her back to him. She was on the phone, pacing back and forth by her desk. She had on a loose red top, with a spiky, orange necklace that had, to Rollins, a stirring, jungle aspect.

But after Henderson's warning, he didn't dare go to her cubicle. He was about to send an e-mail when he started to worry about that, too. For all he knew, Henderson had been snooping through his electronic correspondence. He wrote out a note by hand. *Meet me at Georgio's at 12:30. Don't tell anyone. Urgent. Can't talk. R.* Then he added a P.S.: *Pls. return this to me when you come.* He was about to fold the note and place it in an envelope when he reconsidered and added a final *P.P.S. I'll explain when I see you.*

After checking to make sure the hallway was clear, he strode by Marj's cubicle. He took one step inside, just long enough for Marj to look up at him from her phone conversation. Her eyes were not as forbidding as he'd expected. He dropped the envelope on the chair by her desk and ducked out again. He continued on to the kitchen nook for a fresh cup of decaf. When he returned to his desk, he steeled himself not to look in her direction.

He left for Georgio's well ahead of time so he and Marj wouldn't be seen leaving together. He made straight for the restaurant—the small, industrial-chic place off Federal Street he liked—and took a seat in a booth. Because of the high dividers between booths, he would be nearly invisible from the street. He dabbed at his paper cut with his napkin, leaving tiny kisslike stains on the absorbent paper, then waited with mounting anxiety as the minutes ticked by on the oversize wall clock toward 12:30, and then past it, with no sign of her. At quarter of one, the plump Georgio, in his spattered white apron, swung by his table.

"Not eating?" he asked.

"I'm waiting for someone," he said quietly.

"The redhead?"

Rollins nodded.

"Yeah, I'd give up food for her, too." He gave Rollins a dimpled smile and slapped him on the back.

Then the front door opened, and Marj appeared. She seemed cautious, almost fragile, as she glanced about the two dozen diners at the little eatery. Finally, her eyes lit on Rollins, but her face showed no particular pleasure at seeing him. Rollins' stomach tightened.

"Now you can eat," Georgio whispered to him before returning cheerfully to the kitchen.

Marj stood by his table, her fingertips resting on the top.

"Great to see you," Rollins said, trying to boost her enthusiasm. "Please, sit down." He gestured toward the far side of the table.

"Rolo, I—"

"Please," Rollins repeated, gesturing again across the table.

Marj took a seat, but she seemed no happier. "All right. So what's the big secret—you pregnant or something?"

"Henderson heard about us being in the men's room together. He read me the riot act about the company's no-romance policy."

"Well, maybe that will restrain you."

Rollins looked at her. "He was serious."

Marj met his gaze. "So am I."

A bad feeling gathered in Rollins' chest as he thought back to the conclusion of their last encounter on Friday night. "Look, I'm sorry about the note. It was a mistake. I should never have done that."

"It wasn't the note." Marj's eyes flashed. "That was okay. Not great. But okay. It was the way you left it—a whole hour after you dropped me off, and *after* that whole thing at the Sloanes'! Scared the *shit* out of me. I was standing there inside the door—in my nightie, thank you very much—when I heard these footsteps coming real soft down the hall. I was sure it was Sloane or that skinny guy you say is following you around. I nearly screamed! Then I saw this tiny little white card slide under the door. I was shitless, Rolo."

Rollins had never imagined that she had been so near. Even after all the apartments he'd seen, he couldn't picture Marj's beyond those few sharply angled glimpses up from the street. He couldn't imagine what she did when he wasn't watching.

"I hadn't meant to scare you," he said.

"But that's the thing: You're sneaking around all the time. I don't know who you are!" She tapped the base of her fork against the table-top to accent the key words—*know* and *are*. "Okay, sure, you're this preppy guy. Grew up around here, good schools, all that. But who are you, really? I don't know. I don't know if you do." The way she looked at him, she seemed to be waiting for him to say something, but Rollins remained silent. It was either that or talk forever.

"And I'm not even talking about the driving stuff," Marj went on. "I'm talking about everything. Like at Johnson, you do this shit job for years. People ask me, 'Why is he doing this?' It's like a topic of conversation. I tell 'em you like it. But I don't know. Do you?"

"There are worse things."

She pounded the table. "That's what I mean! 'There are worse things.' What's that supposed to mean? Of course there are worse things. I worked the late shift in the lingerie section at Filene's Basement for six fifty an hour for three years while I put myself through school. That was worse, believe me. But there are better things, too." She folded her napkin, then smoothed it out again. "I guess what I'm asking is, what is it that you want?"

"From a job?" Rollins wasn't sure he followed.

"Out of *life*, Rolo. What are you after? What are you searching for?"

"Can't we eat first?" Right then, he wasn't sure he had the strength to force out an answer, if he could even think what the answer was.

"Okay, okay. Forgive me. I'm just a jerk from the Midwest who didn't know you weren't allowed to ask real questions around here." She plucked the menu off the table and snapped it open in front of her face.

"Hey, relax, would you please? I'm sorry. I'm not used to this." He gently eased her menu down flat onto the table so he could see her better. "The answer is, I don't know," Rollins began, stalling. He wasn't much good at defining himself. He took a deep breath and exhaled slowly. "For what I'm missing, I guess."

That seemed to slow her down a little. "Okay, that's a start." Marj looked at him again. "But what might it be?"

"If I knew, I wouldn't be looking, now would I?" Rollins allowed himself a small smile, but Marj offered no reaction.

"My mother told me to call the cops, you know," she said. "After the note."

An unpleasant feeling spread through Rollins' chest, like ink in water.

"She thinks you're dangerous." Marj swept away a stray hair that had settled over her brow. "Course, she thinks everyone's dangerous."

Rollins was relieved to hear her tone lighten, but his palms still tingled. "Look, I'm sorry. I shouldn't have done it. I just wanted to let you know how I felt."

She took a sip of her water, and fidgeted with her knife, absentmindedly running her fingertip lightly down the blade. "Somehow I get the feeling you're hiding something. Like you have a wife somewhere."

Rollins allowed himself a laugh. "Nope. No wife."

"No girlfriend, even?"

Rollins shook his head. He thought of Tina and vowed never to let her into his apartment again.

"So what aren't you telling me?"

Rollins might have said something. Not everything, but something. He might have mentioned Tina, although, thank God, there was precious little to say about her. Or he might have taken Marj back into his past, spoken of the bitterness he felt for his parents, revealed his sorrow over the dead Stephanie and the vanished Neely. It might have been a relief to lighten his load. He wouldn't tell Marj much, but he figured he wouldn't need to. He figured that emotions were a bit like a new neighborhood. You didn't have to explore more than a block or two to get a sense of what lay farther in. But he hesitated, reluctant to weigh Marj down with his burdens. Before he could say anything at all, the waitress arrived to take their orders, breaking the spell.

Rollins had wonton soup and crab cakes. Marj said she wasn't hungry; Rollins ordered crab cakes for her, too. "To have the full Georgio," he told her.

By the time the waitress moved off again on her spongy-soled shoes, the moment for intimacy had passed.

"So you checked me out?" Rollins asked, a bit of jauntiness back in his voice.

"I suppose you could call it that. Sure. You say all these things—that a cousin disappeared, that you were a reporter. . . . So, yeah, I checked you out." Her eyes flickered very prettily. "I just wanted to see that article of yours. I wanted to find something about you I could hold in my hand."

"That what a person does when her father walks out on her?" Rollins watched carefully, but Marj showed no particular distress.

"Don't bring him into this, please," she said. "This is not about my father."

"No?"

"Notice—you didn't tell me any of your secrets."

"Maybe I don't have any."

"We all have secrets."

Marj let that sit there for a second, but Rollins didn't bite. "Okay," she admitted. "Maybe the thing with my dad makes me careful with men. I don't know, all right? I never knew the guy. And I've only seen, like, one picture."

"You're not too close to your stepfather either, I notice."

"Why do you say that?"

"I just figured. You hardly ever mention him. It's always your mother."

Marj peered into his eyes. "Well, listen to you. Yeah. Okay. I can tell you. Why not? No, we weren't close. That's one of the reasons I didn't stick around."

Rollins' soup arrived, and he dipped his spoon into the pale broth. "Something happen?" He felt as if his view of her had always been blocked somehow, and this was his first good look at her in the full light, up close.

"I didn't *let* it happen, if you want to know. But I could tell that it was going to if I didn't get the hell out of there."

"He made some kind of advance?"

"I think that's what you call it when a guy comes up behind you and sticks his hands on your boobs. He was drunk, but I didn't want to wait around long enough to see what he'd try when he was sober."

Rollins took another spoonful of soup. "Did you tell your mother?"

"No. I just left. I still don't think she has any clue, either. I think she thinks I just got too big for Morton, Illinois."

When the crab cakes arrived, Marj nibbled at the corner of one of them and told him the full story of her coming east. It was three days after her seventeenth birthday, and she used the money her grandmom gave her for a bus ticket. When she got to Boston, she'd stayed in the YWCA downtown for the first six months, then moved in with three other girls to a tiny little place in Cambridgeport, where she'd supported herself working in a used clothing store. She passed her high school equivalency exam, and swung a full scholarship to Lesley College. "Then I graduate, get more shit jobs like that beaut at Filene's Basement, jobs that are no better than the one I had before my precious college degree in business administration, and finally I end up on the bottom rung at Johnson." Marj smiled. "So—we even now? I tell you one, you tell me one?"

Rollins set down his spoon. His senses were all concentrated powerfully on Marj. "Sorry," he said. "I didn't know it was like that for you."

"That's because you didn't ask. That's what a relationship is. It's about asking. Asking and telling, asking and telling. It's called conversation."

Rollins pushed his soup dish aside. He said nothing. The obstacles in his life were not nearly so well defined, nor had he done anywhere near as much to overcome them. He had the feeling that if he started to speak now, he'd go on forever and still not tell her the first thing about what he'd been through.

Marj tapped her hand on the *Beacon* story. "That's all your cousin left behind—just a few footprints in the mud? Then—*wssht*?" She flicked her hand in the air. In the *Beacon* piece, Rollins had mentioned that, a little ways down from Cornelia's house, police had found a footprint in the roadside mud that corresponded to an L. L. Bean boot that Cornelia had been known to possess, but was missing from the house.

"And she left some money." Rollins explained about having lunch with his mother at the Harvard Club, a place Marj (bless her) had never heard of. He left out the more uncomfortable portions of the conversation. No need to burden Marj with his troubles with his mother. Instead, he told her about Cornelia's big inheritance.

That part got Marj's attention. "Really?" she asked, forgetting her anger for a moment. "Even though she's not even, like, around?"

Rollins explained that it had come from Cornelia's grandmother and that it had gone directly into her trust account.

"How much?" Marj asked

"A few million anyway. Maybe ten."

"Whoa."

Rollins took a sip of water.

Marj speculated that perhaps this was just the sort of thing that Cornelia wanted to get away from. "Maybe she was tired of being Cornelia Blanchard, the heiress. Maybe she wanted to be somebody different—move away, start over."

It sounded oddly like Rollins' own fantasy from the other night at the Sloanes'. But then, Marj had done something similar by coming east. Was that the real American dream, to run off and be somebody else?

"She had no obvious reason to leave," Rollins insisted. "She'd published two books of poetry. She'd gotten an offer to be a writer in residence at the University of New Hampshire. Her friends all said she seemed happy."

"You can never tell," Marj declared. "How was her sex life? Lesbians aren't always that active, you know."

Rollins felt himself color. Maybe because his own sex life was so limited, he'd been squeamish about investigating this part, even though Bowser had been adamant that he get all the details he could. "Fine, I guess."

Marj laughed. "As if you asked about it."

"Perhaps you should have handled that part."

"Damn straight. I'd have asked the right questions." She raised her voice, as if she were doing an interrogation: "All right, who's she been fucking, and for how long?"

Rollins glanced around, relieved to see that none of his fellow diners had caught this outburst. His cheeks felt unusually warm. "All I picked up was that Cornelia had gotten involved with her gardener."

"Elizabeth Payzen, that one?" Marj remembered her from the story as the woman who lived in the converted barn down the road from Cornelia's place. As Rollins had reported, Elizabeth had been doing some gardening work for Cornelia. Apparently the two had fallen in love.

"The UPS man saw Elizabeth and Cornelia sunbathing nude down by the pond," Rollins added offhandedly. "Lots of people mentioned it."

"You should have put that in the story."

Rollins flushed again. "She's my cousin, you know. Or was."

"Not to mention your old baby-sitter," Marj shot back. "So what do you think happened to her?"

Rollins shook his head. "No one knows for sure. The cops figured somebody must have driven by and grabbed her when she was walking down the road. They brought some dogs out there—and that's where the trail just disappeared."

"And no evidence of a struggle."

Rollins was impressed with Marj's memory for the details of the case.

"No screams, either," he said. "And there were a fair number of houses around." This was the part that had always bothered him. He'd checked out the spot. It was by the side of the road, in a patch of mud between a row of hedges and the asphalt, maybe fifty yards from her driveway. Elizabeth lived down that road, and Cornelia had often walked over to see her. There were at least four houses close enough for someone to have heard something. "Whoever it was had to have known her, or she would have resisted."

"So who was it?"

"That's the big question."

"And then her car disappears, too." That had happened three weeks later. A Volvo sedan.

"Yeah, strange, isn't it? It's like the car picked up and followed her."

The waitress came to swap Rollins' soup bowl for the crab cakes. Rollins dug into his, but Marj just picked at hers.

"You're really not hungry?"

"I had some cookies at my desk. Oh, here." She slipped a hand into her pocket and handed him his message back. "You said you wanted this."

"Thanks. I didn't want Henderson to find it."

"Getting a little paranoid, are we?"

"I didn't tell you—that gaunt man *did* come looking for me last week."

Marj's face went slack. "No."

"Yeah, last Wednesday, as close as I can figure. Apparently, he asked about me at the cafe near my place." Rollins described his encounter with the waitress there, Leeann.

"So that *was* him you saw that night," Marj said.

"Probably."

"They are following you." Marj said this quietly, to herself as much as to Rollins. She picked up her knife, drummed it on the tabletop, then slammed it down with a loud smack. "Doesn't this get to you, Rolo? Some strange guy following you places?"

Rollins nearly told her how he'd been afraid the other morning that his car was wired with explosives, but decided that might be too alarming. "It's upsetting, sure."

"Well, *do* something about it. I mean, God!"

"Such as?"

"You've got his license plate number, Rolo. Maybe you can get the guy's name." She spoke to him as if he were a child, which was irritating. "Then we'd have something."

"And how exactly am I supposed to do that?"

"I don't know, maybe if you went to the registry of motor vehicles."

Rollins was not keen to submit himself to some faceless bureaucracy. "Well, I used to know a private investigator."

"*You?*" Finally, she looked at him with a little respect.

He explained about meeting Al Schecter when he was doing the story on Cornelia. "We got friendly. I suppose I could call him."

Marj's eyes seem to hang on him a little. "And what about that fax number?"

"I'll run that by Schecter, too. Maybe he can trace it."

Outside, Marj stepped briskly along the Federal Street sidewalk, and Rollins hurried to keep up. "Look, there's something you should know about me," she said as they huffed along. "I don't hop into bed with just anybody. It's, like, a policy of mine."

Rollins almost lost control of his legs for a moment.

She turned back to him. "Does that surprise you?"

"No," Rollins managed to force out. "I have the exact same policy myself."

Marj stopped, causing Rollins to stop, too. "Do you?" she said, searching his face.

They continued on. It was lovely to walk along with her. Rollins felt that he had somehow entered the aura of warmth and optimism that always seemed to surround her. As they were nearing the Johnson building, Marj stopped one last time and flicked her silky hair back off her collar, her necklace clicking lightly. Rollins' whole body tingled with the possibility that she might reach for him, say something intimate, memorable. He'd seen women do such things before with men in the last quasi-private moment before returning to the office. But Marj did not touch him. Instead, she asked: "So what's the E. stand for anyway? In your byline, I mean."

Rollins could scarcely remember. It had been years since he'd used his first name.

"I bet it's something awful like Egbert," Marj added.

This was a bigger secret than she could know. "Actually, it's Edward."

Apparently, he hadn't said it quite loud enough, for Marj inclined an ear toward him. "Say again?"

"*Edward*," he said firmly. This time, he was loud enough to cause a grimy bicycle messenger who happened to be passing on the street to crane his neck about and gawk. Rollins lowered the volume again. "Edward Arnold Rollins. The first name"—he couldn't bring himself to repeat it—"comes from a grand-uncle on my mother's side. The second is my mother's maiden name."

"Edward," Marj repeated, mulling it over. "Edward Rollins. Eddie Rollins, Teddy Rollins." She shrugged. "I don't think that's so bad."

"I just stopped liking it, that's all," Rollins said.

The big, tiled bathroom echoing his name. "Edward! Edward!" His mother screaming it, raking the sides of her face with her scarlet fingernails, as if her insides were on fire. His father groaning it into his big hands. And little Stephanie on the tiled floor all cold and wet and silent. Looking, back and forth, from Mother to Father to Mother to Father to Mother. Then their shrinking away as he ran and ran. Out the basement door. Into the cool night. No moon. Creeping through bushes. Watching once more, this time in through a window.

"Real touchy about the name, aren't you?" Marj went on. "I can see it all over your face. Names are weird. I never used to like Marj. Kids used to call me 'Barge'—like a boat, you know? I think it was because I got my boobs early." She headed across the street, toward the Johnson building. "I told them to go fuck themselves." She looked back at him. "Aren't you coming?"

"I don't think we should be seen going in together."

"Oh yeah, okay. Whatever." Marj kept on across the street. He got a fine view of her from behind, what with the tightness of her black skirt. He particularly liked the rounded gap just above her knees, bounded on either side by what looked like parentheses.

She paused on the far side of the street and turned back to him. "See ya later, Eddie," she shouted. Then, as she went down the side-walk, she raised her left hand over her shoulder and wiggled her fingers good-bye.

Ten

Schecter's card in Rollins' Rolodex was slightly yellowed. It had his number in Hingham, down on the South Shore, in the tight three-bedroom that he'd worked out of. But when Rollins called, he got three chimelike beeps and an automated message that said the line had been disconnected. He checked with information, but there was no listing for him in the town, or anywhere else in the region. Ditto for all of 617 in greater Boston, and the new area codes to the west, 508, 781, and 978. Rollins tried the Boston office of the Hartford Indemnity Company, which had hired the detective for the Blanchard investigation. After bouncing around several departments, he finally reached an agent who had worked with him on the case. "Oh yeah, Al Schecter," the agent said. "Last time we talked, he said he was getting out of investigations. Sounded real blown out."

"He say where he was going?"

"No, but he always used to talk about moving to Rockport, Maine. That was like a thing of his."

"And do what?"

"Start a little fishing concern up there, if you can believe it." The man gave out a sly cackle. "Now, I don't know if he ever did it or not. Lot of 'em say that from time to time."

Rollins thanked the man for the information. He found it hard to picture Al Schecter out in a boat of any kind, but he dialed Rockport information anyway and found a residential listing. No one answered when Rollins called, but a woman's voice came on the machine. That threw him, since the voice sounded too old to be one of Schecter's daughters (he had two, who must be teenagers by now), but too young to be his wife, Pat. Rollins left no message, but made a note of the number and resolved to try again that evening.

He had just hung up the phone when an interoffice e-mail came in.

U traced that licnse plte yet??????
m

Rollins was too pleased to be irritated at this indiscretion. He quickly responded:

Still working on it. Seems Schecter has moved to Maine. Please, though: no more e-mails.

Marj replied a few minutes later:

OOOOps. Sorry. Aerobics tonite. Call latr?

Rollins wasn't sure if that meant he should call, or if she would. Either way, he was proud of himself for not even thinking of driving by her apartment building to try to catch a glimpse of her in her leotard. But he still felt charged up after work, and, for the hell of it, he decided to pursue the first car he saw with either a 3 or an F in the license plate, in honor of Marj's apartment number. The eighty-six hours were finally up, and a pursuit always helped to blow off steam.

The first car matching his search criteria proved to be an orange Volkswagen Cabrio convertible, license plate number 603-TLB, hurrying past the Faneuil Hall marketplace, aswarm with tourists as always. He had to do a quick U-turn by the back side of City Hall to catch up with the car. This time, it was stuck in the left-turn lane at the next lights. The convertible's top was down, and the driver was plainly visible from all sides: a man in his early twenties with shoulder-length hair and oily-looking skin. "Musician type," was the way Rollins described him in the brief audio note he recorded on the Panasonic, along with the time, 6:12 P.M.

As he waited at the light, Rollins' attention wandered to the light blue Dodge Colt one lane over, where a young blonde was peering into her rearview mirror as she touched up her lipstick. But Rollins had a rule never to break off a pursuit that conformed to the day's internal code, and he dutifully kept after the Cabrio. He kept to himself his complaints about the longhair's stop-and-go driving. But he did note the likely age, twenty-seven or -eight, and then felt a pang to realize that this was probably the sort of person Marj dated.

Rollins followed the Cabrio intently as it wove through the clogged Boston streets up and up and onto the expressway, a complete misnomer at this hour, and then veered north over the Charles and angled left onto Interstate 93. He had an almost pulsating sense of déjà vu: this was, of course, the route to North Reading. Was he being lured *back* to the dark house by this longhaired stranger? Was this hippie somehow associated with Sloane and/or the gaunt man? "I'm heading north again on 93, just like the other night with the Audi," Rollins told the tape recorder. "Didn't think I'd be coming this way again so soon."

The traffic thinned just over the bridge, and "Mick Jagger"—as Rollins dubbed him, after the only living rock star he could visualize— shifted into the fast lane and gunned it, his stringy hair flapping behind him. Rollins struggled to keep up, one lane over and several cars back. As far as Rollins could tell, the driver didn't take any particular notice of him—or any of his surroundings. He didn't seem to be checking his side or rearview mirrors unduly, or sending out sidelong glances. Rollins was too far back to hear anything, but he sensed the Cabrio had loud music playing—probably the type that Marj listened to—for he could sometimes see the driver bob his head in time to a fast rhythm. The Cabrio continued on for miles; to pass the time, Rollins mentally ticked off the socioeconomic implications of the exit signs that flew past. He tensed up as the Cabrio finally drew close to the North Reading exit. Rollins remembered the Audi signaling for the turn. But the Cabrio kept cruising along in the passing lane, Mick Jagger bobbing as before. "Six twenty-three," Rollins noted with relief. "Cabrio has passed North Reading. Still headed north. No connection to the Elmhurst house, looks like." He clicked off the recorder. "Thank God."

The Cabrio sailed on toward New Hampshire, past countless signs advertising food stops that brought hunger pangs from Rollins, who normally had a snack after work. He soldiered on, turning his attention from the Cabrio only long enough to make an occasional audio note about time and location. About twenty miles past the New Hampshire border, the Cabrio slid across to the right lane without signaling, then zipped onto the off-ramp for 102. It was the Londonderry exit, and Rollins' neck tightened as he turned to follow. "What do you know?" he told the machine. "Londonderry." Rollins had been back to Cornelia's old haunts many times since her disappearance, but never on a pursuit.

To avoid drawing attention to himself by flaring his brake lights, Rollins downshifted instead of hitting the brakes—another trick he'd learned from Schecter—to slow himself. But he still had to pull hard on the wheel to avoid the guardrail as he swerved onto the off-ramp.

Safely on 102, Rollins had the eerie feeling that his rock star might lead him back to Cornelia's down Pelbourne Road, west off 93. But instead the Cabrio kept right and bombed straight through Derry and then turned in to a Getty station just before the old Wellington shopping center, where a new Kmart had gone in, on the far side of town. Rollins pulled up across the street, grateful for a rest. He rolled down the window and adjusted the side-view mirror to observe his man in its reflection.

The Mick stepped out while the attendant gassed up his car. Rollins noted the tight cut-offs that revealed a lot of hairy upper thigh and the T-shirt that advertised one of the many overpriced microbrews Rollins avoided. Was this really Marj's type? The longhair strolled to the station's pay phone where Rollins swung his head around to watch him talk animatedly, all the while cocking his hips from side to side. "I bet our rock star is speaking to a girlfriend of his," Rollins whispered into the Panasonic, violating his self-imposed ordinance against speculation. "He seems pretty happy." Finally, the Mick pressed his finger down on the telephone's disconnect button and kissed the receiver before hanging it back up. Rollins noted that fact on the machine and added: "Must be love."

He returned to his car, but drove it only a few feet to park it by the air pump and draw up the top; he got out and leaned against the side of the car to soak up the last of the sun's rays. In moments, a pink Chevy swooped in. The female driver had long, flowing hair and sunglasses. "Hey, get your butt over here," she yelled to the rock star, but he'd already started running. He hopped into her car, brought both his arms around her and gave her a big, tongue-mingling kiss. The two of them drove off together, leaving the Cabrio behind. Rollins had watched all this without a sound. As soon as they headed out of the station, he recorded everything he'd seen while it was still fresh in his mind.

Technically, Rollins was now released from his obligations. He had followed the Cabrio to its destination here on 102. But it was early. Marj would still be at aerobics, so there would be no point in hurrying back just yet. As a matter of personal curiosity, he revved up the Nissan and pursued the two lovebirds about ten miles, just shy of 95, where they pulled in at the Overnighter Motel. It was a tawdry-looking place with a big neon sign, a tiny pool out front, and weeds growing up through the cracks in the asphalt parking lot. Rollins turned in to a photocopy shop across the street, parked in the deepening shadows by the building, and, after digging out Marj's binoculars from the glove compartment, squeezed through to the backseat to hunker down and watch through the rear window. From there, even without the lenses, he could see the Mick kiss the blonde on her lips, cheeks, and forehead, and he saw his man slip a hand under the waistband of her jeans after they finally stepped out of her car. She let him leave it there as they crossed the lot toward the long row of motel rooms. She led him to room number 29, five from the end, and wriggled a key out of her pocket. She unlocked the door, and then the rock star swept her up into his arms and carried her inside. She kicked her legs in the air as she passed over the threshold.

The Mick kicked the door shut behind them. But through the picture window that looked out onto the lot Rollins could see that a light was on inside. The rocker set the girl down on the bed while he swept the curtains shut. In his haste, he left a sizable gap between them, through which Rollins—the binoculars now deep into his eye sockets—could see the man pull his T-shirt over his head and then slide his hands up under the shirt of the blonde.

A groan, a parted door, bare flesh . . .

The tape recorder was still at Rollins' mouth, still turning, but he had stopped speaking. Hadn't he seen all this before somewhere? Then the blonde's head lolled back, and her lips parted—whether from pleasure or surprise, Rollins couldn't tell—before Jagger toppled her onto the bed. From his angle, Rollins could see only the top sliver of the man's arched back over the windowsill. But the back rose and fell like a swimmer's.

. . . Strong hands on a slim, bare back, scraping. The whiteness, and the angry streaks of red. A hand in a man's hair. And the thrashing, the thrashing.

Occasionally, a slender hand would reach up into view, or, once, a bare shoulder. The movements came faster and faster until, suddenly, the blonde lurched up almost into full view, her mouth wide open, facing the window with a startled look that nearly caused Rollins to drop the binoculars from his eyes and duck. Her shirt was off, and her bra was down around her waist, and Rollins could see her breasts, which were pale and wobbly, with tiny nipples. One arm across her chest to try to cover herself, she reached with the other for the edge of the open curtain. As she did, the rocker sneaked out a hand to cup her left breast from behind. She twirled around to free herself, then, as she fell back, lunged again for the curtain and flicked it the rest of the way across the window, closing out Rollins' view.

Rollins watched the curtained window for a half hour in some turmoil. He'd seen it all before. Not this exactly, but something very much like it. But where? He shut off the tape recorder. Not on a pursuit, he was almost certain. In all his years of watching, he'd never seen a sex act before. A remarkable fact, but true. There'd been a drooping erection in the light of a table lamp, and an old woman's flabby backside, but that was all. Yet something about this scene here at the Overnighter seemed so familiar. Was it the people? Did he know them somehow?

Once he was in the clear, Rollins doubled back on route 102, crossed over 95 again and, famished, turned in at a pizza place in a row of stores off the highway—the closest thing Londonderry had to a downtown. He hungrily downed a Neapolitan Special with everything. He should not have done what he did. That was obvious. It was a terrible intrusion, a serious violation of his personal code, and risky besides. Still, the sight of the girl stirred him, undeniably. Was it merely because she had awakened a memory? There was something familiar about the way she'd reached desperately for the curtains with her fingers splayed. Perhaps she'd simply awakened his desire to touch Marj, to kiss her, caress her, or more.

Rollins had had a few sexual escapades back at his old place in the Back Bay. But it always took him a few cocktails to get in the mood. That's probably why he remembered little beyond the vigor of the act and a short-lived feeling of accomplishment when it was over. Still, he was fairly sure that he himself had never done anything with anyone like the woman in room 29. It was nothing he'd done. Something he'd seen. But what?

He sat by the plate-glass window, with his back to the counter, where he could sense the burly pizza chef eyeing him occasionally, contemplating a conversation, no doubt. Rollins looked out through the glass to a brightly lit CVS and a small tax preparer's office that lurked in the blurry distance behind his own pale image. Farther down, just past his reflected shoulder, he noticed Lorraine's Haircutting Studio, with its tattered mauve awning. It had been pale green before, he was pretty sure. He'd been in there a few times. He must have entered every shop in town in search of people who knew Cornelia and had an idea about what might have happened to her. A good two dozen people recognized the name, but it was distressing to discover how little they knew about her. Mostly, they knew her enough just to say hello at the post office, or in the library, about the only two places she was seen at all regularly. A few had heard she was some kind of writer. (They usually said this with a squint.) Almost no one had been inside her house, or read her poems, or been able to say with any certainty what she was "like," beyond the default modifier that she was "nice."

After he was done with his pizza, he climbed back into the Nissan. It was coming up on eight o'clock. He found a pay phone, and dialed Marj this time. He just wanted to say hello, to reassure himself that he wasn't as peculiar as he had just begun to feel. But he got her answering machine and didn't leave a message.

He tried Schecter again. This time, he got a man's voice. "Hell-o," the man said in the brisk way that Rollins had always remembered.

"Al?"

"Yep."

"It's Rollins."

"Well, fuck me. It's been a long time. Where the hell are you? Sounds like a pay phone."

"In Londonderry, New Hampshire." He had to raise his voice to cover the roar of a truck going by.

"Shit. Just like old times. That broad hasn't turned up, has she?"

"No." Rollins hesitated. "It's . . . complicated."

"With you, it always is." Schecter gave out a dry chuckle.

Rollins let that go. "I was hoping for a favor."

"Shoot."

"Some guy's been following me."

"He cute?" The investigator laughed again.

"It's serious, Al."

"He there now?"

Rollins' stomach tightened at the thought. He glanced around. "No, I don't think so. But I keep seeing him places. He's been asking questions about me. About where I live, my routine, that kind of thing."

"Is there some problem? You screwing his girl?"

"I don't even know him."

Schecter took this in without comment. "Okay," he said finally.

"I've got his license plate number. I was hoping you could get me his name and an address."

"I'm not in the business anymore, you know."

"So I heard. What happened?"

"A lot." He didn't elaborate, except to acknowledge that his wife, Pat, was not with him up there. Rollins felt bad about that. He'd always been fond of her, a slender, big-haired brunette who'd helped out typing up Schecter's reports. Schecter said nothing about their two children.

"I got a little boat-taxi business up here," Schecter said. "But that's for a couple of martinis, or whatever the hell you're drinking these days. You got any more information on this guy?"

Rollins gave him the plate number. Schecter said that he still had a few contacts and to call him back in a half hour. Before hanging up, Rollins asked if he could trace fax numbers.

"A fax number now? What the hell is going on down there?"

"I told you, it's complicated."

"Faxes are a bitch. But I'll try."

Rollins had that number memorized, and he recited it. Schecter said he'd do what he could.

To kill some time, Rollins climbed back in the Nissan, took Mammoth Road going north by the Homestead Restaurant, and drove down to Pillsbury, where in the thickening dusk a few children were still playing in the front yards. He remembered the road well. He must have taken it dozens of times driving to Cornelia's old house. Now, with the windows down, he could smell the sweet honeysuckle scent in the air. He drove on, as he had so many times before, forked left onto Pelbourne, and wound past a series of historic clapboard houses, all of them set well back from the road. Rollins slowed after the narrow bridge and, about a hundred yards down, pulled up by a gravel driveway that was bounded by a pair of stone pillars, thickly covered now with English ivy.

He parked by the side of the road. It was quiet and dark along here, overhung by rustling maples and elms. Only the occasional car loomed up, its headlights blinding him as it rushed past. Rollins stepped out of the car and walked over to the mouth of the driveway. He reached through the ivy to touch the rough stone of one of the pillars, just to feel something solid. He peered up the long driveway. Always before, the drive had been vacant, but there were a couple of cars parked at the end this time. Could the house have been sold? Or—the thought came to him like a rifle shot—had Cornelia somehow returned?

His pulse quickening, he moved up the gravel drive. With each step, the grounds opened up wider before him—the rolling lawn that went down to the pond, and, up to his right, flanked by a low hill, the handsome Victorian house, its high roof and sharply pointed dormers silhouetted against the late-evening sky. He'd been here as recently as two months ago, and the house had always been dark before, but now light blazed from the windows and spread across the lawn, clear to the trees, and some music—Haydn, perhaps—spilled out into the evening air.

Rollins ducked down as he reached the cars, to conceal his profile from the glowing house. Neither of the cars was the blue Volvo that Cornelia had owned, but that had disappeared after her. No, these two cars were stolid American makes—a bulky Chrysler and a Ford Taurus. Of course, it was certainly possible that Cornelia had come back driving a different car. Rollins' mind raced: Wouldn't he have heard about her return? The news would certainly have made the papers. Surely, someone would have told him.

He tried the cars' doors, but they were all locked. He slid a hand under the front and rear bumpers, and around the wheel casings, but he found no Hide-a-Key, at least not in any of the places that Schecter had taught him to look.

Rollins turned back to the house. The first time he'd come back, when he was doing his research for the *Beacon*, he'd climbed a downspout for a crack at the upstairs dormers. (He was more daring then.) All but one of those windows had been curtained, but that last one afforded him a glimpse of what looked like a spare bedroom. He could make out a hairbrush, comb, and hand mirror, all laid out formally across a cloth on the bureau. An heirloom set, he assumed, come down from the monied side of her family.

Another time, he'd gone tramping through the woods with Al Schecter, who pored over small disturbances in the landscape—a mounded rise, a slight dip—trying to determine if they marked a shallow grave. In a few places, Al had actually dug down several feet in search of a corpse, while Rollins stood by watching intently, not sure what to hope for. They never found anything.

Now the house was so bright that Rollins had to squint as he gazed up at it. Virtually every window blazed with light. Shrouding himself in the bushes, hiding behind the fringe of trees, Rollins circled the house from a safe distance. Few curtains were drawn, and Rollins was finally able to get a good view of all the downstairs rooms—the modern kitchen, the antique-laden living room, the book-lined study, even the bathroom, which was done in blue. A few upstairs rooms were lit, but Rollins couldn't get a good angle on them to see more than a portion of an upper wall here and there.

The only people he saw were sitting about a coffee table in the living room, their faces softened by the subdued lighting. As far as he could tell, the individuals all seemed to be country types—three couples in their forties or so. None of them looked much like Cornelia, but she might have changed a good deal by now. He wanted to run back to his car for Marj's binoculars to get a better look, but he didn't dare risk being caught on the property with such equipment.

Rollins was fully aware that he should leave. He had already pressed his luck at the Overnighter. But then he looked again at the house, so alive now, and he needed to be sure. Instead of retreating quietly back up the drive, he followed the curve of the cobblestone walkway to the black front door.

The babble of voices and music rose as he approached. Rollins reached for the door knocker and brought it down on the door with a boom that quieted the voices and produced some hurried footsteps his way. The heavy door swung open with a rush of air, and an elegant, bony woman in pearls stood before him. "Yes?" she asked.

"Excuse me," Rollins said. "I'm looking for Cornelia Blanchard."

He'd hoped for a glimmer of recognition, but the woman kept her distance, turning only her ear to him. "Who did you say?"

Rollins went hollow. "Cornelia Blanchard. She used to live here." Saying it that way was like killing her, but he kept on. "I'm sorry. I shouldn't intrude. I was driving by, and I saw the lights. She's a cousin of mine. We've been kind of out of touch." He let his voice trail off.

Her eyes eased slightly. "I'm afraid I don't know anyone named Cornelia. You say she lived here?"

"Yes, until a few years ago, anyway."

"And what's your name?"

"Edward Rollins. Most people just call me Rollins."

"Edie Stanton." They shook hands awkwardly across the threshold. Then she relaxed a little. "I used to know another Rollins—years ago—Richard I think his name was."

"I have a brother named Richard. But he's out in Indianapolis."

"He didn't go to Penn by any chance?"

"Yes."

Edie seemed suddenly delighted, turning this unexpected encounter into something closer to a family reunion. "How *amazing*!" she practically shouted. "You're Richard's brother?"

Rollins bobbed his head in acknowledgment, as he tried to accommodate the fact that Cornelia was no longer the topic—*he* was.

"My roommate, Jennie Sturgis, went out with him. But that was a million years ago. I suppose he's married now."

Rollins pictured his brother in Indianapolis, the Christmas cards. "Yes. Two children."

"Imagine that. Well, why don't you come on in, have a drink. We're having a few friends over. Gosh, perhaps you know *them*?" She laughed a little at the wild improbability of it all.

Edie motioned for Rollins to come on through a small, dark ante-room into the living room, where the cocktail party was going full force. But the sound ebbed as the guests turned their attention to the late-arriving stranger in their midst. Rollins had the sensation of passing through some invisible barrier. He'd tried to peer into this house so many times. The living room was done in the earth tones that had just become fashionable, with solid furniture and a large woven rug across the broad planks of the wooden floor. Five people were sitting about, and Rollins felt terribly self-conscious to find them all peering at him as if he were an alien being. But then Edie explained, loudly, with possibly a little too much enthusiasm, that he was the brother of an old friend from Penn, and, like magic, all the apprehensive looks suddenly dissolved, replaced mostly by equally disconcerting familiarity. Edie introduced everyone, and Rollins shook hands all round, but, aside from her burly husband, Ben, and the smallish, well-dressed woman to his left, Nicky someone, Rollins lost track of all the names. Ben handed him a drink. Rollins took a gulp of a gin and tonic, grateful for the tangy release it offered.

"Nice guy, Richard," Edie was saying. "And so handsome! I had a bit of a crush on him myself."

Rollins smiled noncommittally. He and his brother had been out of touch in those years. All he'd known was what his mother had sent him from the Penn newspaper, detailing Richard's exploits on the baseball diamond as the varsity shortstop.

"He and Jennie were mad for each other for a few months there. Inseparable. But then Jennie found Roger Morton—you know, the stud on that cable show, *Wall Street Today*?—and that was it for your brother."

"Were you at Penn, too?" Edie's husband Ben asked, apparently discomfited by his wife's talk of college romance.

"No, Williams, actually," Rollins said.

"Play any squash there?" A wiry, bearded fellow—Allen was it? Alex?—piped up from across the room. "They're big on squash at Williams."

"And Mt. Holyoke girls," added another man, whose name Rollins had missed completely.

Rollins felt himself color, remembering his own drunken fling with a Mt. Holyoker—a chain-smoker named Andi McCallister—one weekend, which involved his sole experience with cunnilingus. "Richard was the jock in the family." Then he added, lest he be thought completely useless, "I was head of the film society."

Allen or Alex let that pass. "We played Williams, that's why I asked," he said.

"Please, not those Yale squash triumphs again, Alex," said a mousy woman beside him.

There was a pause in the conversation, as the initial burst of curiosity about this stranger in their midst subsided. "Rollins is just passing through," Edie explained. "He says his cousin Cornelia Blanchard used to live here."

"That's the woman I was telling you about." It was Nicky, sitting on the ottoman immediately to Rollins' right. "Last month, when you moved in. She's the one who disappeared. She used to live here."

Edie's features darkened. "Well, the realtor didn't say anything about it."

"Was that Jerry Sloane?" Nicky interrupted.

"Why, yes, I believe it was," Edie said. She called out to her husband. "Isn't that right, dear?"

"Isn't what right?"

"The realtor's name was Sloane."

"Yes, that's it. Sloane. Jerry, I think it was. Very helpful, obliging kind of guy."

Rollins felt a spasm; he thought he must be hearing things. "Not the one in Boston."

"Yes!" Edie brightened. "Apparently, he does work all around New England. I don't know how he does it. I told him, is that *legal?*" She laughed. "He assured us it was."

"You all right?" Nicky asked. "You seem a little pale."

"I'm fine. Thank you." Rollins loosened his tie. "Allergies."

Nicky turned back to Edie Stanton. "All I meant to say was, Jerry's not likely to say anything, now is he? After all, there's the strong possibility that she was murdered." That remark silenced the murmuring side conversations that were starting to spring back up, and all eyes followed as Nicky turned to Rollins. "You look a little like her, you know," Nicky said, examining him closely. "Around the eyes." She paused again. "Oh dear. I hope I haven't upset you."

"You say, she was *murdered*?" Rollins hoped he struck the right note of incredulity.

Nicky assumed a sorrowful look. "That's what I've heard."

"I knew she hadn't been seen for a while," Rollins said quietly, still shocked by the name Jerry Sloane. "That's why, when I saw the lights, I wanted to stop in. I thought she might have returned."

"Sorry to disappoint you," Edie's husband, Ben, said.

Rollins turned to Nicky, who seemed to be the most reliable conversationalist. "Did you know her?"

"Oh yes. Not well, of course. No one knew her well, I don't think. I'm in the house down past Lizzie's old barn. You must have known Lizzie. Cornelia's *friend*." Elizabeth Payzen—Lizzie—was the woman said to be Cornelia's lover.

"I thought you said she'd moved," Edie interjected.

"Yes, a while ago." She turned back to Rollins. "Perhaps you'd heard."

Sloane—again? He couldn't put the thought out of his mind. "I—well, I've been out of touch, I'm sorry to say." Several times, Rollins had driven by her converted barn about a half mile down the road, hoping to catch a glimpse of her, but he never had.

Payzen had always been somewhat secretive. When he was doing his interviews for the *Beacon* story, Rollins had called her repeatedly and hooked up with her only when he'd driven by one evening unannounced and found her fixing dinner. She was slender, with short hair and a vaguely elfin demeanor that, at moments, had reminded Rollins of Cornelia. But, to Rollins' frustration, Lizzie was mostly unresponsive. She had turned most of Rollins' questions back on him, or answered with only a yes or a no.

"So funny to think of them down there fucking by the pond," Nicky added.

"*What?*" the bearded Alex fairly shrieked.

"That's the story from the UPS man," Nicky said.

"Sunbathing, I'd heard," the mousy woman said.

"Oh no, fucking. Or, well, as close to fucking as they can. They were on top of each other, apparently. But backward, you know."

Edie looked away and dug into the cheese.

Rollins turned to her. "Excuse me, but I have to ask: You didn't buy the house from Cornelia, did you?" It was an extremely direct question, and a deep and somewhat frightening silence followed. Marj would have been proud.

"No. Not Cornelia," Edie replied. "From what Nicky's saying, I don't know how we could." She snapped off a bit of cracker. "But it was another Blanchard, now that you mention it." She called over to her husband, now busy fixing a drink at a table at the far end of the room. "Darling, what was the first name of that nice man who sold us the house?"

"George, I think it was."

"Oh yes, George."

"George Blanchard? An older man?" Rollins asked.

"Mid-sixties, I'd guess."

"That would be my uncle. Cornelia's father." Rollins hadn't seen George in years. He had received a brief note from him after his story ran in the *Beacon*, quibbling with some of the family details, but thanking him, in the end, "for taking an interest."

Edie smiled. "Well, there you are."

Rollins sensed that this was his cue to be going, and that, despite the web of associations, he was markedly less welcome than he had been before. Still, he persisted: "But how could he sell you Cornelia's house? I mean, it wasn't his!"

That silenced the room again, and this time he could feel several sets of eyes boring into him. But Rollins remembered distinctly that Schecter had checked on the deed of the house at the registry in Nashua. He'd even made a photocopy of it. The house was in Cornelia's name.

Edie was positively chilly now. "It must have been, or he wouldn't have been able to sell it to us, now would he?"

"Rich parents often hold the title of houses they buy for their children," Nicky piped up. She alone seemed to be enjoying the drama playing out over cocktails. "I heard that Cornelia's parents were quite wealthy."

"But it wasn't his to sell," Rollins repeated firmly.

"You suggesting there's some problem?" Ben Stanton asked.

Rollins looked about, but the only face that seemed to look upon him with any kindness was Nicky's. "Not at all. I'm . . . Never mind. Forgive me for intruding. I should be getting along now." He stood up to go.

Edie set down her drink and rose also. "I'm sorry to hear it." But she didn't try to dissuade him.

"It's terrible about Cornelia," Nicky added solicitously from her perch by the cheese. "All this must be hard on the family."

"Yes, well, thank you." Rollins continued to the door.

"She was a lovely person," Nicky called out after him.

"Yes, she was." Rollins pulled open the door and felt the darkness rush toward him. He tightened a little when he used the past tense.

"Your car in the driveway?" Edie asked from the foyer.

"No, back out on the road. I walked in." He headed out toward the cars now, moving quickly.

"How'd you happen to find yourself way out here, anyway?" Edie's voice was raised a little, to carry.

By now, Rollins was far enough away that he didn't need to answer. "Good night," he called out, as if he hadn't heard this last question. "Thanks for the drink." He was halfway down the drive when, to his relief, he heard the front door shut tight behind him.

Eleven

Back in the Nissan, Rollins continued on down the road for only about fifty yards and then pulled over by some overhanging maples. He left his high beams on, and he cast a long shadow up the road when he stepped around to the front of the car. Moths and tiny no-see-ums flitted about his headlights.

Years back, when Rollins was doing the *Beacon* story, he'd leaned a flat rock up against the stone wall along the road here to mark the spot where Cornelia had left a footprint in the mud sometime on the evening of September 17, 1993, the last day she was known to be alive. It was the closest thing Neely had to a gravestone, and Rollins always felt comforted to spend a few minutes by it, reminiscing, whenever he came around. One time, he'd recalled how Neely had played a new Rolling Stones record for him on the playroom stereo (although not too loud), and then actually hop-danced with him in the new sixties way, barefoot on the rug, her blond hair flouncing wildly with each step. He'd moved a little from side to side, remembering. But the weeds had grown up over the summer, and this time Rollins had trouble finding the marker. He was bent over, sweeping aside some thick clumps of grass along the wall when a car slowed on the road behind him.

A voice called out, "Lose something?"

Rollins looked up. It was Nicky again, in the white Taurus he'd seen in Cornelia's driveway. She was leaning out the passenger-side window, half her pale face blazing in the headlights.

"Oh, hi," he shouted, hoping that would be the end of it. "No, nothing like that," he added to answer her question. Nicky continued to wait there, watching him, and Rollins tried to think of some other plausible reason why he might be combing through the weeds like this. Nothing came to mind. "Well, maybe," he said finally.

"Well, maybe I can help you," Nicky said. Before he could object, she'd pulled over a little ways ahead of Rollins' car and stepped out of her Taurus.

She was in a silk dress and white heels—not the most sensible outfit for hunting through high weeds—and she took only a couple of steps onto the roadside before she stopped, the grass licking at her calves.

"I'm not following you, if that's what you're thinking," Nicky declared. "I've got dinner waiting for me in my oven just up the road." Rollins returned to his search, and she must have been able to tell that she had not captured his complete attention. "I must say, you sure stirred up a hornet's nest back there," she added, raising her voice a little. "Edie is ready to kill. And I bet Ben will call half the lawyers in New Hampshire tomorrow—and they'll call the other half, trying to cover their hides." She paused. "So, what, did you lose your wallet or something?"

Rollins glanced back: She was peering out at him, her eyes shielded from his brights. It was pointless to lie. "Actually, I was trying to find the spot where Cornelia was last seen. It was right along here."

Nicky's face, previously so confident, seemed to fall a little, and the hand shielding her eyes dipped for a moment. "Right here? Really?" she asked.

"I set a stone up against the wall to mark the spot where the police found her footprint." With his shoe, Rollins continued to push aside the weeds to check along the base of the stone wall. "It's somewhere around here."

"How do you know?"

"The detective on the case took me out here and showed me."

"Well, wasn't that nice of him."

"He didn't do it because I was a relative. I was here as a journalist, doing a story about her for a paper down in Boston."

"So you're some kind of reporter?" Nicky looked disturbed at the thought. "I thought you were Cornelia's cousin."

"I'm both, actually. Or was. I'm out of journalism now, but I did a story about her disappearance for a Boston tabloid called the *Beacon*."

"Oh, I read that one!" Nicky exclaimed. "You wrote that?" She looked at him quizzically. "I didn't think you were *related*."

"I didn't want to play it up," Rollins said.

"You should've." Nicky's glasses glittered in the bright light. "It's interesting. Especially now that I know you."

"That's what my editor said. But it didn't seem right somehow."

Nicky looked at him again, as if she saw something new in his features. Rollins wondered what it could be. Some sign of his mindless dedication, was it? Or was it possible that Nicky could pick up on the love (if he dared use that word) he still felt for his vanished cousin after all these years?

"I have to say, I was wondering about you back there," Nicky said, nodding toward Cornelia's old house.

"Me?" Rollins brought a hand to his chest.

"Yeah. You didn't seem exactly blown away by the idea that your cousin had been murdered. It wasn't until you heard the name of that realtor—"

"Sloane?"

"As if you don't know," Nicky teased. "My God, you went white as a sheet. I thought you were going to keel over!"

"I wasn't feeling—"

"Right, the allergies. That's a good one." She looked very mischievous, just then. "So you think Sloane's in on the disappearance? Is that the deal?"

"Let's just say his name's come up."

"I've seen him around here a lot, you know. Always checking into things."

"Like?"

Nicky turned evasive. "Oh, I don't know. A little of this, a little of that." She reached down and plucked a wildflower from among the weeds at her feet, and brought it to her nose to smell. "Goldenrod. Want a smell?" She tipped a shoot toward Rollins, who obliged her. Anything to change the subject. The flower had a vague, sugary scent.

"I heard Cornelia was going to Lizzie's house," Nicky continued. "That night, I mean."

"But Elizabeth herself—Lizzie—said she wasn't expecting her."

"So you spoke to her."

"Briefly. She made it sound like she hardly knew Cornelia."

"That sounds like Lizzie. She could be a little remote."

He flicked away a mosquito that had landed on his left wrist, just past the hem of his blazer. "Anyway, police figured someone picked her up along the road here." He glanced along the narrow road, the trees bending over, their trunks hung with ivy. Now, with night upon them, the insects rising, it seemed like a terribly lonesome place. "Whoever it was could have taken her just about anywhere."

"It's all so dreadful," Nicky said. She clutched her arms to her sides against the cooling air.

"Police figured it was someone she knew," Rollins went on. "There was no evidence of a struggle. No blood, no scuff marks, no dropped sunglasses or anything like that. And no one heard any screams."

Nicky looked startled. "It's so awful to think that she might have screamed. I mean, to have been that scared. Especially someone like Cornelia, who always seemed so fearless."

"I know." Rollins turned back to the wall and resumed his search.

Behind him, he could hear Nicky walk back toward her car. But the sound died out when she reached the pavement and picked up the conversation again. "I always wondered about Lizzie." When Rollins expressed curiosity, Nicky explained that her husband had died a few years ago, and after his death Lizzie would have her over sometimes for coffee or a drink. She never said very much—that's how Lizzie was—but it was apparent by the few things that Lizzie did say that things weren't entirely right between her and Cornelia. Nicky attributed the trouble to the way the relationship started, with Lizzie being Cornelia's gardener. "I really don't know if Lizzie could ever be sure she was a lover, and not just a hired hand, pardon the pun. Especially since Cornelia herself was always so free—taking on other lovers and all. You knew about that, I assume."

Rollins had heard rumors.

"Well, I think that drove Lizzie wild. Oh, she'd try to be cool about it, but you could see it hurt. A lot of the time, she just looked so terribly sad."

"It's a long way from there to murder, if that's what you're suggesting."

"Maybe, but why was it that Lizzie didn't come home that night till three in the morning?" Nicky leaned back against the side of her car. "I know, because my bedroom window faces her driveway. Ever since my husband died, I've slept with the shades up, or tried to. I don't sleep much anymore, I don't mind telling you. I saw the headlights, and I heard her car."

"Maybe she went out."

"That would have been quite unusual for her. She kept regular hours. The lights in her place are normally out by eleven at the latest. She's a gardener, for goodness' sake. She gets up with the sun. No one knows why she was out so late that night, or where she went. The cops never even talked to her, so far as I know. I asked her one time myself, and she got this very cold look on her face. She looked like she wanted to kill *me*. I don't think we ever had another conversation beyond 'hello' again." She paused as a new thought struck her. "She was quite chummy with Jerry Sloane, by the way. He's selling her house for her, too. But I think their relationship went beyond that."

Sloane again. Rollins sensed a tide rising all around him. Not of water, but something murkier and more dangerous. He needed to retreat to higher, safer ground. "So Lizzie's moved?"

"Oh yes, a year or two ago. Health problems, I heard. But as I say, she'd stopped speaking to me." She waited, watching him. "Well, aren't you going to ask?"

Rollins was genuinely puzzled.

"About the relationship? With Jerry? Jeez, no wonder you quit journalism. I don't think it was sexual. Lizzie didn't do men. Cornelia did, here and there. That was part of the problem between them. But Lizzie didn't, at least not so far as I know."

"So what was it between Lizzie and Jerry Sloane?"

"I was hoping you'd find out, because I'm dying to know. I think it's the key to what happened here." A car went by, and Nicky suddenly looked past Rollins to the stone wall, perhaps ten yards up. "Is that your rock over there?" She pointed. "I just noticed something shining."

Rollins went over and pushed aside a thick clump of black-eyed Susans. "Yes, of course. Here it is." With a heave, he tipped the stone toward the glow of the headlights. Some moss had grown over the face of it, almost obscuring the initials *CB*, and the numbers 9/17/93, that he had scratched in pen five years before.

Nicky picked her way through the overgrowth toward him. "And you put that there?" She stood beside him, looking at it.

"I thought it would be sort of a memorial," Rollins said. "Not much, I guess. The actual footprint was over there." He pointed to a spot by the edge of the asphalt. "Police figured it was the sole of a boot about Neely's size."

They both fell silent.

"Would you mind if I said something, now that we've found it?" Nicky asked, taking up a position beside him.

"If you like," he said politely. It made him uncomfortable to have this slim stranger so close to him in the cool night air. It seemed unfair to Cornelia, somehow. She who was now, in all probability, so alone, so permanently alone. He'd much rather have been by himself there by the stone.

Nicky bowed her head and clasped her hands in front of her. "Well,

I'd just like to say that I miss you, Cornelia. Things haven't been the same since you left. And, wherever you are, I hope you're all right."

Nicky spoke softly, but somehow her words hung all around them, dressing the roadside in sadness. Rollins sniffled quietly to clear his nose. "Yes," he said. "Quite." He got down and carefully pushed the stone back into place again, so that it would be upright and respectable, and the two of them made their way back up to the road.

"I live just down the street past Lizzie's old place," Nicky said. "Drop in if you ever come back this way." She extended a hand, and Rollins shook it. To his surprise, she held on to his hand for an extra moment. "Please, let me know if you find out anything. Especially about our friend Mr. Sloane." Rollins nodded assent. She finally withdrew her hand and headed back to her car. "It's the damnedest thing, this whole business," she called out to him. "It's driven me half crazy trying to figure it all out."

Elizabeth Payzen's converted barn was three driveways down on the left. All the windows were dark, and they reminded Rollins of Cornelia's place before it was sold. Another dark house. Rollins turned in to the driveway, his headlights glinting off the small windows on either side of the front door, then backed around. As he doubled back, he passed Nicky's car just before it turned in to a driveway marked Barton. Rollins had lowered the window to let in the evening air, and he reached out a hand to wave good-bye, and Nicky tooted her horn in response. He continued back up Pelbourne Road and then switched onto Wilbraham and returned to the pay phone by the pizzeria on 102. He snapped the folding door shut, pulled out his telephone credit card, and called Maine again.

"Where the hell have you been?" Al Schecter asked when he came on the line.

"At Cornelia's."

"Wait—she's back?"

Rollins cleared that up, then delivered the real bombshell: The house had been sold. "The new owners let me in," Rollins said. "But get this—they bought it from Cornelia's *father*. My uncle George."

"But the deed was in her name. I checked that, remember?"

"I *know*. That's why I mentioned it."

"So Daddy pulled a switcheroo." Schecter chuckled.

"It looks like it."

Rollins wanted to tell him about Sloane, but that would have required explaining how he had come to meet Sloane in the first place. And that would have entailed revealing his secret driving habits, which would have brought Rollins nothing but grief. So he kept the news about Sloane to himself. But it burned inside him like something ulcerative.

Through the telephone, he heard Al take a pull on a cigar. Rollins could almost see him: the shaggy eyebrows over black eyes narrowed on his favorite Macanudo as he hollowed his cheeks. He must have exhaled, because a rustling noise came on the line. "When the money comes out, they all grab for it, don't they?"

"I suppose." Rollins didn't like to think about the deceits practiced by one generation against the next. It was getting stuffy inside, and he opened the telephone booth door slightly to let in a little of the cool night air.

"How long has it been, anyway?" Schecter asked.

Rollins thought for a moment, counted back to 1993. "It'll be seven years this September."

"Well, there you go."

Rollins felt a slight chill of annoyance. Schecter always liked to make those sorts of oracular pronouncements that left him scrambling. "I don't follow."

"Probate's coming up. In most states, if a person is missing for seven years, they're considered dead for the purposes of probating the will. It's fourteen in Massachusetts, but seven's the rule in New Hampshire. No wonder the mice are starting to scurry. Your uncle Georgie must have figured he had to make a move, or he'd lose the house. It must be worth a shitload by now."

"Half a million, anyway, with all the land." There were over fifty acres.

"There you go," Schecter said again, and took another puff.

"There could have been family heirlooms and all sorts of shit inside, too, that they didn't want to get away."

And Sloane the go-between, Rollins thought. An image of him, with his thick hair, stocky build, and tight smile spread across Rollins' mind.

"Who'd Cornelia leave her stuff to, you ever find out?" Schecter asked.

"Her lawyer wouldn't talk." It was an older man, very starchy, as Rollins recalled. Eliot someone. He'd agreed to an interview, much to Rollins' surprise, and then wouldn't tell him a thing.

"They're not supposed to, but sometimes you can get to them."

A fingertip on his chin, then on the tip of his nose, and the brightest smile. The whole universe swirling around Neely's fingertip, wherever it touched. At the beach, is that where they were? Or on the lawn? Or was it indoors? Just a fingertip, that's all. Her fingertip, on him.

It could be irritating to have such memories bubble up from nowhere, especially the ones he couldn't quite track. Some aspects came through so clearly—an expression, a feeling. He could still feel that fingertip on him, as if it were there even now. But other points, like the exact place or time or person, were lost in the watery blur that marked the limit of his awareness. They made him long to go back and relive the experience, so he could see everything more clearly.

"You still there?"

"I'm here."

"Thought I lost you for a second. Look, the will's basic, kiddo. Find out. The family must know, or they wouldn't be doing this. I'll bet my left one Cornelia named somebody outside the family. Obviously, it isn't one of them."

"What about the fax number?"

"That's a son of a bitch and it's going to take some time. I got to take a boat in tonight for an overhaul, and you don't want to hear the rest of it. But I got the name of that guy with the Audi for you. Got a pencil?"

Rollins ripped a page out of the directory and pulled out a pen from his jacket pocket. "Okay."

"Wayne R. Jeffries. He lives in Somerville, at two forty-three Braddock Street. He last renewed his license just six months ago, so the address should be pretty fresh. I got a phone number if you want it."

"Please."

Schecter gave him the number, and Rollins jotted it down, too.

Schecter took another puff. "You don't recognize the name, I take it."

"No."

"I did a background check on the guy for you. Get this. He served some time in Concord for aggravated assault. A beef over some broad in a bar. Your guy Jeffries pulled a knife, stuck it in the other guy's eye and got himself five years. Got out couple years ago."

Rollins winced. "Into his *eye*?"

"That's my information. Maybe he didn't like the way the guy was looking at his girlfriend. Who the fuck knows? Here's the better question: Why's he after you?"

"I told you—I haven't any idea."

"I smell bullshit, Rollins. Real heavy bullshit."

"Honestly, I don't." It was the truth, and yet it was not the truth. It was simply all the truth he could know or say right then.

"It doesn't have to do with this Cornelia thing, does it?"

And there it was. He shivered to hear Cornelia's name mentioned in this context. It was as if he were watching her get snatched right in front of him: She's walking down Pelbourne in the rain. A car comes out of nowhere, wipers beating. She's drawn inside. The car vanishes.

"I wish I knew," Rollins said finally.

"Well, watch yourself. Don't try anything smart. Get me? And let me know what happens. I could use some excitement. I already got laid this month."

The Somerville exit off 93 was marked by a car wash. Coming from the other direction, Rollins had last taken it the night he first followed the Audi to the dark house. This time, he felt he was traveling back in time, tracing the string of events back to their source.

A flash of red in the trees, and golden hair streaming behind, and a high, laughing voice. "Catch me, Eddie! Betcha can't!" And his own breath, and tiny thumping heart, and his high-tops beating on the forest floor as he rushed along. Search, she'd called it. She'd empty her pockets, leaving a trail of coins for him to follow her deep into the woods behind their house. Summer evenings, usually. Dusk settling around the trees. He'd pick up coin after coin. But just as he was about to reach her, she'd take off on her long legs. Squealing with laughter while he chugged after. He'd chase and chase.

Braddock Street lay off Highland Avenue, just past Somerville City Hall. Rollins slowed as he turned down the narrow street, the front yards bounded on either side by hurricane fences. It was nearly ten, but a few people were still out on their front steps, sipping a drink or having a smoke in the listless night air. Rollins drove slowly enough to hear the murmur of conversations and the buzz of the air conditioners as he tried to pick out the house numbers. Number 243 was four blocks down on the right-hand side. The shades were pulled on the front, but Rollins could see that a few lights were on behind. There was no sign of the Audi. It made his heart pump to see the place, and he had to drive once around the block to calm himself. He parked in front of the next house past Jeffries', killed the engine, and turned off the headlights. He twisted the rearview mirror so that he could zero in on the front of 243, and waited.

Fifteen minutes passed, then twenty. No one came or went; no more lights came on, and none turned off. It was coming up on 10:30. Rollins needed to check on Marj. It troubled him that he hadn't reached her this evening.

He revved up the car again, took a right, and continued on down to Union Square where Rollins had first encountered the Audi. There was a pay phone by the Exxon station across from the newsstand where he had been idling that night. He tried Marj's number, but, once again, he got only her answering machine. Its chirpy outgoing message was no consolation for him now. He dialed 911, and a brisk dispatcher got on the line.

"I'd like to report a murder," Rollins replied.

"Can you give me your location please?" the dispatcher asked with new urgency.

"Somerville. Two forty-three Braddock Street, near the corner of Ivory."

There was a pause on the line, and Rollins could hear the dispatcher relay the information. Satisfied that it had been recorded accurately, Rollins replaced the receiver on its hook and returned to his car. He hooked a right, and then cut back over to Highland and retraced his route to Braddock Street. This time he parked around the far corner from 243. He waited until he heard the approaching sirens, then got out of his car to watch from beside a drooping acacia tree at the corner. There were two police cars, and they both pulled up by the house, their lights flashing, and three uniformed policemen raced up over the grass with guns drawn. One pressed the buzzer while another rapped heavily on the front door. Finally, the door opened, and a slim, tall man appeared. When the bright light swinging around from one of the police cars caught his face, Rollins could see the slight mustache. It was the gaunt man, after all. With that, Rollins returned to his car and took a right back up Braddock, staying well within the speed limit so as to attract no notice.

Twenty minutes later, he pulled into his space at the Hanover Street garage, grateful, as always, to find it there, untrespassed upon by some out-of-towner. Out on the sidewalk, he had to cross Hanover to avoid a drunk weaving past the metal-shuttered storefronts. Rollins' own head was heavy from fatigue, and he instinctively glanced behind him a couple of times, even though he had just left the gaunt man in ticklish circumstances in Somerville.

He slid the key into the lock of his apartment building and pushed open the front door. He swept up a couple of items of mail from the foyer table and placed them in his inside jacket pocket without opening them. The hall light was still out, and, with some annoyance, he'd groped about halfway up the creaky stairs in the near darkness when the door to the Mancusos' apartment blew open and, in the bright light from the doorway, two streaks of color came his way. "Here he is—

finally!" exclaimed the first one, a deep brown. It was Tina, he could see once she stopped by the banister, her dark face tipped down toward him. "We were waiting for you."

Rollins had vowed to keep clear of Tina, and he would have kept right on going except for the other color, an unmistakable auburn, that hung by the apartment door. It was Marj. She seemed slightly flushed, from the heat he imagined. She was wearing a rumpled T-shirt and running shorts, and one hand was up by her mouth. The realization that Marj was *here*—in the upstairs hall of his own apartment building—was almost more than he could bear. "Marj!" he shouted, and surged up the stairs toward her.

He might have repeated the name again if Marj hadn't replied, without any exuberance, "Hi."

"I didn't know you had a girlfriend," Tina said.

"I'm not his girlfriend," Marj said.

Rollins wished she hadn't said that quite so quickly. Now, he didn't dare go any closer to her. "It's good to see you," he told her, although his words sounded stiff even to him. "I tried to call, but you didn't answer. Is everything—is everything all right?"

Tina put her arm around Marj. "She had a scare, poor thing."

Rollins took a step toward her. "What happened?"

"I got a call, Rolo, at my apartment," Marj explained hesitantly. "A man's voice. It said, 'Hello, Marj.'"

"Maybe you shouldn't go into this in front of—"

"It's okay, we've talked," Tina assured him.

"It was him."

Rollins didn't follow. "Who?"

"*Sloane*." Marj was angry now.

Sloane, *again*.

"It sounded just like that prick." Marj fell silent for a moment. "'Hello, Marj.'" she repeated. "That's all. Click." She mimed hanging up the phone. "It scared the *shit* out of me. He used my *name*, Rolo. He knew how to *reach* me. He knows where I *live*." Her lower lip quivered as if she was going to cry. "He's in on these weird faxes, I just know it. This whole thing, Rolo, is getting to be too fucking much."

Rollins moved toward Marj to comfort her, but Tina stepped out and blocked his path. "She's not feeling too good right now."

Rollins glanced over at Marj; she did not meet his gaze.

"But hey, you should've seen her when she got here." Tina rolled her eyes. "Whew."

"What do you suppose he wanted?" Rollins asked.

"To scare the hell out of me," Marj said. "Which he did. I was just coming out of the shower, Rolo. I hardly had any clothes on. I zipped right out of there."

"And you came here?" That was the only hopeful sign.

"I didn't know where else to go."

Rollins could tell that Tina was listening intently, and it annoyed him.

"Actually," Tina interrupted. "Marjie and I've gotten to know each other real well." She retreated toward Marj and dropped an arm over her shoulder. "Haven't we?"

"We've talked."

"About you, Rolo." Tina landed on the name, causing Rollins' blood pressure to rise. "You're a pretty interesting guy. Seems you like to go driving."

"Marj!"

"Come on—what difference does it make now?" Marj said. "Everybody knows all about you."

Rollins sat down on the top stair. He was so close to his apartment door right now. He longed to pass through that door, set his locks and burglar alarm, and drop into bed. It would be so wonderful to lie between cool sheets right now, with nothing but silence and darkness for company.

"There's something else, Rolo." Marj came over to him quietly. This time, up close, Rollins could see that her eyes were rimmed with red, and a huskier scent dulled the sweetness of her perfume. "This came in on the office fax after you left." She pulled out a folded-up sheet of fax paper from the pocket of her rumpled shorts and handed it to him.

Rollins took it from her. The words were handwritten. "Seen your father lately?" the note read in a loosely flowing script.

His *father*? He rubbed his temples again.

"Well, have you?" Marj asked.

"No. I told you. He's out West someplace. We're out of touch."

Marj took a moment to digest that. "It doesn't make sense, Rolo. What is going on?"

"Maybe it's *your* father."

"Mine? God. I haven't even met him." She picked up the note again. "It's the same handwriting."

A woman's hand, Rollins was still convinced. But he found it hard to focus. He remembered how his father had popped up unexpectedly on his Johnson file, too.

"Well?" Marj asked.

"I was just thinking," Rollins replied.

"*Don't think*," she said angrily. "You think too much already. You've got to do something!"

Tina turned to Marj. "Is he always like this?"

Marj sighed, then turned back to Rollins. "Look, Rolo, we may need to go to the police."

"Marj, please—"

"Don't worry, I didn't call anybody yet," she told him. "I figured you'd like some time to think over what you wanted to say."

Now Rollins was seriously alarmed. "What do you mean by that?"

"Rolo, we can't keep going like this."

"I never should have gotten you involved," he said.

He reached for her hand, felt the gentleness of it, the soft palm, the delicate fingers. She didn't move, and he gently drew her to him. He wanted to plant a kiss in the soft hollow of her neck. He ached to, but he held himself back. He knew it wasn't what she wanted. She was through with him, he could tell.

"Christ, I need a drink," Tina announced. "Want one, Marjie?"

Marj stood, slipping free of Rollins' grasp. "Sounds good."

As she retreated from him, Rollins became aware of the space all around him in the hall. He took in the newel post, the banister, the muted floral print on the wallpaper, the thin carpet. Marj was slipping away, leaving him alone with these things. Rollins could tell he was not wanted in Tina's apartment. No invitation had been extended to him. The proper course would have been to turn toward his own door, undo the locks, step inside, and close the door behind him, setting the burglar alarm, as always, against intruders. And that would be it. Marj would call the police, Rollins would be ruined, and she would be a memory.

He watched her go, the sadness thickening in his chest. She was nearly to Tina's apartment by now, the door open. She was moving through it, as if in slow motion. The door was swinging lazily toward him. He had only a moment.

"Wait!" he called out. He leaped down the hall and caught the door just before it closed. He slipped inside without a word, shutting the door behind him as Marj disappeared around a corner.

He passed through the narrow foyer into the sparsely furnished living room, a sharp contrast to his own. Heather was curled up under a blanket on the lumpy couch, her mouth open, her frayed teddy clutched under one arm. Marj watched her and paid him no attention.

"I finally got her to sleep," Tina told Marj quietly. If they were surprised to see Rollins, neither let on. They had become their own private sorority. Tina passed through a swinging door into the kitchen. Marj went in after her, and, aware that he was pushing his luck, Rollins followed.

The kitchen was nearly empty, with none of the appliances and cookbooks that Rollins had come to expect. It was also extremely hot, as if the oven had been left on. Tina fetched a bottle of Southern Comfort from the cabinet over the refrigerator and poured out a couple of glasses.

"How can you wear all that?" Marj asked Rollins. He was still in his blazer and tie. "I'm about to melt." She pushed open the window over the sink, then flapped the bottom of her T-shirt to circulate a little air. "Why's it have to be so hot all the time? God! Boston is the *worst*. Why did I ever come here?" She turned the tap to release a torrent of cold water into the sink, then put her head under, sending spray in all directions.

"Here." Tina handed Marj a rumpled dish towel when she finally turned off the tap and straightened up. Marj dried her hair, then draped the towel over her shoulders to catch the last drips. Her hair falling every which way, her clothes disheveled, Marj looked all the more fetching to him. He imagined she needed his tending.

Tina passed a glass to her. "Drink up. You'll feel better." Tina filled one for herself, then another for Rollins.

"Mommy?" a voice came from the other room.

"Oh, jeez," Tina said. "Excuse me." She passed out of the kitchen.

Marj took a slurp of the whiskey liqueur, then wiped her mouth with the back of her hand.

"So, now what do we do? Any bright ideas, big guy?"

"I think you should stay with me for a while," he said.

With a sudden, frightening motion, Marj grabbed the dish towel and smacked it down on Rollins' shoulder, sending a bit of spray onto the side of his face.

Rollins thought for a moment that he might break, burst like porcelain into a thousand pieces. Not just from the blow itself, but from the blind rage on her face when she delivered it. Marj had caught a bit of the flesh on the side of his neck, too, and it stung. He blinked to clear the moisture from his eyes.

"You just don't get it, do you?" she shouted at him.

"Look, you don't dare go back to your place, so I figured you could stay with me." He tried desperately to sound calm, reasonable. "That's why you came, isn't it?"

She smacked him with the towel once more, letting go of it this time. "I'm *not* going to sleep with you. Can't you get that through your thick head?"

"I wasn't suggesting that." He picked up the dish towel and draped it over the lip of the sink. He hoped she wouldn't see that his hands were trembling.

"I'm staying here."

"With Tina?"

"She offered, and I said okay."

"But you don't even know her."

"I don't know you." She glared at Rollins until the hinges on the swinging door squealed and her eyes moved to the doorway.

Heather stood there, yawning, her teddy bear in her hand. "You okay, mister?" she asked sleepily. "I heard somebody shouting."

"I'm fine, thanks," Rollins answered, calmed a little by the sight of her. "You should be in bed."

Tina came in. "That's what I keep telling her."

Heather came over closer to Rollins and looked him over. "You're not sick?"

"Just tired."

She came closer still. "But you're all sweaty."

Rollins smiled as he looked down at his jacket, darkened at the shoulder where Marj had swatted him. "It's tap water, actually. We had a little accident." He glanced over at Marj, and Heather's eyes followed his.

"Mommy said I shouldn't get near you because you were sick." Heather touched the back of Rollins' hand. "But you don't feel hot."

"Actually, I didn't want her to make *you* sick," Tina clarified.

"No," Heather protested.

"Ssh. That's enough, little lady." Then, to Marj: "She had a fever just a few days ago."

"It's all right," Rollins said. He reached for the girl, but Tina came over to pull Heather away. "Okay, now out of here, you." She led her firmly by the hand toward the kitchen door.

The little girl turned back to Rollins before she left. "You can show me baby pictures again sometime, if you want."

"I'd like that," Rollins replied.

Heather waved to him, one quick sweep of her little hand. "Bye." Tina gave out a groan, as if she were sorry to miss the action. Then they were gone, and the door swung shut behind them.

"Baby pictures?" Marj asked Rollins.

"My little sister," he said. "Heather reminded me of her."

"You didn't tell me you had a sister."

Rollins let the silence gather for a moment. She was right there, just a few feet away, but seemed so much farther, with plate glass separating them. He wasn't sure he could reach her, but he took a breath all the same and started in. "She died when I was very young. I should have told you, but it was such a long time ago. I don't think it matters anymore."

"Then why can't you look at me when you say that?"

It was true: He'd dropped his head to stare at the floor, a speckled linoleum. He looked up at her.

"How'd she die?" Marj asked.

"She drowned." He could hear his mother's screams ringing faintly in his ears and feel his father's stony, accusing stare. But the feeling was dimmer now, with Marj there.

She looked at him skeptically. "Don't toy with me, Rolo. I'm not in the mood."

Rollins dug into his back pocket for his wallet. He pulled out Stephanie's photograph and passed the photo to Marj, who studied it.

"Where'd it happen?" Her voice was softer now.

"In the bathtub," Rollins said quietly. He had to concentrate on the words, since he'd never used them out loud before. Not with anyone, not even with the child psychiatrist, Dr. Ransome, he'd seen for nearly a year afterward. They talked about a lot of things, but never about that. "She drowned in the bathtub," he repeated. It was a terrible strain to push the words out toward her. Marj was still so very far away. He thought of reaching for her hand, the one holding the photograph. He needed something to grab on to, something warm, with life in it. But he didn't quite dare.

No one had ever looked at him so intently as Marj did right then. "Tell me about it."

Stephanie's tiny back all white and slick-looking.

"It was horrible." Stephanie was drowned again right in front of him, and it frightened him all over again. "She was floating, facedown in the—" He wanted to reach for his sister, plunge into the water, scoop her out.

Her hair like spilled ink. Her little rubber ducks—bright yellow—bobbing slowly around her.

"You saw her?"

He nodded. "From the doorway." He was there again, watching. It was a terrible sight. "My mother pulled her out."

A great wave of water over the bathtub wall, drenching her clothes, as Stephanie flew up in his mother's arms toward her chest . . .

He had to steady himself to speak. "She set her down on the floor and tried to resuscitate her."

Stephanie's little all-white body down on the tiled floor, his mother gasping, wailing as if she were drowning herself, pressing down sharply on Stephanie's belly with the heel of her hand, then brought her lips down to her child's.

Rollins didn't think he could go on. It was too awful. He closed his eyes, hoping to clear the memory, but it was still there, brighter even, when he opened them again. "She pushed on her belly, all that. I thought she was doing it too hard. That she'd hurt her."

"Oh God, Rolo."

His mother's pearls draped across Stephanie's throat when his mother bent down, then lifted again when she rose up.

Rollins reached a hand up to his face; he needed to remind himself that this was the present and that was the past. "Then she yelled for my father, and he came running in and kind of jerked my mother away," Rollins mimed the motion. "And he tried to bring Stephanie back."

Blowing and blowing. His mother holding her, so she wouldn't slip across the tiles.

Rollins gripped the edge of the kitchen table. Otherwise, he was afraid he might collapse.

"It's okay, Rolo." The sound of Marj's voice made him want to cry, but he managed to control himself.

"Finally, they called the medics, but by the time they got there, there was nothing they could do."

"Oh, Rolo, I'm so sorry."

She moved toward him a little, and, after some hesitation, reached out to him, curving a hand around behind his neck.

He noticed the ends of her hair, spilling down to her shoulders. "Stephanie's hair curled at the tips just like yours. When it was wet."

The two of them fell quiet, watching each other. "I've messed up your jacket," Marj said at last. She ran a finger down one lapel, then tapped on it. "You just make me so crazy sometimes." Marj got up to pour herself another drink. When she returned to the table, she stood behind him and returned her hand to the side of Rollins' face. "That whole thing with your sister—God. That sounds really hard."

Rollins nodded, suddenly unable to speak. He reached up to touch the back of her hand as she lightly caressed him. But by then, she'd withdrawn it.

"I'm sorry, am I interrupting something?" Tina declared when she burst back through the swinging door and found Marj standing so close to Rollins. She reached into the freezer for some ice.

"We were just having a conversation." Rollins drew out the last two words.

Tina dropped the ice into her glass and poured herself another drink. "Oh yeah. I used to have those, before Heather was born." She turned to Marj. "Did you ask him about the tapes?"

That was a shock. No one was supposed to know about his tapes. Rollins was afraid he might be sick.

"Oh, now—don't look so surprised," Tina said. "Mrs. D'Alimonte told me all about them. She thinks you're so interesting. She said they were stacked up on this big long shelf over your bed. Hundreds of them."

Rollins brought his hands to his temples. He feared a migraine coming on. "When did she—?"

"Don't sweat it, Rolo," Marj reassured him. "It's not like I couldn't guess a lot of this stuff." She leaned back against the counter, her pelvis protruding.

This was precisely the scenario that Rollins had dreaded for years, the reason that he had been so careful about locking his door, setting the burglar alarm. Certainly, he had other valuables in his apartment, but the tapes were by far the most precious of all. They were his secrets. "How did Mrs. D'Alimonte—?"

"She had to go in there one day because of some roach problem."

"Oh, Christ." Rollins remembered surrendering his keys one morning about a month ago. "But I told her she was to go only into the kitchen. I made that very clear to her." He should have put a lock on his bedroom door, just as he'd always meant to.

Tina shrugged. "Yeah, well. I guess she got curious."

"Look, don't worry about it," Marj said.

"Don't worry about it?" Rollins declared. "Those tapes were private."

"So what's on them?" Tina asked.

Rollins nearly hit her before he realized she'd delivered good news. "She didn't tell you?" He had assumed the worst.

"No, she said there was this big long shelf of them, all with dates. May second, nineteen ninety-seven, October fifth, nineteen ninety-nine, like that—that's all. She made it sound very mysterious."

"So that's why you wanted to look in my bedroom." Rollins stared right at her.

Tina shrugged noncommittally.

"I bet it's part of that driving thing," Marj said.

He had the sensation of falling and of things crashing down around him.

"I already told her all about it." Marj turned to Tina. "It's just something he does. It's like his way of going to the movies."

"The porno flicks is more like it," Tina said with a laugh.

"You make a tape about going to that dark house that first time?" Marj asked him. Then, to Tina again: "I told you about that place."

"The one with the Jacuzzi," Tina said.

"Right. Did you, Rolo?"

Rollins needed to lie down. "I really don't want to talk about it."

"Bingo," Marj said. "Maybe we should hear it. Maybe we'd pick up something."

For the last five years, Rollins had indeed created his tapes with the idea that he might, someday, play them for someone. Someone very much like Marj, in fact. But now that the moment was at hand, he felt nothing but terror. He had been completely violated. That's all he could think. It was as if he were being told to strip himself naked and bend over in the middle of Government Center.

"Come on, Rolo," Marj said. "There might be something about that guy you followed, or Sloane maybe. Something that will clear stuff up."

Rollins waited, praying that this nightmare would pass by itself.

Tina seemed to lean toward him a little.

"Well?" Marj said.

Twelve

"I should have all these locks," Marj said as Rollins struggled with the third dead bolt on his front door. It was just the two of them, finally. Rollins had insisted that his tape not leave his apartment, and Marj told Tina that maybe she'd better stay with Heather. "I'll be waiting up," Tina had told her. Now, with Marj standing so close beside him, Rollins' head spun so, he couldn't remember whether the key to the third lock was round or jagged.

"I'll do it." Marj plucked Rollins' keys from his hand. In moments, the lock turned with a click, and Marj straightened up, smiled, and dropped the keys back into Rollins' moist hand. He stepped inside to deactivate the burglar alarm, then ushered Marj in after him with a sweep of the arm. He hoped the gesture wasn't too grand.

For some time now, Rollins had been fretting about how Marj

would respond to his antique-laden decor, but she made her way straight to the living room window. "Smells like mothballs in here," she said. "And it's so hot, how can you stand it?" She pushed her hands between the heavy green draperies and raised the sash easily while he admired her long, straight back, and her trim legs that tapered down to tiny white socks and battered running shoes. He just wished she weren't so visible from the courtyard.

Marj turned back to the room. "God—it's so *dark*." She clicked on a porcelain lamp in the corner, then glanced around, taking in the furnishings for the first time. In the lamplight, she looked like some sort of finch. There was her hair, of course, but also the pale pink of her T-shirt and the bright red of her running shorts. She made the room's dark hues seem like various shades of mud.

"Well, you *are* rich," she declared.

"Comparatively, I suppose." He watched her carefully, curious to see how this admission went down. He'd come in for some teasing about his wealthy background at Williams, which was itself a joke, considering that almost no one there was genuinely poor.

"Compared to a hick like me, you mean." Marj fingered the plush material of the draperies, then glanced up at him. "But hey, take a breath, all right? I mean, I kind of suspected. The rich relatives, the preppy clothes. Plus, you never talk about money." She ran a finger along the top of the Moroccan carved-wood chair, then checked it for dust under the lamplight. "It doesn't bother me." She looked at him again. "I bet your dad is some big computer guy."

"Hardly. He had a little investment business for a while, but he blew it." He thought better of mentioning the possible SEC investigation. "All this comes down from my mother's side of the family. My great-grandfather financed some of the Rockefeller oil business, early on. These are mostly his things."

"They valuable?"

"The rugs and the paintings probably are, but I've never had them appraised. I don't plan to sell them, so I don't particularly care what they're worth."

She opened the humidor on the sideboard, then quickly snapped the case shut again. "Oh, sorry." She giggled. "I thought it was a music box."

"Cigars," Rollins explained. "That detective, Al Schecter, gave them to me, years back, but I don't smoke."

"Thank God," Marj said. "My stepdad does. Or at least he used to. He really stank, the creep."

A few moments passed. Rollins settled himself in the wooden chair by his fold-up desk and clasped his hands over his knee. "I should tell you where I went tonight."

Marj turned her head slightly, making herself look very fetching. "Maybe I don't want to know."

But there was no stopping Rollins now. He explained that he'd been in Somerville at the gaunt man's house. Marj went very still, and possibly a little pale (the light wasn't too good), and dropped down onto Rollins' fat leather chair, which gave out a crackling sound. He told how Schecter had gotten him the address, but carefully left out the part about the criminal history. He could tell that Marj was frightened enough as it was; there were certain things that Rollins figured he would have to bear alone. She listened attentively until he got to the part about sending the police to Jeffries' house. Then she laughed, or barked, more like, involuntarily, eyes wrinkled.

"Don't worry. I didn't give them my name." He paused for a second. "I dialed 911 and said there'd been a murder at his house. Then I hung up. It was simple, really."

Marj brought a hand to her mouth. "Shit, Rolo. I thought *I* was crazy." She shook her head, as if her mind was balking at the whole, impossible idea of what he had done. "Whoa."

Rollins told her how he'd watched the police converge on Jeffries' door. "You should have seen the look on his face," he told her proudly.

Marj was more concerned that Jeffries had seen him, but Rollins assured her he couldn't have.

"Still, he's going to be so pissed, Rolo," she told him.

"Maybe, but he's on notice now. He's not going to fuck with me any longer."

Marj's eyes flickered at Rollins' choice of words. "What about Sloane?"

Rollins shifted in his chair. "That's something we'll have to decide."

Marj stood up and walked over to the painting on the wall. It was the English landscape; its rural calm seemed very quaint at this moment. "Rolo, what do these people want from you? That's what I don't get. You say you don't know them. But why do they seem to know all about you?"

Rollins nearly mentioned his trip to New Hampshire and the shady dealings he'd discovered between Sloane and his aunt and uncle, but he was on shaky ground with Marj already. He thought it safer to say nothing than to risk her ire.

Marj returned to him. She stood beside his big chair. "It's Cornelia, isn't it?"

Rollins was taken aback: almost Schecter's exact words. "Why do you say that?"

"You told me she's got all this money, right?"

"But she's *gone*. Dead for all anyone knows."

"Maybe Sloane and his friend Jeffries think you think differently."

"But I don't!" Rollins said with a vehemence that surprised him. He stood up, crossed the room, and, with a tug, closed a small crack between the draperies. "I wrote that one story about her, and that was it. That is absolutely all I know."

"Maybe you know more than you think."

Rollins pushed his fingers into his hair in exasperation. "I don't know *what* I know."

That hand clawing a bare back. The thrashing.

It was infuriating: His own life suddenly seemed like the lives he watched. He had only a partial, temporary view. Vivid at points, but nothing more.

Marj moved to him, grasped his shoulder. "But you do know, you *do*! Like when I found Cornelia's picture." Marj looked into his eyes as if she were searching for something. "That didn't surprise you, Rolo. I was watching you. You didn't look shocked or amazed. It was more like, 'Oh.'"

"I was stunned," Rollins insisted. "I didn't know what to think." He was softening; he could feel it. His voice had lost some of its force. Something was giving way deep within him.

Marj must have sensed it, because she pressed her attack. "Bullshit, Rolo. A thought went through that head of yours. I watched it happen. You just didn't want to tell me." She paused a moment, thinking. "I still don't get why she's such a big deal to you. All right, she disappears and it's a big mystery, I get that part. But I keep wondering why every time her name comes up you get this weird look on your face. You go blank—it's like I'm not even here."

She turned back to him. "You ever, like, do anything with her?"

"Marj, I was only six." He was grateful that this claim, at least, was easy to refute.

"What about later—when you were a teenager, or off at college? You told me how she came to your room that night."

"No." Rollins was quiet but firm.

Marj gave a calm-down gesture with her hands "O-*kay*! You didn't sleep with her. But what's with her, then?"

"I liked her, that's all." He saw her again in her light, summer clothes, her gremlin smile that drew him to her to be hugged and, sometimes, tickled. (His sides, just below the ribs, would produce hysterics every time.) She touched him. Except for Stephanie, she was the only one in that family who ever did. Was that it? Was it that simple?

"Oh, please. Liked her. Gimme a break."

It was the sound that drew him first. Dripping water. Ka-plink. Ka-plink. The bathroom door was ajar. The white, dirt-smudged door of his room to the bathroom he shared with Stephanie. He followed the sound, moving silently, as always. He pushed the door open, so quietly. Just a little, then a little more. Steam was rising off the water of the big tub with claw feet, the only one in the house. He saw Neely's blond hair up on top of her head as she lay back, eyes closed, sleeping. Ka-plink. He came closer, fascinated to see her, to peer into the bright mystery that was her. Her neck widened to bare shoulders. Then he looked down from the bathtub rim to a pair of breasts, pink from the hot water. Little scrunched-up nipples poking up like raspberries. Were they as soft? As sweet? Ka-plink. *Staring and staring, his mouth dry. Her knees were up; a light fuzz between her legs, fluttering. He stayed a long time, watching.* Ka-plink. Ka-plink. Ka-plink.

"It's happening again, Rolo. You're, like, out of here. You're thinking something. What?"

"Oh, nothing." The memories belonged to him, inside him. But they had such force, he wasn't so sure he could hold them in any longer. He felt suddenly dizzy.

Her face reddened by the heat of the water. One knee out of the water, like a tiny island.

Marj gave him an imploring look, and he had to speak.

"You're right. Something did happen."

Thirteen

Marj was silent, hand to mouth, waiting.

"I saw her once," Rollins said finally.

"What do you mean, 'saw her'?"

Rollins felt terribly light, as if he might fly away. "In the bath."

"You mean—?"

Rollins nodded.

"Well, that's something. See the whole deal?"

Rollins nodded again. He started to tremble. He was there again, back in the big house. He was very young. Frightened, but so eager.

"She let you?"

"She didn't know I was there. She'd fallen asleep. The door was ajar. I pushed it open and went in." He felt the steamy air on him, heard the drips, saw her.

Her glistening breasts, surrounded by lapping bathwater.

"She pretty?"

Rollins said nothing. He'd never thought in those terms. It was just her—Neely. But the real her. "Sure. I mean, I suppose."

"You touch her?"

He'd wanted to touch those raspberry-like nipples, the fluttering pubic hair. But he hadn't dared. Rollins shook his head quickly. "God, no."

"That's it, Rolo? You saw her, nothing more?"

Rollins nodded.

"I saw my mom and my stepdad fucking. I came home one night, and they were bare-assed on the living room rug. Not a pretty sight. But it's no big deal, Rolo."

A bad feeling spread through Rollins' gut. This memory had led to another. He spoke quietly. "Mother caught me."

A click and a rush of cold air and his mother charging toward him from Stephanie's room. And a slap—hard—and an angry shout. "What are you doing?" Then Neely splashing a towel into the water, and it swishing about like thick rope. Then a hard shove, and he was back in his room again, his mother's finger in his face.

"Don't you ever *do that again."*

"Ye-yes, Mother. I'm—I'm—I'm sorry, Mother."

Rollins turned his face to the wall and clenched his eyes shut, trying desperately to lock out the memory of the moment that had ruined everything. He tensed, bracing himself for a blow.

"I'm losing you, Rolo. Talk to me."

"I thought she was going to hurt me."

Her hands on his chest, pushing him.

"Who?"

"My mother. She was absolutely furious. I'd never seen her so angry. She scared me to death."

"How'd Neely take it?"

His jaw quivering. His face pushing into his pillow. Wet footsteps out of the bathroom through to Stephanie's room. Then quiet again.

"Rolo? How'd Neely take it?" Marj repeated.

"I don't know. She never said anything about it. She was embarrassed, I guess." Afterward, Rollins had crept back into the bathroom. There were wet spots on the floor from where Neely had gone out. The tub was still full, but the water cool. He'd felt it.

"Maybe she liked it—that you saw her."

Rollins looked up at Marj in amazement.

"Girls do, sometimes, you know." Marj looked at him. "So, then what?"

Rollins shook his head. "Nothing. That's all I remember."

Marj got up and headed to the kitchen. "Mind if I get some water?"

"No, go ahead."

Marj passed through the kitchen door. Rollins could hear a couple of cupboards open. "The glasses are over the sink," he called out to her.

"Got it," Marj shouted back.

Rollins went to the doorway. "There's some Pellegrino if you like."

Marj ran the water for a moment, apparently waiting for it to get cold. "This is fine." She filled herself a glass. "I take it there haven't been any more Cornelia sightings." In the *Beacon*, Rollins had referred to reports from Schecter of various people who had supposedly seen Cornelia after the disappearance. There was one at a dog track, another at a mall.

"No, that's pretty standard in missing persons cases, especially if there's publicity involved. Cornelia was beautiful, but something of a classic beauty. There were a lot of women who looked like her." Rollins reached into the refrigerator for the Pellegrino. "Actually, I've seen her a few times myself. I thought I did, I mean."

"Really?" Marj seemed amazed.

Rollins hadn't realized how unusual this might sound. "At a restaurant once. Another time on Fifty-seventh Street in New York. I followed her for three or four blocks before I decided it couldn't be her. And there's even a woman up at Johnson who looks a lot like her. Every time I see her, I get this pang." Rollins pounded his chest with his fist.

"But couldn't she have, like, gone somewhere? Malaysia, or Iceland, some place like that?"

Rollins poured himself a glass. "Not without changing her name. Schecter checked. No one with her passport had left the country. Plus, her bank account was untouched, and same with her credit cards. So what was she going to do for money? And why wouldn't she have told anyone?"

Marj shook her head, then drained her glass. "I still want to hear that tape," she said finally.

"Oh, right." Rollins had almost forgotten. "It's in the bedroom. I'll get it."

Rollins took a couple of gulps of water, then set their glasses in the sink and crossed through the living room to his bedroom. Inside, he climbed onto his bed and brought down the second case from the end—the one detailing his trip to the dark house—and placed it beside his bed.

"Hey, where's the TV?" Marj shouted from the living room.

"In the closet," Rollins yelled back.

"Figures. And what's all this—Greek?"

"Latin. I was a classics major," he called back. "I should toss them out. I almost never look at them anymore."

Rollins slid out the case two from the end and opened it with a soft click.

"You can come in if you want to," he called out to Marj.

"I'm not sure I dare."

He'd left the door open about a foot, and he was watching as Marj pushed the door open and stepped quietly inside. For a moment, she seemed like a complete stranger, it was so startling to see anyone in his bedroom, especially a young woman in running clothes. But then he could see that it really was Marj, and he felt better. She didn't seem to notice the tapes as she glanced about. She crossed to his bureau, and reached for a photograph of himself as a child on the bureau top. It was a small photograph, one he'd made even smaller by cropping his mother out of it. His eyes were downcast and his suit ill-fitting, but there was an uneasiness to the image that captured him in those days.

"This you?" she asked.

Rollins moved closer. "From when I was eleven. A few months after my parents' divorce."

"You look a little out of it." She looked at the picture again. "I've heard that when a kid dies, it can really mess up a marriage."

"Father left the day after Christmas." Rollins spoke the words as if in a trance. "I was in the kitchen having breakfast with my mother and brother. Poached eggs. My mother was never a morning person, but she was particularly quiet this morning. She wasn't eating, not even reading the paper, which was very unusual for her. I asked when Father was coming down. 'He isn't,' she said. Then she ran out of the room in tears. *Ran.* She knocked into the corner of the table when she left, spilling some orange juice. She just ran off. I didn't know what to think. My brother and I looked at each other. Then we went to search for my father, started calling for him all around the house. Mother had locked herself into the bedroom. Later that afternoon, I saw Gabe, our handyman, putting all my dad's clothes out with the trash."

"God, Rolo."

Rollins said nothing. He didn't have the strength to speak, just as he hadn't all those years ago.

Rollins looked up and saw Marj staring at the long shelf of tapes over his head. He had always been proud of his tapes, just as he had been proud of his collection of toy cars as a child, and for some of the same reasons. He'd viewed the tapes as a unique accomplishment; in the deepest possible sense, they were his. He'd hoped, at some point, to share them. But now, Rollins could see through Marj's eyes how strange they were. And he had the horrifying realization that he himself, the maker of those tapes, must seem strange, too. Marj edged closer, tipping her head sideways to scan the dates along the spines of the cases holding the earliest tapes.

"'November twelfth, nineteen ninety-five, nine-seventeen P.M.,'" Marj read out slowly. "'November thirteenth, nineteen ninety-five, ten-twelve P.M.; November fourteenth, nineteen ninety-five, seven-fifteen P.M.'" She paused for a moment, gaping. "I don't believe this. It's just like she said."

Rollins looked at his tapes. They seemed so different now, with Marj there. He hadn't quite realized there were so many. There probably were several hundred. He wasn't sure he dared speak. "I've never— I've never shown them to anyone before."

"Oh, like this is supposed to be an honor."

"Well, kind of."

Rollins expected some sarcastic rejoinder, but none came.

Marj turned back to the tapes. "*All* of them about following people?" she asked. "No music or anything?"

"No music."

"Man oh man." She shook her head slowly. "So these are all, like, notes?"

"You could say that."

"For what?"

"I don't know. To remember, I guess. And maybe to explain to somebody . . ." His voice trailed off. It suddenly seemed ridiculous to think that these tapes could produce understanding. Revulsion seemed much more likely.

"Explain what?" Marj prompted. "What you're really like? What you're about?"

The sarcasm was gone from Marj's voice. Rollins' heart banged in his chest, and there was a rhythmic thudding in his ears. Understanding was out of the question, obviously. He might understand himself one day, if he worked at it. But no one else ever would. That was obvious. "Something like that," he said quietly, hoping to end the conversation.

Marj raised her voice slightly. "You lonely? That what we're talking about here?"

"I'm just interested in seeing what other people do."

"Seeing—that's all?" She looked over at him. "You don't like to be touched, is that it?" She was by his bed.

Rollins eyed her from the bureau. "I like to feel safe, if that's what you mean."

"Well, you can't always be safe, now can you?" Marj returned her attention to the row of tapes. "So where's the one about the North Reading house?"

"Right here." He picked the tape up from the bedside table and popped it into the recorder.

"Wait—I need a pencil."

"I'll get you one." Rollins retrieved a pen from the fold-up desk in the living room along with a few sheets of his stationery.

"I didn't disturb anything, you know," Marj said when he returned. She brought a chair over from under the window, kicked off her running shoes, and took a seat with her feet up on the edge of the bed. "Okay, fire away." Rollins set the tape player down on the bed near her and hit the PLAY button. The tiny wheels of the cassette started to whirl, a light hissing sound came up, and then a rustling noise.

"Turn it up a little, would ya?" Marj asked. She had the paper on her knee, the tip of the pen at the edge of her mouth.

Rollins cranked up the volume knob high enough that the recorder buzzed slightly when it hit a certain pitch. Still, it returned him to the Nissan, where he was setting the newspaper down on the passenger side beside him, hearing once more the rush of cars through a dreary Somerville intersection.

Rollins' voice rose up from the tape: "It's eleven-twenty-four. I'm by a little newsstand called the Mid-Nite Convenient in Union Square. I've got an Audi up in front of me at the light. Dark blue, black maybe. It's a little hard to tell. Just the driver, middle-aged I'd say, a little hunched over."

"You sound so different," Marj shouted. "Your voice seems older."

"It's not the best machine." It was the spare, one he used just for playback.

The recording lasted only about five minutes, interrupted by occasional blips as each new entry began. Marj listened attentively, jotting occasional notes in a loose scrawl. He clicked off the tape when he posted his final remark about needing to find a toilet.

"Well, I'd have been shitless, too. It's all pretty incredible, Rolo. Your doing that, I mean. Following that guy. And then him not turning on the lights. My God! I'd have been terrified."

"It made me nervous, sure." He remembered how his bowels ached.

Marj looked down at her notes, which ran half a page. "Doesn't leave us with much. You got a decent description, and some of his habits." She glanced down at her notes. "'Drives with one hand on the wheel. Pulls on his ear.'" She looked up quizzically at Rollins.

"Like this." Rollins demonstrated, tugging gently at his left earlobe. "I just wanted to record a few details so I'd remember. It brings it back."

"'Shifts lanes without signaling.'" She looked up again.

"That made him hard to follow. But a lot of people don't signal, as you've probably noticed." He remembered that Marj herself didn't signal.

"And you said he made all these 'extra' turns at the end," Marj said.

"I thought he was trying to lose me."

"Why?"

"That's what I didn't know. I couldn't be sure he was." Rollins remembered now how surprised he'd been to see that. No one had ever been evasive before. "I figured I was imagining things," he told her.

"You could have made a note of the license plate number."

"It's just a number! It doesn't tell you anything. Now, a vanity plate—"

"Well, we got it now, along with the guy's name," Marj interrupted. "So what were you doing before you started following the guy? The tape didn't say."

"Just reading the paper."

"Just reading the paper." Marj shook her head. "So why'd you follow *him*?"

"I don't know. He was there when I looked up."

"So there wasn't, like, anything special about him. No 'Follow Me' sign on his rear bumper?"

"I told you. It's arbitrary. I see someone and maybe I think, okay, that's the one. Or maybe I don't. It's all about how I feel." Rollins wasn't sure she appreciated what a confidence this was. "It's unconscious, I guess that's what I'm saying."

Marj set down her pen and shifted in her seat. "Okay, Rolo, here's the thing. Here's the part I've been wondering about. Did it ever occur to you that this guy might have been *expecting* you to follow him?"

"But he couldn't have."

"Why not? It's not like this was the first time you did this." Marj glanced toward his row of tapes again.

Rollins considered this a moment. "But how would he know?"

Now Marj seemed exasperated. "Maybe he'd seen you." She said it slowly, pausing between each word.

"But he *couldn't* have," Rollins repeated.

"How would *you* know? You just told me you were reading the paper. He could have been watching you."

"That's impossible."

"Let's forget impossible, okay?" Marj slapped a hand down on the bed and stood up. "We're way past impossible here. You tipped this guy off somehow. There's no other way! He was on to you. I mean, Rolo, come on. You think you're invisible, that nobody notices you." She laughed, to Rollins' annoyance. "Like in the office. You think nobody gives you a thought, but you are the number one topic of conversation in the ladies' room. Number one, Rolo." Marj's voice was raised now, and she'd left her chair to move back and forth by his bed, gesturing. "So I don't think you were just sitting there, and this guy just *happens* to drive by and lead you back to, like, the one house in all of Massachusetts that's connected to your old friend Cornelia. I don't buy that, okay?"

"So, well, what then?"

"I think he was watching you and waiting. And I think you know why."

Rollins felt a slight pulsing in his temple that might augur a migraine. He stood up and went to the window. He needed to break free from Marj's eyes. "Okay." He glanced at his grandfather's Pierce-Arrow. "Okay," he said again. "Now just calm down for a second, all right? Just calm down." He continued to face the wall. "There is something else you should know. I didn't want to tell you before because, well, I just didn't. I'm not used to this." He turned back to her, swung a hand back and forth between them.

"Conversation," Marj prodded.

"Right, conversation. Okay." He took a breath. "I told you I went to see Jeffries' house tonight, right?"

"Yes."

"I didn't tell you where I was before that."

"Nooooo."

He told her about going to Cornelia's house in Londonderry, although he scrupulously did not say how he'd happened to to do that.

"You saw her, didn't you?"

Rollins told her no, happy to disabuse her of at least one of her fantasies. Still, she was astonished that he had actually gone inside. Rollins made fists of his hands inside his pockets as he told her about discovering that the house had been sold to the Stantons by Cornelia's parents—illegally, he was fairly sure. He looked over at Marj: Her face was all confusion.

"Well, that's bizarre," she said at last.

"And get this. Guess who the realtor was."

Marj's eyes shot open. *"No!"*

"Yes."

"Sloane's hooked up with your aunt and uncle?"

Rollins shook his head sorrowfully. "Seems to be."

"That guy is everywhere, Rolo. He's connected to Cornelia's parents, to you, and now he's hitting me with these fucking phone calls—" She stopped, midsentence, and looked at him strangely.

"What?" Rollins asked.

She spoke calmly, which made her words all the more frightening: "I keep remembering the way he looked at you at the North Reading house."

"*I don't know him, Marj.* I don't know why he did that, okay? I've never seen him before in my life. Really. You've got to believe that."

"Okay, whatever you say. But why Cornelia's parents?"

"I talked to Schecter. He thinks it's because it's coming up on seven years that Neely's been gone."

"So?" Marj looked at him blankly.

"If someone's gone seven years, then they're legally assumed to be dead, and their property goes to the heirs."

"Then who gets all Cornelia's stuff?"

"That's what we don't know. Neely's lawyers wouldn't tell me. But obviously it's not my aunt and uncle, or they wouldn't have gone to all that trouble to phony up the deed."

"Well, maybe it's you, you ever think of that?"

"*Me?*" A stunning prospect, and a flattering one. He felt a little bubble of joy rise through him as he considered it. But why him? It had been so long since he'd seen Neely. Plus, she was so much older. He'd never meant as much to her as she had to him. He was always the one chasing her, never the reverse. "I doubt it," he said finally, feeling a pang of sadness as he did so.

"Then why is Sloane so focused on you? That's the question." She sounded impatient.

Rollins stretched his hands out toward her. "Just wait a second. That's what I was going to tell you." He lowered his gaze to his shoes, which seemed about the only safe place to look right then. He took a breath and told her about visiting the little memorial marker by the side of the road. As Marj's eyes widened in amazement, he realized this was not going as he'd planned. He'd intended this confession to convey his undying loyalty to Neely, but instead he could tell he was coming across like some kind of nut.

"The point is, I've been there before," he finally declared.

"At the side of the road?"

"On her property."

"You go in there, like, regularly? Even after you finished the story?"

Rollins nodded. "I didn't think anyone would be there. The house had always looked empty."

"Why didn't you tell me?" She sat down on the bed.

"I didn't think it was important."

"You thought I'd think you were even weirder than I do, is more like it."

Rollins said nothing.

"So what would you do?"

"Nothing much. Just walk around."

"You drive in?"

"I'd park by the side of the road."

"Where anybody could see you?" Marj said. "Don't they call that trespassing?"

"But she was gone!"

"But you just told me Sloane was the guy selling the place. He could have seen you there." Marj's eyes went wide. "He probably thinks you're still on the case. Maybe he thinks you've found out something. Something important."

"Like—?"

"Like what happened to Neely. Like where her body is. Like who killed her. And he's watching you to find out what you know."

"But come on! I don't know *what* happened to Neely. I'm not investigating a murder. I don't even know for sure that she's dead, let alone killed."

Marj weakened, turned away from him. "I'm just trying to think this thing through, okay?" She sounded plaintive this time, desperate. Rollins felt for her. It wasn't so much that Sloane was trying to understand him. *She* was. That's what this was about. And he was more than she could figure.

There was a knock on the door. "Marj? You in there?" It was Tina.

"Oh, shit. Her."

Marj went to the door. Rollins had to help her with the locks.

"I'm sorry to interrupt." Tina's eyes went from Marj to Rollins and back again. "I just wanted to tell you I'm going to bed, and I thought we should probably get you set up."

"Oh, yeah. It's getting late, isn't it?" Marj turned back to Rollins. "Listen, I better go. We'll talk about this in the morning, okay?"

"Didn't you leave something in the bedroom, Marj?" Rollins asked.

"I don't think so." But she followed him back, anyway.

Inside the bedroom door, Rollins pulled her to him, spoke quietly. "Don't tell her anything about Sloane or Jeffries, okay?"

"Now who's paranoid?" Marj asked.

He held her arm. "Please? Just don't."

She gave him a troubled look. "Sure, Rolo. Whatever."

Neely's hair was on him, so light, as she bent over his bed to kiss him good night. Just the lightest touch, but promising more. A light, lovely kiss, on his forehead, and then, if he was lucky, she'd rough up his hair.

After Marj left, he returned to his bedroom. Had Sloane sicced the gaunt man, Jeffries, on him? Had his trip to the dark house been their plan, not his? A way of protecting themselves from—what? A murder inquiry? It was a terrible, wrenching thought, not least because it made so little sense. It turned the world inside out. Had he been watched? He who had always been the careful, attentive observer? Could he have missed this essential truth that transformed everything, turning him from subject to object, from observer to observed? The idea ate at him. Rollins couldn't put it out of his mind, not while he brushed his teeth, not while he changed into his pajamas, not while he lay under a sheet with the lights out, trying to sleep.

Inside the fear, a memory. Dim at first, then flickering into brightness. He'd been on Main Street, in Medford. The previous month. He had been following a white Caprice south from Melrose. There had been a jam-up on College Street by Tufts University, and the Caprice had veered off onto Main and then pulled up in front of a drugstore. The driver—an overly made-up, middle-aged woman, as Rollins recalled—had left the Caprice double-parked while she went in to the store. Because of all the congestion, Rollins had had to circle the block waiting for her to return. But it wasn't the Caprice he was remembering. It was the car the Caprice had blocked in.

As he'd come back around the block, Rollins had heard the insistent blast of a car horn coming from the part of the street where he'd left the Caprice. But—this was the bothersome part—the driver had stopped hitting the horn as soon as Rollins came around, even though the Caprice's driver had not returned. A rather large car, too. A disturbingly familiar one.

In exasperation, Rollins threw off the covers and switched on the light. He stood up on his bed, and dragged a finger across the last few tapes, stopping at the one labeled "7:18 PM, June 8, 2000." As connected as Rollins felt to these recordings, it had never occurred to him that they might actually be useful, provide a resource. His pulse quickened as he opened the box and plucked out the tape, then stepped unsteadily back down onto the floor. He leaned over his tape player and pushed the new cassette into the slot. He pressed the PLAY button.

The first sounds came out as a roar. The volume was still cranked up, and he quickly turned it down. The pursuit had taken him to Medford. He heard himself describe the white Caprice's muffler problems, and a poodle dashing out into the street, two details he'd forgotten completely, and then he reached the part about the double-parking. *She's pulled over, right in the middle of traffic*, Rollins' voice declared. *Blinkers on, must be going in to the CVS there on the corner. I'm going on ahead. See if I can circle the block.* In the background now, he heard the usual street sounds, the rush of passing cars, the rumble of trucks going by, a shout or two from a pedestrian. Then he heard it. The insistent honking—over and over. *What's* that *about?"* Rollins heard himself say. *Oh, someone's parked in. One of those big SUVs, a Land Cruiser looks like. Big green thing.* On the tape, the honking stopped abruptly.

Rollins shut off the tape player. A green Land Cruiser! Had Sloane been in that car? He must have been. Rollins tried to picture the scene: Sloane, frustrated, rides the horn as he tries to get out of his parking space. Then he sees Rollins and stops abruptly. Why? Rollins had been up in Londonderry only a week before. Had Sloane seen him at Cornelia's house, made the connection to the *Beacon* article? He must have. He must have assumed that Rollins was on him somehow, just as Marj had said. That was the only explanation.

Rollins was not invisible, after all. He had been seen.

Fourteen

That night, Rollins was certain he'd never felt so hot, so uncomfortable. He threw open all the windows, but no air stirred in his apartment: The heat seemed to be coming from inside him. He kept imagining himself being roughed up, shoved this way and that by strangers who shouted at him with gruff, unintelligible voices. Then he felt Tina's hands on him. They were reaching under the waistband of his pajamas, clawing at him. It was a frenzied, indecent dream that left him tangled in his sweat-dampened sheets. Around four A.M., he got up and took a cold shower to try to cool his mind.

Afterward, when he looked at himself in the mirror and saw his limp hair, soft belly, and bleary eyes, he realized that it was no wonder that no one ever reached for him except in his nightmares. He was old, or at least older than he'd remembered. Those creases on either side of his mouth—he was pretty sure they were new. And could he always press a finger that deep into his abdomen?

He was just stepping out of the bathroom when he heard a knock on his door. He was afraid it was Tina again. He pulled on a pair of pants and a shirt, hurried to the door. "Rollins! You there?" It was Marj, thank God. She knocked again. "Quick, Rolo, let me in."

Rollins fumbled with the lock, and Marj burst in the moment he opened the door. "Grab your car keys, Rollins, quick. We're going."

"*What?*" This was happening too fast. She was in her running clothes—bright-colored, skimpy. Seeing her there—so real, so thrillingly beautiful—he wanted her to wait a moment so that he could caress her face, maybe even kiss her.

"Now! Get 'em!"

Foggy-brained, Rollins returned to his bedroom and grabbed the keys from the top of his bureau and, while he was at it, stuffed his wallet into his back pocket. He shoved his bare feet into his loafers. He would have turned back for a pair of socks, but Marj had grabbed his hand and yanked him toward the front door. "We've *got* to go—right now," she insisted. He barely had time to lock the door behind him before she'd disappeared down the stairs.

In a few moments they were out on the quiet, rose-colored street; it was cooler, now, at daybreak. Marj squinted at him against the low sun. "Where's your car?"

"In a garage up the street." He pointed the way. "Would you mind—?"

"Well, come *on*," she interrupted, and took off in that direction.

"What is *happening*?" he shouted after her.

But Marj didn't answer. She was well up the street, beckoning for him to follow. Rollins had no choice but to hurry after her, his loafers slapping the uneven bricks. Finally, he caught up to her and grabbed her shoulders to stop her. "Tell me," he begged her, gulping air. "Tell me now."

"The *car*, Rolo. Where is it?" She was panting, too.

"Up ahead," he gestured up the street. "What's the matter?"

"She's in with Sloane."

"Who is?"

"Tina."

Rollins went cold.

"*Tina*, Rolo. I found a note. I couldn't sleep last night. So I got up and I'm looking around, and I find this to-do list. And one of the things was, 'Get next four hundred dollars from Jerry.'" Marj started moving again up the sidewalk. "This way, Rolo? The car?"

"So that's it?" Rollins asked. "Just 'Get four hundred dollars from Jerry?'"

She stopped again. "I found her address book. *Jerry Sloane's in it*. Address, phone number, the whole fucking thing. She knows him, Rolo."

Rollins' skin went cold. Sloane was everywhere. He was even here, casting his shadow across the two of them.

She turned toward the garage across the street and pointed. "That one?"

"Yeah," Rollins shouted.

She darted across the street—just missing a Buick that came squealing to a halt in front of her. The driver gave her a shout, and Marj gave him the finger back. She was in the shadows of the garage when Rollins finally caught up to her.

"What floor?" she demanded.

"Third. The stairs are over there." He pointed to the entrance.

"Come on!"

"So that's when you left?" he asked, once they were inside the dim staircase. His words echoed around and up the bare stairwell.

Marj climbed ahead of him, her running shoes making angry sounds on the steps. "Not right then." She was breathing harder now. "I was still looking at it when the kid, Heather, asked me, 'What are you doing?' I didn't even know she was awake and then, *bam*, she was right there." She paused to catch her breath. "I nearly died. I thought she was going to start screaming. But she went real quiet, staring right at me. So I said, 'I didn't know your mom knew Jerry Sloane.' And she says, 'Yeah, we spent the night there just last week, when I was sick.'"

Rollins, scrambling to keep up, remembered how Heather had said she'd stayed "near water." Of course! The Mystic River flowed right by the Sloanes' house. And Tina had been so pushy, so curious about everything.

"Then Heather said, 'But you're not supposed to know that.'"

"And that was all?"

"She said, 'I'd better go tell mister.' That's you, right?"

"Yeah."

"Cute. That's when she started pushing me out the door."

They'd reached the doorway to the third floor. "It's down this way," Rollins said, and he grabbed Marj's hand and led her down the row toward his Nissan.

The garage was silent at this hour, except for their shoes beating on the concrete floor as they moved along. The morning light slanted through the soot-smudged windows, casting long shadows. He expected complete vacancy all around him, with all these empty cars. But, as he hurried along with Marj, he sensed a human presence somewhere to his left. One of the cars wasn't empty. He could feel it. He turned, and he saw a shadowy head outlined against the incoming sunlight in one of the sedans in the row to his left. It was hardly anything, just a dark shape where there should have been nothing at all. But it sent a wave of electricity through him.

"What?" Marj asked.

"Keep going," Rollins said evenly.

He unlocked the Nissan, and the two of them climbed in.

"He's here."

"Who?"

"Jeffries."

"*Who?*"

"The gaunt man."

Marj's face bore a look of panic. Rollins jerked the car out of its slot and sped for the down ramp. He'd lowered the window a few inches, to listen. A car started up somewhere behind him.

"Okay, hang on," Rollins said. He gave the car the gas and careened down the ramp. He braked only for the exit, shoved his ID card into the slot, and spun out onto Hanover Street, cutting off a Yellow Cab. Behind him, the furious blast of the driver's horn, which he ignored.

"He back there?" He glanced up into the rearview.

"I don't see—wait, there it is. An Audi, right?"

"That's him."

Rollins took a right, then a quick left. "How 'bout now?"

"No. I think he's stuck at an intersection."

Rollins started to breathe again. "Okay. Good." He swung back onto Commercial Street, his eyes darting about the different rearview mirrors in search of the Audi.

"Where are we going?"

"Up onto the expressway. He won't see us up there." He hooked a left onto Causeway by the FleetCenter, then climbed up onto the elevated highway that cut through downtown Boston. "Now?" Rollins asked.

"I don't see him."

"Good."

The highway was nearly deserted at this hour. Rollins floored it, and the Nissan flew ahead.

"Now what, Rolo?"

"I don't know." He looked at the dashboard clock. Five forty-five. "We sure can't go to work."

"Not dressed like this." Marj looked down at her running clothes.

"Let's think—" Rollins tapped the wheel. "What do they expect us to do?"

"Leave town, probably. Go to Indianapolis or to Morton, which is looking pretty good right now, I've gotta say."

Rollins turned to her. "So we stay."

"But I don't want to be anywhere near those people! They're all over us, Rolo. Every time we turn around, they're right there."

"Okay, okay." Rollins checked in the rearview, then slowed and pulled into the right lane. "We'll check into a hotel."

"Oh, Rolo, I don't know." Her voice had defeat in it.

"A nice hotel."

"Oh, God."

"With room service."

"This is too scary."

But Rollins had already put on his blinker.

"Wait, where are you going? Where are you taking me?"

"To the Ritz."

The Ritz was at the corner of Arlington and Newbury, facing the Public Garden, a deep green now except for the black waters of the duck pond. It was almost six when Rollins pulled up in the Nissan, but two uniformed valets were on duty, and one of them rushed smartly out to greet him. "You'll be staying with us, sir?" He started to write up a claim ticket for the car.

"That's right."

"Luggage in the back?" the valet asked.

"No luggage today." Rollins got out of his car. They were seriously underdressed, but the valet seemed not to notice and merely handed Rollins the ticket. "Have a nice stay."

Rollins and Marj stepped together up the thick red carpet that extended over the sidewalk, then pushed through the heavy glass door and into the long, ornate hall that led to the reception counter in the lobby. The elegant wallpaper, the heavy sconces, the glittering respectability all reminded him uncomfortably of his parents' house.

Rollins approached the sole receptionist on duty at this hour. "We need two rooms, please."

"Actually, one would be fine," Marj piped up at his side. "But make it a really nice one, okay?" She turned to Rollins. "I don't want to be alone right now, all right?"

"Perhaps we can make do with one," Rollins told the receptionist, an earnest young man with a buzz cut.

"Do you have a reservation?"

Rollins shook his head.

"We just came from a fire," Marj explained. "We lost everything."

The receptionist glanced down at his computer screen. "I'm afraid we have only suites left."

"Perfect," Marj said.

"How much is it?" Rollins asked.

"Five twenty-five."

"A *night*?" Marj interjected.

"Yes, sir."

"We'll take it," Rollins said bravely.

"What name?"

"Sinclair," Marj said, nudging Rollins slightly.

"Yes, ah, Peter Sinclair," Rollins said.

"Would you fill this out, please, Mr. Sinclair?" The receptionist handed Rollins an address card. Rollins filled in the name as Peter Sinclair, and gave his old address on Commonwealth Avenue.

When Rollins handed over his American Express card, however, he braced himself for some questions about the discrepancy between the name he gave and that of the cardholder, but, to his surprise, the receptionist said only, "Sorry about the fire, Mr. Sinclair."

A uniformed bellhop named Rafael led them to their room, which was down at the end of the hall. "There you are," he said. The suite was indeed quite splendid—a sitting room and bedroom, both done in the classic English manner. The bedroom had a nice view of the park, and the Common beyond, ringed with Federal-style town houses that were barely visible through the trees. While Rafael explained to Marj about the operation of the TV remote control and the location of the mini-bar, Rollins went around to all the windows, checking the sight-lines, then drawing the blinds and pulling tight the drapes against the now-bright morning sun. He took comfort from the fact that the street was four stories below, making it impossible to see in from that angle.

"Do you think we should rent a VCR?" Marj called over to him. "It's only twenty bucks a night. It seems to have a pretty good list of movies." Marj held up a page from the hotel's welcoming brochure.

"Whatever you think."

The bellhop said he'd bring the VCR by as soon as one became available. "We can have some spare clothes delivered to your room, soon as the stores open," he added. "What are you, a thirty-nine, forty regular?" he asked Rollins.

"Forty-one."

Rafael made a note. "And I'm guessing, thirty-five waist?"

"Thirty-six."

"Thirty-four inseam?"

"That's right."

Rafael smiled. "I used to work at Louis', that's how I know," he said, referring to a prominent Boston haberdashery. "I'll have you lookin' good." He turned to Marj. "Anything for you, ma'am?"

"No thanks. I'm fine."

"All right then." He headed for the door, then stopped. "Sorry about the fire."

"Thank you." Rollins handed him a ten-dollar bill.

"Thank you, sir."

When he left, Marj locked the door behind him. "You sure no one will find us here?"

"Not today."

"Smart of me not to use your name, huh?"

"Extremely." Rollins said it mindlessly as he glanced around the room. When he looked back at Marj, some of her usual radiance seemed to have gone out of her.

"You have been very smart about—about a lot of things," he said quietly.

"Well, I'm glad to get a little appreciation." She glanced around at the furnishings again and took a seat on a faux Queen Anne chair by the wardrobe in the corner. "Pretty fancy. But they'd better be at these prices."

Marj shifted in her chair. "She was spying on you, you know. The whole time, your neighbor was spying on you. I can't believe it. That *bitch*." She stood up and went to the TV console, and flicked on the remote control that was on the top.

Rollins watched Marj's eyes, which were bright with the reflected image of the *Today* show. "It is hard to believe." He thought of Tina's hands on him, from his dream.

Marj clicked off the TV again, and slapped the control down on the countertop. "Have you thought about why?"

"It's what you were saying last night. Sloane must think I've been following him." He hesitated a moment, his eyes downcast.

"What?"

"You were right. I remembered something. I'm pretty sure I saw Sloane about a month ago." He explained about the Land Cruiser being parked in by the Caprice he was following. "It was about a week after I'd been in Londonderry."

"That's just what I was talking about! He thinks you're following him."

"But why?"

"Because he murdered your cousin. It's gotta be."

"Now he's a murderer?" Rollins asked. He'd been puzzling about this ever since he heard the Caprice tape. "What's the motive?"

"Maybe her money."

"But she hardly had any at that point. Seven hundred fifty thousand, tops."

Marj looked at him. "Well, how much does it take?"

Rollins didn't like the direction the conversation was going. "What I mean is, the real money came later, *after* she disappeared. But he was never going to get it, anyway. That money goes to her beneficiaries."

Marj shrugged. "Well, maybe he's one of them."

"I doubt it. It's more likely she'd name me."

"Well?"

"And she didn't. I'd have been contacted by now."

"So maybe they were lovers, and she dumped him and he got mad."

"She's not interested in men, remember?"

"Simple. He wanted sex, she didn't, and he killed her."

"I don't know, Marj."

"There's got to be *some* explanation." Marj retreated to the bed, and dropped down onto her back. She lay there for a few moments. "So, what do we do now, Rolo? Any bright ideas about that?" Marj kicked off her running shoes and sat down on the bed with her feet up straight out in front of her, like a child on a swing. Rollins was standing by the bureau. He noticed that, where he'd draped his hand, he left behind a foggy imprint of his fingertips on the bureau's shiny top.

"It's a nice big bed, at least." Marj's voice was quieter, as though she were closer to him, physically, than she actually was. Marj slid her hand out across the mattress. "Want to try it?"

Rollins felt his stomach tighten.

"Maybe we could relax a little?" Marj scooted farther back onto the bed. "Come on, sit down." Rollins did as he was told. The mattress lurched, and he felt her hand on his shoulder. Her thumbs pressed deep into the flesh about his collarbone, the fingers reaching, fanning out to his shoulders. "Feel good?" She gave off a light, soapy sweetness, with just a hint of sweat, as she worked the muscles in his neck with her hand. "God, you're so tight. All through here." She reached under his shirt collar with her fingertips. "Hot, too, feels like."

"It's been quite a morning," Rollins said.

"We're safe now. You said so yourself."

"For a little while."

A slender hand reached around to pop the buttons of his shirt. A nail scratched him, where it dug underneath.

"You won't need this," Marj said. She came around, and deftly loosened the buttons all the way down.

Neely had taken off his clothes. Late one night after she'd taken him to the movies. He lay on the bed, pretending to be asleep. He felt the clothes slide off him, one by one. So cool, his skin then, before the wrinkled pajamas came on. So warm, her touch.

Marj's tongue protruded slightly from her tightened lips as she undid the rest of his buttons. Finally, his shirt parted in front of him. Marj slid her hands inside and up, slipped the shirt off his shoulders and dropped it to the floor. "Better?" she asked.

"Marj, I—" He felt nervous, vulnerable without his shirt.

Marj pressed a finger to his lips. "Sssh. It's better if you don't talk."

She moved around beside him. "You can relax a little." Marj kissed a shoulder, then nuzzled his neck. The ends of her hair were on him, and her light hands, dropping lower and lower, down his sides. She removed her hands for a moment. Then a rustling sound of what could only have been her pulling off her own clothes. But he didn't dare turn to look.

"There," Marj said. "Lay back down, Rolo. Close your eyes. Just keep breathing, real easy."

Rollins did as he was told, and he could feel his pants sliding off him, then his underwear, too. He was conscious of the rough cloth under him, and nothing above. He reached for Marj's head, to bring her close to him, but she was out of reach.

"Hey," she said from the foot of the bed. "Uncircumcised. Cool."

Rollins looked up: She was naked, too. Slender, with smallish, up-curving breasts, a narrowing slimness that gave way to a slight swelling at her waistline, then a scraggly triangle of dark fur below.

Marj was looking down at herself, cupping one breast, then the other. "What do you think—my boobs okay? I sometimes think they should be bigger."

"They're, ah—they're fine like that. I mean, they're perfect. Absolutely perfect." Rollins' mind was going too fast. "Really." He reached for Marj again. He placed a hand softly between her breasts, closed his eyes again to try to calm his thoughts, and stroked her downward along her belly, grateful for her cool solidity, her Marjness.

"Careful."

Rollins withdrew his hand.

She gave a little purring laugh. "Just joking, Rolo." She crouched down by the bed. "Come on, relax." He could feel her hands caressing his feet. Gradually, slowly, she drew her hands up between his legs, releasing a torrent of fiery sensation. "Feel good?"

His eyes shut tight, Rollins inhaled sharply through his nose.

"That all you can say?" Marj spoke teasingly, her voice nearly all breath as she reached over, pushed a hand between his legs, and slowly drew it forward. Rollins felt one breast surrounding his shoulder as she leaned against him. Rollins' thoughts contracted to the scalloped line of her nails advancing towards his privates.

Rollins' eyes roamed to a reproduction of a gaudy Renoir over the head of the bed. He thought of Tina, his dream. Thought of Neely and what he'd seen so many years ago, and all the horrors that had led to. Thought about the scene at the Overnighter. Thought of Stephanie, floating. His brain pulsed: too many jarring visions flashed before his eyes. He watched himself watching. Marj's electric touch was on him, now, the very base and center of him, slithering lightly over his testicles. He glanced up at her, and her face suddenly loomed huge as she trained her eyes on his groin, of all places. Then she was pulling the foreskin back, lightly, as if she were removing a tiny sock. It was the most tender, most beautiful moment of his life, but instead of pleasure, Rollins felt something closer to pain, as if he were being scratched where he did not itch. His prick remained limp, wounded.

Marj played with him lightly, stroking him. "We can fix this," she said finally. Then she ducked her head down toward his middle. She had just started to kiss him, right there, an act of such generosity it nearly brought tears. But, knowing the whole thing was hopeless, he nonetheless eased her away.

"Oh, it's like that, is it?" Marj asked. The bed quaked for a moment as she lifted off it, just long enough to jerk the bedcovers up over her front.

"It's not what you think."

"Can I ask you a question?" She was staring at him again, he could feel it. "Are you one of those guys that just watches, like that's all you can do?"

"No."

"Don't you do it with *anyone*? Not even, like, small children or something?"

Rollins almost slapped her. He yanked the sheet over himself and curled into a ball.

"Well, I just can't figure you, then. God knows, I tried. I thought, Maybe if I just close my eyes and fuck him. Maybe he'd turn, like, normal." She was talking as if Rollins weren't even there. "What an idiot. What a total fucking idiot." Still covering herself, she groped on the floor for her bra. Rollins heaved himself around to face the wall while she hooked it on. His vision had started to blur, and he needed a chance to clear his eyes.

She'd just finished pulling on her clothes when there was a knock at the door. Rollins rolled off the bed and slipped into a bathrobe while

Marj answered the door. The bellhop had returned with Marj's VCR. "There was one down there after all," Rafael announced, as he came in with a big electronic box in his hands. He looked at the rumpled sheets, then at Marj and Rollins. "If you're still interested."

"Sure," Marj said.

As the bellhop busied himself plugging in all the various wires, Rollins stepped into the bathroom and locked the door behind him. There was a bathtub inside, a large, handsome one that, even if it lacked claw feet, seemed to be fully in keeping with Rollins family standards. He opened the taps up full and a torrent of water poured out. Rollins watched the waters rise for a moment, then went to the window. Through the trees, he could just make out the swan boats paddling about the pond. He'd taken a ride on one with Stephanie a few weeks before she died. His mother had let him hold her briefly, even though he was occupying the outside seat, just inches from the open water. Stephanie had given out squeals of joy and clapped her hands when Rollins pointed out the ducks that swam toward the boat. Possibly, Stephanie was the only one in the family who had ever been happy. Rollins looked down below to the street, watched a Wagoneer pass by the Ritz and disappear down Arlington Street. Then he pulled the shade.

By now, the bathroom was filled with fog, and Rollins turned back to the tub. The water had nearly reached the level of the overflow valve. He turned off the taps, removed his bathrobe, and stepped into the steaming water. He slowly eased himself down, his skin tingling. All around him, the room had gone white, as if he had ascended into the clouds. Color, weight, solidity—they were all gone now as he floated in the whiteness, feeling only the gentle burning of his skin. Guilt, fear, desire—they were all gone, too. He felt peace, completion. He poked his legs out over the far edge of the tub and slid his torso down so that the water lapped at his ears. With each swell of the water, all sound closed off, as though life was over. Then, as the wave receded, life returned with a pop. He lay like this for a while, passing in and out of the nothingness. Then he slumped backward a little more to bring the water up to his nose. With his ears and eyes submerged, the bathroom went liquid, and the whole universe itself became only the vaguest memory. He slid his head down farther and let the water rush in his nose. A queer, burning sensation, but tolerable. He plunged his head to the floor of the tub, peered up at the silvery blur one last time, and inhaled again.

Fifteen

There was a pounding from somewhere far away, then a shout and a ruffling of water, and hands reaching down to him, seizing him under the armpits, pulling on him. Then air, and a great heaviness rising from within, and water spilling out of his mouth and down his chest, and coughing, and fists banging on him, and his name being called, over and over, by an angel. Her voice was much more beautiful than his mother's, which was the only voice he could remember. Then sight again, blessed sight, of white walls and the chrome of the fat faucet and the two sparkling little taps, and the bare flesh of a woman's arm. He clung to the arm with both hands, and stroked it with his bristly cheek. Only then did he register on the other voice, the deep one. "You think he's all right?"

Then the angel again. "Yes, seems to be. Lucky you had a key.

219

Jesus. You never know with some people, what they'll do. He must've fallen asleep or something."

"You sure he's okay?"

"God, I hope so. He's breathing, anyway."

Then the angel's voice in his ear. "Rollins, you all right?"

And his nodding, "Thank you." He clutched her arm and shut his eyes tight, grateful for her, as never before.

The angel, loudly, "Yeah, see, he's okay." Then, more softly, to him, "You sure you're all right? You scared the shit out of me. Jesus."

"Yes, yes. Certainly. I'm okay. Yes. Thank you."

"There, see? He's okay."

"Okay, then." There was a wind on him again as the door opened and shut, and then he reached up to draw the angel down to him. He wanted to kiss her, if he could, and he pulled on her neck, and she said, "Hey, wait a sec." But he didn't care, because his feelings had never been so powerful, and he was pawing at her, and he was big and Neely wasn't there and Tina wasn't there and Stephanie wasn't there and his mother wasn't there, and no one was there but him and her, and he was pushing his hands into her soft parts, and she wasn't pulling away. "Oh, shit," she was saying. "There you go again." Then "Oh, what the hell," and she was pulling her shirt and shorts off, too, and he was seeing absolutely all of her once more, only it was so beautiful this time, so stunningly beautiful, and she was climbing in with him, her gorgeous dark part spread open over him, and she was on him in the water, and she was giggling a little, as if she didn't mean to but couldn't help it, and then her dark part rubbed against him, and he was so big, and so hot, that he nearly burst right then, and she moved a little, sending the waves again and eased him inside her, and he slipped in so smoothly, as though he'd always belonged there, and he felt so hot all over, but particularly there, and he was gasping, drawing the still-steamy air deep into himself, and so was she, into herself, although a little less, and she was wet and slippery wherever he put his hands, and he put his hands everywhere, even on the beautiful little red pips of her breasts, even inside her gaping mouth. The water was slurping out over the tops of the tub walls, and he didn't care, and she didn't seem to care, and he had never felt anything like this before, ever, and he shouted her name as though it were the very word for happiness. "Marj!" he shouted. "Marj! Marj!" He shouted it again and again, slapping the water with his hands, sending up spray onto the tiled walls. Her breasts wobbling, her skin glistening, Marj laughed and tipped her head back and she was giving out little squeals and saying "Oh, God. Oh, God," as she moved her hips on him, and she looked so far away, so lost, but everything was so slithery and indecent it was hard to think, and then the feeling built up and the feeling built up and he started going absolutely stiff everywhere not just there and then he really wanted to shout, but no sound came out, no sound *could* come out, and she straightened and gave out a squeal, then two more, her neck veins swelling blue, and then she slumped down onto him, and her hair was matted and dripping and he brought his arms around her, and now, finally, the bathwater was still, and she said, "So, I guess you are alive," and then she kissed him and he said, "Yes, I guess I am. I guess I am."

Damp and cozy on the big double bed, Rollins groped for Marj again, but she just patted him. "We'd better give your cock a rest or it might fall off." She reached down and gave his penis a shake as a gesture of friendship, but this only made it spring to life once more. "Oh, God," she said. "I just can't." She did let him kiss both breasts, though, before she rolled over and, while he inched his hands down her vertebrae all the way down to the very bottom of her, where the soft flesh parted, she stopped talking and, with a yawn, fell still. He waited a little, staring up at the ceiling, listening to her breath come and go, then he eased himself off the bed, came around to her side, where the covers didn't quite reach. He saw how her breasts drooped sideways, how her hip bone protruded. Her nakedness seemed so tender, so trusting. Maybe she did care about him after all. Then he pulled the covers over her and, with just the softest pat on her shoulder, let her sleep.

He returned to the bathroom. The tub was still full. Some pubic hairs floated on the surface. He reached into the now-cool water and pulled the plug, then picked up the telephone by the toilet—such a strange place for it—and called room service. He ordered crabmeat sandwiches for the two of them, plus champagne, orange juice, straw-berries, and coffee. He had never been so hungry. Then he stepped back into the bedroom, enjoying the air on him.

Marj was standing by the door, eyeing him. "You should probably get dressed, you know. If the room service guy is coming."

"I didn't want to wake you." Rollins was conscious of the deep pile of the rug pushing up between his toes.

"It's okay. I wasn't asleep." She went into the bathroom.

"Not at all?"

"Nope." Rollins heard a tinkling sound, then the rattle of the toilet paper dispenser. "I don't really mind if you look at me. Actually, it's kind of flattering."

Marj returned with her clothes from the bathroom and put them on by the bureau, then sat down beside him on the bed. "Besides, I wanted to make sure that if you were going to go swimming again, you had your life jacket."

From where he was sitting, he could see across to the bathtub. He shifted back onto the bed, and drew his knees up to his chest. He felt cold again.

"I wasn't trying to drown myself, if that's what you mean," he said finally.

"Then what?"

Rollins tightened his arms around his legs.

"You're thinking something, Rolo. What?" She looked into his eyes. "Look, if we're gonna fuck, we've gotta talk. It's a rule."

"Stephanie died facedown." To give details was to bring the scene back—the eerie stillness of it, especially. It was to open the bathroom door again. But Marj was with him now. With her at his side, perhaps he could return inside.

Marj's eyes flared. "Oh, God!" She brought her hand to her mouth. "Your sister! Oh, Rolo, I'm so sorry. I totally forgot."

Rollins' throat hurt just below his Adam's apple. He pressed his chin down against his kneecap; the tops of his thighs pushed against his chest. He had to hold his body tight together, or it might blow apart. "I just wanted to see her again. Just once more."

Marj angled her face toward his. "Well, did you?"

Rollins remembered the glassy sheen of the water as he stared up. "No."

"But you stayed under, Rolo. We had to pull you out."

Rollins spoke as if in a trance. "I saw Neely." She had loomed over him, big as the sky. That was his last thought. Rollins let go of his own legs and reached out for Marj's shoulders. He needed to cling to her if he was going to make it through. "That's why Stephanie died, you know. Because I didn't go in."

She wriggled slightly. "Please, Rolo. Don't hold me quite so tight."

But Rollins barely heard her. He had to push with all his might to say what he had to say. "And I didn't go in because I'd seen Neely."

"Rollins, *please*." Marj finally jerked away. She reared back from him, rubbing her neck and shoulders, which were red where he'd been squeezing. "You were hurting me."

"You didn't understand!"

"You didn't explain!" The words exploded out of her. "God!" There were tears in her eyes.

Rollins climbed off the bed, crossed the room, and stepped into his pants.

Marj reached through the air for him. "Don't go, Rolo. Talk. Please. Talk to me."

Rollins leaned his head against the wall, glad to press against something hard and flat and unforgiving. He didn't want to hurt her, only himself.

Still, he could see Marj watching him. Her shoulders were slumped, and her cheeks glistened with tears. "What am I—your new baby-sitter?" She pounded her hand against the mattress as she spoke. "Or am I just some stupid jerk who doesn't know better than to climb into the bathtub and fuck a person to make him happy?"

Rollins barely heard her. He was going back. He turned back to the wall again, its floral print a complete blur at that distance. What he was about to say he couldn't say to her. It was too awful. He could only say it *with* her. "After my mother put Stephanie in the bath, the phone rang." The words came out slowly. "She told me to watch her while she went downstairs to answer it. But I didn't watch her. I just sat on my bed." He bumped his head lightly against the wall. He deserved the pain. "My mother was downstairs talking on the phone. I don't know who she was talking to. She shouted up to me, reminding me to check on Stephanie. But I didn't. I stayed right where I was. *I didn't think I should go in, do you understand me?*"

"Why not?"

"Because of what she'd said when she saw me with Neely. No, not what she said. I don't even really remember what she said. It was the way she said it. The hate." Rollins closed his eyes. He saw his yellow bedspread, decorated with cowboys. "Finally, I heard Mother say good-bye to whoever she was talking to, and hang up. This time I went to the bathroom door. I listened for Stephanie's shouting, her splashing around, those funny gurgling sounds she made when she was happy. Stephanie was always happy in her bath. She always made a lot of noise. But—" He could see the dark smudges on the door's edge where he had opened it so often with his dirty hands. "But I didn't hear anything in the bathroom. Nothing. All I heard was my mother, coming up the stairs."

"So you went in."

Rollins hesitated. "I opened the door."

If Marj hadn't been with him, he'd never have been able to look through that doorway again, to see the drowned Stephanie, her little head down in the water, her hair billowing around her, and then to go further, to say what he did next, to speak of the thing that, more than any other, had always tormented him.

"You went in, didn't you, Rolo?" Marj prodded.

"No." Rollins rolled his head back and forth against the wall. "I didn't."

"Rolo!"

"I couldn't! I was too scared. I thought if I just shut the door, it wouldn't be true. It wouldn't have happened. She'd be alive. Everything would be fine."

"So you just shut the door?"

Silence.

"Oh, Jesus."

Rollins was having terrible trouble with his eyes. He had to turn his head away from Marj, to stare at the corner of the room, where there was nothing to see. He draped his hands over his head again. His eyes felt wet, his nose was clogged, and he found it impossible to speak.

Then, through the blur, Marj was beside him, turning his face toward hers. "Here." She'd brought him some tissues from the box by the bed. "Try these." She dabbed at his eyes with Kleenex. He had trouble standing, he was quaking so, and he slumped down onto Marj. "It's all right." She helped him back to the bed. "Lie back down here," she told him. "Come on. It's okay." She went to the bathroom for a wet towel and wiped his face.

"I should have been watching her." He could feel the wetness from his eyes spilling down his face, dampening the pillow; his nose was stuffed, and his head pounded. "I should have done something."

"Look, it was an *accident*." Marj spoke so softly. "You were just a kid." She leaned over him, wiping his face. Rollins curled himself around her. He wanted to make himself small again, small enough for her to pick him up and rock him in her arms. But, of course, he was too big for that. Instead, he reached up to cup her breasts through her shirt, and then he pushed the shirt up, and her bra, too, and brought his mouth to her nipples, first one, then the other. Marj took in a breath and pushed her hands into his hair. "Oh, Rolo, Rolo, Rolo. What am I ever going to do with you?"

Then there was a knock on the door. "Room service!" declared an accented voice.

"Damn!" Marj pulled her bra and shirt back down. Rollins pulled the covers up over his head. Through the sheets, he heard the door swing open. He heard the tray go down on a table in the adjoining room of the suite, then a "Sign this, please, miss," and a clipped "Thank you."

When the door closed again, Rollins pulled back the sheets, just in time to see Marj lift the T-shirt up over her head and toss it onto the floor. Rollins lay curled up there on the bed, and she cuddled around him. He loved feeling her soft skin on his back, smelling her sweet breath when she bent down over him. "That's so awful, Rolo," Marj told him. "No wonder—"

"I'm so fucked up."

"Don't say that. That's not what I was going to say."

"That's the truth of it. I never told anybody about this, you know. Even the crappy psychiatrist my parents sent me to, Dr. Ransome. I wouldn't tell him. I couldn't! How could I have just shut the door? Just leave her? It's so . . . evil."

"So why did you?" Marj spoke softly, without blame.

Rollins had to think for a moment to remember that he'd ever had a reason. "Because I loved her. She was the best thing in the family. Absolutely the best thing. I figured if I went in, I'd make her death real." Rollins took the Kleenex from her and blotted his eyes, then he drew another one and blew his nose. "I'm sorry. I shouldn't be doing this."

"Crying, you mean? Gimme a break, Rolo. Everybody cries, especially over stuff like this. You didn't see that, out on your travels?"

Rollins lay there, with his head on her lap, while Marj ran her fingers through his hair.

"But why'd your mother leave you in charge?" she asked him. "That's what I want to know. You were only six. Where was Neely during all of this?"

Rollins took another Kleenex and blew his nose. "I've wondered about that."

"Was this a weekend?"

"It was Saturday, October seventeenth, nineteen sixty-nine. I'll remember the date till I die."

"A Saturday. So your father was home?"

"Yeah, he came running in, too. A few minutes after my mother."

"And Neely? Was she with your brother?"

"No, he was downstairs watching TV. It was a big house. I don't know where she was. She came in a little after."

"How come *she* hadn't been watching Stephanie?"

Rollins turned around in the bed to face her. "I don't know. I always assumed it was because I was so close by. I was playing with my toy cars in my bedroom."

Marj shifted onto her side. "How'd Neely react?"

"She started crying, just bawling. Screaming. My mother actually slapped her, not that it helped, to try to pull her together."

"Jeez."

"The whole scene was so wild—you have no idea. Stephanie on the bathroom floor, the ambulance people rushing around, my parents screaming at me. 'Edward! How could you just leave her there? Edward! Edward!' Like that, over and over." He sniffed, to take in a little air.

"No wonder you don't like the name." She said this quietly, as if to herself.

"I should have told you," Rollins said. "I meant to. But I wasn't sure you really wanted to know."

"I do." Marj stroked his hair. "I want to know everything, Rolo."

Later, after they drained the last of the champagne and licked the final shreds of crabmeat off their fingers, Rollins began to feel a little better. He drifted back to bed, took a deep breath, and folded his hands in his lap as he lay back against the pillows.

"Sleepy?" Marj asked.

He murmured agreement. He rested his eyes for a moment and his body lightened and he was floating. On a calm, blue sea. So peaceful. There was nothing to fear below and, above, there was only a radiant sky from which a yellow warmth beat down upon him. It was like sunshine, only better, more like love, bathing and caressing him all over, suffusing his loins with liquid fire.

The sound of Marj's voice brought him back. She was talking on the telephone at the desk by the window. "Oh, shit," Marj was saying. "*Really*? But it's only a little past noon. Yeah, okay. All right, you send that along. I gave you the fax number, right? Okay, thanks. Bye." Then she hung up the receiver. "Shit," she said again.

Rollins had trouble focusing. Hearing Marj, he wanted to reach for her. He realized that the warmth of his dream had come from her. From her touch: her touch was love, the light touch of her soft skin. "Who was that?" he asked sleepily.

Marj turned toward him. "Lena." A curly-haired girl of that name worked in the cubicle diagonally behind Marj at Johnson. "The market's way off today. That growth fund of Kent McMillan's? It's down like fifteen *percent*. And Henderson is bullshit."

He was still lost in the erotic warmth of his dream. At first the words just washed over him. But then, seeing Marj's distress, Rollins rubbed his scalp with his fingertips, to try to rouse his brain to take in more of what she was saying.

Marj went on: "Five people in the department are out sick today because of some stupid flu that's going around. He asked Lena where I was. Lena didn't know. Then he wanted to know where you were. Lena didn't know that, either. Henderson had that personnel guy, Jackie somebody, call us. When he got no answer at your place, and the machine at mine—well, Henderson lost it." She looked at him more intently. "Are you listening to me?"

Her words struck like ice water. He blinked to clear his mind. "Yes. Of course. Sorry."

"I'm not sure we got *jobs* there anymore, Rolo. Lena said Henderson was sure we were out fucking around. He really used that word, *fucking*! Lena tried to stick up for me. But she said she'd never seen Henderson so pissed."

Rollins eased back onto the pillows. Fired from Johnson? For himself, he didn't really care. Not now. Henderson, Johnson . . . the whole business seemed like ancient history, involving primitive people, petty rituals. And his parents at the bottom of it. Ops was a shit job, just as Marj had said. He couldn't believe he'd ever done it. "Screw them," he said.

But he regretted it when he saw the worry on Marj's face. Obviously, life was different for her, with no trust fund to fall back on. "I should never have gotten you into this," he told her. Then he sensed that such a confession might not be enough. "Look, Marj, if you need any . . . well, you know."

"I'm not going to charge for having sex with you, Rolo, if that's what you mean."

Rollins' jaw dropped to hear those words, and to feel the anger behind them. "No, Marj. Please. That's not what I meant." He wanted to rush to her, to repair this breach between them, but he was still aroused from his dream, and he just *couldn't* approach her right then, not in that state. He never should have fallen asleep. This was turning out all wrong. "I just thought that you might need some money, that's all."

"Well, I don't, all right?" Marj flipped the notepad onto the desk. "Look, I've been shit-canned before, and I'm sure I'll be shit-canned again." Then she dropped down on the chair and fell silent. "Don't worry about me, all right? Just . . . don't. I'll get through this somehow. It's no big deal. I've been through a lot worse." As he watched, Rollins could see her hand grope for the Kleenex box on the desk and bring a tissue to her eye. He couldn't bear that. For her to suffer because of him—that was too awful. Without another thought, he threw off the covers and hurried to her.

Marj turned, and then rolled her eyes at the sight of him. "Oh, God, it's Eddie again."

Rollins looked down—his erect penis was poking out through the opening in his boxers like a man waving from an upstairs window. Mortified, he spun away to rearrange himself, then slumped back onto the bed and drew a sheet over himself, his cheeks flaming with embarrassment.

"It's all right, Rolo. I've seen it before, remember?" Then she sniffled, dropped the tissue into the wastebasket, and turned toward him, her voice full of the sympathy he'd come to love from her. "You want some help with that? I suppose I could, you know, like, do something if you want."

"No, Marj. Really. It's just that I—" Rollins could feel himself flushing, and he turned toward the draperies. If he continued to look at her, he was afraid his erection would never go down.

"What?" Marj prodded. She came and sat next to him.

Her proximity, her remarkable tenderness, the sudden shifting of the sheets, the memory of her in the bathtub—all this provoked him terribly. He tried to think of extremely cold things—ice, snow, winter—and he took a deep breath that he hoped might prove cooling. But she was right next to him, and she deserved an answer. "Well, I guess I was dreaming about you."

"Really?" Marj smiled shyly. "About me?"

His erection was rock-hard and pulsing. But still, going slowly, he managed to tell her about his dream, about floating, bathed in her love—only he didn't use that word, which might have seemed presumptuous. Instead, he settled on "feelings for me."

Marj seemed to melt as he spoke. "That's sweet," she told him. She leaned over to him. "Really." And she kissed him on the side of his neck.

Feeling her lips on him, Rollins couldn't contain himself anymore. He inhaled sharply, and then came all over the sheets.

Rollins was speechless, this moment was so far beyond what words could handle. But his expression must have alarmed Marj.

"God, Rolo, are you all right?"

Everything felt wet and sticky down below, and he was sure that she could smell something. "Marj, I—"

"What?"

He slowly, uncertainly, peeled back the sheets, revealing the mess he'd made.

Marj laughed—a wonderful, carefree laugh. "Well, that's a first," she said. Then she must have feared that she'd hurt his feelings, because she quickly added: "Actually, it's kind of impressive." She went to the bathroom, ran the taps for a moment, and then returned with a wet washcloth. "Here." She handed it to him.

As he wiped the come off himself and the bedding, he didn't, to his surprise, feel particularly ashamed. As for Marj, she hardly seemed to notice. She simply took the washcloth from him when he was done, dabbed at a few places on the sheets that he had missed, then took it to the bathroom, where she washed it out under the tap.

He was sitting on the side of the bed when she came back.

She stood just inside the door. "I didn't mean that, you know—what I said a minute ago about being paid."

"I know," Rollins assured her.

"And this thing about getting fired. That's just something that happens. That's the way I look at it. It's nobody's fault."

"I still feel that if it hadn't been for me—"

"I'll be all right," she interrupted. "I'm pretty good at getting jobs." She smiled bravely. "Had a lot of practice." She turned toward the mirror and fluffed out her hair. "Oh, I forgot to tell you, Rafael dropped off your clothes. They're in the closet."

"You should get something for yourself. I'd pay for it. I mean—if you don't mind."

Rollins thought Marj was about to object. But instead she said only, "Okay. I'll keep that in mind."

Rollins found the clothes on a Louis' hanger inside the closet. There was a pair of cream-colored trousers and a tangerine shirt.

"Hey, a new you," Marj said, looking on by his shoulder.

Rollins put them on right there in front of her. The fit was perfect, but, looking in the mirror, he wasn't sure he was ready for the breezy Californian staring back at him. Marj handed him a pair of tassled loafers and silk socks. "I forgot to tell you, he left these, too."

Rollins pulled them on, felt the slippery stiffness of the new leather through the light silk. He stuffed his hands in his pockets.

"Looking good, Rolo," Marj said, and added a cluck of approval from the back of her mouth.

"I guess it will have to do."

A knock at the door: the bellhop, Rafael, who looked admiringly at Rollins' new outfit. "Fax for you sir," he said, handing over an envelope. Rollins pressed a tip in his hand, then closed the door.

Marj hurried to his side. "I forgot to tell you—Lena said another fax had come in. I had her forward it."

Rollins ripped open the envelope.

You look just like him. The message bore the same rounded script as before.

Rollins and Marj both stared at it.

"Like who?" Marj asked. "What's this about?"

Rollins let his hand go limp. He felt weak. The hits were coming from everywhere. Rollins looked at his image in the mirror, imagined a young businessman on the make.

In these clothes, he might indeed look just like him, now that he'd gone out to the coast.

Marj snatched the fax from his hand. "Who are you?" she shouted at the paper. "What do you want?" She slammed it down on the desk. "God!" She paced across the room in a sudden rage. "Who is it, Rolo? Do you have *any* idea? Is it some creep from college who's trying to bug you? An old girlfriend? Who?"

Rollins sat down on the chair under the window. "It's somebody who knows my father."

"Your father? Why him?"

"I haven't a clue."

"Maybe it's an old girlfriend of his, trying to get back in touch with him."

"Maybe." Rollins heaved himself out of the chair and crossed the room. "I'm going to check with Al." He reached for the phone. "Maybe he's traced the fax number by now." He dialed the Maine number he'd kept in his wallet while Marj lay down on the bed.

Rollins turned away from her, the better to concentrate, when the phone started to ring. In moments, Schecter's voice came on the line. "Al! Thank God I reached you."

"Where the hell are you? I've been calling your apartment all morning."

"I'm at a hotel—"

"A hotel?" Schecter interrupted, chuckling. "What, a little business travel now?"

"It's in Boston."

"Oh, the broad."

Rollins could hear Schecter blow out some cigar smoke. Rollins glanced back at Marj, who was watching him from the bed. "Any progress on that fax number?"

"I've called my guy in California three times now. He tells me it takes time, because there's a lot of shit to go through with these things. You screwing her?"

The crudeness of the verb silenced him.

"Oh, I get it, she's right there!" Schecter laughed again, obviously enjoying himself.

Rollins was not in a joking mood. He told Schecter about Tina being planted in his apartment building to watch him. When he said that, the seriousness of the situation seemed to get through, and it did all the more when Rollins added that he'd found Wayne Jeffries staking out his car this morning. "I'm betting that Sloane hired both of them, Jeffries *and* Tina."

"All right, Rollins, it's time to unload on me now. Three people are on you? What the hell's going on here? What have you been doing?"

"Nothing!"

"Cut the shit, would you? Start at the beginning."

Rollins started to explain about following the Audi in Somerville, but Schecter interrupted him with a roar: "Wait a second. You were doing *what*? You FBI now?"

Rollins' heart sank. Clearly, he wouldn't be able to breeze through this. "No. This is not a job, if that's what you mean. It's just something I'd started to do—in my spare time."

"*What* is, exactly?" Schecter always zeroed right in on any evasions.

Rollins wasn't sure what word to use. He doubted that his own preferred term, "pursuits," would wash. He braced himself. "Tailing people, I guess you'd say."

Schecter blew out some smoke. "You're kidding."

"I've only done it a few times," Rollins insisted. But then he sensed Marj listening in, and he remembered how he'd told her the same. "Well, more than a few, I suppose."

"So it's like a hobby," Schecter said.

"Yes, I suppose you could say that," Rollins admitted, relieved to find a word that was acceptable to both of them. "It's just something I started doing. It helps me unwind."

"Fucking wacko."

"Yes, probably," Rollins admitted.

It was a painful concession, as Schecter must have sensed. "Okay, so you followed this car." He puffed on his cigar. "Then what?"

Rollins described following Jeffries to the dark house, then meeting Sloane there, and spying on him. Schecter listened quietly, taking a pull on his cigar now and then.

"Well, that's the craziest fucking thing I ever heard," Schecter said when Rollins was finally done.

"No one was ever supposed to know, all right?" Rollins said with some irritation.

"No one ever is."

"I called you for help, Al," Rollins reminded the investigator.

Schecter went quiet for a moment. "Just tell me one thing. How's that dykey cousin of yours fit in?"

Rollins told him about Marj's finding the photograph of Cornelia in the *Globe* file on the North Reading house.

"So that's why you went up to Londonderry?"

"Partly."

"What's the other part?"

"I'd rather not go into that now." He wasn't willing to confide everything. There were some aspects of this drama that simply seemed too personal. He could tell Marj, but he'd had to work at it. They came from a part of him that was painful to reach.

"Rollins," Schecter prodded.

"I was just there, all right?"

"Okay, you were just there. And you found out that her house had been sold. So there seems to be some movement there."

"Some."

"Like the maggots are starting to squirm." That was a favorite Schecter expression.

"You could say that."

He took another puff. "And what's the deal with North Reading— Cornelia never lived there, did she?"

"Not so far as I know." Rollins told him that a next-door neighbor had hinted about some wild goings-on in the house, and the *Globe* had reported Sloane's drug arrest. "So there may be a link there," Rollins said. "Cornelia used drugs—marijuana, anyway. Maybe there's a drug connection of some kind."

"Could be," Schecter said, but he didn't sound satisfied. He asked for the street address of the Elmhurst house, then said he would put in a call to the chief of police down in North Reading to see what he could pick up. "We go back a ways." Then he added: "Now, what are you doing tonight? Aside from you know what."

"No plans. We're kind of holed up here."

"Good, because I'm coming down to see you before you get yourselves killed."

"We'll be all right, Al."

"Course you will. Meet me at Joey's at six." That was a Waterfront restaurant he'd always liked. "I'll be in the back. Bring the broad. I'd like to meet her. Deal?"

Rollins cupped a hand over the receiver. "He wants to meet us for dinner."

Marj nodded.

"Fine," Rollins said.

"See you there."

Sixteen

Joey's was an old-fashioned fish place on Atlantic Avenue, a block from the wharves, where the air was wet with the smell of the sea. It had an aquarium just inside the door, and Marj paused a moment to watch the colorful, big-eyed fish swim about. "Look at them," she told Rollins, pointing. "All eyes, just like you." Then she laughed, and Rollins led her inside. She was wearing a long, slinky skirt and matching vest that she'd purchased at the shop downstairs at the Ritz and charged to the room. He was excited to feel the vest's gold brocade under his fingertips, especially knowing that he'd paid for it— and that her bare flesh was on the other side. He imagined that he'd staked a claim to her publicly. As he entered the restaurant, he raised his chin and thrust out his shoulders slightly, conscious of his profile beside this beauty whom he had dressed in gold.

It was just before six, and the restaurant was nearly deserted, except for a few salesman-types at the bar getting an early start on happy hour. Some light jazz was playing, and there were a few neon logos on the walls.

An Asian woman in black came out from the kitchen. "You the ones with Al?" she asked.

"That's right." Rollins nodded. "He said to be here at six."

"I'll take you to your table. He called to say he's running late."

The woman led the two of them back through the dining room to a corner booth, lit by a flickering candle. Schecter had met Rollins here at this very table many times back when Rollins was doing the Blanchard story. Schecter had always dined with his back to the rear wall, so he could scan the crowd, just as he had always ordered the veal. He hated fish, he told Rollins more than once. He came only for the atmosphere. "Every other place seems so new," he'd said.

"You feel all right about this?" Marj asked after the hostess had seated them. "You seem a little edgy."

"A lot's happened today."

"Yeah, well, I'm not too happy to be back near Tina, but I'm trying to at least act calm. She's not that far away, you know."

It was true: Rollins' North End apartment building was just a few blocks away. Rollins had insisted on coming by cab so as not to advertise his presence. "She'd have to be psychic to find us here," he told her.

"She found you before," Marj said.

"That man Jeffries found me. He must have followed me back from North Reading, then told Sloane, and Sloane got Tina to keep an eye on me. That's my guess anyway."

Marj flagged down a waiter and ordered a strawberry daiquiri, and Rollins asked for a glass of iced tea. Marj fell silent, waiting for her drink, while Rollins continued to check his watch and scrutinize the faces of the other diners as they arrived. Finally, the hostess gave out a squeal, and Rollins spotted a heavyset man in a wrinkled raincoat by the front door. Al Schecter. He acknowledged Rollins with a wave. As he handed his raincoat to the hostess, he leaned over to whisper something that caused her to squeal again and then to slap him playfully on his bulky shoulder. "You're terrible," she teased.

Smiling, Schecter made his way down the dining room toward Rollins and Marj, stopping occasionally to say hello to a couple of his fellow diners. The distinctive Schecter scent—a mixture of sweat, cigars, and aftershave—reached Rollins a moment before the detective himself did.

"Edward Rollins!" Schecter bellowed as he swung his thick hand into Rollins' and pumped it a couple of times. Rollins felt comforted to see this big bull of a man. Broad-shouldered, barrel-chested, Schecter had been a football lineman in college, and he still looked like he could go headfirst through a brick wall if necessary.

Conscious of Marj beside him, Rollins started to introduce her, but Schecter broke in. "Hey, she *is* cute." Then he took a step back to survey Rollins' colorful attire. "And she's dressing you, too?"

Schecter winked at her. "What say we dump this guy and go someplace?"

"I can't," Marj replied coolly. "I've already ordered a drink."

Rollins suddenly felt oily inside his new clothes, but Schecter let out a deep-throated rumble of pleasure. "Oh, she's a live one." He slid into the open booth by the wall and set down his briefcase on the seat beside him, then hailed the waiter for a beer. "And he'll have one, too." He pointed toward Rollins.

"I've got some iced tea coming—"

"Fuck that," Schecter said. "I just came from the chief. When you see what he gave me, you'll need some booze in you. *Lots.*"

"What did you find?" Rollins asked.

"Drink up, Rollins." Schecter turned to Marj. "He needs to loosen up, don't you think? So uptight all the time."

"We've been working on that," Marj said.

"I'll bet you have." Schecter grinned, then glanced around at the restaurant walls. "Place has been spruced up a bit. I'll have to speak to Joey." He reached for one of the toothpicks that were set out in a little dish. Silence descended on the table for a moment, but then the drinks came, and Schecter downed some of his beer. "You spoken to Pat at all?" he asked Rollins, referring to his wife.

Rollins shook his head. "No, should I have?" He'd always liked Schecter's wife—a quiet, easygoing woman with a gentle sense of humor, which was key to getting on with Al.

Schecter thought Rollins might have talked to her in trying to get in touch with him. "I was just curious to see how she was doing."

"I take it you're divorced," Marj said.

"Yup." Schecter reached for his beer and took a long chug.

"So what happened?" Rollins pressed.

Schecter looked at him. "I didn't think you cared about personal stuff." He turned to Marj. "This your influence?"

"Maybe I banged on him a little," Marj admitted. "But he's been going through some things."

"So I gather." Schecter finished off his beer and told them the story. Everything had been reasonably steady until the kids were grown and his wife hit fifty. "Pat started going through some changes, getting peevish. Nothing was right for her. Then it was arguments, real bitchy stuff that surprised me. She started giving me shit about the hours I keep. You know how it is, detective work takes time. She started telling me, what's the point of being married if I never see you, blah, blah, blah." It went on like that for a year or two. "Then one night, I come home and no Pat. No note, no explanation. I had to call all over the place to find out that she'd started shacking up with somebody she'd met at the club."

Pat had never struck Rollins as someone who'd take such a risk, and, for all his grumbling, Schecter had seemed happy with his marriage. But then, Rollins had never thought his own parents would break up, either. He glanced at Marj, whose eyes peered out at Schecter over the top of her daiquiri.

"It killed me. We tried to work it out, but she told me she was in love with the guy. Seventeen years we were married. I was in the middle of something like twelve different investigations. But I stopped everything. I went up to Rockport, just for a few days I thought, to try and get my shit together. Been there ever since. I'd always talked about going up there one day. Course, I always thought I'd be there with Pat. But it's just me. I run a little taxi service, shuttling tourists around the islands. It's okay. Been there a year and a half now."

"Who was the woman on the phone?" Rollins asked.

"Oh, that's Annie. I met her last summer. Nice kid. Real sweet. You'd like her. Doesn't give me any trouble."

"God forbid," Marj said.

Schecter looked at her and then to Rollins. "Oh, yeah, a live one," he said again, with a slightly different tone this time.

The waiter came to take their order. Schecter ordered the veal, while Rollins and Marj both went for the trout special.

"Well, I'm sorry." Rollins finally took a sip of beer. It was a watery, American variety, a shade too warm. He thought of Pat, off on her own, with two teenagers whom Schecter had barely mentioned. He felt sorry for himself, seeing Schecter diminished, and for Marj, who had to hear all about it. Breakups, deaths, endings, and departures of any kind—they always made him feel small and helpless.

"Father! Father! Don't go!"

Marj reached under the table and gave his hand a squeeze.

"We had seventeen years. Who knows? Maybe that was enough." Schecter opened his briefcase. "But now drink up." He tapped Rollins' beer glass. "Go on, finish it off. I got pictures here, and some of them are a little rough."

Rollins reluctantly downed the last of the watery brew; he could feel his head lightening.

"Okay," Schecter said when Rollins was done. He withdrew a manila envelope from the briefcase and handed it across the table to Rollins. "Take a look at these. Turned out the chief knew all about that house of yours."

Rollins spilled out a dozen black-and-white glossies. The top one was nearly all skin, bare flesh that looked like plastic in the dim light. Rollins picked it up. His fingertips were soon moist where they touched the photo paper. There was a naked man with his bare buttocks raised over a woman spread-eagled under him, her skirt bunched up around her waist. The couple is down on a rug, and, at this angle, the lower portions of a few clothed onlookers—a pair of shoes, a trouser leg, a short skirt—are visible around the naked couple. Rollins gazed at it with astonishment. "My God, what is this—some kind of orgy?" It seemed to be the stuff of tawdry magazines. "You sure this is the right house?"

"Number twenty-nine Elmhurst, right?"

Rollins nodded, still staring down at the photograph.

"God," Marj said from beside him, her eyes still on the photograph. "Quite a party."

Schecter took another swig of beer. "Chief said it was some kind of swingers club. Saturday night kind of thing. Get in there and fuck whoever." He must have seen Marj's pinched expression. "I know, with all the diseases around?"

Rollins stared at the picture, stunned by its crude starkness. He thought about that ring of onlookers, and now himself, here, watching them. It seemed like a vicious parody of his own night work. He'd tried to capture the whole picture, understanding where the anonymous drivers on random roads fit in to the social landscape. He wanted to know who they were. But these shots simply bore in on the gruesome truth of *what* they were—rutting animals, nothing more.

"They all like this?" Marj reached over and flipped to the second one: A chubby woman wearing only a party hat is sitting on a balding man in a leather chair. His hairy arms encircle her, his fingers squeezing the nipples of her immense breasts. Her mouth is open, her eyelids half-shut, in apparent communion.

"That's so gross!" Marj said. She turned to the third and quickly brought a hand to her mouth. "Oh my God—*look* at that guy." It showed a man in a T-shirt with his pants off, writhing on the bare floor, while a slender woman squats down on his face and a woman with long hair bends over his midsection.

That was all the pictures that Rollins could bear. He reached over, stacked them up again, and passed them back across the table to Schecter.

"Beauts, aren't they?" Schecter said, shaking his head. He caught the eye of the waiter and ordered another round of drinks.

"Who took the pictures?" Marj asked.

"Some neighbor. He shot 'em through a back window with some low-light film. That's why they're so grainy. Then he went around front and snapped all the license plates he could see." He dug through the pile of pictures again. "He got some outside shots, too, of the people coming out."

"How come?" Marj asked.

"Just to bust their balls. It was screwing up the neighborhood, all the cars and activity." He burrowed into the pile again. "Okay, here's where it gets interesting. Check these out."

Rollins didn't move. He wasn't sure he could take this. The images were so coarse, the sex so loveless. He kept imagining a print of him and Marj in the bathtub. Would their own ecstasy look any less dreary?

"Go on," Schecter said. "These are tame. See if there's anyone you recognize."

Schecter picked a few of the exterior shots out of the pile and slid them before Rollins. The house looked slightly different in the bright light of the flash camera, which produced some glare off the metal siding, and turned the shrubs into rubber. But it was definitely 29 Elmhurst: Rollins recognized the medieval door, and the limestone walkway.

The photographs had been taken in close succession, from the side of the neighboring house. In the first one, the faces are all turned toward the street. The next one is closer-in, and two men have turned in shock to face the camera. And in the last one, one of the men is lunging furiously at the photographer, fists clenched.

Rollins looked closer, astonished. "Christ—is that Jeffries?" he asked.

"Where?" Marj leaned into him, hunching over the picture for a better look.

Rollins pointed at the angry man going at the photographer with his fists.

"Oh, my God!" Marj screamed. "It is. It's *him*."

"Thought so," Schecter said. "Check out the back."

Rollins flipped it over and found a label bearing the words WAYNE JEFFRIES in all caps.

"Apparently, Wayne beat the shit out of the photographer. Guy hung on to the film, though, and ID'd him by his car." Schecter reached across the table and tapped his finger by the second snapshot. "I told you, he's a serious hothead. He's lucky the photographer didn't press charges."

"Am I missing something here?" Marj asked.

Schecter looked at Rollins. "You didn't tell her?"

Marj: "Tell me what?"

Finally, Rollins spoke. "He has a criminal record, Marj. He served some time in Concord State Prison for aggravated assault."

"What did he do?"

"Apparently, he stabbed someone in the eye."

Marj gave Rollins a look.

"I didn't want to scare you."

"Well, maybe there are things I should know, even if they do scare me."

Rollins thought about fear, how it had paralyzed him all these years. "I wanted to protect you, Marj. That's all."

"Well, maybe you can't."

Schecter had been watching them, his eyes moving from one to the other during the argument. "Okay, ease back, you two," he said finally. "You're going through some tough stuff here. So let's just take it slow." He pulled out a photograph. "Take a good look at this one. Recognize anybody?"

Rollins looked carefully at the faces. He didn't recognize the two men out front, and two of the people cowering in the background were completely obscured by either a hand or an arm. But there was a woman on the far left, just stepping off the front steps and onto the brick walkway. Her face had been hidden behind one of the men in the first picture, but now, even though she had lifted a hand to conceal herself, Rollins could see some short hair swinging loose as she jerked her head away, and the outline of her face was plainly visible around the edge of her rising fingers. "Jesus," Rollins said.

"*What?*" Marj demanded.

"It's Elizabeth Payzen."

"That's what she looks like?" Marj asked. "I thought she'd be younger."

She did look somewhat haggard, Rollins realized. Graying. "Maybe it's the light."

"I thought it was her." Schecter thumped his hand down on the table with a big, self-satisfied smile.

"But what's she doing there?" Marj asked. "I thought she was a lesbian."

"Who knows?" Schecter said dismissively. "Looks like it was pretty much a free-for-all." Schecter gulped some beer. "But now wait, there's more." He picked through several photographs of license plates. "Okay, take a look at this one."

He pushed the glossy photo toward Rollins. A dark Saab. An antique. As he looked at it, Rollins could feel the blood drain out of his face, and there was a strange buzzing sensation deep behind his eyes.

"It's Father's car. A Saab '96." Rollins shook his head slowly. "What's it doing there?"

"So they were right." Shecter flipped over the photograph. HENRY ROLLINS said the label.

Rollins felt things swirling around him. "Now wait a second, that doesn't mean *he* was there. Somebody could have taken his car and—"

"Then you might want to take a look at this," Schecter said and dipped into his briefcase for a second envelope.

He slid that one toward Rollins.

"Don't open it, Rolo," Marj told him. "You don't need to know any of this." She pushed the envelope back in front of Schecter. "Come on, let's leave. Let's just walk out of here." She raised her voice to Schecter. "Thank you. It was good of you to be so helpful. But I think we're done now. Come on, Rolo. Let's go. We're out of here."

Rollins could feel her hands on him, pushing him out of the booth.

"Okay, have it your way," Schecter said. He reclaimed the envelope with his thick hands.

Marj continued to press against him, but Rollins did not budge. "No," he said evenly. "You were right before. There are things I need to know, even if they scare me."

"But not this, Rolo."

Again Schecter pushed the envelope to Rollins' side of the table. "It's your choice, my friend."

"I know."

"Rolo," Marj said.

Rollins said nothing. His fingers felt stiff as he opened the envelope, and slid out the photograph. Like all the others, it was in grainy black and white, with poor lighting. As he nervously scanned the scene, he saw only skin and shadows at first. But then he saw the man in a suit and tie, sitting in an upholstered chair in the far corner of the room. The hard eyes, the resolute jaw—the sight plunged into Rollins' heart.

"That's him in the chair?" Schecter asked.

Rollins couldn't speak. His mouth and throat were dry as paper.

Do me up, darling?" from his mother, sweet-scented in the front hall, turning her back and lifting her hair away. And his father beside her in his evening clothes, his tassled shoes sparkling, reaching for the fastener at the back of her neck.

"This is just too—sordid," Rollins declared, and he looked across at Schecter, searching his eyes for confirmation.

"I'm with you there," Schecter said.

The sight of his father in the chair lived inside him now, feasting on him.

His eyes burned into the image on the photograph: A fleshy, heavily made-up woman is perched on his knee facing the camera. She is wearing nothing but a pearl necklace, which dangles down over her flabby breasts, while she paws at his cheek with her left hand as if trying to win his attention.

"At least he isn't doing anything too gross," Marj added hopefully, patting Rollins' thigh under the table. "Just watching, looks like."

Rollins twisted around to her, and Marj dropped her eyes, plainly regretting her choice of words.

Schecter cut in: "But now, you see who *that* is, don't you?"

Rollins returned to the photograph, where Schecter was pointing to a couple his father appeared to be observing rather coolly. They are off to his right, a topless woman with short hair leaning into a thickset, shirtless man in the doorway. Looking more carefully, Rollins could see that she's fondling him through his unzipped fly.

"Oh, God," Rollins said.

"It's your friend Jerry Sloane," Schecter said.

"It *is*?" Marj looked again.

"And you see who that woman is, don't you?"

Rollins had. "Elizabeth Payzen again."

"You're joking," Marj said.

Rollins brought his hands over his face, cupping his palms over his eye sockets. He needed to close the world out for a minute, to think.

"So she had something going with Jerry?" he heard Marj ask.

"For a couple seconds anyway."

"And his father *knew* these people?"

Rollins finally removed his hands. "I guess he must have." The world looked soft and blurry now.

"I thought he was, like, classy."

His laundered shirts in a box as if they were brand new, all his shoes shined every Monday, whether he'd worn them or not.

"So did I."

"Chief knew all about Jerry," Schecter said. "He used to deal a little drugs, but mostly he was a good-time guy who showed up wherever the action was."

"Did your friend ever do anything about these?" Rollins tapped the photographs. He felt like he was suffocating. "The police chief, I mean."

"Nope. He didn't go after any of 'em. He didn't really care, so long as it stopped. He pegged Jerry as the organizer, and he put in a call to him reminding him of his drug record. That was the end of it. The party went elsewhere. Chief put all this shit in the file and moved on to other things.

*   *   *

Their dinners came, and not a moment too soon. Schecter pushed the photographs aside and plunged right into his veal, but Rollins just stared at his fish. The head was still on it, the eyes like glass beads, wide open even in death. What had those eyes seen? He pushed the plate away. "How about Cornelia? You ask him about her?"

"The name rang no bells. Course, the chief doesn't get out much."

Marj told Schecter about finding Cornelia's photograph in the *Globe*'s file on the house.

"Can't figure that," Schecter said. "Unless she'd showed up here herself at some point. Chief said this shit had been going on for years. Maybe somebody ran to the *Globe* to try to shut it down. That's all I can think."

"She's not in any of *these* pictures, is she?" Marj asked.

"These were just taken last year."

Rollins looked over at him. "So?"

Schecter stared right back. "Rollins, I keep telling you. The woman is dead."

Rollins reached across the table for the pile of photographs anyway. It was painful to see them all—all the bodies, all the anonymous sex, and his father on the big chair in the corner. He scrutinized the women's faces. None belonged to Cornelia. He passed the photographs back, glad to be free of them, but sorry, too. He didn't want to find her to be in with such a sleazy crowd. But he didn't want her dead, either. He wished he had other choices.

"You ever find out who owned the house?" Marj asked.

Schecter took another bite of veal. "Some people named Glieberman. California types, apparently. Free-living." He turned to Rollins. "That's her on your father's lap, by the way. The *third* Mrs. Glieberman. Chief recognized her. Formerly Mrs. Reid."

"The previous owner?" Rollins asked.

"You heard of her?"

"Neighbor told us." He remembered Mrs. Beuley's account.

"I guess she came with the house." Schecter laughed. "She does some business with the town, I forget just what. They finally bugged out a few weeks ago. I guess they had their old friend Jerry handle the sale."

"Elizabeth's the one that puzzles me," Marj said. "What was *she* doing there?"

Schecter sliced up the last of his veal. "Maybe she got into Jerry. Maybe she's trying to lose herself in the fuckfest. Maybe she's there for the drugs. It could go a lotta different ways."

Rollins straightened up in his seat. "One of Cornelia's neighbors told me that Elizabeth had gone out the night that Cornelia disappeared and come back very late, around three. Did you know that? She made it sound very suspicious."

"I never did get a really good explanation of where she was that night," the detective admitted.

"That doesn't bother you?" Marj asked.

"Only a little. People's lives are messy. Look at yours—hanging out with *this* guy." Schecter took another bite. "A lot of people wondered about Payzen. But I know the cops talked to her at least once."

"The neighbor said they never did," Rollins said.

"Neighbors never know anything. Which one was it? That tight-ass, the stay-at-home?"

"Nicky Barton."

"Right. Nicky Barton." He grinned again. "Personally, I think she had something against dykes." He took another gulp of beer. "There may have been some history between the two of them. Neighbors can be like that. Real bitchy. But I checked Lizzie out. There were some problems there. She said she wasn't in Londonderry that night, but she wouldn't tell me where she was. But still, I had trouble picturing her as a murderer. I mean, where was the heat?" He wiped his fingers and picked out the photograph of her from the manila envelope again. "Okay, check this out. You see a couple of animals coming at the photographer, but Payzen's pulling back, all wimpy like. That's not the face of a killer."

"Maybe that's what Wayne Jeffries is for," Rollins said. "Or Jerry Sloane."

"Or your father," Marj said.

"Now cut that out!"

That brought silence to the table. For the first time, Rollins was conscious of the noise all around them—the clattering of knives and forks, the chatter of conversations. It was like the roar of a vast ocean.

Schecter broke the tension. "Why hire anyone to kill her? Why go to all that effort?"

"And why would these people zero in on you later?" Marj added, with a look toward Rollins. "It's not like you saw anyone do it, right?"

"Me?" Rollins touched his chest. "No. God."

"You have to keep asking him these things," Marj told Schecter. "You know how he is. He won't say anything otherwise."

"I've noticed that, yeah." Schecter's head bobbed in laughter, then he popped a last slice of veal into his mouth.

"So what do *you* think happened to Cornelia?" Marj asked him.

Schecter set down his knife and fork. "I spent a solid year on that case, and I've thought about it a lot since."

"And?"

"And frankly? I don't have a clue."

After dinner, Rollins offered to put Schecter up in their spare room at the Ritz. "What, and listen to you two humping all night?" Schecter said. "No thanks." He'd already made arrangements with an old friend in Belmont. He'd do what he could to track down the Gliebermans, to see what light they could shed on the connection between Sloane and Lizzie Payzen, and he'd keep after his California connection about the fax line. "Now, you sure you don't want me to put the squeeze on this Tina Mancuso for you?" he asked Rollins as he was leaving. They'd discussed her a little over dessert. "Ask her what she's trying to pull?"

"Leave her alone," Rollins told him. "She's minor."

As a precaution, Rollins had the restaurant call a cab so they wouldn't have to wander out into the night on their own. But after Schecter had driven off, and they were in the cab by themselves, Marj told him he should reconsider Schecter's offer.

Rollins shook his head.

"Why not?"

"It wouldn't go well for Heather, okay?" Rollins finally said.

"Okay," Marj said quietly. "I can see that." She nodded slowly, taking this in. "You might have said something to Al. But yeah, I can see that."

He rode along in silence. "My aunt and uncle might help us more."

"Why's that?"

"They made their own deal with Jerry, don't forget. And they must know about the money." Seeing a pay phone along the Common, he had the cabbie pull over.

"You're going to call them *now?*" Marj asked.

Rollins checked his watch. "It's only a little past ten." He climbed out. Dark leaves rustled in the slight breeze, some kids were gathered around a pounding boom box, and a few pedestrians hurried along the lit pathways that crisscrossed the park. He grasped the phone and pressed 411 for information in Weston. When the operator came on, she had to ask him which number he wanted for Dr. and Mrs. Blanchard. (Only Rollins' uncle would make such a big deal of a Ph.D.) "There's one for The Barn, another for The Pond, and Main House." Rollins settled on the last and pressed in the numbers. A cultivated voice answered on the fourth ring.

"Aunt Eleanor?" Rollins asked. "It's Rollins." He waited a moment. "Your nephew."

"Oh, yes, of course. Rollins. I'm sorry. I keep thinking of you as Edward."

They discussed the health of Rollins' mother and the whereabouts of his brother for a few minutes before Rollins was able to get to the point. "I was hoping to come see you," he said. "Something has come up."

"Oh?" Her voice seemed to catch. "You haven't heard anything—?"

"No, no. Nothing about Cornelia. Not directly, anyway. It's just that I've learned a few things about the case that I'd rather not discuss on the phone."

"Well, George is down in Pennsylvania."

"Actually, I was hoping to see you." Rollins had never gotten along very well with his blustery Uncle George. Aunt Ellie could be stiff, but at least she listened.

"I'm not doing too much tomorrow."

"How about now?"

She hesitated a moment. "It's awfully late."

"We'll be there in fifteen minutes."

The Blanchard place was a solid colonial, set well back from the road, with a fenced-in paddock and a big barn beside it. The light was on under the side portico, and, when Rollins pressed the buzzer, what sounded like a small pack of dogs came scampering to the door. After a few moments, a weary voice cried out "Coming, coming, coming." And then the door opened to reveal Rollins' Aunt Eleanor in a mono-grammed bathrobe, her white hair down to her shoulders, restraining three or four collies with her hands. She looked older than Rollins had remembered, thinner, with dark bags under her eyes, but it had been years since he'd last seen her.

She seemed a little startled to see Marj there, and she brought a hand up to her robe. "I wasn't expecting you'd bring anyone."

Rollins introduced them. "This is my friend Marj," Rollins said.

Eleanor showed a half-smile. "Oh? Well, your mother will be pleased. Come on in." With a shout, Eleanor ordered the dogs to back off while she opened the door to let Rollins and Marj pass into the spa-cious kitchen with sparkling marble countertops and brilliant tiles, and every cabinet brimming with crystal and flatware. "We'll go into the dining room."

Rollins passed through the swinging kitchen door to a high-ceilinged, dark-paneled room where a silver tea tray had been set out on the mahogany table, and a few Pepperidge Farm cookies were arranged artfully on a Chinese plate beside it. "I asked Ginger to put out a little something for us," Eleanor said.

"Very kind of you." Rollins took a seat on one of the heavy, Shera-ton chairs, and Marj pulled out another one beside him.

Eleanor sat at the head, then leaned forward to Rollins and clutched his arm with a bony hand. "Please. I have to know. I'm sitting down now. Have they found her?"

"No. It's nothing like that. I'm sorry. I thought I'd explained."

Eleanor slumped back into her chair. "Oh, God. You did. But I couldn't think why else you'd come." She balled up her linen napkin and looked away for a moment. Then she looked across to Marj. "It's such a terrible situation." Eleanor blew her nose into the napkin, then steadied herself and poured out some tea for the two of them into beautiful Wedgewood cups. "Go on," she urged Rollins and Marj. "It's herbal. It won't keep you up."

Rollins set his cup down in front of him. "Look, Aunt Ellie, I went to see Cornelia's old house." He looked at her carefully. "It's been sold."

She dropped a lump of sugar into her tea and swirled it around with a silver spoon.

"You don't seem surprised."

"Why should I? Your uncle George and I put it up for sale ourselves."

"But you didn't own it."

Eleanor set her spoon down in her saucer with a clink. "Of course we did. It just wasn't something we wanted everyone to know."

"When I was doing—that story, I spoke to a private investigator on the case, who told me that the deed was in her name."

"So?"

"So you couldn't have sold the house. It wasn't yours."

"That's ridiculous." The words bore the sound of something breaking. "Of course it was ours. Look at the deed, you'll see that George signed it over to the new people. I was there at the closing. I saw the whole thing."

"The Stantons, you mean?"

"Yes. That's it. Quite good people, I thought. We were so happy that house ended up in good hands."

"And not Elizabeth Payzen's?"

Eleanor fixed Rollins with an icy look. "Whoever said anything about her?"

"Neely left her everything, didn't she?" Rollins could sense Marj staring at him hard.

A shot in the dark, but a hit.

Eleanor brought her hands from her lap to the tabletop, a gesture that seemed somehow aggressive. "That detestable lawyer of Neely's, Mr. Eliot, wouldn't breathe a word about that. Not even to her parents!

Oh, he was vile. You should write an article about *him*."

"That's why you turned to Jerry?"

"Do I know a Jerry?" The voice was lofty, contemptuous.

"Your realtor, Jerry Sloane."

"Oh, yes, of course. Mr. Sloane." A slight smile crept over her features. "He seemed to know things. Yes, he was very . . . helpful."

"Wasn't that a little risky, Aunt Eleanor?"

"Whatever do you mean?" Her eyebrows raised.

"I wouldn't have thought that Jerry Sloane was your type."

"Oh, but he came very highly recommended."

"Really?"

"Yes, by your mother." She said this airily, as if discussing trifles. "She seemed to know him quite well."

Rollins glanced at Marj, who met his eyes with a startled look of her own.

Aunt Eleanor gave out a delicate laugh. "You seem so surprised! But your mother—she knows lots of people, you know."

"I wonder how you happened to ask her."

"We talk occasionally, your mother and I."

Rollins replied quickly: "Anything to keep Elizabeth from getting the house, and all her things, is that what you mean?"

Mrs. Blanchard set down her teacup. "She was our only child." Rollins braced himself for a furious outburst. Instead, she reached to enclose Rollins' hand in hers.

Paper beats rock, Neely always told him. And rock beats scissors.

"Your family suffered a terrible tragedy of your own when your darling little sister died. I know that. But at least you could put a headstone on her grave." Mrs. Blanchard dabbed at her eyes again. "Oh this is terrible," she muttered to herself. "I vowed I would not let this happen."

"It's okay, Mrs. Blanchard," Marj told her.

Eleanor's lips quivered. "Neely was under a cloud there for so many years. She took the death of your sister so hard. She blamed herself. It took her years to recover. She had nightmares. She had to take another year off before college. And she spent a long while trying to find herself afterward. I just wish she'd never gone to Londonderry. A mother can tell—this wasn't her way."

"Lesbianism, you mean?" Rollins asked.

Eleanor put down her napkin. "I suppose that's the word for it. I'd always loved her early poems. Not that nonsense about vaginas. Nature was her subject. That second volume . . . Well, you saw who it was dedicated to."

"Elizabeth."

"Neely was trying to free herself when she died. She told me so. I went to see Elizabeth once in Londonderry after the disappearance—perhaps you heard?"

"No." Rollins was surprised he hadn't.

"I wanted to meet the woman who'd had such a powerful effect on my daughter. I never had met her, you see. I sometimes think that Neely had deliberately kept me away. So I went there, and I knocked on her door and told her who I was, and, to my surprise, she invited me in. We had coffee there on the deck behind the house. You know what she asked me?"

Rollins shook his head.

"She asked me about Stephanie. She asked me if Neely really had had a cousin who died in the bathtub. I said, yes, that happened. She said that was good to know. Neely had talked about it, often. It had weighed on her. I knew that, of course. But the thing was, Elizabeth said she could never be sure that it really had happened, or whether it wasn't cover for something else. That was her word, 'cover.' I asked her, 'Whatever do you mean?' She said she didn't know, exactly. She just thought that the dead baby was some sort of emblem." Eleanor lay down the napkin. Her eyes were red. "I don't know what I was expecting from her that day. A confession, perhaps, or maybe an explanation. I didn't get anything like that. When I'd finished my coffee, she walked me back to my car. As I was leaving, she said she was sorry. I said, 'For what?' And she said, 'For everything.' And then I drove off. And that was the only time I ever saw her."

Seventeen

At the hotel that night, Rollins and Marj cuddled together under a sheet, listening to the AC hum as the shadows from the street below played across the ceiling. The air-conditioning had been Marj's idea. They'd left their clothes out to be laundered overnight and gone to bed naked. It was wonderful to feel her skin on him—a bare arm, a hip, sometimes a leg thrown over his, but Rollins must have finally drifted off because he woke up to find Marj on top of him. "I thought you were awake," she whispered as she eased herself down on him, sliding his erection deep inside her. "You're hard as a rock."

Afterward, they drowsed again until dawn, when Rollins let his fingers stray down to her pelvis, and they went at it once more. "It's been a while for you, hasn't it?" she asked him when they were done. "I mean, before me." When Rollins nodded, she kissed him. "Poor baby."

Rollins played with her nipple. "Do I have to go through hell to get you?" he asked. "Is that how it works?"

Marj pressed a fingertip down on his nose, just as Neely had. "If you do get me."

The words frightened him, but they were quickly dispelled by her hand, which reached down to encircle him once more.

They were both sound asleep when the telephone rang at nine. It was Schecter. He'd gone out to Wayne Jeffries' house in Somerville, a piece of information that Rollins had trouble processing right then. "I thought if I had a talk with him," Schecter went on, "I might be able to clear this whole thing up." Unfortunately, Jeffries had driven off the exact moment Schecter pulled up, and Schecter had followed him to a small two-family in Melrose. The detective was parked outside there now, talking to Rollins from his cell phone. Rollins realized he could hear the street noises in the background.

"But get this," Schecter told him. "I checked the name on the mailbox. It's Mancuso. No first name, but I figured it's got to be that neighbor of yours."

Rollins was horrified to think that a temptress like Tina and the frightening Jeffries had formed such a tight alliance against him.

"I can't see if she's inside there, too, and I'd like to know what I'm dealing with." Schecter wanted Rollins to find out if Tina was in her North End apartment. "I tried to call, but the number was unlisted, and I don't have time to hustle it down. Check on her, would you please? Because if she's not there, I bet she's here with loverboy."

Rollins leaned back against the headboard, thrust a hand into his hair. As Marj eyed him uneasily from the other side of the bed, he tried to calm the panic that was rising in his chest.

"Al, are you sure this is the way to go?" he asked. "Jeffries seems a little wild to me." Schecter was going right at Rollins' pursuers, when every instinct told him that it was better to keep quiet, to watch and wait.

"I can handle wild," Schecter said. "Crazy, now that's something else."

Rollins pointedly didn't ask what Schecter had in mind. With the detective, he'd always sensed there were certain aspects to his investigations that he'd just as soon not know about. All he knew for sure was that Schecter got results. "All right," Rollins told him. "I'll go right over, and I'll call you back."

"Be quick about it."

Marj did not like the idea of paying Tina a surprise visit, but she didn't want to stay behind, either. The two of them pulled on their clothes—Rollins in his Californian outfit, and Marj in her running clothes, all of them cleaned and pressed by the Ritz. And they tidied themselves up as much as they could. Then they grabbed a couple of pastries from the continental breakfast buffet downstairs and climbed into the Nissan the moment the valet brought it around.

It gave Rollins a strange feeling to be behind the wheel again. The car seemed a little tighter than he remembered, and older, too. He'd had it only six years, and it still ran fine, but there were 350,000 miles on it, and he realized the engine sounded rougher than it used to, impeding conversation, and the clutch point was lower than it should be. Of course, it was wonderful to see Marj in the passenger seat beside him, her slim bare legs making sticky sounds on the vinyl, her hair fluttering in the breeze of the open window. But it was odd, too, inexpressibly so, as if her presence required a different car altogether—a larger one perhaps, or possibly a different model, something more in a family line than this tiny Nissan.

It was a lovely summer morning, the rising sun beginning to burn off the moist coolness that had settled in overnight. Rollins drove up over Beacon Hill and around the back of Government Center to the North End. He pulled up on a side street around the corner from his Hanover Street apartment; the Nissan would be less conspicuous there. He told Marj to wait in the car and lock the doors. She did so, glumly. He was beginning to sense that she resented being told to do things, even if they were obviously for her protection. She also lowered the visors, and slumped down low in her seat.

Rollins walked up Hanover, the street glowing a peach color in the morning light, and unlocked the front door to his apartment building.

He stood for a moment in the hall, listening for any sounds from the second floor. Then he quietly climbed the stairs. At the top, he checked to make sure his own door was still securely locked. Then he made his way down to the Mancusos'. His plan was simply to listen at the door, then slip away the moment he heard Tina's voice. He was cautiously inclining his ear toward the door when it flew open with a shout. "Boo!"

Rollins recoiled and shot his hands up in the air. But it was only Heather. She leaped onto him and clung to him like a monkey. "Hi, mister!" she said. "Scared you, huh?"

"Sssh." Rollins whispered, quickly setting her down behind him. "Is your mother inside?"

Heather shook her head. "Nope. She went out."

"She say where?"

"I think she went back to our house."

"You have a house somewhere?"

"Yup." She wrinkled her nose. "I wasn't supposed to tell you that."

"And she just left you here?"

"Yup," Heather said again, pouting. "*After* she promised to take me to the beach."

Rollins could see now that she was wearing her bathing suit, a bright blue one with green stars.

"Can you take me, mister?" She folded her hands in prayer. "Please?"

His mind formed several excellent reasons why he couldn't, but before he could voice any of them, Heather had dashed inside. In another moment, she was standing in front of him again, towel and teddy bear in hand. "I'm ready."

Rollins groaned inwardly and told her to wait a moment while he went to call Schecter from his apartment. Heather followed him in, anyway, and made straight for his refrigerator. This time, he shut the door behind her.

On the phone, Schecter thanked Rollins for the information. He'd wait there at the house until he could catch either Jeffries or Tina alone. "Him or her, I don't care."

Rollins hoped it wouldn't be Tina, but he was in no position to tell Schecter that. "Just to find out why they've been following me?" he asked.

"To figure out what they know about what happened to Cornelia. That's what this is about, Rollins. I spoke to Rose Glieberman yesterday night. Took me ten phone calls, and I woke up half the city. But I got her. She's split up now with that douche-bag husband of hers. That's why they're selling. She'd known your dad out in Oregon, years back. I guess they'd had something going out there."

Rollins had heard more than he wanted to know about his father's love life, as Schecter must have sensed because he switched back to Cornelia. "I don't like the fact that she was mixed up with these low-lifes. That Jeffries is an animal. He could have killed her and never given it a thought."

Rollins closed his eyes. He couldn't believe he'd ever taken Jeffries for an insurance agent. He had been watching so carefully all those years, making such shrewd deductions about the strangers he pursued, and yet he hadn't grasped the first thing about them. It was jarring to think how much he had missed, how much time he had wasted with his absurd suppositions.

"And get this," Schecter went on. "Rose had the impression that Cornelia had come into some more dough *after* her disappearance."

"She did," Rollins replied. "From her grandmother. Might be as much as eight or ten million by now."

Schecter was silent a moment. "Are you kidding me? Are you *kidding* me? Maybe ten million bucks and you didn't think this might have been worth mentioning? You got shit for brains or what?"

It wasn't good to talk about money. The numbers commanded attention they didn't deserve. "I didn't think anybody would know about it. The family's kept it pretty quiet."

"They obviously didn't keep it too quiet if the fucking Gliebermans know!"

"That money doesn't have anything to do with me," Rollins insisted.

"That's what you think."

Once again, Rollins resented his superior tone. "So you tell me—what's the link?"

"To you? I don't know, but I'll pull it out of 'em, don't worry."

When Rollins hung up the phone, Heather was standing right in front of him. "Ready?"

Marj was slumped down deep in her seat when he returned. "Took you a while," she said as he opened the door. Then, seeing Heather, she added, "Well, look who we have here."

Rollins explained to her about Tina's absence, and then, more hesitantly, about the beach plan.

"I don't think we're dressed for it, Rolo," Marj replied, and she set her mouth in a sulky expression that Rollins had learned to watch out for.

"I am," Heather said. "See?"

"I don't believe this," Marj mumbled, turning away.

"So I thought Heather would like to get out of the house for a while," Rollins wound up. "Have a little fun. Besides, I think we could all use a break."

Marj turned to him again. "You might have asked me first, all right? Not told. Asked. I'm in on this, too, you know."

Heather piped up from the backseat. "Is everything okay, mister?"

Rollins glanced back at her. She'd fastened her seat belt over the hump, and she'd belted in her teddy on the seat beside her. "We still going to the beach?" she asked.

"Sure," Rollins said.

"Yay!" She clapped her hands.

Marj glanced back at Heather for the first time. "Hi, honey, I guess we're going to the beach."

In Rollins' estimation, the only beach worth visiting was the one by his grandmother's big house in Gloucester. After crossing the Charles, he veered off 93 onto Route 1, where he pointed out to Heather all the cartoonish highlights along the roadside: the bright orange dinosaur on the miniature golf place, the giant cows at the Hilltop Steak House, the forty-foot Leaning Tower of Pizza. Rollins was pleased with himself. Maybe he had a way with children, after all.

It took about forty minutes to get to Gloucester, which was out Cape Ann on the North Shore at the very end of route 128. The center of town was a seedy fishing village, its air thick with noisy seagulls scavenging for garbage and heavy with a briny sea smell. But his grandmother's was away from all that, by Coffin's Beach, well to the north. Along the way, Rollins told her what Schecter had in mind, although he had to do it obliquely since Heather had perched herself on the armrest between the two rear seats and was watching the two of them very intently. Rollins didn't think that Heather should hear too much about the possibility of Schecter grilling her mother.

As Rollins pulled into the driveway, its shattered clamshells crunching under the Nissan's tires, he could see a few cars with New York license plates parked by the barn. Some of his Arnold cousins must be visiting, children of his mother's brother, Lloyd, a big New York investor and his second wife, a pretty Parisian named Marie.

Rollins had filled Marj in about the greater family on the way up. And he'd tried to impress her with the scale of the house itself, which was commensurate with the size of the family. As a child, he'd always been delighted that it afforded him so many places to hide. It probably wasn't much bigger than the Brookline house, but it had an entirely different feeling. The Brookline house was filled mostly with empty space, but the Gloucester place was crammed with adventure. There were over fifteen bedrooms, each one seemingly filled with a cousin or two, and any number of sitting rooms, parlors, pantries, nooks, and intriguing back halls. There was even a bowling alley in an annex off the barn, where hammerhead sharks and barracudas were mounted on the walls. And all of it was commanded by Rollins' late grandmother, invariably enthusiastic and carefree and not at all the stiflingly proper society matron that her daughter, Rollins' mother, became. Neely had visited with them once, that last, lovely summer before Stephanie died, and, with Rollins' grandmother leading her on, she'd led many a game of Capture the Flag on the sand flats at low tide. But the gloom that had enveloped the family after Stephanie's death had extended even to here, and Rollins had never had anywhere near as good a time afterward. The family continued to come for a few years, but finally stopped after the divorce when everything seemed to become such an effort for his mother.

"It *is* big," Marj said as she stepped out of the car. "It's like the Ritz."

Heather said nothing, merely craned her head up at an extreme angle to take in the whole structure.

A stiff breeze was blowing. Some flags flapped on their high pole out front, and Rollins' shirtsleeves fluttered as he stepped onto the wide wraparound porch to the front door. "Anybody home?" he shouted. When no one answered, he pulled open the screen door and stepped inside. The big front hall was cool and dark, with musty air that seemed to have been preserved for generations like everything else. All around, there were red and blue winners' pennants, crisscrossed tennis rackets, water-stained prints of yachts, and other testaments of the active summer life hanging off the high pine walls.

"Anyone home?" Rollins called again. Finally, he heard footsteps slowly coming his way through the dining room and an elderly woman in blue appeared. There was a moment's pause as Rollins strained to recognize her, and, evidently, vice versa. "Edward?" she called out at last. "Gracious sakes alive. Is that you?"

"Alice?" Rollins replied.

It was indeed Alice Farnsworth, the house's longtime caretaker. Rollins remembered her from his own childhood, although she must have been well into her sixties now. She gave him a hug, then took a step back from him to declare that he hadn't changed a bit, while they both smiled at the obvious untruth of such a statement.

Alice's gaze turned to Marj and Heather, standing together a few steps back. Rollins quickly introduced his "two friends." Then, seeing Heather's impatience, he added: "We're very eager to go to the beach."

"Well, come on, then. Tide's just coming in." Seeing they lacked towels, Alice went to get some from the linen cabinet upstairs. When she returned, she explained that his Arnold cousins were off sailing at the yacht club, and she filled him in on exactly which members of the family had come. The older two, Whit and Geena, had each brought "special friends," Alice said with raised eyebrows. "Your grandfather would never have stood it." Unlike his grandmother, his grandfather, also long dead, had always been a strict constructionist where propriety was concerned. Rollins thought he should translate for Marj, explaining who was who, but her eyes seemed slightly glazed, and he let it go. Finally, Heather plucked loudly at the hem of her bathing suit, and Alice handed him the towels. She offered to find some trunks for him, but he didn't think he was up for a dip just now. Alice said nothing to Marj, but she told Alice, "I don't need anything either, thanks." Alice looked mystified for a moment and sent them on their way.

"I don't think that woman liked me," Marj told Rollins as they set off across the road and down a narrow earthen path through a field of wildflowers to the beach. The sun's warmth seemed to radiate off the hard-packed ground as they ambled along.

"She just doesn't know you," Rollins reassured her.

"You didn't do too much to fix that, now did you?" she snapped, and then, leaving him to ponder that, she went on ahead with Heather.

Rollins caught up to them at the bluff, where they took in the view of the long beach, very wide now at low tide. Although the Arnolds owned the meadow, the beach itself was public, and there was a motley array of bathers with parasols, radios, Frisbees, and air mattresses scattered about. Marj led Heather down a weather-beaten staircase, and, with Heather beckoning, Rollins followed. He found a secluded spot to lay out a couple of the towels. But Heather ran on down to the water, with Marj trailing after. Holding his hand up against the sun, Rollins watched Heather hop up with a shout when a wave splashed over her feet, then run shrieking from what must have been a sand crab. He could see Marj hold up a tiny wriggling creature and make reassuring gestures. In moments, Heather came racing back to him to plop her teddy bear down on Rollins' towel and beg him to come down with her. "You have to!" she cried as she reached down and gave Rollins' hand a yank. "Please?"

"Oh, all right." He reluctantly removed his shoes and rolled up the pant legs of his new trousers, and followed her down. Neely had played here as a teenager, years ago. She was fleet-footed and a wonderful swimmer. But with Heather there, and Marj watching, he couldn't form a clear memory. Did she wear a bikini? Flip-flops? Did her nose burn? Any image of her kept dissolving to the sight of Marj in her running clothes bending down to Heather, now holding up a starfish. Distracted, Rollins nearly jumped when an icy wavelet splashed up toward him and lapped at his toes. He couldn't believe that the water had always been this cold.

Marj started laughing.

"What?" Rollins asked.

"You! You're such a geek." Marj mimed him reacting to the frigid water.

"It's cold."

"Oh, please."

"Come *on*, everybody!" Heather grabbed Rollins' hand, then Marj's, and tugged them a few more steps into the water. It wasn't too bad, once his feet went numb, and Rollins enjoyed feeling the water swish past his ankles. But after a rogue wave drenched a few inches of his pants, he declared he'd had enough and retreated to higher ground.

He returned to his towels on the soft sand with Heather's teddy beside him. The nearby boom boxes were annoying, and it was irritating to have a wet dog shake itself dry right next to him, which soon happened. Yet, as he stretched out his legs, and drew his hands up under his head, and felt the sun beat down on him, he recalled the long games of Frisbee, the kite-flying and sandcastle-making from his own childhood vacations here, invariably delicious breaks from the lonesome monotony of home, and he realized just how pleasant it could be to pass a summer day at the beach. He could see why his grandparents had bought the house, and why the family had kept it all these years. He might try to come back here himself one summer. With Marj, perhaps, now that they seemed to be out of jobs. Maybe he'd even figure out a way to bring Heather along.

Down by the water's edge, Heather and Marj flitted about like a couple of butterflies—Marj in her pink and red, Heather in her shiny blue suit. Both of them flapped their arms girlishly as they chased after the retreating water, then, with nearly identical squeals, scurried back ahead of the onrushing waves. They seemed to be enjoying each other, Rollins was glad to see. He glanced up once or twice. But the sun's warmth was soothing, and the sea sounds were oddly restful, once you ignored the shouts of all the other sunbathers. Rollins rolled up his sleeves, and pulled his pant legs up a little more, and lay back again to let the warm summer air lull him. The sky was a deep blue, with wispy clouds sailing across it. He mused sleepily about the three of them. Were they a kind of family? He felt himself smile at the thought.

He must have dozed off, because the next thing he knew, the sun was much higher in the sky, and the left side of his face felt raw and hot with sunburn. He raised himself up a little and saw that he, the teddy, and the towel he'd been lying on were surrounded by a narrow trench that was half-filled with water. And Heather was squatting beside him, laboring with a clamshell, busy diverting the rising tide from his little circle of sand. "You better not move, mister, or you'll get wet."

Rollins tried to focus on his watch. Could it really be almost twelve? Had two whole hours passed? "Why didn't you wake me?" He worried about Tina coming back and finding Heather gone.

"The lady said she'd worn you out last night." Heather continued to deepen the moat around him. Still, the tide sent occasional waves up over the moat's interior restraining walls, soaking the backs of Rollins' heels.

How could he have been so careless? He recalled, now, that he'd just been contemplating his own paternal status when he drifted off—and then he'd jettisoned his paternal responsibilities. He squeezed his eyes tight to push the sleep from his mind, then climbed to his feet and looked about. "Where is she, anyway?" A knot of worry tightened in his gut.

Heather stood beside him and shrugged. "I don't know."

An upwelling of irritation. "What do you mean, you don't know?"

"I don't."

"She didn't tell you where she was going?"

"I was kinda busy." She squatted back down to return to her work.

Shielding his eyes from the bright sky, Rollins scanned the beach more carefully, but there was no sign of Marj. He made a megaphone of his hands and shouted for her—"Marj! *Marj!*" Heather put her fingers into her ears and a number of the bathers around him turned toward him. Rollins' bowels felt as if they were twisted.

He led Heather farther down the beach, searching for Marj and calling. They went well past the last clump of bathers, two or three hundred yards distant. But he saw no sign of her. He called for Marj again, and waited for a return shout. But he heard only the sound of the sea pounding on the beach, and the cries of seagulls. He shouted again, louder. His yell sounded desperate, even to him. Teddy in hand, Heather shouted, too, at a higher pitch.

Fear gnawed at him, and Rollins turned to the little girl. "You remember that friend of your mother's, Jerry Sloane?"

Heather scowled. "He's mean. He called me 'kid.'"

"You didn't see him on the beach, did you?"

"Nope."

"Did you see anyone else you recognized?"

She nodded. "Yup."

Frightened, Rollins grabbed her with both hands. "Who was it?"

"You!" Heather gave him a big smile. "Fooled ya!"

Rollins glanced at his watch. It was twelve-thirty now. "Damn." He led Heather back the other way, searching and calling. The little girl chugged alongside, kicking up little puffs of sand as she went. Rollins' feet were raw from the sand, and his lungs heaved.

"Uh-oh!" Heather pointed to the moat as they passed it by. Rollins had left his shoes and socks inside it, but the tide had risen up over its banks to lap at the soles of the shoes.

Rollins hurried past without a word.

With Heather scrambling after him, Rollins continued on down the beach, past one spit of sand reaching down to the water, then another. Finally, Heather pointed. "Look!" Then she scurried ahead. When Rollins caught up, Heather was holding Marj's pink top in her hands.

Rollins took it from her without a word. The material was so loose and light in his hands.

"Hey, look, over there!" Heather pointed to Marj's red shorts that were just a few feet above the reach of the water. Rollins looked out to sea, and he saw a figure out in the surf, barely outlined against the fierce glint of the water under the high sun. Rollins saw an arm flash, then he heard a shout. "Hey, what time is it?"

"Marj?"

A glistening woman, obviously female, pushed through the water toward him, rising as she came. She was in her underwear, but, soaked through, they did little to cover her.

Rollins put his hand over Heather's eyes.

"Hey, I'm decent." It *was* Marj. "Jeez."

Rollins nearly threw himself on her, even though she was soaking, he was so glad to see her. But Marj stepped away from him, and flicked her head back to shake the water from her hair. "You bring one of those towels?"

Rollins had left them inside the moat; they were probably sopping by now, or gone. Heather handed the top to Marj, who awkwardly pulled it over her wet, sticky skin. She had to hop a little on the sand to get into her shorts. "God, the body-surfing's incredible here! With all the wind, the waves were *perfect*."

"We were worried about you, you know," Rollins said.

"We were calling and calling," Heather added.

"I'm sorry." She said it lightly, as if their fears couldn't have been a big deal. "I had to go way off since I didn't have my suit."

"You might have borrowed one."

"It would have been a hundred years old."

"We thought maybe some guy got you," Heather said.

"Out here? Nah. No way." Marj plucked her shirt loose from where it stuck to her skin.

Despite her assurances, Rollins and Heather each held a hand of Marj's as they made their way back up the beach to retrieve Rollins' things.

The Arnolds had returned from the morning races and had settled themselves around the big table for lunch when Rollins, Marj, and

Heather returned to the house. He needed to call Schecter, but the cousins, a little boisterous after what must have been a good showing out on the water, gave out a big shout when they saw Rollins come in. Uncle Lloyd demanded that he come over and introduce his "family," as he put it. Rollins explained that he and Marj weren't married, actually, nor was Heather his daughter. "Marj works with me at Johnson," Rollins explained, remembering Marj's annoyance that he hadn't been so forthcoming before, "and Heather's a neighbor."

"Got the day off today, have you?" Lloyd asked.

"Something like that." He glanced at Marj.

"Oh, playing hooky?"

From the loudness of their inquiries, Rollins figured they had been making good use of the sweating Heinekens that were grouped on a silver tray in the middle of the table.

"I didn't think you'd run off and gotten married on us," said Wick, a robust-looking thirty-something whom Rollins last remembered as a pimply adolescent.

"Not like your father," Lloyd added. "Where's he hiding out these days? It's been years since I've laid eyes on him. What's going on there, you have any idea?"

"Actually, I have kind of lost touch with him myself." He thought of his father in Schecter's photographs. The whole table quieted, and a few heads shook sorrowfully.

Marie, in her soft French accent, followed by asking about Cornelia, as if there were a natural link between one disappearance and another.

"Neely?" Rollins asked, to make sure he understood correctly.

Marie nodded in that brisk French way, and the room went still once more, except for Heather, who was swinging Marj's hand. Rollins tried to close out the conversation by saying that he didn't know anything more than he'd written in the *Beacon* story, which he assumed they'd all seen. But the family only asked more questions. Even the "special friends"—a stunning redhead who seemed to belong to Whit, and a handsome blond fellow who sat beside Geena—chimed in. They all wanted to know: Where could Neely be? Was she really dead? Perhaps Rollins' status as an expert on the case freed them to raise a topic that would otherwise have been off-limits. Nevertheless, it distressed him to hear the vast house—a place where Neely still seemed so alive—ring with such questions. The very sounds seemed to be driving her away again, out into oblivion. Rollins was able to silence them only by declaring that he was about to call a detective who might, in fact, have news for him about the case.

"Right now?" Whit asked.

Rollins nodded.

"Well, how dramatic," Marie said.

Rollins used the telephone in the game room, settled onto the wicker settee, with a view of the surrounding marsh.

"And where the hell have you been?" Schecter asked the moment he came on the line.

Rollins had to tell him he was in Gloucester, which caused Schecter to sputter with amazement, and that only got worse when he said he had Heather with him. But his voice moderated as the detective thought the matter through. "Well, hang on to her," he told Rollins. "Who knows? She might come in handy. But get your ass down here. If you ever want to get any answers on this case, now's the time."

Rollins returned to the dining room, where Heather was now sitting on Geena's lap while she took bites out of her chicken salad sandwich, and Marj looked on tentatively from beside the mantelpiece, adorned with a model of a clipper ship. Perhaps she didn't belong in such a place, with these people.

"Well?" asked Uncle Lloyd as he popped a slice of hard-boiled egg into his mouth.

"We should go," Rollins said.

"Has something happened?" Whit asked eagerly.

"Not yet. But it might soon."

The group all professed disappointment that Rollins and his "friends" had to leave so soon. They were going to put up the net for badminton after lunch, and Marie was organizing an expedition into town to buy lobsters for dinner. Geena would have liked to show Heather the upstairs.

"Do you play bridge?" the redhead asked Marj. "We were trying to get up a foursome."

Marj shook her head. "Sorry."

"How about canasta?" asked Whit.

"I don't even know what that is."

Geena did her best to sound reassuring. "Well, I'm sure you have lots of talents that we don't know about."

By then, Rollins had led Marj and Heather into the front hall, where Heather retrieved her towel and teddy bear, and then, shouting one last round of good-byes, they headed out to the car.

Rollins' face was sore with sunburn, and his discomfort was not less-ened by the sullen looks that Marj, still damp and sandy, gave him as they drove south. He thought he'd done a little better to fit her into the group, but now Marj made it sound as if she wasn't sure it was worth the effort. "Are they all like that?" she asked.

"Like what?"

"Rich, I guess I mean." She swept the hair off her forehead. "They don't seem very nice."

"They're okay, just a little loud."

"You sure you're not just trying me out like those new clothes of yours? I keep thinking you'd be better off with a preppie like that Geena."

"You mean, I should stick to my own kind?"

"Maybe."

"Thanks a lot!" Rollins thought if he said it in a joking way, then she'd dismiss the whole idea as a joke. He shifted gears. "We don't have to go back there if you don't want. I don't have much to do with my family, as you may have noticed." He waited a moment, unsure if this was the time to say this. "I liked seeing you with Heather."

"Oh, we're having kids now, is that it?"

Rollins prudently remained silent, but, out of the corner of his eye, he could see Marj staring at him, shaking her head as if she couldn't believe what she was seeing. "Sex really gets to you, doesn't it?" she said.

"I'm serious."

"I know you are. One thing about you, Rolo, is you are always serious." There was only a slight edge to her voice, which Rollins appreciated.

Marj turned to check on Heather, who was snoozing in the backseat.

"She is cute, isn't she?" Rollins said.

"Look, Rolo, maybe we should talk about this some other time, okay?"

Rollins returned his eyes to the road. "Of course."

Schecter had given Rollins the Melrose address, which was off Upham Street near the center of town. Rollins had driven through the congested downtown a few times before, on one pursuit or another, but it seemed like a new place now that he knew Tina Mancuso lived here. He turned down a narrow street lined with modest two-story houses bounded by tiny yards.

"Hey, that's *my* house!" Heather shouted when Rollins drew near a gray dwelling topped with a TV antenna.

"That's right. A friend of mine and I are going for a visit."

"Can I come?"

"No, I think you better wait with Marj."

Heather made a long face and slumped down in her seat. "I wanted to show you my room."

"Maybe later," Rollins said.

"We'll have a good time," Marj assured her.

Schecter's silver Cressida was parked up ahead, a short ways down from the house. Rollins tapped on the window on the passenger side, and Schecter popped the lock. Rollins took a seat beside him. Schecter was wearing a University of Maine baseball cap, and he was working a cigar, which had filled the car with smoke.

"Took her swimming, huh?" Schecter tamped the ash into the tray under the radio.

Rollins didn't want to discuss it. "Tina leave yet?"

"No, Wayne did."

After spending the day with Heather, Rollins wasn't sure he was ready for an ugly confrontation with her mother.

"Just a couple minutes ago," Schecter went on. "I tried to follow him, but I got cut off by a fat-assed truck. Maybe you should give me surveillance lessons. I seem to be losing my touch." He glanced at Rollins, as if to see how such a rare gesture of self-effacement was going down. "I was going to see if I could pick him up at his house, but I didn't want to lose the broad. She's still in there, as far as I can tell."

Rollins must have frowned because Schecter asked, "Why, you got a problem with that?"

"I'm worried about Heather."

"Nothing's going to happen to Heather."

"Tina's going to figure out that Heather told us about the Sloane connection, and she's going to take it out on her."

"So?"

Rollins had adjusted the rearview so that he could see Heather and Marj in his car behind them. Heather was up in the front seat, flipping the sun visor up and down. "She might get hurt, Al."

"Rollins, look, don't go soft on me, all right? The kid'll be fine."

Rollins looked over at him. "Are yours?"

"Cut the shit, would you?" Schecter said angrily. "You want to keep running all your life? Is that what you want? And what about that girl-friend of yours? You want her to keep running? You can't even live in your apartment anymore. I mean, my God, Rollins, where does it stop?"

Rollins shifted uncomfortably in his seat.

"Go ahead. Wimp out." Schecter stubbed out his cigar. "I'll go in there myself." He opened the door and climbed out of the car, headed across the street to the Mancuso house.

To gain something, did you always have to risk something else? Rollins slammed his hand down on the seat beside him, then opened the car door to follow. "Okay," he called out to Schecter across the street. "Just wait a second, will you?"

Schecter took Rollins by a high fence where they couldn't be seen from the house and he laid out the plan. They'd go in together. Rollins would get first crack at asking the questions, then Schecter would follow with his own. "I've got my gun, in case anything happens." He pulled back his jacket to show Rollins the small automatic in the discreet leather holster on his belt. Rollins had seen the gun before, but it stunned him to see it again in a situation where he might use it. "Oh, quit worrying," Schecter told him. "I'm just going to throw a scare into her." Schecter went on a few steps, then stopped again. "She was fucking with you, don't forget. She was really jerking you around."

Schecter led the way up to the front door. The house could have used a little work. The shingles looked battered, and a couple of window panes were cracked. Up on the concrete landing, Schecter had Rollins press the buzzer while he himself stood well off to the side, out of view.

It took forever for the door to open, and when it did, it only cracked open a few inches, secured by a thin brass chain at about eye level. "Well look at this," Tina said. "What are you doing here?"

"I've got some questions for you."

"Sorry," Tina said. "Not buying today." She started to close the door, but before she could lock it, Schecter stepped across and rammed his shoulder into the door, ripping the chain off the door frame with a splintering sound. He bulled his way inside, and Rollins followed behind.

Tina gave out a shout and started to run upstairs, but Schecter grabbed her by the wrist and dragged her over to a swivel chair in the living room. "Sit down." He shoved her into her seat.

"I was just going to get my robe." She was dressed only in a thin, silver nightgown that barely reached her knees. It didn't look like she had anything on underneath. She crossed her arms in front of her.

"You won't need it," Schecter told her. "It's nice and warm today." He nodded to Rollins, and he shut the door behind them, and turned the bolt.

"Get some tape, would you?" Schecter called to Rollins. "Check in the kitchen."

Frightened, Rollins didn't ask why. He went into the kitchen, a meager space, and tried a few of the drawers. He found some duct tape in the cupboard over the refrigerator. He brought it in to the living room, which was largely unfurnished and had no rug on the floor. Tina was in the swivel chair, with Schecter standing over her.

"What do you want from me?" Tina demanded. "Why are you doing this?"

"We just want some answers to a few simple questions," Schecter said. Then, to Rollins: "Tie her hands."

Rollins didn't think he could participate in anything like this. "Are you sure—?"

"Do it!"

Rollins started to pull off a few feet of tape.

"I've got some questions for *you*." Tina swung an arm toward Rollins. "What were you doing following my boyfriend all over the place? Answer me that."

Schecter leaned down toward her. "Shut the fuck up."

Tina said nothing, her chest heaving. She glared at Schecter.

"Now, put your hands behind the back of the chair," Schecter told her.

Tina left her arms where they were. "Go to hell."

Suddenly, Schecter grabbed Tina by the front of her nightie and yanked her out of her chair. Schecter drew her to him and took her left ear and twisted it sharply, forcing her head back. "Ow, ow, ow," she yelled, gasping. Her chin was pointing nearly straight up, exposing her neck, and some of the whiter skin down her front.

Rollins pulled on Schecter's shoulder to get him to stop. "Don't, Al. Please. Don't hurt her."

Schecter shoved her back into her chair. The neckline of the nightie was torn, exposing the top of one breast. Tina tried to cover herself. Schecter leaned down toward her menacingly. "Hands behind your back, I said."

Tina did as she was told, and Rollins bound her wrists—slender, with silver bracelets he hadn't noticed before—with several rounds of tape as she made fists.

"Now the feet," Schecter said. "One on each chair leg."

Rollins hesitated. "For God's sake, Al."

"Just do it." Schecter pushed her knees open.

"Oh, into S and M, huh?" Tina asked. "You are really sick."

He ignored her. "*Now*," he told Rollins.

Rollins pulled off more tape and, crouching down, affixed each ankle to one of the chair's two front legs. In his hands, he could feel the slight stubble of her shaved legs. Her feet were cold to his touch.

When he was done, Rollins stood behind Schecter, looking down at her. It gave him no pleasure to turn the tables on Tina, to toy with her the way she had toyed with him. He only felt sorry for her as she strained in her chair, her shoulders contorted so awkwardly to accommodate the hands bound behind her. And her torn and rumpled nightie barely covered her.

"All right, how do you know Jerry Sloane?" Schecter demanded.

"Fuck off," Tina said.

"Well, a tough one. I hope you said a nice good-bye to your little girl this morning."

Finally, there was some distress in her voice: "What have you done with her?"

"Nothing yet." Schecter pushed his hands onto either side of her face and gripped her ears again. His face was just inches from hers. "But there's no telling what I might do."

This time, when he withdrew his hands, a tear trickled down the side of Tina's nose. She flicked her head to the side, as if to dispel it.

"That's much better," Schecter said. "Now, why don't we start by your telling us about Jerry."

Tina looked down at the floor.

Schecter started to reach for her one more time.

"Okay, I'll tell you what I know. Just don't touch me, all right?"

Schecter drew back his hands. "Jerry," he repeated.

She started to speak, timidly at first. She confirmed things they already knew, like the fact that Sloane sold real estate and lived in Medford, then moved on to how Sloane had been in charge of the operation. "He got Wayne and me to watch him," she said, nodding toward

Rollins. "We were supposed to report his movements, every day. Make a note of where he went, what he did. Wayne handled everything outside, I did the inside." As she spoke, Tina's eyes rarely left Schecter's face. Her breath did not come smoothly. And the nightie was so thin, Rollins could see it flutter with each beat of her heart.

"So, how'd you get involved?" Schecter asked.

"Through Wayne." He'd sold real estate part-time for Sloane Realty, Tina explained, but he was always available for extra jobs if the money was right. "He was the one who figured out you had this crazy driving thing, following people," Tina said, finally looking up at Rollins, just for a moment. It gave Rollins a chill to hear his pursuits described like that. While Schecter listened with his arms folded across his chest, she explained that Jeffries had been watching Rollins' car one evening when he saw the Nissan suddenly take off, then keep on for ten miles, then pull up across from a house where a car had just turned in. Sloane had thought Wayne was "totally fucking nuts," as Tina put it, when he'd suggested that Rollins followed people pretty much at random. So he'd gone out to prove it by driving by Rollins' car several times when he was idling that night in Union Square. "It was like he was throwing out a hook," Tina said. "And finally you bit." But Jeffries had panicked once he'd found Rollins behind him. "And he couldn't shake you! He goes here, he goes there, but you stay on him like a bloodhound." In desperation, he'd gone back to the one house beside his own to which he had a key, the one in North Reading. It had just gone on the market. He hid in the basement for hours, hoping Rollins would go away. Sloane was furious about that. "I guess that house was owned by somebody he knew. He was afraid you'd trace it."

At that, Schecter reached out and grabbed a handful of her hair and jerked her head back.

Tina gasped, and her eyes widened.

"But why?" Schecter demanded. "Why'd you pick on my friend here?"

Tina's breath came faster, and her head was at an awkward, painful angle. "Because Jerry *told* me to. The money was good. Two hundred dollars a day, plus expenses, each."

Schecter twisted her hair, making her gasp. "I don't give a shit about you—you got that? I know everything I want to know about you. You're a fucking whore. End of story." Schecter bent down to her, thrust his face into hers. "What did Jerry get out of it? Why'd he want to fuck with my friend?"

"We didn't ask questions."

Schecter let go of her hair, stepped back and slapped her hard across the face, leaving an angry red mark. "Don't give me that."

Tina squirmed and whimpered a little. Tears spurted down her cheeks. "Okay! Okay—just don't—just don't hurt me anymore. There was money."

"Whose?"

"I don't know."

Schecter whacked her again. Harder this time. A slim line of blood trickled down from her left nostril. Rollins winced, but he didn't dare try to restrain Schecter, who loomed over Tina. "I'm not going to ask you again," Schecter said.

Terror was in Tina's eyes as she looked up at Schecter now. "Okay, goddamnit. Okay. It seemed like a big inheritance or something like that. Somebody was dying, and there was a lot of money involved. And you"—she lifted her eyes toward Rollins—"might screw it up somehow. That's all I know."

"Go see if you can find a pair of pliers," Schecter told Rollins. "We're not getting anywhere with this bitch."

"Wait," Rollins said. He dabbed at her nosebleed with a tissue he'd found. "Who was dying?"

"Like I said, he never told us."

Schecter leaped at Tina, ready to smack her again, but Rollins held him back.

"Was it Cornelia?" Rollins asked. "Cornelia Blanchard?"

"He never gave any name."

"She's holding out on us," Schecter scowled.

"It was a woman," Tina added hastily. "It was a woman, I know that much." Her eyes stayed on Schecter.

"But where?" Rollins asked. "Where was she?"

"Shit, I don't know. I can't even think straight anymore. Some place near Boston. Waltham, Brookline. One of those."

Schecter moved closer, his hand raised.

"Al, please," Rollins stepped between Tina and the detective.

Tina looked up at Rollins imploringly. "Please, Rollins—Ed—don't let him hit me again! Jerry was always going in to town. That's all I know."

"He ever say anything about a fax?" Rollins asked.

"A fax?" Tina scoffed. "Shit no." Then she braced herself, obviously terrified of Schecter.

"Hang on a second, Al." Rollins pulled up a wooden chair and sat down beside her. There was something he had to know, and he thought he might get more if he spoke to her from her level. "Did Jerry ever mention my father to you?" Just to say the words "my father" in this room under these circumstances made Rollins feel that he had committed a terrible betrayal. His insides went hollow as Tina squirmed, but she said nothing.

"I'll get the pliers," Schecter said. "I'm getting tired of this." He started to go into the kitchen. "Rip her nightie off—we gotta get going here."

"No! Wait!" Tina shrieked. "Yes. Yes, he did. Once."

Rollins' whole body filled with dread. "You're sure?"

Tina nodded.

"What exactly did he say?"

"I went to his house one time a few weeks ago, and Jerry was just getting off the phone, and he looked real tired, and he said your dad was a hard man to work for."

The words seemed to have disabled Rollins' brain for a moment.

"Jerry Sloane's working for my father?" he asked. "For my *father*?"

"That's what it sounded like." She said this casually, as if it were an insignificant detail.

Schecter yelled at her: "Give it up, you fucking bitch!"

"That's all I know, I swear." She started to whimper again. "Please don't hurt me." She turned back to Rollins. The blood from her nose had started to flow again, over her upper lip this time, but he merely stared at her, transfixed. "He called him Henry," she went on. "I had to ask him who Henry was, and that's when he told me, your father. That's right, isn't it? Your father is named Henry, right?"

Rollins nodded, but he still didn't follow. "What do you mean, 'work for'? How could Jerry Sloane possibly be working for my father?" Even after the photograph from the dark house, it seemed inconceivable. Sloane could have known his father, sure. Sloane could have talked to his father. Sloane could have attended drug-infested orgies with his father. But Sloane could not have worked for his father. Not on this.

"For the money—the inheritance," Tina said. "At least, that's how Wayne figured it. We sent Jerry reports."

"Reports?"

Those tortoiseshell glasses of his father's, very thin and elegant, and the unusual way he read, his head up slightly, trying to maintain the correct focal distance, as if disdainful of text.

"Yeah, sometimes written, sometimes over the phone. Telling him what you were up to. Who you'd been with, where you went, like that."

"But why?"

"He didn't tell us why! Okay?"

Schecter stepped closer.

The blood was trickling down over her mouth to her chin. Rollins swiped it away with the tissue. "All right, listen to me," Rollins said, boring in on her. Another question had been building inside him. "One last thing. Did Jerry ever mention my mother, Jane Rollins?"

"Your *mother*?" Tina looked startled for a second, then her eyes softened into a fleeting look of sympathy before she shook her head. "Not that I heard. Just the dad, and just that one time." Then, more quietly, she added: "Anyways, it's all over now, whatever it is."

"What makes you say that?" Rollins asked, puzzled.

"Jerry told me I was all done."

"Why?"

"I keep telling you—*I don't ask questions*. He paid me my money.

I'm done. I'm moving my stuff out of that apartment this afternoon." She looked at Rollins, then Schecter. "That's it. Everything. You gotta believe me."

"Course we believe you," Schecter said. He went into the kitchen, and Rollins heard him rummaging through drawers.

"What's he doing?" Tina asked, frightened all over again. "What's he gone to get?"

"I don't know," Rollins told her.

Schecter came back into the room with a long, serrated knife.

"Don't let him hurt me!" Tina shouted when she saw it.

"This is all I could find," he said, casually. "Lucky for you."

"Al, please," Rollins said. "I think she's told us all she knows."

But Schecter brushed off Rollins and held the knife in front of the bound Tina's eyes. "Take a good look." He brought the tip of the blade down her nose, then down across her lips to her chin, then, trailing a thin white line down behind, dragged it down her throat to the neckline of her nightie. "You can fuck with him," Schecter told her, "but you better not fuck with me." He scraped lightly at the pale skin between her breasts. "You understand me? This is the end of it, right here. No more. Got it?"

Tina nodded.

Turning the knife sideways, Schecter brought the tip of the blade down the light fabric. It descended with a purring sound, over her belly, down to her crotch. Tina squirmed slightly to see it there, deep in the fold between her open legs. Schecter picked at the hollow with the knife tip, dimpling the fabric by her vagina. Tina's eyes were fastened on the knife as her chest heaved. She strained, trying to wriggle farther back in her chair, but the tape securing her ankles held her rigidly in place.

"Scared?" Schecter asked.

Tina nodded.

Schecter got a better grip on the knife and gently pressed. "Really scared?"

Tina flinched and sucked in some air. She nodded again.

"Good. Remember that feeling."

Schecter bent down before her, blocking Rollins' view. He heard a ripping sound, then another. He expected screams, but heard none.

"There," Schecter said, standing up. He'd released her feet. He went around to the back of the chair, and with another slice of the knife freed her hands.

Tina stood up, clutching her rumpled nightie to her chest. Scraps of tape still surrounded her wrists like a pair of bracelets. "Fucking bastards," she said. The tears were streaming down her face, and the blood was dribbling from her nose onto the carpet

"It was nice to meet you, too," Schecter said as he led Rollins out the front door.

Schecter shut the door behind them, then lit up a cigar as soon as he was outside on the walkway. "Decent piece of work, that," he said.

Rollins could barely contain his fury. "You didn't have to hit her. You heard her—it was over. She was willing to tell me what she knew."

"What do you know?" Schecter said, taking a satisfied puff. "She's a piece of shit. Okay? That's what she is. You want to get the truth from a piece of shit like that, that's how you do it. You don't act nice. You scare the crap out of 'em. It's the only way."

"You lied to me."

"Listen to you," Schecter said, chuckling.

"You said you wouldn't hurt her."

"So she cried a little. Big deal. Maybe she'll smarten up next time. The point is, we got what we needed. You can stop running now. We're hitting back. And if you ask me, it's about fucking time."

Rollins would have argued with him, but he didn't see the Nissan where he'd left it behind Schecter's Cressida. He was suddenly afraid that something terrible had happened, but then he heard a horn honk, and he saw the Nissan come up around the corner, with Marj at the wheel. "I thought it would be better to wait around the corner, out of sight," she told him when she pulled up.

Rollins told her they'd found out everything from Tina that they could, but they didn't tell her how.

"Can I see my mom now?" Heather asked from the backseat.

"Of course," Rollins told her. He helped her out of the car, and took her by the hand up the sidewalk. To his relief, Tina didn't appear when he rang the doorbell. But the door was still unlocked, so Rollins opened it and stepped inside with Heather.

"Mommy?" Heather called out from behind him.

Tina appeared at the head of the stairs. The nosebleed had stopped, but her eyes were red with tears, one side of her face was still raw from where Schecter had struck her, and her whole body looked limp.

"Hi, Mommy," Heather said. "Mister took me to the beach."

"Get the hell out of here," Tina told Rollins.

"He took me to the beach, Mommy. We had a nice time."

"Look," Rollins said. "I'm sorry. I didn't mean—"

"Just go."

Heather looked at him. "It'll be okay," she whispered to him. "She gets like this. Don't worry."

"I said, go!" Tina roared from the top of the stairs.

"If anything happens, leave a message for me with Marj Simmons." He gave Heather the number and spelled the name for her, just in case. "If you forget, the number's in the Boston phone book, or call 411 for information. Okay?"

"I'll be okay." Heather gave him a hug. "Bye, mister."

Marj and Rollins had a quick lunch in the Ritz cafe while Rollins filled her in on Tina's revelations—carefully omitting the part about Schecter's rough tactics in obtaining them. Marj went pale when he told her that his father might be actively involved. "Jesus, Rolo," she told him, slowly shaking her head. "Your *father*? He's behind all this shit?"

Rollins could barely speak. "It looks that way."

Seeing her narrowed eyebrows and tightened lips, Rollins was afraid he was losing her. He reached for her hand. "Hang in with me, Marj, please," Rollins begged her. "I need you."

"Okay, Rolo. But God—"

When they returned to the room, the message light was on. "From a Mr. Schecter," the Ritz clerk said when Rollins called down. "He says he traced the fax number. It belongs to the Holy Name Hospice, six twenty-eight Franklin Street in Watertown."

"Hospice?" Marj asked when Rollins relayed the information. "What the hell is that?"

"It's where people go to die," Rollins said.

Eighteen

It was well after three when Rollins and Marj reached Watertown square, its ancient millworks by the Charles surrounded by modern office buildings and strip malls, and everything bright in the afternoon sun. Franklin was a side street a few blocks from the center of town. He spotted a parking space on Arsenal, the main thoroughfare, and he was pulling over to parallel park when he noticed the Audi behind them. A dark blue, he could see now. Not black. It was idling by the side of the road a half block back. And a slim man was driving.

"What?" Marj started to glance back behind her.

"Don't turn around. He's straight behind us. The Audi."

Marj gave out a groan.

"I'm pulling out." As soon as Rollins started to move again, he could see in the rearview that the Audi was starting up, too. "He's following us."

"Goddamnit!" Marj slapped her thigh. "What is wrong with them?"

Rollins clenched the wheel as he sped down Arsenal to the next light, then, with a quick glance behind to the Audi in his rearview, he pulled into the Arsenal Mall. At this hour on a weekday, the parking lot was nearly empty.

"Where the hell are you going?"

"There." Rollins bobbed his head toward a narrow passageway between the mall's two wide buildings. It led to a second lot behind, Rollins knew, and he made straight for it.

"Look out!" Marj pointed to an eighteen-wheeler rumbling toward the passageway ahead of them.

Rollins jammed down the accelerator and felt himself thrust back in his seat as the Nissan charged ahead. A few pedestrians turned and stared. Trailing a cloud of exhaust, the delivery truck roared on toward the passageway.

Marj grabbed the dashboard.

Rollins floored it. The needle tipped toward seventy.

"You're not going to make it!"

The truck was just about to pull in to the passageway, leaving no room for the Nissan.

With one last burst of speed, Rollins charged forward and nipped in front of the truck, which braked and let out a furious blast from its horn as the Nissan flew past. The earth fell away as the passageway dipped underneath them, and then a terrible scraping thud as the belly of the Nissan smacked on the slight rise on the far side.

He almost didn't see the little VW coming.

"Rolo!" Marj whipped her arms up in front of her face.

He slammed on the brakes and pulled hard to the right. There was a screech of tires under him, and he could feel the Nissan slipping sideways, out of control. The Nissan's rear was spinning out toward the Beetle, but Rollins twisted the wheel back the other way, regaining some purchase. He braced himself for a crash—but none came. By a miracle, the Nissan slipped by, leaving another cacophony of honking behind him.

"What about the Audi?"

Marj dropped her arm from in front of her face and craned her neck around. "Gonzo. No, wait! There!" She pointed behind them.

Tina must have called Jeffries, and he was taking out his rage on the only enemy he knew. The gaunt man made no effort to conceal himself now. It was personal. Rollins could feel the hatred, rising up like the heat off the asphalt. The terror that Schecter visited upon Tina was being returned to them.

Rollins stepped on the gas, and the Nissan shot ahead to the far end of the mall. Tires screaming again, he pulled a sharp left around the building, and sped to the rear mall entrance. But the light was red and Rollins had to slow. His heart pounded, and the side of his neck throbbed.

"He's catching up!" Marj said, her head twisted around behind. "He's almost on us!"

The cars were streaming by in front of them, but Rollins saw a slight gap in the traffic and gunned the Nissan across the wide avenue, causing drivers from both directions to slam on the brakes and lean on their horns. On either side, Rollins could see their faces contort in fury as the sound of squealing tires rose up all around him. But, again, the Nissan slipped through unscathed.

"He still coming?"

Marj twisted back around again. "I don't see him."

Rollins hooked his first left, sped down two streets and then cut right. "He there?"

"No."

Rollins pulled in behind a Dumpster and eased back into his seat. Sweat poured off him, and every pulse was racing. When he closed his eyes, he still saw cars careening toward him, but, as he sat there, breathing, the sight gave way to other flickering scenes from farther away—distant houses, shadows, and then Neely again, darting through the trees, her blond hair streaming behind her.

Catch me, catch me if you can!

Marj massaged her temples. "Now *I'm* going to get a migraine."

Rollins glanced back, but his view was blocked by the Dumpster. "We lost him, right?"

"Yeah. Back at the light." Marj unbuckled her seat belt and shifted around in her seat to face him. There was sweat on her cheeks and across her forehead. "Christ Almighty. I thought for sure we were going to get blasted." He saw something different in her eyes when he glanced over. Before, she'd always seemed to look slightly askance, as if she were trying to make up her mind about him. But now, as she stared at him straight on, it seemed that she'd decided something. "You're a helluva driver," she said.

Rollins waited there, resting, trying to find the calmness that would allow him to continue. He closed his eyes for a moment. Then he leaned over and planted a kiss on Marj's hair. "Thanks."

He started the car back up and, still watching for the Audi, wound back to Franklin Street. He pulled into a municipal garage. "I doubt he'll look for the car in here," Rollins said.

"Wait—you're not still going in."

"It's the only way, Marj." Schecter had been right about one thing. He couldn't keep running forever. He took the ticket from the automatic dispenser. "We have to find whoever was sending those faxes."

"He might be waiting for us inside. He must know why you're coming here."

"It's a hospice, Marj. He can't go after us in there. It's too public."

"I think we should call the police."

"And tell them what?" He could imagine the smirking reports on the evening news—*A stalker today came to the police with bewildering claims of being stalked himself.* He'd be lucky if the police didn't arrest him on the spot—if they didn't put him in a psychiatric hospital for observation. "No, thank you." Rollins pulled in to a space up on the second level, toward the back. He undid his seat belt and pulled back the door handle, then turned back to Marj. "Coming?"

Marj slowly undid her seat belt. "We could have gotten killed back there, you know. That VW, Rolo—did you see how close it came?"

"I did," he said. He closed his eyes for a moment.

He climbed out of the car and went around behind to help Marj out. But she'd already gone on ahead, her running shoes squeaking slightly on the glossy floor of the garage. He hurried after her and caught up to her just inside the doorway to the stairs. She reached for his hand, pulled him to her, and hugged him tightly. "Just hold me for a second."

He patted her back, stroked her hair. "It'll be all right," he whispered. Finally, her grip eased.

"I get scared sometimes," Marj told him. She opened her hand as if grasping for something. "I mean, *Jesus*. I don't care about this dying person, Cornelia. I just want to get away from these people."

Her eyes had reddened, and her nose had started to run. Rollins dug his handkerchief out of his pocket and he helped her blow her nose. That made her smile a little. "I was thinking of having your friend Schecter try to trace my dad for me, you know. I was going to ask him last night at dinner. But then I thought, no. I really don't want to know. Wherever he went, he has his reasons. I don't want to drag him back." She looked over at him. "You're being very brave, you know. When I said you were serious before, well, I meant it as a compliment. Most people keep their eyes closed their whole lives. They don't look because they're afraid of what they might see. But not you, Rolo. Your eyes are always wide open." She raised herself up on tiptoe. She kissed his eyes. First one, then the other. Her lips were soft against his eyelids. She leaned against him. "Can't we go back to the hotel, Rolo? I'm *really* scared. Let's just forget about this whole hospice thing. I don't *care* who's there. I don't care about the faxes." She whispered in his ear: "I'd kind of like to be in bed with you right now."

That stirred him. He stroked her cheek and swept some hairs off her forehead. Still, he said: "Later, all right? There's one more thing we have to do."

The hospice was a three-story Victorian about three blocks in from Arsenal Street. It must have been grand once. Now, the front door was patched with plywood. It was a terrible place to die. Rollins held Marj's hand as they hurried up the sidewalk. He scanned the streets, but saw no sign of the Audi. He pulled open the door without pressing the buzzer and found himself in a small, paneled vestibule where an industrial fan moved the humid air. A nun in a black habit sat behind a desk reading a paperback.

Rollins glanced back through the window to the street behind him to check for Jeffries one last time. The nun was watching him intently when he turned back to her. "Everything all right?" she asked in that overly solicitous way that Rollins associated with the religious. Rollins assured her he was fine and explained that he was here to see someone.

"Might I ask who?" The nun pulled out a typed sheet from a manila folder.

"Cornelia Blanchard." He could barely force out the words.

The nun glanced down at the sheet, then looked up at Rollins again. "I'm sorry. I don't see that name here."

"She may be here under another name," Rollins said desperately. He tried to steal a glance at the sheet, but the nun pulled it back toward her ample bosom. "I'm sorry, but this is private information."

"But I need to see her. It's terribly important."

"I'm sorry. Without a name—"

"Look, someone has been sending us strange faxes from this address," Marj began.

The nun looked from Rollins to Marj and then back again. "I think I'll need to speak to Monsignor Crandel." She picked up the telephone.

"Thanks for your help." Marj pushed through the door just to her left.

The nun put down the receiver and stood up. "Excuse me. You're not allowed in there, miss."

But Marj did not stop. Rollins could hear her footsteps continuing on as the door closed behind her.

"Wait here." The nun threw out a hand and froze Rollins with a fierce look, then passed through the door after Marj, calling out for her again to stop. The moment the nun was gone, Rollins climbed the staircase to his right, beside a portrait of a cardinal. The steps were covered only with a thin rubber mat, and they creaked slightly with each step. He ascended slowly, so as not to alarm anyone.

A male nurse with a ponytail was standing by the door at the top of the stairs. "I thought I heard some sort of disturbance downstairs."

"Oh, some girl barged in acting crazy," Rollins said.

"Yeah, we get that here," the nurse replied wearily.

Rollins kept on, saying he mustn't be late because his mother was expecting him.

"And who's that?" the nurse called after him.

But Rollins pretended not to hear. He continued briskly down the narrow hall, which opened into a common room where a few older people in bathrobes sat slumped in the chairs. Rollins thought of his mother's retirement center in Hartford, and the ghostly pallor of its residents. It was awful to see death hovering over everyone like a black angel. Rollins approached an elderly man, unshaven, who was reading a book with enlarged type. "Excuse me, sir, I'm looking for Cornelia Blanchard. Is she here, do you know?"

The man looked up at him, his eyes glassy, his skin cinched tight about the bones of his face. "What's that?" An ear stuffed with a hearing aid swiveled toward Rollins.

"My name is Rollins. Someone from here has been sending me faxes," he repeated. "I believe they're from my cousin, Cornelia Blanchard. We called her—"

"Rollins, you say?" the man asked hoarsely.

"That's right."

"Pleased to meet you."

The male nurse caught up to Rollins and asked him his mother's name. "Maybe I can help you find her." There was an edge to his voice this time.

When a few other people turned to look, Rollins ignored the nurse and turned to them and identified himself. "I'm looking for Cornelia Blanchard. Slim, average height, brownish hair. It may have gone gray." It was so pathetic that he didn't even know what she looked like. "She might be here under another name. She's been sending me faxes." He looked from face to face, hoping to see someone he recognized. "Any of you?"

They all slowly shook their heads, obviously mystified. They might have been a herd of cows.

"Her *name*, sir?" the nurse demanded.

"Cornelia Blanchard!" Rollins shouted back. "We sometimes call her Neely."

"I'm sorry, sir, there's no one—"

Rollins turned away. Farther on down another hall, he could see a room with a lot of plants hung in the windows, and afternoon light pouring through. He moved toward the light, as toward the opening of a cave. He came to a small kitchen area, and a few younger people, not much more than fifty, were having breakfast at a table by the stove. "I'm looking for a woman who's been sending me faxes."

"Those went to you?" one of them interrupted. It took Rollins a moment to realize that it was a woman. Her head was bald, but she wore lipstick and stud earrings. She was sipping coffee out of a lipstick-stained mug. "Hell, I didn't think anybody actually *got* those," she said in a raspy voice.

"Did you send them?" Rollins knelt before her in her chair, looked carefully, trying to find Neely in this bald woman's face. "It's Rollins," he told her. "Eddie Rollins. You remember me, don't you?" He searched her eyes for some hint of recognition. "Cornelia, is it you? Neely?" He held her tightly, ready to hug her to him if she said yes.

Nervous laughter came up around him. "Maybe he needs the psych unit," someone said.

"The name's Evelyn," the woman told him. "I didn't send anything. Sorry—don't know any Cornelia." She gripped his wrists, to remove his hands from her. "I think it's Liz you're looking for."

Reluctantly, Rollins released her. "Liz?"

"Yeah—you know her?" She turned to her friends at the table. "What's Liz's last name? I can't even think of it now."

No one spoke. All around him, Rollins could hear the sound of television sets at low volume, with occasional bursts of canned laughter.

"Could it be Payzen?" Rollins asked quietly.

The woman clapped her hands together. "Yeah, that's it. Payzen. I swear, my mind's going along with everything else." She knocked on the side of her head.

A shadow fell. All that was so bright about Cornelia suddenly went dark. In his mind, there was a rustling sound, as of branches closing behind someone dashing through the trees, and then nothing. Silence and stillness filled his mind. Neely was gone.

"Elizabeth Payzen," Rollins said, trying to adjust to this truth. It had been foolish to hope differently. But he couldn't stop now. "So she's here?"

The woman looked downcast for a moment. "For now."

The ponytailed nurse spoke softly: "She's very sick. Her cancer has spread to her lungs. She's having a lot of trouble with her breathing."

"But she sent me a fax just yesterday."

The woman shrugged.

"I'm sorry, sir," said the nurse. "But I'll have to ask you to leave. Elizabeth is not receiving visitors right now." The nurse took Rollins by the arm and started to escort him back down the corridor.

"Where's Lizzie's room?" Rollins called back to the bald woman.

"Over there," the woman shouted back, pointing to a half-open door a short ways down the hall.

Rollins could see Payzen's name on a card by number 12. He pushed past the nurse and pushed open the door. Inside, the shade was drawn halfway, dimming the light to the drowsy hue he associated with hot weather. An ashen-faced woman lay in bed under a thin blanket, her head propped up on pillows, her arms limp by her sides.

A bulky, uniformed nurse stood up from a chair in the corner when Rollins burst in the room. "Excuse me—"

"It's Rollins," he announced, and rushed toward the bed. "Lizzie?"

The figure on the bed stirred, her head turning in his direction. "Rollins," she repeated hoarsely. He saw a flicker of a smile. It was definitely Elizabeth Payzen. He could tell by the eyes, which were the same piercing blue he remembered from before. But she'd lost weight; her flesh, once so taut and radiant, hung off her. She must have been in her fifties by now, but she looked twenty years older. Her hair, once a gloriously thick chestnut brown, had gone white and patchy, and her face was frighteningly pale.

The ponytailed nurse was at his side. "I'm sorry," he said. He grabbed Rollins by the arm. "He's not supposed to be in here."

"It's all right, Daryl," Elizabeth rasped out.

"You're in no condition—" Daryl objected.

Elizabeth raised an arm slightly. It seemed to take all her strength. "Please."

Daryl looked at Payzen and then at Rollins. "Okay then." Shaking his head, he left the room.

Rollins turned back to Elizabeth. A great weight seemed to have settled over her. With some effort, she reached a hand up to touch his arm. Her fingers felt like a tiny bird landing on him. "I was expecting you," she whispered. She looked over to the day nurse. "Could you give us a moment alone, please?"

"If you like," the woman replied in an Irish accent. "She's very weak," she told Rollins. "Try not to tire her. And only a few minutes, all right?" She stepped toward the door. "I'll be just outside."

"So those were your faxes?" Rollins asked when they were alone. He spoke gently, she was so frail. He was afraid he might hurt her otherwise. Perhaps he already had.

"Yes, from the office." She raised a finger weakly toward the hallway. "I shouldn't have been so coy." She took another moment to breathe. "I needed to talk to you, but I—well, I wasn't sure I dared. So I just kind of put it out there and let God decide." The edges of her mouth lifted into a half smile. "Forgive me. I've become quite religious in my last days." For a moment, her eyes sparkled.

"You knew my father?" Rollins asked.

Elizabeth brought a slim finger to her dry lips. "Later."

The first time Rollins had met her, he couldn't imagine what Cornelia had seen in her, Elizabeth had been so brusque and evasive. But now, as she labored to draw the breath to speak, he had a different impression. She was obviously trying so hard to connect. But there was something else, a wryness that reminded him of Neely's own off-kilter quality, which he had nearly forgotten. Neely rarely came at anything quite straight. She was always dashing about, bright-eyed, emitting gales of laughter over jokes and antics that flew over his head as a youngster. She'd eluded him then, he realized, just as she was eluding him now.

"Cornelia spoke of you," Elizabeth went on with some difficulty. "Often. I think she was in love with you a little."

Rollins' heart swelled: Cornelia seemed to be hovering there before him like an angel. "But I was just a boy."

"Oh, heavens. Age doesn't matter. She once told me that the thought of you made her want to have a child."

"I had no idea." Rollins dropped down on his knees beside her, to bring his head close to hers.

"Oh yes. You—" she paused for a moment, looked down at her hands—"*and* your sister."

"Stephanie," Rollins said quietly. For a moment, she was in the room, too.

"She died, didn't she?"

"Yes."

"For years, I couldn't be sure. Cornelia was often—what's the word? Metaphorical." She breathed quietly for a moment, as if she was trying to find her peace with that realization. "Cornelia actually tried to get pregnant. She told me so—on her fortieth birthday. She cried, telling me. I guess she realized then that she never would." She smiled again as she looked over at Rollins. "But I enjoyed our own mating dance." Elizabeth's eyes glittered. "So suspenseful." She looked up at the wall beyond the foot of her bed where, Rollins saw now, a slim crucifix hung, its Jesus hanging in silent agony.

There was a commotion in the hallway. "I need to go in there!" Marj shouted, then lurched inside the room. "Rolo! I didn't know where—" She stopped still when she saw Lizzie.

"It's Lizzie Payzen," Rollins said. "She's been sending the faxes."

"And Neely?"

Rollins shook his head.

"It's all right, Nancy," Elizabeth told the nurse, who was hovering nervously in the doorway.

"Okay then," the nurse replied, and withdrew once more.

"Do I know you?" Elizabeth asked weakly, gazing up at Marj.

"I saw your picture," Marj explained shyly. "At that house."

"*Marj*—" Rollins broke in. "This isn't the time—"

"Oh, the Gliebermans'," Elizabeth interrupted. "Yes, that was wild." She paused again, then looked up at Marj, who seemed very nervous all of a sudden. "It's all right," Elizabeth assured her. "Heavens! Dying, you'll find, is very liberating. Cornelia—" she stopped—"I gather you know about Cornelia?"

Marj nodded.

"I'm glad." Elizabeth smiled. "I was just telling Rollins that she was hoping to get pregnant. That's what drew her there—all that sperm." She smiled again, more weakly this time. Then her face clouded over. "Well, partly. It was also the drugs, the lunacy. She went a little crazy toward the end." She fell silent, her chest slowly rising and falling under the bedclothes.

"Crazy in what way?" Marj asked.

Elizabeth pondered that a moment. "Crazy from sadness, I suppose. She always carried this deep sadness that no one could ever reach. Your sister's death, Rollins—that ate away at her." More breath, more rapidly this time. Like a fish, Rollins thought, desperately flapping its gills on the shore. "I went with her once, to the house, to see what it was all about. Later, I went back." Elizabeth closed her eyes. "God forgive me."

"For what?" Rollins asked, suddenly worried.

"For being so *D-U-M-B*."

Rollins leaned in closer. "Lizzie, there are rumors—"

"I've heard them," Lizzie replied quickly. "The whispers. I've had to live with them."

"Did you—?" Rollins pressed.

"No!" Her eyes blazed, but her voice was little more than a whisper. "Absolutely not."

"But you had a reason."

"Why, because we weren't getting along?"

"Her *will*, Lizzie."

She fell silent for a moment. "That was supposed to be our secret." She breathed, more haltingly this time.

"You never said where you were," Marj added.

"I didn't have exactly the nicest alibi."

298

"What do you mean?" Rollins asked gently.

Lizzie's eyes shot over to him. "I've never told anyone."

"Tell me, Lizzie," Rollins said. "Where were you? I have to know."

"It's too awful."

"Please."

Elizabeth Payzen looked up at the crucifix again, then back at Rollins. "I was at the Gliebermans'." She shook her head, as if to free herself from the memory. "Things were not going well with Cornelia. She'd been seeing other people. She told me it didn't mean anything, but I knew it did. I had to show her that I didn't need her either. I wanted to lose myself. Just throw myself into the depravity, the soulless sex. And so I did. And I lost *her*." More raspy breaths, this time followed by heavy coughing that reddened her face and made the veins bulge an alarming blue on either side of her neck. The nurse came in and raised her up in bed. She poured her some water and brought the cup to her lips. Elizabeth grasped it with unsteady hands and took a few sips. She passed the cup back to the nurse, her chest heaving.

The nurse bent down to her. "You need the oxygen?"

There was a steel canister in the corner, Rollins could see, with tubes coming out to a clear plastic mask.

"I'm okay," Elizabeth rasped out.

"I don't want you getting tired now."

"Really. I'll be fine. Another few minutes. Please?"

The nurse looked at her, obviously pondering. "Just a few," she said finally, and retreated again.

Lizzie grasped Rollins' arm and pulled him down to her. "If only I'd stayed home that night, she'd still be with us. I would have—I would have heard Cornelia on that road. She was coming to see me. I'd have had her back, I'm convinced of it." She slumped back against the pillows again, exhausted. Her eyes looked hurt now as they met Rollins'. "Terrible, isn't it, what people do to each other?"

"But you never said anything," Rollins told her. "You never explained."

"I couldn't! I didn't want to lie, and I couldn't tell the truth. The truth was too horrible." Her frail chest swelled under the bedclothes.

"So I said nothing." She swiped at her eyes with her hand, to clear away some tears. "I had to let people think what they were going to think." She turned to Rollins. "People like you."

Rollins looked at her, uncomprehending.

"In that story of yours."

"I didn't make any accusations," Rollins said, panicky. He swung around toward Marj for confirmation, and she gave him a blank look back.

"You made some comments," Elizabeth said. "You said I was 'under suspicion in some quarters.' I'll never forget those words. My mother called me about them. Everyone in town started staring at me."

"My editor added that," Rollins said unhappily. Grant Bowser had assured Rollins that the line was "safely vague."

"I didn't know where you were coming from," Elizabeth said.

"A lot of people have that problem," Marj said.

"But I need to trust you now."

She offered her hand, and Rollins took it. The loose skin was cool, and he could feel the delicate bones underneath. He enclosed her hand in both of his, hoping to give some strength to this poor, sad woman stretched out before him, with death in her lungs. She was his last link to Cornelia. They might have been friends, if only he'd known. "You can trust me."

She looked up into his eyes, as if searching for something inside. "I didn't know what you were after." She coughed again, another hard cough that brought the nurse back to the doorway. But Marj gave Elizabeth a sip of water, settled her down on the pillows, and Elizabeth waved the nurse away.

"What happened to Cornelia that night, do you know?" Rollins asked.

Elizabeth took a moment to compose herself, to wait till her breath steadied again. "The night she disappeared, I got back very late." She spoke in the barest whisper, her voice nearly all air. To hear her better, Rollins had to crouch down, his ear turned toward her mouth. Her breath made a slight wind on his cheek as she spoke.

"I called her, as I always do, first thing in the morning," she told him. "But I got no answer. I thought, 'That's odd.'" She rested again, her chest straining for breath under the sheets. "I went to her house to look for her. I tried the doorbell. Nothing. The front door—it was unlocked. I went inside. I was frightened. I didn't know what I'd find. I'd been very worried about her. She'd been so anxious, those last months. So depressed. Jumpy. I was afraid she might—"

"What?" Rollins asked.

"Might harm herself. She bore so much guilt, don't you see? She could be—so *black*. Oh, it was so terrible, thinking these things."

"What did you find?"

Another long pause. "Her bed was still made, as if she hadn't slept in it. Everything was in its place. From what I could tell, only her raincoat and a pair of boots were missing. It seemed she'd gone out in the rain the night before, and not come back." She started to cough again. Marj reached quickly for the water glass and handed it to her. Elizabeth took a sip and went on: "I went out searching for her, calling her name. I went out into the woods. I checked the pond. I didn't know what I'd find. She'd been so unhappy those last months. . . . Finally, I went out onto the road. I was the one to find her footprints. I saw where the trail ended. That's when I called the police."

"Who took her, do you know?" Rollins asked.

Elizabeth took several breaths, then fastened her eyes on Rollins'. "I thought you might know."

Behind him, Marj reached for his shoulder.

"Me? How could *I* know?" Rollins asked.

Elizabeth's gimlet eyes pierced him, but she said nothing.

The nurse came into the room again. "I'm sorry. It's time, Elizabeth. You need to rest now."

"Just a moment, please," Rollins implored her.

The nurse looked at Elizabeth, who nodded. The nurse bowed her head. "Two minutes. No more."

"Those faxes," Elizabeth whispered. "They did their work."

"What do you mean?" Rollins demanded.

"I need to give you something—something that fills in a part of the mystery that was Cornelia." Elizabeth shifted in the bed and turned to Marj. "Do you see my shoes there?"

Rollins watched as Marj's eyes found a pair of black shoes on the floor by the bureau.

"Reach into the left one for me, would you?"

Marj bent down to the shoe and pulled out an envelope that had been curled up inside. "This?" she asked, holding up the envelope.

Elizabeth nodded, and Marj passed it to her. Elizabeth held the envelope in her hand. "This will explain—a part of her. This is why I wanted you to come. This is also why I wasn't sure I dared. But I think it's safe now." She handed the envelope to Rollins. He pressed it down on the side of the bed, and smoothed it out with his palm. The envelope said *Rollins* in blue ink. It was the same handwriting as the original note with the fax number.

"I found it in a book of poems I'd given to Cornelia. John Donne. 'A Valediction Forbidding Mourning' was always one of her favorites. Do you know it?"

She recited, quietly, as if singing to herself: "'Dull sublunary lovers love/ (Whose soul is sense) cannot admit/ Absence . . .'" She stopped, wiped away a tear with a finger. "Ever since Cornelia left, I've thought of those lines again and again and again. I meant for her to keep the book, but she returned it to me one night after an argument. I put it in the bookcase and didn't look at again until a few months ago, when I was sorting out my things before coming here. Cornelia had left a poem in it. Just a little scrap. From the date, she must have written it just before she left us."

Rollins started to open the envelope, but Elizabeth stopped him. "Please, not now. Keep it for later. We don't have time for that. You'll want to have some time to yourself, to reflect."

Reluctantly, Rollins slid the envelope into his pocket.

"But listen. There is something I'd like you to do for me in return. I've been thinking about Cornelia's poem while I've been lying here. It reminded me—we buried some things of hers in her garden, years ago. They're in a strongbox. I need you to bring it to me."

"But the house has been sold."

"Sold?" A look of astonishment came over her face. "But—her will! That house was to come to me. She promised it to me. It couldn't have gone to—not without—" She coughed, a terrible wracking cough. Rollins quickly brought some water to her lips, and she sipped a little. "No matter. There's no time for that. I'll never live there now anyway. Dig up the box, would you? I can't get there, can't dig—but you can. The box will still be there. You'll find it."

"But where?"

"It's in with the peonies in the far right-hand corner of the garden. You understand?" She reached for his hand, held it. "The peonies."

Rollins nodded.

"But you'll have to dig deep."

"What's in it?"

"Something very personal. She wouldn't let me see. This was years ago. She'd been—troubled. Very troubled. Sleeping badly. Cross. Then one night she called and said she wanted to 'bury her past.' Her words. When I arrived, she was holding a strongbox of her grandfather's, a battered old thing with his initials on it." She stopped to catch her breath, loosened her grip on his hand. "It was dark out, but she had a candle and we made a kind of procession down to the garden. Silly, I suppose. But Cornelia took it very seriously. She could be very melodramatic. I did the digging. Cornelia was always hopeless with a shovel. It was like a funeral."

"And that's in the poem?" Rollins asked.

"Obliquely, yes," Elizabeth said. "That . . . and other things. But please—bring me the strongbox. I want to see it before I die."

"I will." Rollins got up to go. Clearly, it was time. It was past time. "Thank you for trusting me." He touched her hand lightly.

"God provides," Elizabeth said.

"He has for you," Marj added.

Elizabeth looked puzzled for a moment. "Not financially." She smiled wanly. "Cornelia was never wealthy. All she had was that house, and it's gone now."

"Oh, but that was then," Rollins added. He told her about Cornelia's grandmother's bequest. "There could be ten million in her estate now."

Elizabeth looked startled. "That's quite a sum," she said finally.

"I assume you've made some provision for it," Rollins said delicately.

Elizabeth seemed quite agitated now. "Why—why yes. I finalized everything just a few days ago. Notaries, lawyers. This form, that form. I couldn't think why there'd be such a fuss about a tiny little estate. No one told me anything had changed. She was gone—how could it have? My heavens—I had no idea there was so much—"

Elizabeth's eyes turned from Rollins toward the door past the foot of the bed. Rollins was expecting the nurse, but a man was there. Even before he could tell who it was, Rollins felt a chill of fear. It was like hitting a film of ice on the highway. He'd lost traction. He was adrift, vulnerable. He prepared for impact.

"So much what?" the man asked. It was Jerry Sloane. He was smaller than Rollins remembered, somewhat slimmer, almost wiry, as if his body had been honed for action. It was stunning to see him here. And so breezily here, as if he'd been here before and belonged here now. Sloane had his salesman's cheery bonhomie, radiating happiness to be in the presence of the two people whose lives he had so unaccountably upended. Yet there was something about Sloane's very comfort here that kept Rollins from saying anything about him to Elizabeth. Seeing the two of them together, Rollins suddenly feared that Sloane's alliance with Elizabeth might run deeper than his own.

"So much money," Elizabeth said finally, with some hesitation. "I had no idea that Cornelia had come into another inheritance. You didn't tell me that."

"Didn't I?" Sloane replied innocently. "I thought I had." Then, as to a child: "You've been under so much stress, my dear. It can affect your memory." He brightened as he took in Rollins and Marj. "Well, look who we have here. Hello again." He reached out a hand to Rollins, who was too startled to do anything but shake it. The hand did not feel human.

"And, Marj, isn't that the name?" He reached a hand toward her, but she didn't take it.

"As if you don't know."

"You all—you all know each other?" Elizabeth asked, sinking deeper into her pillows.

"You know how it is in real estate," Sloane said cheerfully. He came closer to her as if to reclaim her from the two strangers by her bedside.

Elizabeth recoiled from him. "Here for your money, are you, Jerry?" She practically spat out the words. "So that's why you've come around, acting so sweet, so attentive. I can't believe I fell for it. Ten million—is that what I'm worth to you? Is that it?"

"Please, Lizzie. Don't talk like that. The money has nothing to do with it. You know I've always cared about you."

"You—!" Elizabeth's eyes flared. She gasped, then coughed—a terrible wracking cough as if she were trying to expel something that was lodged deep within her. Her face turned nearly purple, and the veins bulged out all over.

The nurse rushed in. "She needs air," she shouted. She wheeled the oxygen tank over to the bed, turned a knob, and clapped an oxygen mask over her face. "Okay, now breathe, Elizabeth. Easy now. In and out." Elizabeth relaxed back into the pillows. "Doctor!" the nurse shouted.

The ponytailed nurse rushed in, trailed by a bearded doctor in a white coat. "You'll have to leave now," Daryl announced, reaching for Rollins and Marj with his hands. "Out, out. Both of you."

Rollins stepped out to the corridor, followed quickly by Marj. They turned back toward the room only to see the door shut with Sloane still inside. The bald-headed woman came up, apparently drawn by all the commotion.

"That man who went in there with Elizabeth—" Rollins began.

"Jerry?"

Rollins nodded.

"He's over here all the time. I figured they were lovers. But Lizzie never said. Nice guy. Seems devoted to her." She looked downcast. "I don't know what he'll do without her."

"He'll manage very well," Marj said.

The bald-headed woman gave Marj a strange look, then went on down the hall. Rollins and Marj were about to follow her to the exit when the door opened again, and Jerry Sloane emerged and closed the door behind him. He came up to Rollins and Marj, then ushered them a ways down the hall, presumably to get well clear of Elizabeth's door.

"Listen to me, Rollins," Sloane began quietly. "I'm only going to say this once."

"So you do know my name," Rollins said. He'd called himself Harris at their only previous meeting.

Sloane ignored that. "Back off. You got that? You're playing with fire here." He turned toward Marj. "And you, too, sweetheart."

"So you get the money," Rollins said.

Sloane raised his voice. "I'm *warning* you—back *off*. Just walk down that hall there and never come back. That's my advice to you."

"I'm going to fight you, Jerry. You're not going to get a penny."

"You—fight me? You? That's good. I know all about you."

Rollins did not back down. "Oh? And what do you know?"

For the first time, Sloane seemed uneasy. "I don't think I should tell you this in front of your girlfriend there."

"Go ahead," Marj said.

"Yeah?" Sloane moved right into Rollins' face. "You're nothing but a fucked-up little prick who doesn't know shit."

With that, Rollins' right fist flew out and struck Sloane in the soft part just below his rib cage. His midsection gave like a pillow where the blow landed. Sloane produced a terrible gargling sound and doubled over.

Marj grabbed Rollins by the shoulders. "I think we better go."

Sloane was still hunched way over, his arms around himself, gasping for breath. "You asshole," he managed to rasp out.

"Nice talking to you, Jerry," Marj told him. The two of them hurried out into the hall. A few other patients, some just in bathrobes and slippers, were headed slowly toward Lizzie's room, obviously drawn by the strange sounds. Rollins and Marj picked their way past them, then made it down the hall to the stairs. An elderly priest was just coming up the stairs. "You have a nice day now," he told them as they went past.

Rollins and Marj had made it to the front hall when Schecter suddenly burst in the door. "Oh, good. You're there," he yelled, seeing

Rollins and Marj. "Don't come out this way. Jeffries is out there." Schecter turned to the nun at the front desk, who was gaping at him in terror. "Where's the back exit?"

"Through there." The nun pointed at the double doors she'd forbidden Marj to pass through. "Down to the right."

Schecter gave Rollins a shove. "Go! Now!" Then he pushed Marj that way, too. "Both of you! Quick!"

"What's going on?" the nun cried out.

"Lock the front door, would you please? Don't let anyone in! You got that, Sister? No one!" Schecter led Rollins and Marj through the double doors and down the hall, past a nurses' station and an administration area. Various professionals looked up at them in astonishment. The last room was a small kitchen, where an older woman held a teakettle in her hand. "Where's the rear exit?" Schecter demanded.

The woman pointed to the hallway, where some mops were leaned up against the wall. "Through there."

Schecter charged past, and Rollins and Marj hurried after. Schecter turned the bolt to open the door. He stepped outside, then gestured for them to follow. The back door led into a narrow alley between fenced yards. Around them, a few dogs started to howl. Once they'd gotten clear, Schecter had them duck down by some trash cans along one high concrete wall, hiding them from the hospice while he figured out their next move.

Over their heads, Rollins could hear a window slide open. Then a voice boomed: "You out there, Rollins? I'm going to get you, and the girl, too. You'll pay for this. I'm going to get you!" It was Sloane.

"What a fucking dope," Schecter muttered. "I've got to teach that guy the facts of life."

"That what you did with Tina?" Marj asked.

Rollins reached out a hand toward her. "Marj, please."

"You hurt her, didn't you?" Marj demanded.

Schecter glowered at her for a moment. "I do things my way, you got that?"

When Marj went quiet, Schecter asked where Rollins had left his car. Rollins told him about the municipal lot, which was only one street over.

"We're going to get you out of here," Schecter said. "Both of you."

Rollins let Schecter lead him and Marj along the high wall, keeping their heads low, and down the side alley to the street. There, Schecter had them wait by some thick bushes while he checked to make sure the coast was clear. He crept out to the sidewalk, then signaled to them to come. "Go through that little deli there," Schecter said, pointing to a glass-fronted shop across the street. "It backs up on the lot. It's less visible that way."

"What about you?" Rollins asked.

"I'm going back to have a little chat with Jerry."

"Look, you sure that's safe?"

"The guy's all bluff. Besides, you're the one who sets him off."

Marj tugged at his sleeve. "Come on, Rolo. Let's get out of here."

"Okay," Rollins nodded. He tried to shake Schecter's hand. He wanted to apologize for Marj, to offer his gratitude, to explain. "Look, Al—" he began.

"You better get going," the detective replied.

"Thanks," Rollins said. Then he and Marj dashed across the street.

Rollins and Marj made it back to the Nissan and returned to the Ritz by a circuitous route, all the while checking to make sure they weren't being followed. Finally they were safely back in their suite with the door bolted behind them. Rollins dropped down on the bed while Marj opened up the mini bar. "We need a drink," she told Rollins.

"Not just yet." He reached into his pants pocket and removed the envelope. It had gotten a little crumpled.

Marj was crouched by the mini bar, but she turned back toward him. "You're sure you're ready for that, Rolo?"

Rollins nodded.

"It could be bad, you know."

"I know." Rollins smoothed out the envelope on his thigh, then slid a finger in under the flap. There was only a thin strip of paper inside, with several lines of what looked like poetry written in black ink. It had to be Cornelia's handwriting; it was more upright and assertive than Lizzie's. The lines were a fragment of poetry. Rollins held the paper under the light of the window, while Marj came over to read it over his shoulder.

September 14, 1993

> *For so long Henry*
> *I dreamed about you*
> *coming for me at night*

"Oh, Jesus," Rollins said. He let his hand drop.

"What?" Marj took the paper from his fingers, and she read the rest out loud.

> *I became the night,*
> *silent, dark*
> *Until dawn at last broke*
> *the memory of you*
> *and me*

Marj turned the paper over, checking to see if the poem continued on the back, which it didn't. "I don't get it," she said. "Who's Henry?"

It took Rollins a little while to speak, his mind was in such turmoil. To steady himself, he gazed out the window, his eyes fixed on the branch of a distant tree.

"My father."

Nineteen

Rollins turned away from Marj to face the wall, where it was calmer.

They were on the couch in the sitting room. The shades were pulled on the Newbury Street side. Rollins had thought he'd be able to rest here for a while, to recover. He could hear the cars on the street below, but they seemed distant, forgettable. Mostly, he was conscious of the stillness and the quiet of the room. He might have stepped into a painting by Vermeer, where everything is silence and light. But he was aware of a great heaviness within him.

Beside him, Rollins could hear Marj get up off the couch. She came around to kneel down in front of him, her head against the side of his leg. "You know what I'm thinking, don't you?" she asked finally.

Rollins could hardly track his own thoughts. He was a child again—innocent, shockable.

"Remember how I asked you where Neely was when you were supposed to be watching Stephanie?"

Rollins tensed. He could feel what was coming.

"And you told me that your mother was on the phone, and your brother was watching TV?"

He nodded.

"Rolo, I think you know where Neely was."

Rollins pushed his palms over his ears so hard that he heard sea sounds, and his fingertips dug into his scalp. He saw it again, that image from the Overnighter. But the image was not from the Overnighter. It was from inside him, where it had been buried long ago. It was just a flash, like so many memories when they first stirred.

Her bare shoulders, and his hands on her.

Rollins could feel Marj's hands tugging on his. "You need to hear this," he heard her say. She must have been shouting, to get through.

Within him, the light brightened, and spread.

On that worn carpet in the billiard room by the couch. Just the tops of their heads at first. Then her bare shoulders, red in places, and breathing, and everything happening so fast.

Rollins clamped his hands down over his ears all the harder—so hard his pulse thundered in his palms—and he squeezed his eyes shut.

The Garbo rule. He had to be alone. Just him, deep inside his head where he was safe.

Still, Marj's voice came through, as if from another world. "You know it, Rolo. You've always known it. She was with your dad."

Father and Neely. As if lit up by lightning.

Marj crouched down before him: "Speak to me, Rolo. When did Stephanie die that Saturday? Tell me when."

A crushing weight on his chest. Still, he had to speak. "Late."

"How late?"

He could hardly draw breath. "I don't remember. It was dark."

Dark outside in the bushes, when he looked in the windows.

"When they were doing it," Marj said quietly.

He dropped his hands, watched her. She seemed so tender, so forgiving.

"And you knew, Rolo, didn't you?"

Rollins slid off the couch and down onto the floor. He pulled his knees up, propped his chin on his hands.

No repeats. See something only once, and you don't get involved. That was the whole idea.

Heads together. Her shoulders bare. The thrashing.

"What did you see, Rolo?"

"Nothing. I didn't see *anything*."

"Tell me. You saw something. What was it?"

Rollins was a child again, a little boy in red high-tops, wandering the dark halls of the too-big house. But Marj was with him now; he could feel her by his side. "I was by the billiard room. No one went there. The pool table was really old. No one played. It was way off in the back of the house. Dusty. Never used. I was in the hall when I heard a noise from there. From inside. A kind of groan. I went closer— to look. The door was open, just a little. I saw—"

The writhing.

"What?"

"I didn't *know*. I *don't* know. It was too fast. It all happened too fast. Just—just a flash. But maybe it was—God! I didn't *know*. I *don't* know. I was only six! I just ran. I put it out of my mind. I put it out. Out!"

Their heads so close.

"Easy, Rolo. Relax." Marj's hands were on him, gently loosening his hands from his ears so she could speak to him. "Easy. Come on, just breathe. Easy, now." Her voice was a lullaby, soothing him.

He spoke more quietly, his voice almost all air. "I ran back to my room. I—just sat on the floor. I played with my cars. I loved those little cars. Then my mother called up to me to watch Stephanie in the bath. But I couldn't."

"You said it was because your mother had yelled at you for seeing Neely the other time."

"That's right. That's what I thought. That's all I thought. Of seeing Neely. That registered. I wasn't supposed to see Neely. And I had. I'd seen her." He could feel the tears trickling down his face.

"And you'd seen her again," Marj said.

Neely's bare back. Father's hands on her.

Rollins felt an icy coldness drip down the inside of his body, and he hugged himself for warmth.

The look on Mother's face when she shouted at him.
"Edward! Edward!"

His nose was clogged, his cheeks were wet, and his face felt puffy around his mouth.

"She knew, Rolo. Your mother knew. Why else would she slap her?"

"It was because Neely was so upset! It was to *calm* her!" He could hardly force the words out, he had so little belief in them.

"Right, to calm her. As if that's going to calm her." Marj took Rollins' hands in her own. "Then tell me this, all right? How long did Neely stay on after Stephanie died?"

Rollins' head throbbed. He'd surely get a migraine now. "Three days," he said finally. "She left the day I went back to school. I remember, she gave me a big hug when I went off that morning. She was crying. But she'd been crying a lot those days. She was gone when I came back." He turned to Marj. "But it was only because we didn't need her anymore. That's what my mother told me."

"But you were still there, Rolo. Your brother wasn't even in kindergarten. What did your mother do about him?"

"She hired somebody else. An old cow named Mrs. Callahan."

"There. You see?"

His father and Neely—and Stephanie floating facedown. And he didn't go in. And his mother knew. She knew! And *still* she screamed "Edward." Rollins was afraid that he might burst. He lurched forward and grabbed on to Marj, and he clung to her while his entire body quaked—frightening convulsions that pulsed from his belly up to his shoulders—and the tears poured down his cheeks and an awful howl rose up from the deepest part of his chest.

"It's okay, Rolo," she whispered. "It's okay, honey."

He closed his eyes and he felt a wind on him from somewhere, and he was moving through empty space, a place without light or love or warmth or anything to touch or see or do. It was nothing, just as he was nothing, had always been nothing.

"Edward!"

But somehow he could still feel Marj cuddling his head in her arms. "It wasn't you, Rolo," she was saying. He felt her warm hands on his hair. "You weren't the reason the family broke apart. It wasn't because you weren't *supposed* to be watching. Neely was. No wonder Lizzie said she was sad. All those years, Rolo, she felt guilty." She paused. "Stephanie would never have died if it weren't for Neely and your father. And your fucking mother knew, Rolo. It wasn't you. It wasn't you. It was *them*." She stroked his head, sweeping her fingers through his hair. "Oh, honey." The strokes stopped and Rollins could feel Marj moving around to face him. She was crouched down before him, the sides of his head cupped in her hands. Her palms pressed against his ears; her fingers dug into his scalp. She had him, just as he wanted her to have him. "You don't have to *watch* anymore," she said, with new emphasis, shaking his head a little. "You don't have to follow any more *cars*. You don't have to look in any more *windows*. You can relax, Rolo. You can relax. You can live your *own* life."

Her voice guided him back. Rollins nodded his head to show her that he'd heard, although he could not speak. Gradually, as he followed the voice, the blackness everywhere turned to purple and then to red and finally to pink. And then he opened his eyes and saw her, just inches away. Her lips were there, and he kissed them, also her eyes and the sides of her face. When he finally pulled away, her cheeks were stained with his tears. Smiling, she wiped them dry with the end of his shirtsleeve. Then she helped him off the floor and guided him toward the bed. He felt like a child as she eased him down on top of the covers, and then pulled off his shoes and socks. "Just a sec," she told him. She went into the bathroom and came back with a cool washcloth and bathed his face. When she was done, he reached for her and kissed her again. And she said: "Actually, I was thinking a bath might help. But then I thought, noooo, maybe not." She brought her finger down on the tip of his nose just the way Neely had, and then down over his lips. "How about a shower, though? Might make you feel better."

He still had trouble walking, so she helped him into the bathroom. He sat down on the toilet seat and she helped him remove his clothes, then she opened the shower door and got the water going. She steered him into the stall. He closed the door behind him and he leaned against the tiled wall and he let the water beat down on his back and his shoulders.

Then there was a rush of cool air as the shower door opened, and Marj was naked beside him. "Hey, scootch over," she said.

Rollins made room, and Marj reached for the little shampoo bottle on the small shelf by the shower nozzle. "We just need to clean you up a little." She shampooed his hair, her soft belly pressing against his rump, then turned him around to soap him all over, slowly. Her hands on him, everywhere, made him feel better, more himself, more the self he'd always wanted to be.

"Marj," he said. "Oh, Marj." He pushed his hand down her belly and between her legs. She met his eyes as he stroked her fur, which was wet and scraggly. He felt adventurous, as though he was exploring a secret part of her, as he rode his hand up and down through the tangles. Running his hand along, he could feel the cleft of her vagina loosen under his touch. She tipped her head against his shoulder as the shower water beat down upon him. He could hear her breathing deepen. "Inside," she whispered, lifting her pelvis toward his hand.

He slipped his middle finger inside, feeling the beginnings of the slithery wetness within. She leaned against his chest as if they were slow-dancing. "Deeper," she whispered.

He pushed his finger in, and the slipperiness opened, inviting him.

She clung to him, pressing her breasts hard against his chest, and he could feel her lean her pelvis toward his hand.

He slipped another finger inside. It thrilled him to sense that he wasn't just touching her, but actually *reaching* her somehow. He was leaving his past, leaving himself. And he was getting inside to where the true Marj was.

She tensed for a moment, held him still, as he continued to slide his fingers into her. He'd never felt so connected to anyone. He slid his hand in harder, rougher. "Oh," she cried from deep in her throat. Then her breath caught, and she tightened her grip on him, and shuddered. Finally, she relaxed with a sigh and kissed the side of his neck.

His erection brushed against her side. It was so hard it ached, and she reached for it and leaned back against the shower stall. "I still want you inside me," she whispered as she raised herself up. Her mouth open as if she were stepping into cool water, she guided him to her.

His arms about her shoulders, he slid himself up inside her and held himself there without moving for some time. He wanted to live in this moment forever. "This is where you belong," she told him as she hugged him to her chest. "This is us." Her eyes on his, she brought herself up and down on him. Meeting her gaze, he pushed and pulled against her. A kind of dance. Soon they were both moaning, and then gasping, and then shouting, and then Marj was screaming in his ear until, with one last frantic thrust, he burst up inside her.

* * *

The phone rang when they were drying off. Marj answered it and passed the receiver to Rollins. "It's Al. He's on his cell phone."

The detective had a cigar going. "Sounds like you made it back okay."

"Yeah, we're here."

Schecter's voice was cool, with little of its usual cocky ebullience. "You better watch yourself. You're playing with fire here. I tried to cool Jerry Sloane down for you. I told him to put Jeffries back in his cage, and I said if he didn't lay off I was going to tip the feds about the illegal sale of Cornelia's house. Jerry didn't bite. He told me to get lost. Then he pulled a gun on me—right there in the hospice. I don't know what you did, Rollins, but he's definitely aggravated." Schecter took another puff from his cigar. "Say, you all right? You sound like you're only half there."

Rollins told him about his father's affair with Cornelia. "That's why Elizabeth was trying to get in touch with me. She thought I should know."

"God, you just keep getting in deeper and deeper, don't you?"

"I guess." Rollins wasn't paying much attention to what Schecter was saying.

"Look, I'm still by the hospice. I'll keep track of the two of them for you."

"Don't bother." Death behind him, death ahead. Rollins was exhausted. He could barely hold up his head. "What's going to happen is going to happen," he told the detective. "There's no point trying to stop it."

"Where'd you get that?" He mimicked Rollins, "'What's going to happen is going to happen.'" The intonation sounded snotty, which Rollins didn't appreciate. "These guys are bad guys," Schecter insisted. "They can hurt you. And they can hurt the girl, too."

"My father—"

"Listen to me," Schecter interrupted. "You're tired, you're not thinking well. Let me do this for you, all right? I'm in my car. I got Jerry's car up the street. Big one. Land Cruiser, right?"

"Yeah, that's his."

"He came out to use the car phone. Jeffries was with him. I'll try to keep track of them for you, let you know if either of them starts heading your way. Nobody else knows you're there, right?"

"Just you."

"Good. Keep it that way. Just lay low. If we're real careful, maybe we can ride this thing out."

"How about Elizabeth—she okay?" Rollins asked.

"I didn't see a body come out, if that answers your question. Stay put, all right?"

"Sure, Al."

After he hung up, Rollins gave Marj a sanitized version of Schecter's update on Sloane, emphasizing the part about how the detective had offered to keep an eye on Sloane and Jeffries for them.

"Both?" Marj asked skeptically.

"Nobody knows we're here, Marj."

"Nobody was supposed to know we were going to that hospice, either." Marj sat back on the bed and pulled her legs up under her. "I wish I liked him more."

"Who?"

"Your friend Al. All the macho crap. I'm not sure I like being 'the broad.'"

Rollins moved to her. He needed to reassure her, boost her spirits. "Marj, we need him, and he's been good to us. If it weren't for him, we wouldn't know anything."

"How badly did he hurt Tina?"

"Not too badly. He slapped her a couple of times."

Marj shook her head. "While you watched, I bet."

Rollins was too tired for this. "No, Marj. Please—don't be like that. Not now. He might have hurt her worse, but I—I stopped him. I held him off her. We had to find out what she knew."

"Okay, Rolo." She smiled sleepily. Rollins was conscious of all the empty space around them.

"I can't believe it about the money," Marj said finally. "Everything goes to Jerry. Wow."

"It doesn't end there, Marj." With some effort, Rollins got up off the bed again. "I've been thinking there's got to be more to it."

"Why?"

"I don't think Sloane's operating on his own. He couldn't have set it up to get all that money."

"I don't follow."

"When Cornelia disappeared, she didn't know that she was going to inherit anything from her grandmother, right?"

Marj nodded.

"And it certainly didn't look like Elizabeth knew, either."

"So who told him?"

Rollins had only to look at her.

"Your father," Marj said.

Rollins nodded. "It's got to be."

"How would he know? He's out of the family."

"Maybe he's not."

Through the narrow gap in the curtains, Rollins could see the fading light outside the window. He could just make out the swan boats in the public garden that were tied up for the night, and the gaslights glowing like fireflies along the pathways. Questions nagged at him on every side, like unseen hands, poking and prodding.

He went over to the couch in the adjoining room, kicked off his shoes, and put his stockinged feet up on the coffee table.

"Your father in with Sloane?" Marj persisted. "I'm really glad I didn't try to trace my dad. God only knows what *he's* been doing all these years. He's probably selling children, or spying for the Chinese, or—"

Rollins raised a hand to quiet her. "I'm sorry, Marj. I need to rest for a moment. I'm really tired."

Marj fell silent, and Rollins eased back and closed his eyes. In moments, he could feel Marj leaning him forward to insert a bed pillow behind his back. Then a light kiss on his forehead.

He was running down a long, dimly lit hall. His sneakered feet were beating soundlessly on the thick carpet; a wind was in his face as he rushed along. Neely was ahead of him, her giggles echoing behind her. Her blond hair tossed as she raced along on her long, tanned legs. He was panting, straining to keep up. The hallway was endless, and it kept turning this way and that. Neely kept laughing and laughing as she darted along. But Rollins kept being surprised by walls that loomed up unexpectedly, and sudden corners, and staircases that dropped out beneath him. Still, he ran and ran and ran.

Something was ringing. An alarm, was it? No, a telephone, far away. And then a voice. "Yes, I'll get him." And then a warm hand on him, and Marj speaking. "The phone, Rolo. It's Al. He says it's urgent."

Rollins got up, rubbed his eyes, and reached for the receiver.

"Listen to me," Schecter said. "I'm in my car, heading north on 16. I've got Sloane up ahead, but Jeffries has split off. It looks like he might be heading to town."

"What time is it?" Rollins was surprised to see that it was pitch dark out, except for the glow from the streetlights. He'd expected morning.

"About ten." He raised his voice: "Rollins, I think he may be headed your way."

"Now?"

"Yes, now."

"You said we'd be safe here."

"Maybe you are. You're using cash, right?"

"Credit card."

"Oh, Christ. Don't you know *anything*? That's traceable. Get out of there, Rollins. You and the girl. *Now*."

"And go where?"

"Anywhere. Just go. Christ almighty."

Schecter gave him his cell phone number. Rollins told him he could leave a message for them at Marj's, and he gave Schecter that number.

"Got it. Okay, my friend. I gotta pay attention here. Now go on. Get out of there."

Rollins set down the receiver. "Jeffries may be coming," he told Marj.

"Here?" She slumped down on the end of the bed. "I thought we were safe here."

Rollins was afraid she might cry.

"It's because of what Al did to Tina, isn't it?" Marj asked.

"Maybe." He pulled on his California clothes again and stepped into his shoes.

Marj was already in her running clothes. She sat there for a moment, her head drooping. Then she stood up, went to the closet where her new clothes hung. She took them off the hanger and tucked them under her arm. "Well, I'm all packed."

He was already waiting for her at the door.

"Your work clothes, Rolo?" Marj asked, gesturing toward the closet where his blazer and flannel trousers hung.

"I'm done with them," Rollins said. They went out to the corridor, then hurried down the emergency stairs and out to the sidewalk on Newbury. The air was still warm and soft with humidity. He glanced about uneasily, checking for Jeffries. All seemed clear. He grabbed Marj's hand and dashed across the street to the Ritz's parking garage. He handed the receipt for the car to an attendant, then plucked two twenties from his wallet and told him they were his if he brought the car up in two minutes. The Nissan was there nearly in one. Rollins handed the attendant the money, Marj tossed her things into the trunk, and they took off.

Rollins drove down Newbury, and then swung around Copley Square a couple of times to make sure he wasn't being followed before heading back through Chinatown to get up onto the expressway to 93.

"Wait—where are we going?" Marj asked.

"New Hampshire."

"Why?"

"We've got to get that strongbox."

"But Jeffries—"

"It'll be all right. He doesn't know we're going there. Besides, I promised."

For a long time, as they drove along, Marj kept checking around them for Wayne Jeffries' Audi. But she gradually wearied of the job as the miles passed without any sign of him. The next thing Rollins knew, Marj was sound asleep, her head slumped over at an awkward angle, her running shorts bunched tightly around her thighs.

It was a few minutes past eleven when Rollins turned onto Pelbourne

Road. A thin moon had climbed up over some distant hills to the west, and the New Hampshire sky was thick with stars. Rollins found the entrance to Cornelia's driveway and pulled over a few yards beyond it. Marj stirred as the car slowed. "We there?" she asked, looking around.

"Yeah, back there on the right."

Rollins reached for the door handle, but Marj stopped him. "Don't we need a shovel?"

Rollins slumped back in his seat. "Damn."

Marj glanced around again. "You know anyone around here?"

Nicky Barton's chunky neo-Colonial was dark when Rollins drove up. But Nicky's Taurus was parked in the driveway. While Marj waited in the car, he tried the doorbell, which sounded some chimes inside. He had to hit it a few times before an upstairs light flicked on. "Who is it?" Nicky called out from inside the door.

"Rollins," he said.

"Cornelia's cousin? From the other night?"

A bolt loosened, and the door swung open. Nicky stood before him in a black bathrobe. "It's a little late, isn't it?"

"We need a shovel."

Nicky looked at him for a moment. "Do you."

"I want to set Cornelia's stone in a little better."

"At this hour?"

"We were just passing through."

"'We?'"

Rollins gestured back toward Marj in the car. "A friend and I."

"All right." Nicky stepped past him, and went across the driveway to the garage. She disappeared inside for a moment, then came back with a heavy shovel.

"Perfect," Rollins said, taking it from her.

"And you got one of these?" She held up a flashlight.

"Actually, no."

Nicky handed it to him.

"Thanks."

"Just leave the stuff in the garage when you're done."

"Certainly." He turned back toward the car.

Nicky called out to him. "This is all for Cornelia's stone, you say?"

"Yes, that's right," Rollins assured her as he returned to the car. He put the shovel in the backseat and climbed into the Nissan, handing the flashlight to Marj. When he flipped the headlights back on, Nicky was watching him from the front steps.

They drove back up Pelbourne and pulled over a little ways past the memorial stone that Rollins had put up for Neely. Rollins and Marj stepped out and shut their doors quietly behind them. Carrying the shovel, Rollins led Marj up the asphalt road.

"So this was Cornelia's?" Marj whispered when they reached the heavy stone pillars guarding the mouth of the drive. The big Victorian was just visible up ahead through the trees, outlined against the starry sky.

Rollins had forgotten that Marj had never been here. He thought by now that their lives had merged completely. "Yeah."

"Another huge house," Marj noted.

Wary of the loose-gravel driveway, Rollins stuck to the grass just to the left, and Marj followed behind him. He carried the shovel over his shoulder. Around him, the wind in the trees moved like an alien presence, one that had somehow been disturbed by their arrival on these grounds.

Before him, the lawn sloped down to his left. The garden was at the foot of the lawn, along a stone wall by the hayfields. Rollins checked behind him, to see if they'd been followed. Seeing no sign of anyone, he continued on. In the distance, the pond glistened a dull silver, and the surrounding forest was a gathering of darkness. Up to his right, the big house loomed, but it was black and still. He passed across the lawn and angled down toward the garden. It was a slim rectangle in the English fashion, divided by the path that led down to the pond. The near half had a few vegetables—he could make out some tomatoes and beans—encroaching into what Rollins had always remembered as exclusively a flower bed. But the far half, where the peonies were supposed to be, was still all flowers. Rollins spotted some familiar leaves down at the end.

"There," he whispered, pointing. "You see?"

The two of them went around to the peonies. Marj handed Rollins the flashlight, and he clicked it on: There were six or seven plants, all of them well filled out. He hadn't expected so many. He wished that he'd brought something besides a shovel to push into the earth around the plants to probe for a metal box down below.

"Try the middle," Marj said. "And hurry, would you?"

While Marj carefully parted two of the peony bushes, Rollins shoved the spade down in between, then stepped on the blade to drive it in deeper. He dug out one shovelful of dark soil, then another, and then two more. He encountered no resistance and heard nothing. "Check with the light, how about?" Marj suggested.

He shined the light down, but illuminated nothing but black earth, with a few worms wriggling in it. He got down on his knees, soiling his new trousers, rolled up his sleeve, and pushed his hand in. His arm went in clear to his bicep. He groped around the cool dirt, feeling for something flat and hard. He touched a few rocks, and more pebbles, but nothing remotely boxlike. "I'm going to try another spot," he said finally.

That hole went no better. Nor did the one after that.

A car went by on Pelbourne, its headlights illuminating some of the trees lining the drive. Rollins stopped, fear flooding his chest. Marj glanced over toward the road, then crept up the lawn to look down the driveway to check to see if anyone was coming. "It's okay," she whispered when she came back.

Rollins jammed the shovel in extra deep this time—and struck something hard. It might have been a rock, except it gave a hollow sound. The two of them froze.

His heart pounding, Rollins scraped around the hole to widen the opening. Then he dropped down on his knees and reached in. He felt a sharp corner, with flat planes running from it at right angles. "Got it," he said. Rollins had to rip out one of the peonies to get at the box, and then dig a virtual trench to free it. He labored over the hole, the sweat flowing, while Marj edged in beside him. Finally, he reached in with both hands and managed to work the box loose. Without a word, he carried it out of the garden and set it down in the tall grass behind, where Marj shone the light down on it.

The strongbox was caked with dirt, but Rollins could see that it was quite old, with a greenish handle on top. The box itself was black, except for a dull gold border framing the top, and the initials A.L.B. under the handle in old-fashioned lettering.

"Alexander Blanchard, must be," Rollins said, clearing away some grime off the top. "Cornelia's grandfather." The box was dented and scraped at one corner where Nicky's shovel must have struck it. He pulled the handle, but the lid didn't budge. "Damn," Rollins said. "It's locked."

"Here, let me," Marj said. She set the strongbox down on its back, then picked up the shovel and, before Rollins could stop her, smashed it down on the box. The blow landed with a loud clank that seemed to echo around the field. The strongbox hopped into the air, tumbled over the grass—and landed with the lid wide open.

Rollins hurried to the box and crouched over it while Marj shone the light in.

The box was filled with loose papers, and some bulging envelopes. The two stared at it in amazed silence for a moment, then Rollins reached in and pulled out a white envelope. It was labeled *Brookline—* *'68-9*, and there were a number of photographs inside. Rollins plucked out the first one and held it up to the light. A young boy in Bermuda shorts and a tennis shirt stared up at him.

"God, Rolo, is that *you*?" Marj asked.

Rollins nodded, lost. "It's our old backyard."

Neely's hands on him, backing him against the dogwood by the garden. "Just stand there, would you? Just for a second?" Then her backing up, her Brownie up by her face. "Hold it. Smile, would you? You have such a nice smile. Please?"

More photos, more memories. A close-up in the kitchen that showed him smiling widely to reveal two missing front teeth: That brought back the tunnel-like feeling the absent teeth left along the roof of his mouth. A blurry one of him running across the lawn in his Keds: the freedom of warm air on him. Richard holding a whiffle-ball bat: a storm cloud of envy, since Richard never missed. And Stephanie in diapers on her changing table, her little feet curled together. That one stopped him. Sadness all over.

"That's your sister, isn't it?" Marj asked.

Rollins nodded.

Marj pulled out a picture of his father. Henry Rollins' face had been blacked out in angry strokes with a ballpoint pen, but his thick hair and lean build were unmistakable. "Look at this." Marj pointed to his father's groin, where someone—Cornelia presumably—had drawn in a monstrous phallus.

Rollins took the photograph in his hand for a moment. He was shocked by the rage in those slashing strokes of Cornelia's ballpoint.

"So, it's true," he said.

"Sure looks like it," Marj said.

He stuffed the picture back in the envelope, which he returned to the strongbox.

He noticed a small cardboard box inside. Rollins plucked off the cover: a yellow rubber ducky.

Stephanie's back glistened where she floated, head down, and the yellow duckies bobbing beside her, like boats by a tiny island.

"I guess." Rollins gave it a squeeze. The ducks had always used to squeak, something that had delighted Stephanie. But, after all this time, this one gave out only a chuffing spurt of air.

Then footsteps. Rollins turned. Out of the night, a figure loomed beside them. Nicky. A yellow raincoat thrown over her black bathrobe. "Just firming up Cornelia's monument, are we?" she whispered.

"Sssh," Rollins told her.

Her eyes zeroed in on the open strongbox, and she moved toward it. "What have you found?"

"Just family stuff."

"Buried in the garden?"

A door opened and a deep voice boomed from the doorway. "Who's out there?" It was Ben Stanton. He shined a powerful flashlight toward them.

Rollins flicked off his own light, but he could feel himself being lit up by the brighter beam. He slammed the box shut and tucked it under his arm. "Come on!" he told Marj. He ducked down and scurried along behind the stone wall bordering the garden, then, beckoning to Marj to follow, he crossed the open field, staying as low as possible, and made for the far trees.

"Who's there?" Stanton repeated. Dogs started barking from inside the house, inspiring other dogs in other houses much farther away. Glancing back, Rollins could see the light trained on Nicky Barton, who was struggling to run with her shovel.

"Nicky? That you?" Stanton shouted.

A heavy tread, frantic rustling, then a shriek pierced the night air. Rollins looked back again. Ben Stanton had grabbed Nicky by the shoulder and was hurling her to the ground. Rollins and Marj had reached the trees by now. They stopped, panting.

"Let me go!" Nicky cried. She swung the shovel at Ben, but he grabbed it and flung it to the ground.

"What in hell?" he demanded. "Who were those two?"

But that was the last Rollins heard. He and Marj pushed on through the trees. They had to tread carefully. It was nearly pitch black, the ground was marshy and uneven, and tree branches and bushes poked out almost everywhere. But they kept forging ahead. Rollins felt oily under his clothes, and his breath came rapidly. "Look—there," Rollins whispered, when a glimmer of starry sky appeared in the distance ahead of them. They kept pushing and pushing, and finally broke through to the road.

Twenty

Rollins called Schecter from the pay phone near the pizza place on 102, but all he got was an automated message saying the cell phone was out of range.

When he told Marj, she stepped into the booth with him. It quickly filled with their combined heat.

"I'll try my machine," she told him, and slipped past him to the phone. She dialed her number, then pressed in more keys. She listened, tipping her head lazily this way and that. "My mother," she whispered. "Her messages go on forever." Then she straightened up. She remained silent for a few moments. "It's Al," she said. "You better hear this yourself." She pressed another button, and handed him the phone.

There was a click, and then Schecter's voice came on: "Hi, Marj, could you give this message to Rollins, please? I've got Jerry holed up in a motel here in Littleton, way out past Concord on Route 2. God knows why. But here's the thing. I just called in to see how your friend Elizabeth was doing. Don't worry—I pretended I was a cousin in San Francisco. She died this evening, Rollins. Sorry. Leave a number where I can reach you once you get settled, okay, buddy? I don't want to have to worry about you."

The answering machine clicked off, and Rollins hung up the phone. His arm felt heavy, weighed down by something he couldn't see. He thought of Elizabeth gasping for breath, coughing so hard, trying to expel death from her lungs.

Marj reached for him, stroked the side of his face. "It didn't look too good for her when we left."

"No, it didn't."

"I guess we keep the strongbox now." She was carrying it under her arm.

"I've got to find him," Rollins declared.

"Who?"

"Father." Rollins picked up the phone again and called his brother in Indianapolis. Richard's wife, Susan, answered sleepily. Rollins told her it was a family emergency. "Just a moment," she told him. Rollins waited without moving, the receiver tight to his left ear.

"I need Father's address," he said when Richard came on the line.

"You need—Ed, do you have any idea what time it is?"

"It has to do with Cornelia."

That calmed him momentarily. Richard asked if she'd been found—the standard question from family members, it seemed.

"No—not yet."

"You're not getting all wound up over this, are you? Mother said you were obsessing about Neely again."

"You were talking to Mother about me?"

"It wasn't *all* about you, Ed. She was concerned. We both are. We know how you get."

"The address, Richard." Rollins' family had exploded all around him, and he was the only one to notice. "That's all I need from you, okay?"

"Look, I don't have it. The last I knew he was in Santa Clara. In California. With that stewardess of his—Kathi. With an *i*, God help us. Why do you need him, anyway?"

"I can't tell you now."

"No sweat, big brother. I know how it is. You've got your stuff, I've got mine."

Rollins assured him that he'd get back in touch with him later.

"If you want," Richard said.

When Rollins closed out that call, Marj pushed into the booth again and massaged his neck. "That sounded a little rough," she said.

"He thinks I'm crazy."

"Yeah? Well, wait till he sees these." Marj held up a thick handful of letters from the strongbox. "They're all from your dad to Neely. Looks like he was still writing to her, begging to see her again even after she left the house."

Shocked, he took the stack of envelopes from her and looked through them. No question—the letters were all addressed to Cornelia Blanchard in his father's swift, forward-slanting script. Some to a post office box in Weston, some to Smith, some to an apartment in Jamaica Plain where, Rollins seemed to recall, Cornelia had lived while doing graduate work at B.U.

"He's a guy, Rolo. Guys do that."

"Begging?" Rollins asked her.

"Demanding, more like. As if she owed him."

Rollins opened a letter he'd sent to Jamaica Plain. It was on a single sheet of white paper, written in longhand with what looked like a fountain pen.

Neels—dearest,

Do you have any idea what I am going through? Do you? I long for you every minute. My life makes no sense anymore, not without you. I'd divorce Jane in a moment if I knew you'd have me. I can hardly bear the sight of her anymore—or of myself. I sleepwalk through the days. My life is so empty without you! I don't know how to be happy. Let's go away together—please! I dream of you, Neels. Remember that secret knock of mine on your door. Do you remember? Remember that pink nightie you

used to wear? The one with the bow? It tortures me. Please—speak to
me when I call. Is that too much to ask?

In memory of what we had,

Love always,

H

It took Rollins a while to pull his eyes away. His father had always seemed so dry and self-contained—lifeless, even, a waxed figure. His hair brushed straight back, his back straight, his chest out. A man made for a dinner jacket, starched shirt, and pressed trousers. He hadn't imagined that Father was capable of such passion, such need. Even when Rollins was literally down on his knees begging his father not to leave, his father had not bent down to him or taken him in his arms. He had merely waited for Rollins to detach himself, as, with the help of his brother, he finally had.

But the letter was so stark, such a naked display of emotion. It was like seeing them together.

The writhing.

"I've got to find him," Rollins said. With trembling hands, he stuffed the letter in the envelope and handed it back to Marj. He called Santa Clara information. An operator came on and said that she wasn't showing any Henry, only an initial *K*—for Kathi, presumably—on Cypress Street. An automated voice gave him the number.

Rollins pressed it in. His pulse jumped when a voice answered, but it belonged to a sleepy female. Rollins identified himself and said he was trying to reach his father, Henry.

"Wait a second, would you?" Sheets rustled in the background. Rollins tensed, afraid his father was about to come on the line. Rollins couldn't imagine what he might say. But the same woman came back on. "What are you asking me now?" The voice had a Texas twang to it.

Rollins repeated himself, and the woman said, "Oh, Hank's son." Rollins had never heard his father referred to as Hank before. "The journalist."

"He there?" Rollins pulled the receiver away from his mouth so Kathi wouldn't hear his nervous breathing.

"With me? Heck no. I'm sorry, hon. I didn't mean to leave that impression. He left here maybe a year ago. He went back east—to Vermont."

Rollins wasn't sure he understood correctly. "Not Townshend." That was the site of the family's country house.

"Yeah, that's it." Kathi couldn't be sure he was still there, but that's where he'd gone.

"But why?"

"You want the whole story?" She didn't let him answer. "Hell, I would if I were you." While Rollins half-listened, she launched into the tale of a love affair that started on a midnight flight to Albuquerque and culminated in a wedding proposal two months later in a candlelight dinner overlooking San Francisco Bay. But life for Kathi changed once she became the third Mrs. Rollins. Rollins' attention rose with his distress as she recounted how Henry Rollins had picked on her housekeeping, her (limited) education, her taste, her accent. "He wanted me to take voice lessons, if you can believe that." She was a brunette, with short hair in a boyish cut, but he'd wanted her to dye her hair blond, and wear it down to her shoulders. And he'd kept wanting her to take tennis lessons even though she was the "sit-around type," she told Rollins. "I thought, my God, he's going to kill me with all this."

"He ever mention Cornelia Blanchard to you?"

The name didn't ring a bell.

"He might have called her Neely."

Rollins thought he heard Kathi sit up a little. "Wait—a novelist, like?" she asked.

"Poet."

"Oh yeah, poet. He mentioned her a few times. I think he had a book of hers. Wasn't she related or something?

"She was my cousin."

It hurt to use the past tense.

"Yeah? I pegged her an old girlfriend."

"She was a blonde, that's why I mention it." A dead blonde, he might have said.

"Well, maybe he wanted me to be her." Kathi barely paused, obviously missing the full significance. "Finally, I got a little tired of all the complaining, and I said some stuff that I probably shouldn't have, and he said some things that he definitely shouldn't have. Then we were going at each other pretty good. He has a temper, your dad. I don't know if you know that."

"He didn't hit you, did he?"

"No, but I had a feeling he might have if he'd kept at it a little longer. I had to do some flying, and when I came back, he was gone. I only found out he was in Vermont because he left me an address so I could forward his mail. No note, of course. No explanation. No goodbye. No nice knowing you. No nothing. Just the address. Sweet, huh?"

"You're lucky," he told her.

"What's that?"

"I said I'm sorry that happened."

"Aw, hell—live and learn. Try him in that Townshend place. He was always going back there. If you see him, tell him his wife says hi."

"He's split," Rollins told Marj after he hung up. "He's come back to Vermont."

Marj reached for Rollins' hand. "What do you mean, back?"

"Apparently he's been there a few times."

"Rolo, was he there when—?"

"Well, I know he spent some time there after he traveled in Europe. Just before he headed west." Rollins suddenly had a sinking feeling.

Marj looked into his eyes. "But when was that, exactly?"

Rollins' fear deepened as he thought back. "That must have been about a year after I last saw him. We had lunch together, a few days after he closed down his investment firm. That would put it in nineteen ninety-three." He stopped for a second. "The fall."

Rollins looked at Marj. She was all eyes as she looked back at him.

"When Neely disappeared," Marj said finally.

Rollins turned away from her. He stared out the window to the empty highway, lit by street lamps. "Hey," Marj said. She brought her hands up to his neck to soothe him.

He reached for the phone again.

Marj pulled her hands back. "You're not calling him."

"I'm just going to see if he's there."

"But it's after midnight."

"I don't care. I've got to know where he is."

"Well, hang up if he answers, okay? Promise me?"

"I will." He called information, then pressed in the number. The phone rang once. Then twice, then three times. Rollins held his breath as an answering machine came on with his father's voice. Drier than he remembered, older, but it still cut into him just as always.

"I'm here, but I'm not here now," said the voice on the machine. Then a long beep. Rollins was just returning the receiver to its hook, when a tired voice came on. "Hello?"

In a flood of panic, Rollins quickly hung up, then stared down at the phone.

"It's him," he told Marj. "He's there."

Twenty~one

They went into the Burger King on 102, hardly Rollins' favorite, but the only restaurant still open at this hour. He needed to eat something, to fill himself up. He was famished, but also hollow. He didn't mind being among some regular people, either, who might make him feel less like a freak.

When Rollins returned with their food, he found Marj engrossed in some papers that she had taken from the strongbox, which lay open on the table before her. Marj dug out a few of the french fries and popped them in her mouth while Rollins spread out a napkin on the table to create a kind of placemat for himself, unwrapped his burger, and took a bite. It wasn't nearly as bad as he expected.

"You might want to take a look at this one, Rolo."

Rollins set down his burger and wiped his hands with a napkin. She handed him a neatly folded carbon copy of a typed letter that Neely had written to *Aunt Jane*. It was dated December 19, 1969.

"That's just before he left," Rollins told her. Just after Christmas: The Christmas tree was still up, its lights twinkling.

"Yeah? Well, this is why."

He returned his gaze to the letter. Rollins pictured Cornelia typing away through the night; the letter seemed to be written by someone made sleepless by memory and anguish. He thought of his mother, donning her spectacles to read it. At her small, antique desk in the library, overlooking the garden. Alone. She was always alone, always set apart somehow, like a portrait inside a frame.

> *Dear Aunt Jane:*
> *There is something you should know about me and Uncle Henry. . . .*

So the letter began. It ran three pages, single-spaced. As he read, his fingertips pinning the sheets to the tabletop, he had the sensation of plunging into it, of immersing himself, so that he could visualize the affair that Neely described as if he had actually been there, watching.

He could see how it began:

> *She's in the drawing room, reading a book of poems by Elizabeth Bishop. It's nearly midnight. The children are in bed. Father breezes in from a party, headed for the stairs. Mother had been sick, unable to attend. So he is alone as he sees Neely there in the green chair before the fireplace; she's lit by the warm light of the table lamp. She is wearing a bright shirt from India that brings out the color of her eyes and hair. Father comes to the doorway, stops. He looks at her without speaking. She doesn't notice at first, then looks up. "Hi," she says. Cheerful as always. "Hi," he says back. Softly. Then he turns and leaves the room.*

Later:

> *A Saturday morning. She's in her bedroom in the back of the house, sleeping, when there's a knock at the door. She wakes, rolls over, says, "Come in."*

Father enters slowly, apologizing. She says, "No, it's fine." But she pulls the sheet up. He says he's brought her something. He's hesitant, like a child. He says he'd like to give it to her. She says, "How nice." He brings out a small package that he has concealed behind his back. He comes to her bed, and he hands her the package. It's wrapped in red paper, with a silver ribbon. She hunches up onto her elbows, the sheet up tight to her armpits. "Really—for me?" she says. He nods. She takes the gift from him. "Aren't you going to open it?" he asks. She raises herself up onto her headboard. The bedsheet slips down to her waist. Her nightie is thin; it barely covers her. She undoes the wrapping, she opens the box. She finds—a gold necklace. She melts, it's so beautiful. He says, "I thought of you when I saw it. Try it on." She takes it out of the felt-lined box, brings it around her neck, but has trouble with the clasp. "Here, let me," he says. Their hands touch as he takes the necklace from her. She swings her back around to him, lifts up her hair. He pauses, savoring the moment, then affixes the clasp. "There," he says. "Turn, let me see you." He steps around to see her better. "Glorious," he says. She climbs out of bed, goes to look at herself in the mirror over the dresser. He watches her admire herself. She is stunned by the beauty of the necklace. Still wearing it, she extends her arms to him, gives him a hug. "Thank you, Uncle Henry." "You're certainly welcome," he replies, smiling like never before. She turns her back to him again and lifts her hair, and he undoes the necklace and replaces it in the box. "Don't tell anyone this came from me, all right?" he says, handing it to her. "I'd like it to be our secret."

And so it began. Before she knew it, she was involved. She was on the hook. He had asked, and she had said yes. So that a week later, when he first came into her room at night, when the whole house was asleep and moonlight slanted in under the window shade, she let him enter. She let him remove his clothes and slide into her bed beside her. She let him lift up her nightie, whisper words to her she never expected to hear from him. Amid the confusion and the fear that first time, there was an element of pleasure for her. It had been her first time. Father had gone slowly, lovingly. She continued to seek that pleasure, but, as their encounters continued, she had more and more trouble finding it amid her growing revulsion. Eventually, the revulsion was all there was. That was all she felt their last time together in the Brookline house, the night Stephanie died.

The letter concluded: *I wish that none of this had happened, Aunt Jane.* It was signed, simply, *Cornelia.*

Rollins held the letter a moment. The Burger King was nearly empty, except for some truckers who seemed to have come in to wash up. But Rollins was back on that cold morning when his father never came down to breakfast. Neely had typed the letter out on a manual. The lines were uneven, the periods thick dots, the angry capitals big as billboards. He could almost hear her rapping out the sentences, the keys smacking against the page. He saw, he felt her agony. He bled for her, and for himself. A marriage ended when she was done. He pictured her mother standing up from her desk, pushing in her chair, then going to speak to Father.

"Oh God," Rollins said, sickened.

"Yeah, poor Neely. But I felt bad for your mom, too. Can you imagine getting this from your niece?"

Rollins shook his head.

"But then I found this one." Marj waved another letter in the air. "Take a look at this."

It was a formal invitation that Mrs. Rollins had sent to Neely two years later inviting her to the family's annual clambake at the old house in Gloucester. Marj pointed to the line written in pen at the very bottom. *And I know Henry would love to see you, too.*

"What's *that* all about?" she asked Rollins.

Rollins stared at it, uncomprehending. He could see his puzzled image reflected in the picture window.

Marj picked up another note that she'd set out on the table. "Or this one?" She handed it to Rollins. It was a stiff card, with JANE ROLLINS engraved on it, inviting Neely to tea. *It will be just the two of us this time, I promise.*

"What's that mean 'this time'?" Marj asked. "Like, who was there last time?"

Rollins shook his head. "I don't know."

"Or this one." She passed him a postcard, bearing a Sargent portrait from the Museum of Fine Arts. *Go see him*, read the card. *He needs a lift. Please. Do it for me.*

"There must be five or six more in here," Marj said, stirring the papers around inside the strongbox. "What's she doing—pimping for him?"

"Marj, please!"

"Well—what do *you* call it?"

"I don't know. I don't know what it is."

"It's like your mom would do anything for him."

Rollins looked at her across the table, hoping he'd see something in her eyes, on her face, that would explain everything. He was behind again, scrambling to catch up.

"To get him back," Marj added.

"*What?*" Rollins looked at her in amazement. "That's ridiculous." After he left, she'd removed all the photographs of him at the Brookline house. His parents had not been in the same room, so far as he knew, ever since.

"Rolo, I've got a mother. She's got to know her husband came on to me. But she didn't chuck him out."

"But my mother did chuck my father out. They got divorced. They spent forever working out the settlement." Rollins spoke heatedly. It was too absurd!

"Okay, okay. But listen to me. None of that got started until *after* this letter." Marj tapped it with her index finger. "And she knew all about the sex before. We figured that out, remember? That's why she slapped Neely when your sister drowned. She knew all about it. She had to. If she was going to divorce him for that, she'd have done it five years earlier. She was okay with his screwing around. Not thrilled, obviously. But okay with it. She probably figured that was his way."

"So why'd she divorce him after the letter?"

She ate another french fry, an action that Rollins found irritating. "Maybe it was the humiliation."

"But nobody else knew, except her and Father and Neely."

"Neely knew *she* knew. That's what made it different. Before, your mother could pretend that she didn't know. Once she got this letter, forget it."

Rollins remembered how happy his mother had been to recount the story of her engagement at the Harvard Club. "Happiest day of my life," he said idly.

"What is?"

Rollins explained that's what his mother had said about the day Henry Rollins had proposed to her. "I suppose it isn't something you'd say about a man you loathe."

Twenty-two

Outside the restaurant, the night sky seemed deeper now, the stars colder, more distant. The highway was nearly silent at this hour, and as he followed Marj to the car, Rollins could hear the ringing of the high-intensity lamps that lit up the parking area. He climbed inside the Nissan. He put his key in the switch, but he left it there. "I thought the same thing as Neely." He turned to Marj. "The other day, in the bathtub, when I was thinking about my sister. I was thinking she was *lucky*, being dead." He looked away again. "That's when I went under."

"So you really wanted to, like—"

"Yeah." Rollins felt ashamed of himself. "Until I saw you. I thought you were an angel, come to save me."

Marj turned away from him for a moment and rolled down the window. "Me? An angel? Hardly."

He sat there for a moment, deeply glad to share his little car with her. He thought how wonderful she was to have stayed with him all this time, to see him through his ordeal, to care. The kindness seemed to radiate from her, like warmth from her skin.

But they were not done yet. "I need to have a talk with my mother, don't I?" he told her.

"That's what I was thinking." She looked down at her running clothes. "But I'm not sure I'm dressed for it."

"Don't worry. She'll be delighted."

He pulled out onto 102 and then headed south on 93, bound for 495. Marj returned her gaze to the highway. For a long while, she rode in silence beside him as the roadside trees flew backward outside the window.

"You are being a good son, you know," Marj said.

"What makes you—?" He stopped, sensing a brightness coming from behind. It filled his rearview mirror, and then it lit up the interior of the car, as if a sun had dawned inside it. Rollins turned, and he saw two massive headlights behind him, no more than ten feet behind him, and closing fast. Rollins hit the accelerator.

Beside him, Marj's head jerked back into her headrest. "What?"

"Behind us. Some jerk—" He glanced back again; two headlights were blazing in his rear window. The road ahead was clear, and he pushed up the speedometer to 75, then 80, then 85. The Nissan shuddered wildly, but the other car stayed with him. With its brights up, it was like a ball of light coming after them. Rollins had to move his head to keep the reflected brilliance out of his eyes. "Can you see who it is?" Rollins shouted over the roar of his engine.

"No—it's too bright."

Rollins jerked the Nissan into the right lane, hoping to see the car go flying past, but it moved to stay behind them as if it were magnetically attached.

"It's Jeffries, got to be."

"That *shit*."

Rollins pulled back into the middle lane, but the brightness stayed with them.

Marj whipped around, her hand shielding against the glare. "Come on, come *on.*" Rollins floored it. Road signs and mile markers flew past, but the light behind them grew ever brighter. "He's coming closer!" Marj shouted.

The Nissan's tires screamed as Rollins yanked the steering wheel to the left. But the brightness followed.

Rollins looked to his left: There was no guardrail and the roadside fell away sharply. He smashed down the accelerator, but the speedometer needle didn't budge past 85.

"He's going to ram—" Marj screamed.

A terrible thud rattled the car, snapping Rollins' head back against the headrest and jerking Marj about in her seat. The Nissan swerved. The yellow line marking the road's edge went at a crazy angle, and Rollins could see the gully beside the road open up wide below him. He yanked on the wheel, the tires screeched, the highway seemed to swerve every which way as the Nissan lurched back toward the middle lane again.

"No!" Marj screamed.

Rollins straightened out the Nissan and glanced back into the rearview. The brightness was on him tight, and there were lights up ahead. A low flat-bed truck, laboring in the center lane, dead ahead.

"Watch out!" Marj shot a hand out toward the truck.

"I see it." Rollins flew ahead. The truck loomed up. Jeffries' lights still filled his mirror. Rollins eased off the gas as he closed on the truck. The brightness swelled behind him.

Rollins spun to the right and hit the gas to speed clear. There was a squealing of tires, and the brightness seemed to push right into the flatbed truck with a terrible crunching of metal. Behind him, Rollins could see sparks spew into the air as the long truck lurched to the right toward the Nissan. Behind it, Jeffries' dark sedan slid to the left. Rollins pulled well clear to the breakdown lane in the far right and stopped to watch in horror as the great truck skidded past, the sedan somehow pinned to the flatbed's rear. A road sign buckled and slapped down on the sedan's roof with a great clang, then another one went as the two vehicles careened along with a roar of angry tires. The two vehicles, linked now, skidded on toward the overpass in a slow twisting motion, a death grip. The truck gave out a frantic blast of its horn as it tried to break free, and then, with an explosion of metal and glass, the sedan slammed into the concrete pillar to the left. The truck swung back to the left and was whipped around the far side of the underpass. The cab disappeared down into the gully beyond. Rollins advanced cautiously by the Audi, wrapped around the concrete wall.

"Keep on going, Rolo," Marj said beside him. "Just leave it. He tried to kill us!"

Rollins kept on, watching. He was in the underpass when he saw a man stagger up the hill toward the road. The truck driver, presumably. Then there was an explosion, and the Audi burst into flames—a great ball of orange that leaped up all the way to the bridge above. The truck driver retreated back down into the safety of the gully as Rollins hurried by. His heart was fluttering inside his chest, and he was bathed in sweat.

"That could have been us, Rolo," Marj said.

Once they were safely past the wrecked Audi, Marj asked Rollins to stop. He pulled over in the emergency lane. Marj unclipped her seat belt and threw her arms around Rollins. Soon, she was quaking, her tears spilling down her cheeks and onto his neck as he held her and stroked her hair.

Twenty-three

The stately Maple Hill retirement center glowed yellow amid its ring of security lights when Rollins and Marj finally pulled up the winding drive a little past four A.M. The plan had been to charge right in, wake Rollins' mother up, and start firing questions at her. But now that they were stopped, and everything seemed so quiet all around them, Rollins could see that such a plan had been born of anxiety and exhaustion.

"Can't we rest a little?" Marj asked, as if she'd read his mind.

Rollins thought that they might sleep in his car, but he didn't see a good place to park there in the maple-lined visitors' lot. Even though he'd seen the Audi smash into the side of the overpass, Rollins still couldn't shake the idea that there was someone shadowing him. He feared he never would.

"They've probably got a ton of security," Rollins told Marj after he took a turn about the parking lot. "I'm going to try someplace else." He drove back out onto the main road and took a right into a shopping mall.

Rollins parked the car under a street light, lowered his backrest almost level, and showed Marj which lever to pull so she could do the same. He eased himself back and closed his eyes. For a long time, the sight of that great fireball filled his mind, but he must have slept, because he was surprised to see blue sky up over the roofline of the mall, and cars driving by on all sides. He straightened up and looked over at Marj. Her face was angled toward his, looking almost unbearably calm and lovely. She still wore her seat belt.

She stirred, stretched, groaned. "You might want to think about a midsize, Rolo," she said. "God, my back."

Marj spotted a Denny's in the mall, and they climbed out of the car to use its bathroom. Rollins hated to be apart from her while she went into the women's room. In the men's, Rollins almost didn't recognize the shadowy, unkempt, bleary-eyed figure staring back at him in the mirror over the sink. His clothes seemed encrusted on him. He used the toilet, splashed some water on his face, tucked in his shirt, and then joined Marj at a table for a breakfast that neither one had much stomach for.

"You okay?" Rollins asked Marj as he watched her pick at her eggs.

"I'm not sure I can do this, Rolo."

"It's only my mother."

"Oh, right. Only."

Afterward, they returned to the car and drove back to Maple Hill, and parked in the visitors' lot. He switched off the engine, but she didn't move.

"I'm just going to *talk* to her," he said. "There are things we need to find out."

"Be careful, okay?"

Rollins came around to open the car door for her, but Marj had already stepped out by the time he reached her. The two made their way through the big glass door to the reception desk. Unshaven and filthy in his California clothes, Rollins felt like an impostor, but the woman at the desk merely asked him to sign in while she telephoned up to his mother to say her son was here. She put down the receiver. "Should she have been expecting you?"

"No. Tell her I was in the area."

The receptionist passed that along.

"Okay," she told him. "You know where it is?"

His mother's apartment was on the third floor, at the end of a long hall that was broken up by loveseat-and-table clusters that looked like they'd never been sat in. A few of the doors they passed were adorned with sprigs of plastic flowers. But his mother's door bore only a metal nameplate with JANE ROLLINS on it.

Rollins straightened his shirt collar and gave Marj's hand a squeeze. Then he knocked. After an agonizing delay, his mother swung the door open. She was dressed informally—for her—in a white blouse and blue skirt. Her thin lips were brightened by lipstick, and she'd rouged her cheeks. Hastily, it seemed.

"Oh, my heavens," his mother declared as she took in Rollins' attire. "*Look* at you."

Rollins braced himself for questions, but none came. Neither did a kiss, a handshake, an embrace. There was nothing between them.

His mother turned to Marj in her running clothes. "And *what* do we have here?"

"This is my friend Marj Simmons, Mother."

"My my," Mrs. Rollins said, looking Marj up and down.

Inside, Rollins recognized some of the artwork—a Flemish landscape, a craggy mountain scene done by a lesser member of the Hudson River School—from the library of the Brookline house. The striped chair by the window had come from his mother's bedroom: she'd always sat in it to brush her hair while she listened to the evening symphony on the radio. But these familiar items were intermixed with some newer, too-bright watercolors and blond-wood Danish furniture that didn't seem to go. Perhaps he and Marj didn't belong here, either.

"I used to know an Alexandra Simmons in Brookline," his mother was telling Marj. "Married a Princeton man, Connie Baxter. Is she one of yours, do you suppose?"

"I don't think so," Marj replied, coloring a little. "I'm from the Midwest."

"No Eastern relations?" His mother sounded disappointed.

"None that I know of. My parents are from Chicago."

"No matter." Mrs. Rollins clasped her hands together, as if to dismiss a subject that had proved unpromising. She sat Rollins and Marj down on the green velvet couch, which Rollins realized had come from his father's dressing room. It was soft and wide, and Rollins suddenly had a hideous vision of his father reclining on it with Neely. Mrs. Rollins plucked the tea cozy off the engraved silver teapot on the low table between them. "It should have steeped by now. I've got some toast here, too." She pointed to a plate with a short stack of sliced toast, and butter and jam beside it. "I didn't know what you'd want."

"Actually, we've eaten," Rollins said.

"Have some tea, anyway," his mother insisted. "Formosa oolong—very healthful." She poured out cups for her guests. They chattered in her hand as she passed them. She followed each cup with a tiny urn of sugar cubes (complete with a tiny pair of tongs) and a small, silver milk pitcher. "Now tell me, Marjorie, are you one of Edward's friends from Williams?" she asked Marj.

Rollins heard the coolly gracious tone of a church social.

"I went to Lesley," Marj replied.

"Oh, yes, of course. Now I remember. You're with him at Johnson." Mrs. Rollins seemed to regain her balance a little, now that she had placed Marj in an acceptable part of the universe.

"That's right," Marj said uneasily, with a glance at Rollins. "We've been working in the same department."

Mrs. Rollins raised an eyebrow. "That's permitted, Edward? Dating a colleague?"

"It doesn't really matter," Rollins said. "We've quit."

Mrs. Rollins pulled her head back as if she had encountered an unpleasant smell. "Well! You *are* full of surprises this morning."

"What, your spies haven't told you?" Rollins asked.

His mother's face was like an arrowhead—nose, eyes, and mouth narrowed toward him. "What on earth—?"

"Oh, Mother. For God's sake—let's quit this." Rollins set his teacup down with a clatter. "I need some answers from you."

"My goodness, you sound like some sort of prosecutor." Mrs. Rollins turned to Marj as if trying to win an ally against a monster that had loomed up in their midst. To Rollins' relief, Marj turned her gaze away.

"Am I on trial on here?" Mrs. Rollins asked. She sounded amused, as if her son's behavior had to be a joke.

"What do you know about Jerry Sloane, Mother?"

"Why, I don't believe I know anyone by that name," she replied airily.

"He's a realtor," Rollins pressed.

Mrs. Rollins still looked blank; she was the picture of innocence. "Sorry."

"You recommended him to your sister when she was selling Cornelia's house."

Finally, a slight glimmer. "Did I?"

"Aunt Eleanor told me you did."

"Well, perhaps I did then." She picked some lint off her skirt, giving it far more attention than she did her visitors. "You'll find when you get to my age, you forget so many things. I'm lucky if I can remember my own name some days." She turned to Marj. "You sure you wouldn't like some toast?"

Rollins raised his voice slightly—enough to lower the temperature in the room noticeably. "He stands to inherit Cornelia's estate."

"Who does, dear?" she asked idly.

"Jerry Sloane."

"Well, isn't that interesting."

"Through Cornelia's friend Elizabeth Payzen," he said, eyeing his mother's response. "She's Cornelia's sole beneficiary. And Jerry Sloane is hers."

His mother said nothing, but her eyes did not leave his.

"Elizabeth died yesterday," Rollins went on.

"I'm sorry," his mother said.

"Of course you are, Mother. Jerry comes in to the money next month." He explained about the seven-year rule, which appeared to be a revelation to her. "Perhaps as much as ten million—isn't that what you told me?"

"Yes, I suppose I did." His mother turned her head away, as if the news possibly weighed more heavily on her than her words would indicate. "How lucky for him."

"And for Father," Rollins said evenly.

Mrs. Rollins turned back to him—the quick, sharp movement, Rollins thought, of a frightened animal.

"They're friends, too," Rollins went on. "Small world—isn't it, Mother? They met under rather scandalous circumstances, at a house in North Reading. Perhaps you've heard of it? A ranch house on Elmhurst Drive. Number twenty-nine? Neely went there, too. I've seen photographs. They'd shock you, Mother. They shocked me."

"Well, thank you for the information." It was the tone she used with salesmen.

"It's nothing you don't know."

Mrs. Rollins turned to Marj, whose glance had been shifting uneasily from mother to son. "You must forgive him. There has always been some strain between us."

"That's family for you," Marj said. "I've got one of my own."

"You're in on this, aren't you, Mother?" Rollins shot out the words like bullets.

"My dear boy, I have hardly understood a thing you've said from the moment you arrived. In on what?"

"Neely's murder!" Rollins thundered.

Hearing those words spring from his lips must have been like seeing the world crack apart. Marj's eyes widened, and Rollins felt himself quaking in unusual parts of his body, like his wrists and the underside of his knees.

But his mother merely shook her head. Rollins had seen that expression before: years ago, when she spoke to his psychiatrist, Dr. Ransome, after his sessions. Bafflement and self-pity that a son of hers should have such regrettable problems; that's what her look said.

Rollins' irritation mounted—a lifetime of slights, indignities, and willful misunderstandings on the part of his mother now rose in his chest. He tried to pierce her with his eyes, to strip away that protective veneer and engage with the soul underneath—a soul, he thought bitterly, he had only inferred. But she looked away.

"He's a real bastard, Mother, and you've been working with him," Rollins seethed.

"That is quite enough."

Rollins leaped up. "My God! I can't *believe* it! You!" The words flew out of his mouth, high-pitched and breathless. He was barely aware of what he was saying. "You! You had Neely killed!"

His mother tensed; her gaze tightened on him. "Would you please talk sense."

"We've seen the letter, Mrs. Rollins," Marj told her.

Mrs. Rollins turned to Marj. "Don't you start."

Rollins came to Marj's aid. "The one that Cornelia wrote to you, telling you of her affair with your husband."

"You couldn't have," Mrs. Rollins snapped.

"And why's that?"

"Because I burned it."

That brought silence for a moment. Rollins could hear some people slowly make their way down the corridor outside her door. "We saw a copy, Mother. A carbon copy from her typewriter. She kept it."

Mrs. Rollins picked up her napkin and then set it down again. "I see." She looked at Rollins, who was standing up just to her left. "Oh, sit *down*, would you?" she commanded. "I think we've had enough histrionics for one morning."

With some irritation, Rollins returned to the sofa.

"All right," Mrs. Rollins continued. "I will tell you about that letter. It's time you knew. It's past time. Hand me that cane, would you?" She directed Marj to the walking stick propped against the end of the sofa. "Excuse me, but I must rise. I find that my hip bothers me if I sit too long." She took the cane from Marj, stood up, and went to the window. It bothered Rollins that his mother should range freely while he was confined to the couch.

"Yes, I received Cornelia's letter." It had not come in a conventional envelope, Mrs. Rollins explained, but in a puffy brown mailer. It arrived in late December 1969 with the words *Do Not Open Until Christmas* on the front, along with the initials *C. B.* Mrs. Rollins didn't recognize the initials or the handwriting. She figured it was a box of chocolates from somebody at the club and set it under the tree without thinking. On Christmas Day, however, she couldn't find the package. Increasingly puzzled, she searched everywhere for it. She finally found it late that night; it was out in the trash barrels behind the house. "Of course, it didn't contain chocolates at all."

Besides Cornelia's letter, the package contained photocopies of twenty or thirty of Henry's love letters to her. Jane Rollins read them all right there in the driveway in the light from the windows, even though it was snowing, and she was standing there just in her slippers. "They were very passionate letters. Rather graphic."

"We've read them," Rollins said. "Cornelia saved those, too."

"Have you." Mrs. Rollins stopped a moment. "Then you know. Your father was asleep by then, and I ran right into his room and woke him up. I'm surprised you didn't hear us, because, my God, I tore into him. I felt such anger. I made him leave that night. Just—out. Good-bye. I simply could not bear to have him stay another minute."

When she finished her tale, there was silence for a few moments—until Rollins started clapping. Slowly at first, then faster. "Well done, Mother," he exclaimed. "A stunning performance."

Mrs. Rollins looked at him, surprised.

"There's only one problem," Rollins went on.

"What's that?"

"You already knew. You'd known for years. You knew the night that Stephanie died. You knew when you screamed at me, blaming *me* for her death. When I was six, damn you. Six! When I was *not* to blame. And you knew when you slapped Neely and sent her out of the house."

"How can you presume to say what I knew?"

"Because Father told me," Rollins said. Beside him, Marj looked at him anxiously. But he felt strong, secure. He had gotten very good at lying.

His mother professed surprise. "When?"

"Just last night, Mother. On the phone. He's in Townshend, you know. I called him. We had a nice talk. We hadn't talked like that in years. Much of it was about you. Oh, yes, Mother. He told me all about your arrangement with him."

Mrs. Rollins eased back slightly onto the windowsill. Rollins had the sense of her falling, as though some powerful support had given way beneath her. Marj had been right. She had known his mother better than he had himself. Now, it was as if he were seeing his mother for the first time. She had granted her husband his fateful affair with Neely: It had gained her the upper hand. She held his secret, and she also got to play the stoic, a role to which she was always much better suited than that of lover.

"So, after the letter, you cast him out," Rollins told her. "You married again. To dear Albert Crossan, may he rest in peace. And Father remarried, too. Not once, but twice. But you couldn't forget him, could you? He was the only man you ever loved—that's what you were trying to tell me at the Harvard Club, wasn't it?" He waited a moment, then decided to give the knife another twist. "And he loved you, too. He told me that."

"He did?" Rollins' mother said eagerly. "He said that?"

"Yes. He loved you. He loved everything about you."

There was hope in her eyes.

She was exposed; it was time to strike. "Especially your money. That was the thing he loved best. And those fabulous parties you got invited to. And, oh yes, he loved your many connections in Boston society. And your family. He just loved your family. Especially Neely."

"The viper!" His mother seemed to be in physical pain.

"He also told me his suspicions about you and Jerry Sloane."

"Me and—?" It was as if he'd struck her.

"That's what he said, Mother. I wanted to speak to you before I reported it to the authorities."

A last flicker of anger. "You wouldn't dare."

"We'll see about that." Rollins stood up, victorious. "I think we can go now, Marj."

Leaning on her cane, Mrs. Rollins lurched unsteadily toward them, her arm outstretched toward her son. "No! Don't go—please!" A new tone in her voice—asking, not telling.

For the first time ever, he thought his mother might actually cry. He pressed his advantage. "As I said before, Mother. I've come here for answers. If I can't get them, I'll let the police do it." He reached for the door handle.

"Wait!"

Rollins stopped, turned.

His mother was leaned toward him, her hand outstretched. Seeing him halted before her, she clamped her free hand down on her cane to recover her balance. She waited a moment, as if to muster the strength for what she had to say.

"All right. Yes, I loved your father. To that, I plead guilty." She waited a moment. "He could be difficult. Every man comes at a price. That affair with young Cornelia was his. Oh, but it was a vile, horrid thing. I suppose I tried to convince myself that she enticed him. There are two sides to these stories, you'll find. Always. But yes, my God, I did love him. We had some wonderful times together." She leaned back against the doorway to the kitchen, as if exhausted by the revelation. "Sometimes, I think that those early years with Henry were the only time I ever really lived." She paused a moment. "Pathetic, I suppose." Her voice found a deeper register. "But I had *nothing* to do with Cornelia's disappearance. The first I heard of it was a week after it happened, when my sister called me in a panic to say that Cornelia couldn't be found anywhere." She reached for her son's hand. "You have to believe that, Edward, no matter what your father says. I am shocked that he would suggest otherwise. That is a detestable lie."

Her eyes fell again; she looked abject, ashamed. "But yes, I do know Jerry Sloane. I should have been more candid with you. I am not particularly proud of the association." She paused. "I met him through your stepfather at a golf event of his on the North Shore. The concrete business attracts all sorts, as you may know. We fell into conversation. He was drinking, I believe. He mentioned to me that he knew my former husband. Gradually, things proceeded from there. He has been very useful to me. He is a man of the world. He knows things that I could never have found out on my own, and would not care to. He was my liaison to Henry."

"Through the house in North Reading?"

"Initially, yes." She closed her eyes, as if seeking absolution.

"Did you have any idea what went on there?"

"I did not want to know, nor did I need to. Your father had certain—needs—that I could never satisfy. That was very clear to me from early on." Her eyes found Marj, who had been listening intently. "What a wonderful introduction to our family this must be for you."

"But Mother, what about Neely's money?"

"I have dealt with the devil," Mrs. Rollins said. "This is what comes of it."

"Were you the one to tell Jerry Sloane about Neely's additional inheritance?"

"No. We didn't discuss such things."

"He knew about it somehow."

Mrs. Rollins fell silent. "Possibly, I mentioned it to your father."

"So you are in touch?"

"From time to time, yes. When he needs me."

"Mother, did you ask Jerry Sloane to keep tabs on me?"

"Absolutely not. My goodness, the *idea*."

"He hired two other people to help him. One of them tried to follow me down here. He tried to hit my car, Mother. Fortunately for Marj and me, his car went off the road and slammed into the side of an underpass."

"How awful!" His mother seemed stricken. "I'm glad you weren't hurt."

"You don't know why he might have wanted to do that, Mother?"

"I can't imagine anyone wanting to do such a thing."

Rollins fixed her with his eyes. "Mother, did you ever think about what might have happened to Neely?"

"I'm happy to say I've put that matter entirely out of my mind."

"Yesterday, I found a poem that she wrote shortly before she disappeared," Rollins continued. "It sheds some new light on 'that matter.'"

"Oh?"

"It's all about Father, about how he used to come for her at night. I think he'd just come back to see her. He was in the East around that time, living in Townshend."

"When did she write this, did you say?"

"On September fourteenth, nineteen ninety-three. Just before she vanished."

"Before—before she vanished," his mother repeated slowly. She seemed dazed, uncomprehending.

"He might have been there that very night, Mother."

Finally, shock as the full implications kicked in, and the woman who had always been in full control finally lost control. Her frightened eyes and gaping mouth gave away her surprise, her terror. "Your father? There that night? But—but he told me he'd given her up. He promised—" Mrs. Rollins gave out a strange, muffled cry, and her face went white with a look of pain and horror, as if she were being strangled by unseen hands. Her legs buckled underneath her, and she crumpled to the floor.

Twenty-four

She landed on her side, her head and shoulder on the Persian rug. Her skirt had pulled up, exposing her slip, and her arms and legs were at awkward angles. Rollins stared down at her, this woman who had dominated his life, now lying on the floor before him. He was several feet away, but he found himself unable to move closer.

Marj crouched down to her almost immediately. "Mrs. Rollins? Are you okay?"

Rollins' mother's eyes were open. Her lips quivered, but no sound came out except a gasping noise as she drew the air into her lungs. An arm shifted and a knee flexed, as if she were twitching in her sleep.

Rollins just watched, transfixed. His world had tipped over.

"Rolo, come *on*. We've got to do something."

"Just lie there, Mother," Rollins said, finally coming to his senses.

He grabbed a pillow off the couch and Marj gently slipped it under Mrs. Rollins' head. "Stay still now. Don't try to move."

Rollins went to the telephone. There was a sticker on it listing the retirement center's emergency number. He dialed it. "It's my mother, Jane Rollins," he said. "She's fallen to the floor. There's something terribly wrong. She can't get up. She needs help. Quickly, please."

A nurse from the center came moments later. She was young, with her hair up in combs; her blue-and-white uniform rustled when she moved. Rollins pointed to the spot just outside the kitchen where his mother lay. Marj was kneeling by her head, touching a cool cloth to her forehead. The nurse tried to talk to his mother, but she got only a babyish whimper in reply.

"We were—we were talking," Rollins hurriedly told the nurse. He hoped he didn't sound defensive. "And she just . . . fell over."

"She have a history of heart trouble?"

"I don't think so."

"Is she on any medication? Heart pills, anything like that?"

"Not that I know of." Rollins weakened: "We've been a little out of touch."

"I see." The nurse fetched a blanket from the bedroom and placed it over his mother. "You'll be just fine, Mrs. Rollins. Just lie there, all right? We'll be taking you to a hospital in a few minutes and getting you all fixed up."

The EMTs arrived a few minutes later. There were three of them, clean-cut young men in pale green jumpsuits, with walkie-talkies blaring. They bent down to her to check her vital signs. Marj stood up to give them room.

"All of sudden, she just went," Rollins told him. The truth was too private—not just that he had provoked her collapse, but that he took grim satisfaction in doing so. It was the dark pleasure of revenge.

"Looks like stroke," one of the men told Rollins. "It can go like that. Just—boom." He asked more questions about medication and medical history. Rollins felt guilty not to know the answers. He knew so little about his mother.

"We better get her to the emergency room," another medic said.

They gently leaned her sideways, slid a slim, metal board under her, and strapped her onto it. They lifted her up onto the gurney, secured her, then wheeled her to the door. She was merely a package now.

"Where are you taking her?" Marj asked.

"Hartford Hospital. Downtown."

Rollins trailed along behind the gurney. He was conscious of the worried stares of the other residents in the hallway. Outside, Rollins was puzzled by the glare; he seemed to have forgotten what season it was, or even what year.

Marj had to remind him where he'd left the car. "You okay there, Rolo? You want me to drive?" she asked him.

"I'll be fine."

Yet as he maneuvered the Nissan out to the street, and then to the highway, he found that it was difficult to stay with the ambulance. Despite its flashing lights, he kept tuning out, losing focus, as he watched his mother fall, over and over. It was so remarkable, like seeing a building dynamited. One moment, a grand, outdated edifice stands there, tall and imperious. The next, it's nothing but rubble and billowing dust.

And Rollins himself had lit the fuse.

The hospital was a massive, gleaming structure in a leafy part of town just off the highway. Nearing it, Rollins drove by some children splashing about an open hydrant. The technicians pulled up at the emergency entrance and wheeled his mother directly into the hospital through a pair of double doors.

Rollins and Marj hurried around to the visitors' entrance, where a nurse behind a glass partition took down Mrs. Rollins' basic information. They settled into the chairs farthest from the overhead TV. Marj reached for Rollins' hand. "You doing okay?" she asked.

"It just keeps going, doesn't it?"

"What does?"

Rollins had to search for the word. "The pain. All the pain in the family. Stephanie's dying, Neely, the divorce, my parents' sick relationship. It's like our family keeps getting torn apart until there's nothing left."

"And now this."

"Yeah. Now this." Rollins turned to her. "Do you think she feels it, Marj? Do you think it finally hit her, everything she'd done?"

"I don't know, Rolo."

Rollins looked into Marj's eyes, which seemed to search his in return. "It always seemed like I was the only one who felt it. The only one who even noticed." He stiffened. "That's why *I* got packed off to the child psychiatrist." He reached for her, brought his face close to hers. "You don't still think I'm strange, do you?"

She brought her hand around to the back of his head, gripped him. "Oh, honey."

"You did, at first. I know you did."

Marj smiled devilishly.

"But you understand me better now, don't you?"

She kissed him lightly on the cheek. "Of course, Rolo."

It took about a half hour before the chief resident, Dr. Adams, a tall, bespectacled man in green surgical garb, emerged from the ER and came up to Rollins. "You Jane Rollins' son?" he asked.

Rollins nodded, and Dr. Adams beckoned him back into the hallway, away from the noise. "Look, there's no good way to put this," he began. "Your mother's had quite a massive stroke." Rollins listened numbly as the doctor reported the grim particulars: mental function difficult to determine; speech impairment severe; the right side of her body almost completely paralyzed.

The facts struck like a stick against some distant drum. His words had the sound of fate, of finality.

"Paralyzed, you say?" Rollins asked finally. It was so hard to believe that he'd heard right, that the damage might be lasting, even permanent.

"On the right side, yes. I'm afraid so."

"Could I see her?"

"Of course."

Rollins returned to the waiting room to get Marj. She seemed so alone there in her seat.

"It's a stroke," he told her. "She's half paralyzed."

"Oh, Rolo," Marj said, her features darkening. She reached for him, and Rollins took her hand and together they followed the doctor back down a long corridor, through a pair of double doors and into the ICU. His mother was in a private room near the nurse's station. She lay on her back, motionless, beside a great stack of high-tech monitors and arrays. An IV tube ran into her left arm. She seemed terribly small in the bed, as if she'd been swallowed up by the sheets and blankets that lay on top of her. A white bandage was wound tightly around her head like a skullcap, and there was an angry bruise over her left eye. She seemed to be sleeping. Her eyes were shut, but her lips still quivered. Rollins wondered if she was being tormented by her dreams.

"We've got her on blood thinners. They'll clear out any blockage," Dr. Adams said, looking down at her. "We're going to keep an eye on her here for the next few days."

"And afterward?" Rollins asked.

Dr. Adams turned grim. "Well, we'll have to see."

Back in the waiting room, Rollins had Marj check her answering machine again for word from Schecter. This time, Marj reported that a message had come in. "He says Sloane is continuing on out Route 2. He's up by the Vermont border."

"Oh, Christ," Rollins exclaimed. "He's probably going to my father's! He's going to Townshend! When did Al leave that message?"

"An hour ago."

Rollins checked his watch. It was 11:30. Sloane and Schecter could be almost to Townshend by now. He used the pay phone to try Schecter's cell phone, but was unable to get through. He slammed down the receiver and turned back to Marj.

"I never told Al my father was there in Townshend. He could be walking into a trap."

"He'll be all right. He can handle himself."

Rollins spoke firmly: "I've got to go up there, Marj."

"And leave me here with your mother?" Her voice rose in anger. "In the hospital, after this huge stroke? When I hardly know her?"

"I've got to finish this, Marj. I've got to get there. I've got to find out what happened to Neely. That's the only way out of this mess. And my father knows, Marj. I've got to see him."

"But he might *hurt* you!" She was near tears.

"I'll be all right. He's still my father."

"And Sloane?"

He had no answer to that. He simply took her in his arms and drew her slim, soft body tightly against his. "I'm sorry, Marj. But I've got to do this." He stroked the back of her neck, wishing that he could do that forever. Finally, he pulled himself away from her. "I'll be back as soon as I can. Then we'll be free of all this for good, I promise." He reached into his back pocket for his wallet. "Here." He gave her his bank card, and whispered his password. "This will keep you going."

"I don't want your money."

"Take it." He pushed the hand holding the bank card back toward her. "Please."

"But I don't want to stay here. I hate hospitals."

"Please, Marj. For me."

"I want to be done with all this." The tears started to fall.

Rollins kissed them away. "You will be—very soon. I promise."

In the end, she'd walked him to his car. She gave him a big hug before he climbed into the Nissan. "Be careful, okay?" she whispered. Then she grabbed the back of his neck and pulled him to her and kissed him on the lips.

From Hartford, Rollins took Route 91 north along the broad Connecticut River up past the old mill towns of Springfield and Chicopee. The highway was fully stocked with cars heading to unknown destinations, but Rollins scarcely noticed them. He checked occasionally for Schecter's Cressida, or Sloane's massive Land Cruiser, but for the most part he thought only about where he was going now. In Marj's honor, he kept the radio tuned to hard rock as he cruised along, and, for a couple of songs he knew she liked, he even cranked up the volume till he could feel the beat in his chest. He imagined that it was Marj's touch on him, as if their bodies were pressed together, even now.

He crossed into Vermont and finally turned off 91 by South Woodstock and pulled in for gas at the shiny new Mobil station, and then, famished, bought a sandwich and a bottle of ginger ale in the accompanying convenience mart.

As Rollins continued on from Brattleboro, there was a blanket of green all around, and an occasional sprinkling of wildflowers; mauve shadows stretched across the foothills. Vermont had always been a frosty, white world when he'd come as a boy. Now, Rollins felt almost hopeful as he drove along with the window down, taking in the fresh, grass-scented breeze and all the scenery. Perhaps the dreadful suspicions about his father, Sloane, and Neely were merely a terrible misunderstanding. Yes, his father might have had an affair with Neely years before, and he might have come by to see her in the days, possibly even the hours, before she disappeared. But that didn't necessarily mean that he'd killed her. His father's hands had never felt particularly soft on Rollins, but they weren't brutal. He could have come and gone without incident—one of the dozens of people who had harmlessly crossed Neely's path shortly before her disappearance. Why single out his father?

After South Woodstock, the valley opened out, cows and horses appeared in the fields, a few hay barns sprang up, and houses crowded together along the roadside. They were mostly white, with steep metal roofs that gleamed in the setting sun. Finally, Rollins reached the village of Townshend itself: a cluster of small shops, a tiny library, a gas station, and a country store with baskets of vegetables for sale out front. He used to trudge along this snowpacked street as a youngster: Bells would jingle when the shop doors opened with a blast of warmth. It was just the four of them back then, since the family was "roughing it," as his mother said, without help. Cooking, skiing, shoveling snow—the family had seemed to Rollins almost cheerful on these winter holidays.

On the far side of town, Rollins took the third left by an A-frame onto Bald Mountain Road, an unpaved cul-de-sac that climbed up to a trailhead ten miles in. The family place was a few miles down on the right. His apprehension rose as he neared it, and he kept a careful eye out for Sloane's SUV as he drove along. The entrance had always been marked by a towering birch that rose up by a snow-covered boulder. But, as he slowly drew near, he could see only the boulder, bare now except for the name ROLLINS painted in black letters that had dribbled a little. Through the swaying pines, Rollins could just make out the shadowy outline of the house. No lights were on now, in the gathering dusk, and, to his surprise, he didn't see any cars in the driveway. Still, he thought it wise to go well past the house, on beyond the next bend in the road. Better not to reveal himself too soon.

He pulled over by a thick stand of slender beeches, their leaves fluttering in the evening breeze. He rubbed his hands together and took a few breaths to calm himself. He'd hide his car here and approach the house on foot. Because of the dead end, neither Sloane nor his father were likely to drive past; he didn't want to give either of them advance notice of his presence. Still, it was better to leave the Nissan facing town, so Rollins could make a quick exit if necessary.

The unpaved road was narrow, and it was bounded on either side by soft shoulders of dirt that was thick with weeds. He pulled on the wheel and carefully inched around to the far edge. But when he backed, he could feel the rear of the car drop suddenly as his left rear wheel slid over the edge of the hardened surface. "Damn." He pressed on the accelerator, but the wheel seemed only to dig in deeper. Any benign feelings toward his father faded with the realization that he absolutely did not want him—let alone Sloane—to find him here, stuck, vulnerable. He tried the gas again. Nothing. In desperation, he mashed down the accelerator one last time. The tires gave out a fierce roar, and the Nissan lurched back onto the road with a squeal. Rollins' blood surged out to his fingertips, but he hit the brakes to keep the car from slipping over the far edge. After checking the sightlines to make sure the car was not visible from the house or the approaching road, he pulled on the hand brake and climbed out.

Heart pounding, on foot he headed back down the road toward the house. After checking again to make sure there was no car in the driveway, and that no lights burned in the house, he turned in to the driveway.

It changed everything to be here. His senses were so heightened, he somehow imagined he could hear the light glinting off the window-panes of the old farmhouse and could feel on his own skin the scraping of the pine branches against the weather-beaten shingles.

Compared to the big house in Brookline, or his grandmother's sea-side palace, the farmhouse had always seemed small. But had it always been this run-down? The trim wanted paint, the brick steps needed repointing, and the few shrubs that grew along the side of the house looked dry.

"Hello?" he shouted. "Father?"

There was no answer.

Whatever optimism Rollins had first felt upon seeing the verdant Vermont hills had left him. It was scary to be here. There were no kind spirits in this house. Rollins moved quietly across the driveway, which was sprinkled with rust-colored pine needles. He might have been a child again, creeping about. As before, the silence reminded him of how much he didn't know.

There was a small shed off to the side of the house, by some poplars. Rollins swung open the door and poked his head inside. In the dim light, he could make out various woodworking tools hanging off hooks along the far wall. Rollins had never seen his father work with his hands, except for an occasional afternoon spent washing his precious Saab. He'd always avoided all machinery, never worn work gloves. All that had fallen to Gabe. Yet on the workbench rested a large red engine with two rubber tubes attached, one of them splattered with what looked like mud. Rollins wiped away some grime from the housing with his fingers. He made out the word HALE in large, angled type. On the table beside it was an instruction booklet concerning the operation of a diaphragm pump, along with several wrenches, some pliers, and a pair of soiled gloves.

He stepped back out onto the driveway. "Father?" he called again. But he heard nothing except the wind swishing through the trees.

Rollins went up onto the small, screened-in porch at the front of the house and peered in the sidelights by the front door. It was so dark inside all he could see was his own dim reflection in the glass. He rapped on the door and shouted, but received no answer. He tried the knob; it turned, and he stepped inside. "Father?" Still silence, except an occasional creak of the floorboards. As Rollins surveyed the shadowy interior, he realized that, for all he knew, his father could be lurking in the darkness like some savage.

The hallway was bare except for a throw rug across the floor. So different from when he was a child and winter clothing was scattered about. The household had never been exactly joyful, but it was usually somewhat active, and there was often a bright fire going in the hearth. Now, it was cool inside, and dark and silent.

"Hello?" he called again.

The living room was just to the right. The adults had taken their cocktails here on the chintz sofa by the old stone fireplace. Now, the room was dominated by a metal desk bearing a dusty computer with a small screen. There were some papers piled up, most of them investment-related: annual reports, newsletters, prospectuses. From what Rollins could make out, few displayed signs of any profitable business activity on his father's part.

Off to the side of the desk, however, by itself, lay a single, folded-up sheet tucked under the flap of an envelope. Rollins slid it free and opened it up. The handwriting was scrawled, and the text began without salutation:

FYI, the woman's name is Marjorie Simmons, called Marj. She's late-twenties, a bit of a looker, and your son appears very attached. I agree, the best way to close out your son's inquiries is to scare her off. Last night, I placed that call to her we talked about. I'll let you know what happens. Remember—burn this letter. Leave nothing between us.

The letter was unsigned, but Rollins had no doubt that it was from Jerry Sloane.

So he *had* made the frightening call that brought Marj to his apartment several days ago.

Rollins jerked open the desk drawers. He discovered office supplies and stationery (with *Henry P. Rollins, investment counselor* on Xeroxed letterhead), plus a few meager bills for necessities like gas and electricity. He checked the credit card statements: payments of under $100 a month, mostly for gasoline and groceries. To Rollins, who rarely passed a month without incurring at least $800 in restaurant bills on his American Express card, it looked as though his father had taken a vow of poverty. The incoming mail was stacked in a holder on top of the file cabinet. Rollins flipped through it. He found mostly the usual solicitations, but one envelope stopped him. It was from *JAR* in Farmington, Connecticut. It was slit open, and there was a note inside. *Perhaps this will tide you over. Call me, would you please? I can never reach you.* It was signed, *Missing you, J.* In the lower left was a notation in pencil. *Rec'ved, $2,000.00*

Rollins' hand trembled to hold such an odious bill of sale. Two thousand dollars for what? A few moments of affection? Was that always his price? And was Rollins himself the product of such a bargain?

He passed through to the small room behind. The bird-filled wallpaper he'd always loved was badly water-stained in places, and there was a small TV (never allowed in his day) in the corner, plus a stack of old *New Yorker*s beside a couch. Rollins went back across the hall through the barren dining room, where oil portraits of his Arnold grandparents hung, and through the open doorway to the kitchen. The refrigerator buzzed, and the large clock over the stove ticked noisily, but otherwise the room was silent.

"Father?" he called again. Yesterday's *New York Times* was spread open across the table, and some dirty dishes were piled in the sink.

There was an answering machine on the counter below the wall phone. The message light was on. Was there a message that would explain his father's whereabouts? Rollins pressed the replay button. "You have one new message," said a chirpy, automated voice. "First new message. Four-seventeen P.M." There was a pause, and a gruff, male voice came on the line. "Hey, you there? Look, I've got some things to take care of, and I won't get to your place until nine. Be there, okay? I need to see you." Sloane's voice.

Rollins checked his watch. It was 7:28. He had about an hour and a half.

He opened the back door, and went out onto the steps. A bad odor—manure, probably—seemed to be blowing in from the far field. Before him, on the grass, slender wickets had been set up for croquet.

Neely's blond hair down over her face. The mallet between her tanned legs. And Father watching.

"Neely?" he called out. A whisper this time, a quiet plea. But the rank smell got to him, and he turned back inside, the screen door snapping shut behind him.

He checked the front window. No car had pulled in the driveway.

Uncertainty had turned to unease, and now was deepening into an almost bottomless dread. It was the thought of Neely again, as she once was, flitting about the croquet balls. That thought in the gathering dusk, amid the silence, the poverty and the stench from the fields. That thought gave shape to the fear growing within him. Death was here, close by. He could feel it.

Where he stood in the hallway, there was a pair of large cabinets. In his mounting terror, all he could think was that they were big enough to store a body in. He grabbed the knobs, and yanked open both doors. But when his eyes adjusted to the darkness, he saw only mops, paper plates, glass jars, and various cleaning supplies.

Farther along that same wall, a narrow door led down to the basement. As a child, Rollins used to go down sometimes with his father to replace a blown fuse in the antique fuse box at the foot of the stairs. That had been a rare thrill, a quiet acknowledgment of shared manhood. But he dreaded venturing down now, afraid of what he might find below. Still, he lifted a small flashlight off a pegboard on the adjoining wall, opened the door, and started down.

The stairs were rickety, and there were some spiderwebs in the top corners of the stairwell. He made his way down slowly, shining his light ahead of him. The old fuse box had been replaced by a more modern one in a shiny bluish case. But otherwise the basement was unchanged. It was as cold and damp as ever, and the rough stone walls were wet in places from condensation. The floor was packed earth, rock hard.

Shining the flashlight across it, he checked for any indentations or uneven places to suggest a shallow grave, just as Schecter had years before in the woods by Neely's house. If she had indeed been buried down here, the floor had long since been smoothed out over her. It was now as flat as poured concrete.

Rollins flashed his light about—to some shelves laden with dusty plates, piles of newspapers, an abandoned washing machine. In the far corner, a stack of empty cardboard boxes were heaped up. He went closer and scattered them with a kick. It took a few more swipes of his hand to clear away the last of the boxes, revealing a massive wooden crate that had been hidden within. It came up to his waist, and it bore stickers saying FRAGILE and HANDLE WITH CARE. It was not empty: When he squatted down and gave it a push, he could barely move it. Reluctantly, he brought his nose down to it, but, to his relief, he detected no particular scent. He tried to pry up the lid with his fingers. But it was sealed tight with heavy staples all the way around. Then he remembered seeing a hammer in the work shed.

Above his head, a narrow ventilation window faced the driveway. He dragged a bundle of newspapers over; standing on tiptoe, Rollins could just see out. No car had come into the driveway. He should be safe if he hurried. He climbed the stairs and ran back outside to the work shed. He quickly grabbed a hammer off the wall and dashed back down the kitchen stairs. Breathing heavily now, he pried up one of the crate's staples, then another, and another. He listened for any sounds from the house as he worked; several times, he stopped to check the basement window. Staple by staple, he made his way around two sides of the box, then three, then four. Finally, he pulled up the lid. The crate was filled with wood shavings. He plunged his hands in—and struck something cold and hard with his fingertips. He scooped out some of the shavings, and shone his flashlight in. He could see something dark inside, way down deep. He frantically dug out some more shavings, and a large, engraved card flew out with them and fluttered to the floor. He picked it up. *Cupid*, it said in flowing letters at the top. The text began: *Congratulations on your purchase of the very finest outdoor statuary available . . .*

He'd found a large, well-packed garden ornament.

He breathed again.

Just then, Rollins heard a thump upstairs, then rapid clicks, suggesting movement. He scooped the shavings back in with both hands, then replaced the lid and piled the boxes back up over it. He held on to the hammer, just in case, and returned up the stairs. Back in the kitchen again, he checked his watch: 7:45. Sloane wouldn't have come this early, would he?

He called out: "Father? That you?" The clicking noise continued, louder now, like shoes crossing a wooden floor. The hammer up to protect himself, he went back through the dining room, then out to the hall. The house was darker now, but he didn't dare shine his light. "Father?" he called again. He looked in the sitting room—nothing. He checked the living room. The same. But the rapping sounds continued. He mounted the stairs, his heart beating madly. There were three bedrooms up there. "Father?" Then a whisper. "Neely?" It felt good—hopeful—to call her name. Perhaps she was held prisoner there. Gagged, bound. Locked in a closet. *Alive.* The sound grew louder as he rose. The click was sharper, more insistent, and he could hear a rubbing sound, too. He went into the end room, where he'd always slept as a child. The same twin beds, with their matching green bedspreads, the same red bureau. For a moment, silence. Then a heavy shape swinging toward the window and a loud crack. In the wind, a pine branch was jostling a loose shutter. Rollins relaxed the arm that held the hammer. Thoughts of Neely receded again.

His brother's room was behind him. It was identical to Rollins' own, except the bedspreads were a matching blue. Closet, bureau—empty. He glanced out the back window as he passed through. In the fading light, he could just make out a small mound of dirt in the hay field past the edge of lawn. The house was on a slight rise, giving fine views of the mountains out the back; the surrounding fields sloped down, so the mound had been hidden from the ground floor. A hose ran into the pit, which—judging by the dirt—must be barely a foot deep. It looked like the hose came up from the brook that flowed through the far trees. His father must be irrigating some new planting with brook water. Hence the toolshed pump. That was all he could figure.

His parents' room was across the hall. It had a double bed, unmade. What strange passion had it held? The closet was filled with clothes, all of them men's. He recognized some of his father's fine suits and jackets in see-through garment bags off to one end, evidently unused. He turned back to the room. A couple of Tom Clancy paperbacks were out on the bedside table by the telephone. The bureau was past the window under the eaves. He checked the driveway once more, then tried the drawers. The lower ones had the usual pants, sweaters, and shirts. All of them coarse and cheap; none were made of the splendid, rich material he'd always associated with his father. The smaller, upper-right drawer was filled with balled-up socks and jockey underwear. As he rummaged through these underthings, his flashlight caught on a patch of white toward the back.

He pulled the drawer open all the way. A small white box was taped to the drawer's rear wall. He peeled the box loose and set it down on the bureau top. He removed several rubber bands and lifted off the cover. Inside, there was a slender gold necklace, a couple of rings, and a woman's wristwatch, a slim Omega. Its crystal was shattered, and the watch hands were frozen at 10:23. The broken glass suggested violence, pain. With trembling fingers, he turned the watch over. The back bore an engraving. *From E. P. to C. B.* it said. *Love, always.* In a flash, Rollins could see his father's blows raining down, hear Neely's screams.

Almost frantic, Rollins stuffed the watch in his pocket, then dropped the other jewelry back into the box and resealed it in the back of the drawer. His lungs burned for air, and his heart pounded. But mostly he was conscious of a sickening feeling in the pit of his stomach. He needed a bathroom, desperately. Hunched over, he clapped a hand over his mouth and rushed down the hall. He pushed open the bathroom door, reached the toilet just in time before he bent over and delivered two heaves of vomit.

Then—the sound of an engine. The crank of a hand brake and the slam of a car door. He turned the tap for some water, but the faucet only sputtered, producing a dribble of water that he swished around inside his mouth then spat into the sink. He pushed the plunger to flush the toilet, but nothing happened. He closed the toilet lid, slid the hammer under the bathtub, and hurried downstairs. He heard a dog yip, and out the front window, he could see a tall man striding across the driveway.

"Hold on there, Scamp," the man said gruffly.

Rollins moved slowly, his stomach uneasy.

The man looked rugged in blue jeans and a faded T-shirt, clothes that had always been foreign to his father. He was reaching into the back of a red pickup truck, a vehicle that was all wrong, too. What had become of his beloved Saab? Stranger still, the man pulled out a rifle. This was inconceivable. His father had never hunted, never shot.

But it was his father, unmistakably.

Rollins yelled out to him: "Father! It's me! Edward!" His first impulse was to run to him, confess everything, and cling to him as he had when he was a boy. But the stiff, purposeful way his father moved, and his tight grip on the gun, caused Rollins to stay by the door.

"Edward?" his father called to him. He sounded as if he'd half-expected him.

A small black dog rushed toward Rollins, growling.

"Quiet," his father commanded.

His father's hair had gone gray, and he was nearly bald on top. His eyes were hooded, and the set of his mouth suggested despondency. He came toward Rollins slowly. "Well, I'll be damned," he said, shaking his head. "Look at you."

Rollins had forgotten about his clothes.

"No car?" his father asked.

"I parked on the road." Rollins paused, unsure how that would go down. "I didn't want to get in your way."

His father eyed him a moment. "What brings you up here?"

"Well, I—I hadn't seen you in a while," Rollins began. The dog continued to growl.

"Scamp!" His father slapped the side of his leg. The dog cowered on the driveway.

Henry Rollins finally extended his hand toward his son, who shook it. The formality felt both strange and familiar. There'd never been any kisses or hugs from his father when Rollins was a child. Now, the skin felt leathery; the contact was brief, perfunctory, meaningless.

"Why the gun?" Rollins asked.

His father looked down at the rifle. "Oh, this?" He smiled. "Just for security. You have to be careful, living alone around here." He led his son inside the house. "How long you been here?" His accent used to be so crisp and properly Bostonian. Now, his voice had dust in it, and some wear.

"Just arrived. I thought I'd find you inside."

Mr. Rollins flipped the switch in the front hall, and the house blazed up. "What—you don't need light?"

"I didn't want to frighten anyone."

For the first time, Mr. Rollins looked at his son suspiciously. "You're not scared of your old man, now, are you?" He went into the kitchen, propped the gun up in the corner, then dropped down into the nearest chair. "There's probably a beer in the refrigerator." His head drooped slightly, as if he'd grown tired of being tall. In the kitchen's harsh, overhead light, his skin—which had once radiated health and confidence—looked worn and sallow.

"I might take some coffee." Rollins checked his watch again: 8:05. He'd pass a little time with his father, then slip away well before Sloane arrived. He'd hide in the shadows somewhere by the turn off the main road onto Bald Mountain Road, watch for Sloane, then warn off Schecter following behind. That was his new plan.

Mr. Rollins went to the stove and put on the kettle. He got out a mug and spooned some instant into it. "Hope this is all right." He showed his son the jar. "It's all I've got."

"Fine."

His father went to the refrigerator and snapped open a can of beer.

Rollins eyed the rifle. "I spoke to Kathi. That's how I found you."

"Oh, yeah?" He seemed amused.

"Richard had her address. She says hi."

"Yeah, she would." He took a slurp of beer. There was a time when his father would never have touched beer, let alone drunk it straight from the can. Silence again as his father surveyed him. It was as if he were trying to decide something about him.

"I was at Mother's this morning," Rollins said.

"Making the rounds, were you?"

"She had a stroke."

"Did she?" The tone was both unsurprised and uncaring. Rollins might have told him that she'd eaten a nice dinner.

"It's serious, Father. The doctor said she's paralyzed on her right side." Rollins felt for her just then. He imagined he *was* her, trying to win this gruff man's attention.

Nothing doing. Henry Rollins tipped his head back to take another draft of beer, then set the empty can down on the counter. "Well, I'm sorry to hear that."

The clock on the wall ticked. They'd had so little time together, and so little time remained. They might have been strangers on a train. "Kathi told me your marriage broke up."

His father's features hardened. "Yes, that's right." He looked out at his son through slitlike eyes. "You're not married, are you?"

Rollins shook his head, although his father must have known from Sloane that he wasn't.

"So you don't know how tight it gets."

Rollins braced himself; he was moving into realms of intimacy with his father that he had never dared penetrate before. His heart churned, and his palms turned slick. "That how you felt with Mother?"

"Sometimes, sure." His father got up and casually cracked open another beer. "But it doesn't have to be that way. Richard, for instance. He's married, and that seems to be going well. How about you—thinking about it?"

"It's crossed my mind." It calmed him to think of Marj.

His father returned to his seat. "That why you wanted to see me? Get my permission?" He seemed to find that amusing.

Rollins said nothing; it seemed safer at that point just to let his father talk.

"Well, don't do anything I did." He took another gulp. "She any good in bed?"

Rollins' pulse jumped. What a question! If anyone else were to have asked such a thing to the father Rollins *thought* he knew, he was sure that the old man would have exploded. And it was all the more horrifying knowing that his father had already sicced Sloane on the question of Marj already. Was Rollins' own relationship just another one to bore into the way he'd watched Elizabeth fondle Sloane at the Elmhurst house? Was he more grist for his father's warped mill?

The water on the stove started to boil, producing a low whistling noise and sending a cloud of steam into the air, but both men ignored it.

"Don't be shy, son. These things are important. I think that's what broke your mother and me up. She was always so uptight about all that stuff." Rollins was astonished to hear this revisionist history. It was as if Neely had never existed.

The kettle grew agonizingly shrill, and his father finally stood up to attend to it. He poured in the water and handed the mug to his son. "How long's it been, since we—?" He flicked a finger back and forth between the two of them.

"Almost nine years."

"That long? Imagine that."

Outside, the sky turned dark, blackening the trees out the window. His father poured his son more coffee and helped himself to more beer. Henry Rollins' words, once so clipped and sharp, loosened further, dropping into vulgarities here and there. His father seemed to enjoy the chance to catch up with his firstborn. He relaxed in his chair, but never did venture far from the rifle. He told Rollins about some of the places he'd been in Europe, and explained about the second wife, Christine, whom Rollins had only barely heard of. "That was pretty much a rebound thing. Didn't last." He'd tried different jobs. He had indeed taken up real estate for a while, in Oregon. "Sold little office buildings, mostly." He never did mention Kathi.

It was nearly eight-thirty, but Rollins still needed answers. "So, why'd you come back here to Vermont?" he asked, trying to make the question sound innocent.

His father's initial wariness returned. "Well, your old man had to go someplace, didn't he?"

"Of course." Rollins tried to keep his voice soft. "I just never thought you were particularly attached to this house."

"I've got happy-enough memories of this place. Skiing, all that. Your mother gave it to me, straight out. Seven, eight years ago, she sent me the deed in the mail. Damnedest thing." Mr. Rollins eyed his son. "And this was *after* she put the screws to me in the divorce. Of course, I don't have the cash to keep it up, but I'm working on that."

"Are you?" His words, with their simplicity and their skepticism, hung in the air.

"Yes," his father said evenly. "I am." He held his son's gaze a moment.

Rollins felt an understanding pass between them—an understanding that both locked them together and blew them apart. The edge to Henry's words and the silence that followed seemed to acknowledge that he suspected his son knew all about his financial dealings involving Neely's inheritance—and dared Rollins to do anything about it. And there was another message, too: I am past caring about your mother. And now I am past caring about you.

Rollins drained the last of his coffee. It was over. This was the time. He'd go to the bathroom off the front hall, start the water running, then dash to his car and drive away. "Mind if I use the bathroom?" Rollins asked.

"Actually, I do."

Rollins tensed. Was there no escape?

"Aw, don't give me that look," his father said. "I've just got a little problem with the plumbing. You'll have to go out back. Just a piss you need, right?"

Rollins nodded.

"Go out in the bushes there past the door. That's what I do."

Rollins got up and went to the kitchen door. It was dark out, but the bushes were lit up by the light from the kitchen. Rollins stepped toward them, settled himself, then released a long yellow stream. He zipped up, turned back, just to look. He saw no sign of his father. This was his chance. He should have run, right then. He might have made it. But when he turned back toward the lawn, he saw the slender croquet wickets. And then a gust of wind sent the stench his way, and he remembered the mound of dirt beyond. He glanced back at the kitchen once more, saw nothing, then crossed the lawn to the hay field. In the moonlight, the dirt pile was a heap of black. He still had the flashlight in his pocket and he shined his beam down into the hole beside the mound. It went in about a foot or so before it bottomed out onto white plastic. He swept away some loose dirt, and made out a word scrawled in Magic Marker. *Septic.* The lid was about eighteen inches across.

Wide enough to fit a body through.

Rollins crouched down, recalling the facts of Neely's disappearance. What had been a notion hardened into an inescapable fact. He flicked the flashlight off, shoved it back into his pocket where it clicked dully against the wristwatch, and dropped to his knees. "Oh, God." He brought his hands to his face as horror spread through his chest.

Above him, a few stars peeked through the lightly overcast skies, and a quarter moon over Bald Mountain shone dully upon him, casting a dim shadow on the field around him. The breeze had turned chilly, and it cut through his shirt. The full weight of the universe had settled down upon him.

Neely was buried in the septic tank beneath him.

He could still get to his car from there. He'd just go. Quickly. He'd be free of his father, and what he'd done, forever. Free of his family, free to start a new family with Marj.

He stood up and started running toward the far side of the house. It was 8:34. *Quickly.* Some change jiggled in his pocket; he reached in a hand to still it, for fear his father would hear. *Quickly.* To the road and then to his car, and then—

But before he even reached the corner, the dog howled from the front of the house, and then dashed around toward him, barking. The screen door screeched, and his father called out through the night. "Edward? What the hell you doing over there?"

Rollins froze. He was near the corner of the house, but not near enough. The dog stood before him, growling furiously. Rollins glanced back toward the kitchen. His father was a dark shape in the light by the door.

"Edward?" he called again. He was holding his rifle.

Rollins didn't move.

"Why don't you come back inside, son?"

Rollins was too terrified to speak, or to move.

"Come back inside, son."

"Yes, Father," he replied. He stepped back toward the kitchen door. He was a child again, forced to obey. It was natural, easy. Whatever made him think it could ever have been any different? He was in his father's grip, now as always. The gun loomed larger as he came closer. The barrel glistened in the moonlight.

"What were you doing out there?" his father asked when Rollins drew near.

"Just—just looking at the croquet course. We used to have one in Brookline—remember?"

His father pointed the rifle right at him. "That all, son?"

Rollins' chest tingled where the gun was aimed. He stepped back inside the kitchen door, and Father shut the door behind him, then bolted it this time. He motioned for his son to take a seat at the table again. Rollins did. Father sat back down, too. He kept the gun on his son.

"Perhaps we should be more candid with each other."

Rollins' eyes were fixed on the gun.

"What were you looking in the septic tank for?"

Rollins said nothing.

"Edward, I saw you point a light into it."

Light was everything at night, as Rollins well knew. He stared at his father. This was no one he knew. The gruff way he talked, the coldness in the eyes. This was a total stranger pointing a gun at him.

The wall phone rang. Rollins jumped.

"I think we'll let the machine take that," his father said.

"Ah, Mr. Rollins?" It was a hesitant female voice that Rollins immediately recognized. "This is Marj Simmons. I'm a, um, a friend of your son's. I'm calling from the hospital in Hartford. You may have heard that your wife—I mean your ex-wife—is here. She's doing okay. I was hoping to get in touch with, um, Edward. Is he there? I just wanted to make sure he got there all right, and that he's, like, okay. Could you ask him to call me when you see him?" She left a number at the hospital. "Got that? Thanks, bye." The machine clicked off.

"That your girl?"

"Yes."

"She sounds nervous."

"She's worried about me. She knows I'm here, Father."

"She thinks you might be here." The rifle remained pointed at his son's chest.

Rollins' hands were out in front of him. "Put the rifle down, would you please, Father?" He spoke calmly. He'd reached the end of a long journey. It was 8:41. If his father didn't get him, Sloane would. He was past fear now.

His father sighted down the gun barrel. "Pow," he exclaimed, then smiled weirdly. "I just wouldn't want you to run off, not after you came all this way to see me." There was a note of mockery in his voice. He did not lower the gun.

"I can't believe you'd ever get involved with slime like Jerry Sloane."

"So you knew about that, huh? Jerry told me you never made the connection, but I figured you did. You're a smart boy, and you always were nosing around in things."

Rollins said nothing, just stared at the tip of the gun barrel.

"I needed money. It was that simple."

"You get a cut of Neely's inheritance, is that the—?" Rollins stopped, his eyes still on the gun.

"It's a deal like any other." Henry Rollins smiled. "Just a matter of turning information into money."

"You bastard." Rage consumed him. He wanted to hurl himself forward onto his father, fists flying. But the gun rooted him in his seat.

Mr. Rollins ignored his son's outburst. "So, how'd you find out—about Neely and me?"

"From Elizabeth."

"That dyke."

Rollins ignored that. "She got in touch with me before she died.

She told me where to find some copies of letters you wrote Neely. And that letter Neely wrote Mother."

"So she kept all those?"

"In a strongbox she'd buried in her garden in Londonderry."

"Buried treasure. That's cute. So that's what brought you up here? Thought you'd check me out?"

His voice turned imploring. "I had to know, Father. I had to know what happened to Neely."

"You'll regret that." He cocked the gun. "So how'd you find out?"

His mouth felt dry. "I found her wristwatch in your bureau, Father." It pressed into his pants pocket. He would die with it on him.

"You always were fond of her, weren't you?"

Rollins couldn't think about that. One word burst up from deep inside. "Why?"

"I didn't mean to."

"Well then, you can *explain*. You can get a lawyer. You don't have to make it any worse than it already is."

"*Explain*. I wanted to take her away from all this crap. I'd had enough of it, and so had she. *That's* my explanation." He kept the gun on his son.

"Well, there, you see?"

"No, *you* don't see."

Rollins stared at the gun. "So what happened?"

Father's index finger was curled about the trigger.

"Tell me. Please. I have to know."

"All right, sure. I'll tell you. Your mother sent me a ticket East a few years ago. I was down on my luck, and I thought I'd look up old Neels. It had been a long time, and I had such happy memories of her. I drove over there to that house of hers in Londonderry, and I saw her on the road, walking. I offered her a ride."

A quick upward glance into his father's steely eyes. "She got in your car?"

"I had a gun with me. Not this one. A handgun I bought out West. Like I say, I was real eager to see her. Guns can be persuasive, now can't they?" He fell silent a moment. "It had been such a long time. I'd never stopped thinking about her. Through two wives, other women . . . Nothing else was like being with her. She was the whole reason for the trip. Nothing else was so—so fresh. I just wanted to be with her one more time. That's what I told her. 'Just once, Neely. That's all I want. Then you'll never hear from me again, I promise.' She really didn't like the gun. She started whimpering, telling me I'd ruined her life and all that." His father's voice turned scornful. "Come on. She was old enough to make her own decisions. I took her down the road, then turned down a smaller road, then a smaller one still. We were miles away from anywhere. I stopped under some trees, turned the headlights off. The rain was coming down. It was late, it was dark. There was nobody around. I was losing patience. She started crying harder, which annoyed me. She didn't have any reason to cry. Not with me. We'd always been such good friends! I mean, the things she used to tell me! And she'd always liked the sex. God, she was an animal." A strange new light came into his eyes.

"I had to bring the gun right up close to her head to get her to understand me. She undid her things, and I got on her, and we did it right there in the car. It was nice. Just like old times."

"And then—and then you *shot* her? You just shot her?" Shocked. Desperate.

"Hell no. What do you think I am? I wasn't going to do anything like that."

"So, what—?"

"She was crying pretty hard at the end. Her face was all red, and she was real broken up. I told her to quiet down. I couldn't take that. That blubbering. It was rude."

Rollins stared at the stranger across from him.

"I thought maybe we'd go up to Canada. It's real pretty up there in the fall. But she wanted out of the car, said she wouldn't tell anyone. I told her no, I couldn't do that. Then she tried to open the car door as we were going along! I told her, 'Don't. It's dangerous.' I didn't want her to get hurt. Well, she came at me and clawed her nails into my face. I'll admit, that made me angry. I still had the gun, and she's damn lucky I showed a little self-control. I could have shot her. But I didn't. I grabbed her and held her. She was struggling. She always was a wild one. So I had to hold her tighter." He paused. "Maybe I shook her a little."

Rollins' father was a blank shape across from him. "She went still. I guess her head must've hit something. I don't know. She was breathing fine. I figured she'd passed out. I started up again. Like I said, I wanted to go clear up to Canada. It's so beautiful up there in the fall. I tipped the seat back so she could rest. I kept on for miles. I kept expecting her to come around."

The world went darker, colder. Rollins had never felt so lonely, so scared. "But that's not murder!" he cried. "You didn't—"

"I didn't kill her, Edward." His father spoke coldly, decisively. "I want you to know that."

"Then you *can* explain!"

"It's too late for explanations, don't you understand? I'd hoped to keep you out of this, son. But you came at the wrong time. I was just emptying the tank. I have to do that every few years. Can't use Red Tag for it—that's the local outfit. I have to pump it out myself. Thought I'd be all done by now, but my pump got clogged this morning. I guess that's our tough luck, now isn't it? I had to drive down to Brattleboro for a spare part."

It was completely black outside. The kitchen was reflected in the windowpanes. It had all come down to Rollins and his father, and a gun between them. It would end here.

"I loved that girl." Mr. Rollins tightened his hands on the rifle again. "And now I need you to forgive me, son. Forgive me my trespasses, just as the Bible says. I've wronged you, Edward. More than your mother, your brother. More than your dear little sister, God bless her soul. More than Neely. She betrayed me, but you never did."

"I didn't know."

"You didn't want to know. It was a mark of your goodness that you didn't. Please, son, forgive me. I need that from you."

Anger gave him strength. "Put down the gun, Father."

"Forgive me."

"Father, *please*. Not like this." Rollins stretched out his hand toward his father and reached for the gun barrel. "Put down the gun, please."

"No!" His father sprang up. Rollins grabbed for the barrel with one hand, and thrust the tip up toward the ceiling. With the other, Rollins tried to free his father's hand from the trigger. The gun was nearly vertical between them. His father strained against Rollins, grunting and panting, his face tight with effort. Rollins could feel the coldness of the gun barrel as it tipped this way and that. "Let go!" he screamed.

"No!" Father's voice was almost all air as he struggled to wrest the gun away. "*You* let go. Goddamnit. I need—I need to do this."

The tip of the gun was just inches from his father's reddened face. "No—don't! Father! Please! No!" But he was losing his grip. The barrel was angling closer and closer toward his father. "No!"

"Just—watch out for Sloane." The words were all breath, cutting through his father's teeth. "He's—dangerous." Then his father's eyes widened and his mouth gaped as if he'd had a vision. There was an ear-ripping explosion, and a bright blue flame leaped upward. His father's head snapped back, and his whole body followed, his chair skidding away, until his father struck the kitchen wall and slumped down onto the floor, blood gushing from the underside of his chin down onto his chest. He lay there, motionless, his head propped up awkwardly on his shoulders, his cold, dark eyes still fixed on his son.

Twenty-five

Rollins stood there for several minutes, staring at his father's blood-soaked body. The sound of the gunshot rang in his ears, and he kept seeing that awful spurt of blue. His father stared at him through glassy eyes. To calm himself, Rollins concentrated on breathing, drawing the air in, letting it out. Over and over. Otherwise, he was afraid that his mind might shatter. Finally, with a sweep of his fingertips, he closed his father's eyes.

Then his chest clenched again. Sloane. He was coming at nine.

Rollins craned his neck around to check the clock. It was 8:53.

He would never be finished until he was finished with Sloane.

The rifle was coated with his father's blood. He started to reach for it, then stopped. He'd never even touched a gun until the struggle moments before. Now he was going to shoot Sloane—kill him in cold blood?

He brought his hands to his face, pushed his fingers in to the bone. "God, oh God."

The fear squeezed him, pressed against his chest, ground into his belly.

He stepped away from his father's body. Slowly at first, then faster. He raced out the back door. He slipped through the trees, the low brush whacking against his legs as he angled back to where he'd left his car on the road. His lungs heaving, he climbed in the Nissan. He was ready to hit the ignition, to flee.

But, safe in his car, he paused for a moment, caught his breath. The sound of the gun blast receded; the image of his blood-drenched father dimmed.

Watch out for Sloane. He's dangerous. What made his father say that? What had he meant? Sloane must have done something, something his father had known. Why *else* would Sloane have agreed to cut Father in on Neely's inheritance? Sloane knew that Father had raped Neely, hurt her. That was his leverage. But what did Father have on Sloane? Had *Sloane* killed Neely? Was that it?

Rollins' eyes jumped about the car—to the passenger seat, the dashboard, the radio, the slot under the radio, which contained a spare tape. A tape. To create a record.

He popped open the glove compartment, pulled out his Panasonic, and stared at it. He needed to get Sloane to talk while the tape rolled in secret. To *confess*. To provide evidence for the police, enough to justify Sloane's arrest and conviction. To put him away.

He pulled out the recorder, weighed it in his hand. The only voice it had ever received was his own. But couldn't it also record others? Like Sloane's voice, telling what he'd done?

Rollins switched on the recorder and stuffed it into his pants pocket. A test: "Can you hear me?" he asked quietly. "Am I coming through?" He pulled the recorder out again, rewound the tape, and pressed Play. *Can you hear me? Am I coming through?* His voice was only slightly muffled. The tape heard.

He thrust the tape recorder back into his pocket. Through the trees, he could see light stream from the kitchen, sending out blades of yellow through the night.

He stepped out of the car. He stole through the trees. He made for the light.

The dog barked at him, but Rollins shushed the animal, and it retreated to the front door, whimpering.

Inside the kitchen door, Father was propped up against the wall. The blood had soaked through his T-shirt, oozed onto the floor. The gun lay across his lap.

Rollins bent down over the body, loosened his father's index finger from the trigger. The skin was cool, the joints stiff. The blood was wet and sticky, like paint, on the gun's underside. Rollins swabbed it off with a paper towel, threw that in the trash.

He looked up at the clock: 8:59.

He'd draw Sloane to the body, then surprise him from behind, then get him talking.

There was a radio on the counter. He switched it on, and classical piano played. A Chopin nocturne. A haunting sound, pale as moonlight. It would lure Sloane.

Quick. To Father's study, gun in hand. Rollins waited there in the shadows behind the door, breathing, his hands tight on the gun. Waiting.

Nine o'clock came and went. 9:05. 9:10. The nocturne ended, and a spirited Schubert piano trio picked up. In the distance, a car rumbled up the road. The headlights lit up a rectangle of flowery wallpaper on the study wall, a patch of brilliance that slid sideways as the car turned in.

A car door slammed; the dog barked.

"Hello there, Scamp," said a cheery voice. It was Sloane. "Your daddy inside?"

Footsteps on the loose dirt of the driveway.

The dog continued to growl.

"Henry—you here?" Sloane called out by the door. The screen door opened and then banged shut behind him. "Henry?" The Schubert played on.

A heavy tread on the hall. "Henry?" Sloane shouted again. The footsteps continued on toward the kitchen, following the music just as Rollins had planned. The tape recorder was running inside his pocket.

Pointing the gun ahead of him, Rollins opened the door and crept after Sloane. He drifted like air through the dining room, then waited, his brain pulsing, just outside the kitchen door.

"Jesus Christ," he heard Sloane whisper as he kneeled before the body.

Rollins passed through the doorway into the kitchen. Sweat blurred his eyes, and his hands hurt from clutching the gun. He pointed the rifle at Sloane's head. "Don't move."

Sloane stayed where he was, facing the body. "Oh, shit. You."

"Come to finalize the deal?" Rollins asked.

Sloane's voice hardened. "Screw you." He started to move his hands to his waist.

"Hands *up*!" Rollins screamed. Every pulse was going.

Sloane jerked his hands up to shoulder height.

The sweat trickled down Rollins' face, gathering at his chin. His left eye twitched. He stared at Sloane's hands—pudgy, bright with thick rings—sure they'd fly at him any second.

"You weren't going to call the police, were you?" Rollins' jaw was so tight, it was hard to talk.

"What the hell are you talking about?"

"You're glad he's dead. Saved you a lot of trouble. You get all the money—and your secrets die with him."

"Fuck you. I haven't got any secrets."

"Look at me."

Sloane turned.

Rollins sighted down the gun barrel at the spot between Sloane's eyes, every muscle tight.

"*He* did her, you dumb fuck!" Sloane was getting edgy now. "Your old man."

Rollins continued to sight down the gun. He needed to concentrate on Sloane. "You helped."

"Bullshit."

Rollins cocked the gun. "*You helped*," he repeated.

Rollins had Sloane's full attention now.

"You left your fingerprints on her watch."

"No fucking way. *He* took off the fucking watch! I didn't touch it."

Dryly, with no triumph in his voice: "So you were there, Jerry?"

Sloane just stared at Rollins.

Rollins could feel the anger. It came at him in waves. He took a few steps farther into the room, keeping his eye down the barrel on Sloane. "Okay. Easy now. Reach the telephone for me, would you?"

Rollins watched Sloane stand up, move toward the wall phone, and pick up the receiver.

"Okay, now dial 911."

Sloane pushed in three digits.

"Now hold the phone up for me." Rollins inched toward him.

Sloane reached out with the receiver.

Rollins didn't hear a voice coming from the receiver, but he couldn't wait. "I need help!" he shouted. "I'm out Bald Mountain Road. There's a man here, trying to—"

Suddenly, the receiver swerved. It caught the tip of the rifle and knocked Rollins off balance. Rollins squeezed the trigger, but the gun made only a click.

Sloane ripped the rifle out of Rollins' hands and hung up the phone. "You stupid shit." Sloane swung the gun at Rollins. It crashed into the side of his face and staggered him. "That's for yesterday," Sloane shouted. "This is for today." He kicked Rollins in the belly, the toe of Sloane's shoe plunging nearly all the way into Rollins' spine. It knocked all the breath out of him, doubled him over, and sent a shock wave of pain through his body. "Doesn't feel too good, does it, Eddie boy?"

Rollins was hunched over, unable to breathe, unable to think. It was all he could do to keep from collapsing onto the floor. He kept his arms down, to protect himself from any more blows. A grunt, and Sloane's shoe smashed into Rollins' side, ramming him hard into the counter. Rollins felt a stabbing pain in his ribs. Sloane's fist cracked into the side of Rollins' head. The room spun and blurred.

Rollins stayed low, like an animal.

"There, we're even," Sloane said. "Now—outside." He gave Rollins another kick. Rollins staggered toward the kitchen door.

"Open it."

Hunched over, Rollins opened the screen door and stepped outside. It was cool now, and gusty. The trees thrashed in the wind. The lawn was glazed with moonlight.

Sloane rammed what felt like a handgun into the small of Rollins' back to shove him ahead. "That way." Rollins stumbled ahead, weaving past the slim wickets, which seemed like tiny grave markers. "You'll go where she went."

"So you—you did know."

"Course I knew. It was my idea. Your old man doesn't know shit about anything. Just like you. What a patsy. I had to kill her. She was groveling around, a fucking mess. I did her with one shot. It got me into your dad big-time."

"And him into you."

Sloane gave him another whack from behind. "Keep going."

The wind eased, and the stench rose from the septic tank.

"It's not—it's not going to work." Rollins' mouth was swollen from the blows; it was hard to force out the words.

"It worked for the girl."

"Too many people know I'm here. They'll come looking."

"They'll figure you shot him and ran off."

"They'll know it's you."

"I'll clean up a bit, then I'll call the cops myself. Tell them how shocked I am to find my good friend dead."

"They've got a record of my call to 911."

"Nice try. I dialed 411. Information, not the cops."

The stench was fierce. They were nearing the septic tank.

Rollins heard growling and looked up to see Scamp coming around the far side of the house. Rollins' hopes lifted as the dog charged up at Sloane, barking furiously. Sloane tried to quiet him with a kick, but the dog continued to growl and bark. Sloane brought his gun down and fired a single blast that echoed around the trees. The dog spun and tumbled, writhing, to the ground. Sloane touched the gun to the dog's head. A second blast finished him off.

"Now get going."

Rollins didn't move.

"Get going!" Sloane thrust the gun into his back.

Rollins' body was there, but his mind had flown. It had taken off into the trees, where it flitted about among the branches. He was with Neely again.

Then a roar of a car engine, coming around the house.

Sloane's gun slid across Rollins' back, toward the sound.

Then lights probing the field, swinging to brightening them. Twin lights. Headlights.

His arm up against the glare, Rollins could see a car. A small car. Schecter's Cressida! It rumbled across the lawn.

Sloane grabbed Rollins by the back of his shirt, yanked him up. "Back off, you motherfucker!" He screamed at the car. *"Back off!"* Buttons popped as Rollins was jolted to his feet. "I'll shoot him! I swear to God, I'll shoot him!"

The car stopped. The lights stayed on. Two spotlights.

"Stay there or he dies!" Sloane screamed. "Don't move!"

Using Rollins as a shield, Sloane slowly stepped back across the lawn. He pressed the gun tightly into Rollins' back.

Rollins stumbled as he moved backward across the uneven ground. His thoughts collided inside his head. His whole body was on fire.

At the far corner of the house, Sloane jammed the gun hard into Rollins' back. "Faster!" Sloane told him. "To my car. Go!" He forced Rollins ahead of him.

The driveway scratched under Rollins' shoes. The moon up above—serene, indifferent. Sloane grunted behind. "Go! Go!" The gun hard against his back. Panting. They reached the Land Cruiser, and Sloane jerked open the driver's door.

"Get in!" Sloane shoved Rollins into the driver's seat. "You're gonna drive." Keeping the gun on Rollins, Sloane stepped around the front of the big car, heading for the passenger side.

His only chance. Shielded by the high dashboard, Rollins slid his left hand down the steering wheel, then groped the control panel. He found the headlight switch, and yanked. A blast of light. Sloane swung his arm up to shield his eyes. Rollins ducked down under the dashboard. Sloane fired, shattering the windshield, spraying glass over the seat. His hand stung, Rollins fumbled for the ignition. The key was in the switch. He turned it. The engine roared to life.

Sloane screamed—"No!"—and fired again. Hunkered down under the dash, Rollins jammed the gearshift into forward, and then shoved a hand down onto the accelerator. The car shot ahead, jerking Rollins backward onto the seat front. A frightened gasp from Sloane, and thunder on the hood, as if a load had dropped on it. Sloane wailed—a hideous, pitiful sound. Above Rollins, the tip of Sloane's hand slapped down on the edge of the remaining windshield. Then the pop of gunshots—one, two, three, four—from far away, but coming closer, and another scream from Sloane. This one guttural, of agony, and the hand slid away. Then Rollins lurched forward again as the SUV smashed into the house.

Twenty~six

"Hey—you okay?"

It was Schecter, underwater.

No, *Rollins* was underwater.

No, there was no water. It was Schecter. Just Schecter, bending down to him. "You all right there?"

Everything felt so tight all around, and it was black behind. Then his eyes started to focus, and he remembered. He was in the SUV, squeezed between the dashboard and the seat. "Yeah." He reached back behind his head, felt a lump. "My head. God, it aches."

"You must've got quite a whack when you hit the house there."

Schecter brushed away some broken glass, then helped Rollins ease himself up onto the seat.

Rollins stared out through the shattered windshield. The house rose up right in front of him. "God."

"You clipped Jerry pretty good, too."

"Sloane?"

"You ran him into the fucking wall."

Schecter held the door open so Rollins could step out. He walked unsteadily around to the far side of the car. Sloane was sprawled out on the driveway. He was barely moving. Blood had drenched his trousers. His face was sweaty and bone-white in the glare of the headlights. His breathing was brisk and shallow, like a dog's in the heat. His life seemed to be draining out of him.

"You stay with him," Schecter said. "I'm going inside to call the cops."

Slowly, painfully, Rollins leaned down and touched Sloane's shoulder. "Take it easy," Rollins told him. "We'll get an ambulance."

Sloane pushed Rollins' hand away with a moan.

Schecter came back out and the two of them crouched beside Sloane. Finally, Rollins heard sirens. Flashing lights were coming up the road. In moments, three cruisers and a pair of ambulances filled the driveway, and the brightness careened about the trees.

Several policemen burst out of the cars. "What have we got here?" one yelled.

Schecter leapt up, beckoning. "Over here! There's a guy down here." He gestured toward Sloane. "He needs help. He's all smashed up."

Two men from the ambulance rushed over and bent down to him. "We gotta do something to stop this bleeding," Rollins heard one of them say.

Schecter called out to the other crew: "And there's another one in the kitchen. He's dead." He pointed toward the house. "In there to the left."

"Jesus Christ—what happened?" one of the cops asked Rollins as he surveyed Sloane's broken body.

"He tried to kill me," Rollins said.

"Kill you?" the officer replied, incredulous.

"He was going to shoot me." Rollins felt the icy chill of the barrel pressing against his back. The fear had frozen his mind around a single thought—that he might never see Marj again. "But I got free and

I—I guess I hit him with that car." He pointed toward Sloane's Land Cruiser.

"You ran him over?" the officer asked.

"Yeah, right here," Schecter said. "Smashed him against the house."

"Jesus."

Rollins reached into his pocket and pulled out the tape recorder. "Here." He handed the officer the tape from his tape player. "This has everything on it. It explains everything."

The officer looked down at the tiny cassette in his hand.

"Yeah—everything that happened here," Rollins said angrily. It was so hard to make the man understand. "I had the tape recorder going in my pocket when he tried to kill me. He told me how he'd killed my cousin. He chopped her up. He—" Rollins couldn't continue. "Look, everything that happened is on the tape." He tapped the cassette with his index finger. "Just listen to the tape."

"Okay—I'll pass it on to the detectives." The officer turned back to Sloane, who was screaming in pain as he was being shifted onto a gurney.

Another officer charged out of the house. "Hey, guys," he shouted. "We got a body inside."

"That's what I was telling you," Schecter said irritably.

"We got a name off his driver's license—Henry Rollins," the officer shouted.

"He's my father," Rollins said.

"Your—" the officer near him said. "Oh, Jesus."

Flies were buzzing around his father's corpse, and the kitchen wall behind him was splattered with blood. The air was heavy with the smell of death. Rollins' stomach burned, every part of him hurt, and his head felt clogged, backed up with tears that would not fall. He was lost and alone. Rollins pulled out a chair from the kitchen table and dropped down into it. He was afraid he might collapse otherwise.

Police photographers were taking flash pictures of the crime scene from a variety of angles. A thin man in a short-sleeved shirt was crouched by the body, his head turned slightly away from the odor.

"We got the son here, Frank," one of the cops told the man.

"Oh, good." The man stood up. He was a lanky redhead. He had on latex gloves, and he stripped them off with a rubbery sound. The man reached out a bare hand toward Rollins, who shook it limply. "Detective Frank LeBeau," the man said. He gestured across to another man by the sink. "And that's my partner, Detective Tom Jencks."

Rollins gave the men his name.

LeBeau had the medics throw a sheet over the body. "We'll take it out in a minute," he told them. "But we need to go through some stuff here first." He turned back to Rollins. "I know it's a tough time for you, but there are some questions we've got to ask." He took a seat in a chair across from Rollins. "Were you here when your father died?"

Rollins nodded.

"What happened?"

Rollins touched his hand to his forehead. It felt wet and clammy. "God—where to begin."

LeBeau went to the sink and poured a glass of water. "Take your time," he said, handing it to him.

Rollins sipped the water gratefully. "He had a gun," he began.

"That one there?" LeBeau pointed to the rifle that was on the floor in the corner of the kitchen. It must have landed there after Sloane knocked it from his hand.

Rollins nodded. "I thought he was going to shoot me. I grabbed for it, we fought, and the gun—the gun went off."

Had he shot his father? Had he?

"What made you think he'd shoot you?"

"He was pointing it right at me."

"Why'd he do that?" the other detective, Jencks, asked.

Rollins took a breath. "Because of Neely."

Jencks again: "What's neely?"

"Neely. She's my cousin. Or"—his voice dropped—"was." Rollins tried to explain about Neely's disappearance and his growing suspicions about his father's involvement. But each line of explanation seemed flimsy and incomplete. As Rollins went along, he kept having to stop, to back up, to add a detail or two to bolster his account. Still, he plodded on, for nearly an hour, parrying questions from these two men. And his father's corpse right there, bearing silent witness to his son's full understanding.

The thought came to him gradually, but it built and built until it had the power of hard fact: He hadn't killed his father, nor had his father killed himself. They had done the deed together. Their hands were together on the trigger. Both had fired the fateful bullet, and therefore neither had.

Rollins held nothing back. The story was over now; what was done was done; he had no secrets anymore. He told about his driving habits, and his tapes, and his discovery of the dark house. He told about Marj and Schecter. He told about Sloane. He told how Sloane had killed Neely, then tried to horn in on Neely's ten-million-dollar inheritance. He told about his mother, about Wayne Jeffries and the crash on the highway. For Schecter's sake, he said nothing about Tina. For his own sake, he left out Heather. These two were behind him now, but they had pushed him ahead. LeBeau mostly listened, taking careful notes in his notebook, asking only for a few points of clarification. But as the tale went on, he seemed to grow more sympathetic. He occasionally shook his head or looked over at Jencks in amazement, or muttered "God Almighty" under his breath.

Finally, Rollins reached the part about becoming convinced that his father was involved in Neely's disappearance and his realization that her body was hidden in the septic tank out in back of the house.

"Wait a second now," LeBeau said. *"Here?"*

"Yeah, in the back." Rollins took him to the window and pointed. "It's out there, just past the edge of the lawn. When my father figured out I knew—that's when he pulled the gun on me. Later, when Sloane showed up, that was where he was going to dump me."

LeBeau glanced at his partner. "Okay," he said. "We'll take a look at it later."

"Oh, and I found this." Rollins pulled Neely's wristwatch from his pocket, and passed it to the detective. "It's Neely's watch. It was in a drawer upstairs."

LeBeau hooked a pencil point under the clasp. "We might be able to get some prints off it," he said. He set it down on the table. "Ten twenty-three," the detective told Rollins. "Think this is when she died?"

"I guess so." Rollins went hollow at the thought of his father raping Neely, knocking her unconscious, then relying on Sloane to finish her off.

LeBeau turned the watch over. "E. P.?"

"That's Elizabeth Payzen, Neely's friend."

"The beneficiary," LeBeau said.

Rollins nodded.

"She still alive?"

"She died yesterday. That's what set everything in motion."

"God, what people won't do for money," LeBeau said.

Rollins led the detectives upstairs to the bureau where he'd found the wristwatch. There, LeBeau carefully bagged up the other pieces of jewelry as well as the box itself. When he came back, they reenacted the shooting, with LeBeau himself taking the part of Henry Rollins. Tracing the angle of the gunshot, LeBeau climbed up onto the chair and, with a penknife, extracted a bullet that had embedded itself in the ceiling. He held it up in a gloved hand. "This is what did it." The bullet seemed almost pristine.

LeBeau finally gave the medics clearance to lift his father's body onto the gurney. Rollins trailed behind it across the driveway to the waiting ambulance. Jerry Sloane had been taken away in the other ambulance by then, but his and Schecter's cars and the whole area around them had been cordoned off with yellow police emergency tape. Schecter was outside, talking to one of the officers. "I was just helping out a friend," Schecter was saying.

After the ambulance drove his father away, Rollins led LeBeau and several other officers outside to the septic tank. He passed the curled-up body of the dead dog, Scamp, on the way. "That was my father's dog," Rollins said. "Sloane shot it."

"Okay," LeBeau said. "We'll take care of it."

As Rollins stood by, a couple of policemen pried back the cover of the septic tank, and then jerked their heads away when the stench hit. "Oh, man. It's full of crap in there," one cop said, his hand up against his face.

"What did you expect?" another one said.

They decided to leave that part till morning, when they could summon the local septic tank service—Red Top, just as his father had said—to drain it.

"It looks to me like you've been to hell and back," LeBeau told Rollins as they returned to the house. He made it clear to Rollins that neither he nor Schecter were under any formal obligation to stay in Townshend that night. "No one's charging either of you with anything," he said. "But I'd appreciate it if you'd stick around."

The detective drove them back to the Mountain View Inn in Woodstock. It was nearly three in the morning, and Rollins barely spoke to Schecter on the way, just gazed numbly out the window at all the dark houses they passed. The place was run by LeBeau's brother-in-law, so Rollins and Schecter were able to secure a couple of small rooms up on the top floor even though the inn was theoretically all booked. Rollins had never been so exhausted when he dropped into bed. Still, sleep did not come. He kept seeing lights flaring, bodies tumbling. Pipes must have gone through the wall right by his bed, because he could hear water flowing and gurgling all night long.

He called the hospital the first thing in the morning.

It took a few minutes for a nurse to bring Marj to the phone. "Oh, Rolo, you're there!" she exclaimed. "God, I was so scared! When nobody answered that phone last night, I—"

"Father was pointing a rifle right at me when you called."

Marj gasped. "He was going to shoot you?"

"It looked like it." Rollins took a breath. "He's dead now, Marj."

"Your father? He's—?"

"We fought over the gun. It went off and—"

"He's *dead*?"

"The bullet went in under his chin. He died right away. Oh, God, Marj, it was—I can't even say what it was. Then Sloane came and—oh, God. I found Neely's body. It was in the septic tank. My father raped her that night, then banged her around and Sloane shot her. They took her up here and stuffed her in the tank. It's all so awful, I can't tell you. Wait—you there?"

"I'm here," she said quietly.

"It's over now, Marj. The police have Sloane, and I'm safe. I'll be done here soon. The detectives need me just a little longer, and that'll be it. I'll be back in a few hours."

"Why didn't you call me last night? I was scared out of my mind. I thought something terrible had happened to you."

"I couldn't, Marj. I was so busy with the detectives, and then, when I got back, it was so late."

"I was up, Rolo. You think I could sleep? You could have called. I was up all night." Her voice caught, and Rollins thought he heard her crying. "I was afraid you were dead. *Dead*, Rolo."

"I'm—sorry—I—"

More soberly: "I don't think I can take any more of this."

"But it's over, Marj. Over."

"It won't ever be over."

Rollins was frightened by her tone. "Please, Marj, don't talk that way."

There was a knock on the door. "Time to go," Schecter shouted to him. "LeBeau's here."

"Just a second," Rollins shouted back. Then he returned to the receiver. "Look, I've got to go. Just hang on a little longer. Okay, Marj? Please?"

"Okay, Rolo. I'll try."

Detective LeBeau handed Rollins and Schecter some coffee he'd picked up at a Dunkin' Donuts. "Thought you might need something." Then he drove them back to the house on Bald Mountain Road. The place looked drab in the early morning light, which revealed more starkly the peeling paint and untended shrubs. It seemed destined for tragedy. Several news vans were in the driveway, their satellite dishes elevated to beam the story back to the home station. Over a dozen reporters and cameramen had gathered behind the yellow emergency tape, which now ran from the side of the house out to the trees. They converged on the three of them the moment they emerged from LeBeau's unmarked Chevrolet, shouting so many questions that Rollins couldn't quite make them out.

LeBeau raised his arms to keep everyone back. "Later, guys, please." He managed to clear a path through them all for Rollins and Schecter, and then raised the yellow tape to allow them to pass through to the backyard.

The two-man Red Top crew was already there. They'd driven their tank across the lawn, flattening several of the croquet wickets on the way. The air stank of raw sewage. "I think we're about halfway down," one of the policemen said, shouting to LeBeau over the heavy chugging of the Red Top pumps and the horrid slurping sounds coming from inside the tank. It took about ten more minutes, but finally the Red Top man handling the thick hose made a signal to the driver, who shut off the pump, bringing silence to the surrounding field.

"All right, let's get this over with," Pete, the hose man, said. He was in faded red overalls, and from the expression on his face there was no doubt this was the last place on earth he wanted to be. The driver retracted the hose onto a big spool on the side of the truck, and then four or five uniformed policemen crowded around the open septic hole while the hose man got down on his knees to look inside. "Hand me that flashlight, wouldja Larry?" he told the driver. Larry climbed out of the truck to pass him a long metal flashlight. The hose man thrust the flashlight into the hole, and then poked his head down into it. "Oh boy," he said when he pulled his head back out.

"What's he see in there?" one of the reporters shouted. Rollins turned: Three or four bulky cameramen had aimed their cameras at him, and a couple of technicians extended long boom microphones his way. Then one of the reporters stepped over the tape to steal a closer look, and three or four others followed. In moments, the whole press contingent was streaming across the lawn. The police chief himself, a burly character named Wexler, raised his arms and shouted to everyone to move back, and then directed a couple of his men to cordon off the area with their cruisers. They came around from the other side of the house, lights flashing, right across the lawn, flattening yet more wickets.

"Okay, let's have a look there," Chief Wexler said once the cruisers were in place and the media were under control. He took Pete's flashlight and crouched down to peer into the hole himself. "Well, it's a body all right."

"How in hell we gonna get it out?" a lieutenant asked.

"You can help us with that, can't you, Pete?" the chief said to the hose man.

"I'm not messing with no bodies," Pete said.

He turned to the driver, who was gazing into the hole. He was extremely slender, with a prominent Adam's apple. "How 'bout you, Larry? You're skinny enough."

"Aw, shit," Larry said. "It's always me." He went back to the truck and put on a pair of heavy work gloves. He sat down by the hole, with his feet in, and then several policemen grabbed him by the arms and lowered him through the narrow opening.

"Careful you don't step on her," the chief shouted.

"I know, I know," Larry said.

Finally only his two arms were visible out the opening, and then they disappeared, too. "Okay, I'm down," came a hollow sound from inside. "Hand me the flashlight."

A cop obliged.

"You see her?" the chief asked.

"Sure do. Goddamn."

"Well, bring her up," the chief said.

Minutes later, as the cameras doubtless zoomed in from behind the squad cars, a bit of grimy skeleton rose out of the hole. A portion of the rib cage, it looked like, with one arm limply attached. "Holy mother of God," Rollins heard one of the reporters say. The bones themselves seemed delicate, like some sort of artwork, but they were blackened with what must have been excrement, and strips of rotted flesh clung to them in places. Rollins watched with a leaden feeling. Neely. The golden hair, the bright smile, the keenness and joy—all gone; only a few scraps of skin and bone remained. Without a word, the policeman standing by the hole took the segment gently in his gloved hands and laid it down on a canvas sheet that had been stretched out by the hole.

"Hang on. Here's some more," Larry said from underground. A butterfly-shaped pelvis with a long piece of one leg bone dangling off it came up. The cop laid that down on the canvas, too. Then, one by one, other grime-splattered bones emerged, some a few feet long, others just an inch or two. Finally, a skull. It might have been a prehistoric pot except for the few strands of golden hair that still adhered. The wisps of hair sparkled yellow in the sun. "Jesus," a reporter said. The policeman set the skull down on its side.

"That's it," Larry yelled up finally. "I don't see no more."

"Okay," Chief Wexler shouted down. "Good work, Larry. We'll haul you out." The policemen reached down into the hole to grab Larry's hands. They braced themselves, then, their faces red with effort, pulled Larry out again.

Larry's boots, elbows and much of his front were black with sewage. "I'm never doing that again," he said. "No fucking way."

Some reporters shouted for him to come over and answer some questions, but Larry waved them off. "I'm done, guys." With his gloved hands, he tried to wipe off some of the thicker blobs, but succeeded only in smearing it. "God, I stink," he muttered. He and Pete climbed back into the big truck and turned it around. The police guided the truck back around to the far side of the house. They undid the police tape, and let the truck pass back through to the driveway.

A man in khakis with the word FORENSIC on his nameplate came up to LeBeau, who was still standing with Rollins. "I've got some preliminaries for you," the man said. "Real rough."

"Let me have 'em," LeBeau said.

"Caucasian female, about five-six or five-seven. I think we're looking at about a three-or four-centimeter indentation of the temporal lobe of the skull."

"You mean she got smacked around?" LeBeau replied.

"You could say."

"This before or after she was dropped in the tank?"

"It's hard to know for sure, but I'd guess before. Has to do with the location and degree of the trauma. I could show you if you like."

"Save it," LeBeau said.

"Also got a bullet hole in the occipital region. About ten millimeters. That's what killed her."

"Right in the back of the head?"

"Execution style."

"How about the fact that the body's in pieces?" Chief Wexler asked.

"I'd say that came after."

"To fit her in the tank, you mean?"

The specialist nodded.

"Larry went in easy enough," the chief said.

"Larry didn't have rigor mortis."

"Well, ain't that pretty," the chief said.

Schecter watched with his arms folded.

By then, the reporters must have figured out the basics of the story, for they started firing questions at Rollins about what had happened. "So what was it?" one man shouted. "Your dad just snap?" Another cried out: "Who's in the tank—your girlfriend?" Still another: "You been arrested yet?" And finally: "I heard there was another man involved. We got a love triangle here?"

Rollins said nothing, and Chief Wexler came over to quiet the throng. "Got anything for us, Chief?" a reporter shouted. "Names? Ages? Motive?"

"Show a little respect, would you please?" Wexler shouted. "This man's innocent. This is a family tragedy, and he's a victim here. We'll be providing some information a little later. This is just for photos, if you want to take them. It's all pretty damn disgusting if you ask me." Then he pulled Rollins away. He shouted over to the detective, who had returned with the forensic specialist to look over the skeletal remains.

"You need anything more from our friend Ed here?" Wexler asked.

LeBeau shook his head. "Nah, I think we're done for now." He came over to shake Rollins' hand. "I'm real sorry about all this."

Then the chief checked to make sure that LeBeau had addresses and telephone numbers for Rollins and Schecter, which he did. "Okay, I think we're all set," Wexler said finally. "You get home to your family." He enlisted several of his officers to escort Rollins to his car. Then he shouted after him: "And make sure these jackals don't follow him, you got that?"

Schecter had to leave his car with the police for a few days, since it had figured in the action against Sloane. They wanted to compare his tires to the tire tracks on the lawn and measure out all the angles involved to make sure the evidence squared with his account. "Sorry, but we've gotta do all the bullshit," Detective Jencks told him sympathetically. The right side of Schecter's car was in bad shape, anyway. He'd caught the corner of the house when he raced back around to the driveway, and Schecter wasn't sure the Cressida would get all the way to Maine in that condition. He'd have to arrange for repairs through his insurance company. Rollins insisted on paying for any damages that weren't covered by his insurance. "Really, Al, after everything you did for me," he told him.

He dropped Schecter at the bus station in Brattleboro. He started to shake hands with the detective on the sidewalk, but Schecter clapped him in a big bear hug.

"You know what you need?" Schecter asked.

"No, what?"

"You need a really good cigar."

Schechter handed him a top-of-the-line Macanudo.

Rollins smiled and climbed back in the car. He ignored all speed limits in driving back down 91 to the hospital. He parked in a loading zone, then dashed inside to the ICU without stopping to check in at the nurses' station. His mother's door was open. She lay motionless in bed as before, tubes drooping down to her. But a man was sitting in a chair by the foot of the bed. He was lean and tousle-haired, and he wore a gray suit, no tie, but a handkerchief in his outside pocket. It was his brother, Richard.

"Hey, Ed," Richard said quietly, as he rose to his feet.

"So you heard—"

"Your girlfriend called me." His eyes were downcast, wary.

"Where is she?"

Richard hesitated. "She said she had to go."

"Go?" Rollins felt panic. "Where?"

"I don't know." Richard shrugged. "She didn't say."

"Did you say something to her?"

"Nope." He turned back to the table where he'd been sitting. "She left a note for you." He handed his brother a small white envelope, and Rollins ripped it open. There was a note inside.

Dear Rolo,

I'm so proud of you. You have more courage than anybody I know. I'm glad you got your answers, finally, even if they weren't the happiest ones. But I'm sorry. We can't go on like this, you and me. I'd cause you too much trouble, and you'd drive me crazy. I could give you reasons, but I think you know them all already.
It's best this way. Really.

Your friend,

Marj

p.s. I borrowed $80. I'll pay you back, I promise.

His bank card was in the envelope.

Rollins had to read the note twice, but even the second time, it didn't make sense. *Can't go on?* What did that mean? Of course they could go on.

Richard spoke: "She didn't really seem your type—if you want my opinion."

Rollins cut him off. "What would you know about that?"

"Sorry. Look, this whole thing—""

"I've got to find her."

"Now?" He glanced up. "With Father dead—and what about Mother?"

"You can manage." Rollins stepped past him to his mother's bedside. She lay on her back, her eyes closed, the breath whistling in and out. Rollins leaned down to her. "And you—God." She continued to lie there, nearly motionless except for the slight rise and fall of her chest with each breath. "See no evil, hear no evil—isn't that right, Mother?" He stared at her, the anger still strong. "When I think about what you shut your eyes to. What you let me think."

"If you're going, go," Richard called over to him. "You're right—we don't need you here. You've done enough."

"Done enough? Oh, like I'm the one who screwed my niece, then raped her when she wouldn't have me anymore, and then—oh, to hell with it. What's the point?" Rollins moved to the foot of the bed. "I'm going." He plucked the jaunty handkerchief from Richard's outside jacket pocket and stuffed it in his brother's hand.

"Use this," Rollins said. "Crying helps."

He hurried back to his car and drove up to Boston at eighty-five miles an hour, the Nissan shuddering. He made straight for Marj's Brighton apartment, parked by a hydrant, and charged into the lobby the moment the first person opened the front door. He felt the suspicion on him, but he didn't care. He rang Marj's buzzer several times, but got no response. Finally, he pressed the button marked SUPERINTENDENT. After several minutes, a sleepy-looking black man in work clothes appeared. "I'm looking for Marj Simmons," Rollins told him. "You seen her?"

"Not for four or five days."

"Would you mind if I went up to check her apartment? I'm her fiancé. I'm afraid something may have happened to her."

"You don't have a key?"

Rollins shook his head.

"Doesn't trust you, huh?" the super said. "Some fiancé."

"I'm really worried about her."

"I can see that," the super said. He led Rollins up to the third floor and opened Marj's door with the master key.

Marj's apartment was a mess, with fashion magazines scattered across the floor and various pieces of lingerie draped over the living room couch. Still, it touched him to see the Marj that existed when he wasn't around. It meant a lot to see the big TV in the living room, the unmade double bed with its handmade quilt, the photograph of what must have been her mother on the dresser. "Like I told you," the super reiterated. "I really don't think she's been around." Rollins went to the answering machine by the telephone and played back the new messages since Schecter's. Two were from an older woman who must have been Marj's mother, each one concluding "Call me, all right?" Another was from the personnel manager at Johnson asking where she was. And a last one was from Lena saying that she'd better call in soon or she was "gonzo." He picked up the portable phone and pressed

REDIAL to see if he could determine the last number she'd called. But no one answered there. It wasn't until Rollins hung up the receiver that he realized the number Marj had dialed was probably his own.

Rollins thanked the super, and gave him $20 for his trouble. Then he returned to the Ritz, leaving the car with the valet out front. "Marj?" he called out as soon as he came into his suite. No one answered, and the place was the way he'd left it, only somewhat neater. The maids must have been in. But the message light was on. Rollins pounced on the receiver. "You have two messages," said an automated voice. Both were from the assistant manager of the Ritz asking when "Mr. Sinclair" was intending to check out. Rollins slammed down the receiver. He collected his spare clothes from the shelf of the closet, bunched them up, and threw them in the wastebasket. He left the suite and took the elevator down to the lobby. "I'll be checking out now," he told the clerk at the reception desk. He received the bill for the five nights' stay, which he stuffed in his pocket without even looking at it. "Have you heard anything from Mrs. Sinclair?" Rollins asked as he signed the credit card receipt.

The receptionist checked the messages in Rollins' file. "No, sir."

"How about a young woman named Marj Simmons?"

An interested look from the receptionist this time. "Sorry, sir."

He called Johnson from the pay phone in the lobby. He spoke to Lena. "You haven't heard from Marj, have you?"

"No. I thought she was with you."

"Well, she was . . ." He let his voice trail off.

"You know you're in huge trouble here. I really don't think Henderson wants you back after you skipped out like that. And now, God, all this publicity. Everybody's talking about the Rollins in Vermont who shot himself after a corpse turned up in his cesspool or something. Henry Rollins, right? Tell me—is he really your father?"

Rollins said no. That was all wrong. He wasn't related to any Henry Rollins.

He drove back to the North End, left his car in a tow zone, and ran back to his apartment building. The light over the stairs was working again. There was some mail for him on the front-hall table. Rollins glanced through it. When he found no letter from Marj, he dropped the whole pile into the wastebasket under the table. He hadn't gotten far up the stairs before the door to Mrs. D'Alimonte's apartment opened, and his landlady came rushing out. "Oh, Mr. Rollins, how *are* you?" Mrs. D'Alimonte sang out.

Irked at the recollection that she had snooped in his room, Rollins continued on up.

"That's not much of a welcome home."

Rollins stopped and turned to her, newly hopeful. "Do you have any news for me?"

"I had a wonderful visit to Baltimore, if that's what you're asking. The most delightful baptism—and the reception afterward! Heavenly."

Rollins continued to trudge on up the stairs.

"But now tell me, Mr. Rollins, what in the world happened to those people in 2A?" The Mancusos, she meant. "They've vanished. Everything's gone."

He thought how she had gossiped with Tina about him. "I can't help you there." He had nearly reached the top of the stairs.

"You seem tired, Mr. Rollins. Everything okay?"

"I'm fine, Mrs. D'Alimonte. Absolutely fine."

He put the key in the lock and opened his door. There was a letter for him. He snatched it up, hoping it was from Marj. But the front of it bore the word *MISTR*, all caps, in pencil. He opened it up. There was a strip of pictures of Heather taken at a photo booth. *ITS FR YER WALLIT*, it said on the back. He looked at it again, then set it down on the bookcase next to his calendar.

The apartment was empty. He scanned the room, hoping to find some hint of her. He couldn't believe she was gone. He sat down in his fat chair by the phone and dialed information for Morton, Illinois. There were over twenty Simmonses listed, and Rollins didn't know Marj's mother's first name, or the name of her stepfather. His love for her suddenly flamed up as if it might consume him. He barely knew the first thing about her.

"I'm sorry," the operator said, "without a first name or street address—"

411

* * *

Rollins was pretty sure he didn't move for the next several weeks. He certainly had no memory of doing so. He slept, he ate. He was aware of placing a number of telephone calls to Marj's apartment, and more to Lena at Johnson. He looked at Heather's picture a few times, and it cheered him a little. The owner of the little cottage that he rented for a week every year in Nova Scotia called up to ask where he was; he'd been due there three days before. "I won't be coming this year," he said, and returned the receiver to its cradle. On several occasions, people yelled up to him from the courtyard saying they were from a TV station. He didn't respond, and they went away after a while. Mrs. D'Alimonte pounded on his door once to tell him his car was being towed, but the news meant nothing to him. He was finished with the Nissan anyway.

He was aware that his brother, Richard, took care of the funeral arrangements for his father, which consisted of scattering his ashes off Bald Mountain, as requested by his will. This was a relief, since Rollins could not bear the prospect of burying him in the family graveyard at Forest Hills where little Stephanie lay, and, for all he knew, he himself would someday go. Detective LeBeau called with a few more questions about Neely, which Rollins answered.

The days came and went. The shadows crossed the room.

Somehow he mustered the energy to attend Neely's memorial service at the Blanchard family plot in Lexington. He arrived by taxi. The plot was on the far slope of a large, private cemetery, and it was bordered by Norwegian spruces, and azaleas and dogwoods grew among the mottled gravestones. Rollins came late, for a clump of media personnel had established an outpost past the iron railing, their cameras trained on the proceedings. Rollins was still numb, but he knew enough to keep his distance from his aunt. Her shoulders sagging, Aunt Eleanor stood by the catafalque upon which Neely's cremated remains rested in a small chest. She clung to her portly husband, George, who stood beside her, ashen-faced. Eleanor was veiled, but he could see that she had been broken by her grief. Her only child, after all, had been seduced and then raped and killed in a plot masterminded by her uncle, Eleanor's own ex-brother-in-law. It was all too grotesque for words.

A smattering of cousins, including some of the New York Arnolds he'd seen at Gloucester, formed a kind of buffer zone around the couple. Rollins' own mother was there in a wheelchair. She was there, motionless, in the shade of a great spruce far off to one side. Richard stood stone-faced behind her, with his wife, Susan, and their two children beside him. Rollins gave his mother a perfunctory kiss. Her lips quivered in reply, but no sound came out.

After some hesitation, Rollins grasped his brother's hand in both of his. "Look, about the other day . . ." he began.

"Don't worry about it." Richard pulled Rollins close and embraced him.

To keep the tears from falling, Rollins slipped free and leaned down to Richard's eight-year-old daughter, Natalie, who'd grown quite tall. Not knowing what else to say, he told her that he admired her dress. He added that he'd been meaning to send her a birthday present, but she needed to remind him of the correct date. "May eighth," she'd said very properly. "And my brother's is August thirty-first."

A young female minister was standing before the square hole that had been opened in the earth to receive Neely's remains, and she was addressing the group with her hands outstretched. "The greatest of your mysteries, Lord, is life itself," she was saying. Rollins paid little attention. His eyes were on Natalie, trying to see if he could spot anything of Stephanie in her. So Rollins was only dimly aware of a little Toyota coming up the drive, of a door opening and closing again with a thump. He didn't actually turn until he heard the sound of someone coming rapidly toward them along the gravel path. It was a young woman in a tight black skirt, a beautiful young woman. Probably the most beautiful young woman ever. One hand was perched atop her head, holding down an immense hat that threatened to blow off as she hurried along. Rollins might have shouted to her, but he could tell there was no need. Marj was coming. She was coming to him. Other heads turned as, with whispers of apology, Marj sidled through the crowd toward Rollins. And then she was right there next to him, the brim of her hat flopping against the side of his face as she whispered, "Hi. Remember me?"

Rollins could sense that people were staring, but he didn't care. Overjoyed, he circled his arms around Marj and pushed his face toward hers. He kissed her forehead, her cheeks, her lips. And her big hat flew right off her head.

Acknowledgments

For much assistance on matters pertaining to missing persons, I would like to thank Charles Allen of Management Consultants, Inc., of Lexington, Massachusetts. For help with other technical details, I'm grateful to Gretchen Young and John Colcord. For literary advice and encouragement, I'm deeply indebted to Sally Brady and all my fellow members of two of her writing groups, but especially to Erica Funkhauser, Tom Lonergan, Caroline Preston, and Judy Richardson. My thanks, too, to Amanda Vaill for some friendly editing. On the business side, Kris Dahl at International Creative Management has proved a brilliant and patient agent. My editor, Dan Conaway, has been a dream, demonstrating, time and again, that the era of careful, intelligent, incisive editing has by no means ended in New York publishing. And, as always, I have been sustained in this work by the unfailing love of my wife, Megan Marshall.